DINOSAUR WORLD OMNIBUS

Adam Carter

First published in e-book format as Dinosaur Prison World (2014), The Dinosaur That Wasn't (2015), Excavating a Dinosaur World (2015) and Dinosaur Fall-Girl (2015).

Cover by Covermint Design. **www.covermint.design**

Visit: https://www.facebook.com/OperationWetFish for news, illustrations, previews and short stories.

For Paul

Jupiter's Glory:
- Book 1: The Dinosaur World
- Book 2: The Pirates and the Priests
- Book 3: The Obsidian Slavers
- Book 4: Just Passing Through

Detective books:
- Detective's Ex
- One-Way Ticket to Murder
- Who Slew Santa?
- The Curse of the Genie's Detective
- The Woman Who Cried Diamonds
- The Murder of Snowman Joe
- The Murder of Loyalty
- The Prostitute Butcher
- The Santa Worshippers

Dinosaur Frontier:
- Book 1: The Lightning Angel
- Book 2: Lightning Strikes Twice
- Book 3: The Law of Ceres
- Book 4: The Silk Caves of Ceres

Operation WetFish, Vampire Detective:
- Book 1: The Power of Life and Death
- Book 2: Chasing Innocence
- Book 3: The Hunt for Charles Baronaire
- Book 4: Christmas on the Kerb
- Book 5: A Necessary Evil
- Book 6: No Comment
- Book 7: Fear and Ecstasy
- Book 8: Call of the Siren
- Book 9: Happy Families
- Book 10: A Step in the Right Direction
- Book 11: What Money Can't Buy
- Book 12: 'Tis the Season
- Book 13: The Power Trip
- Book 14: Trust and Betrayal
- Book 15: A Gathering of Minds
- Book 16: The Pain of Life
- Book 17: The Happy Place
- Book 18: The Terrible Truth of Barry Stockwell
- Book 19: The Apex Predator
- Book 20: End of an Era
- Book 21: He Who Kills the Killers' Killers
- Book 22: Bad Day at the Office

Miscellaneous:
- Holding the Nuts
- One Week to Love: Speed Dating of the Gods
- The Trojan Ant
- Gauntlet of Daedalus
- The Faerie Contract
- Token Love
- Sleigh Ride Slaughter to Saturn
- Have Imagination, Will Travel

The dinosaur books of Ceres form a series of (mostly) stand-alone adventures set on a quarantined dinosaur world. Since the stories are spread across the world (and several generations), there is very little interaction between the books and most feature characters unique to that particular story. The intention is that any book can be read independently, without even realising there even are any others. The main exceptions to this are the Dinosaur Prison World stories which, while each can be read alone, do feature recurring characters. Any Dinosaur Prison World book is marked in bold and underlined on the list below.

I also have a timeline into which all of my books slot, so if you wish to read the books in chronological order, they are as follows:

- Excavating a Dinosaur World
- Dinosaur Fall-Girl
- Dinosaur Plague Doctor
- Ike Scarman & the Dinosaur Slavers of Ceres
- ***Dinosaur Prison World***
- ***The Dinosaur That Wasn't***
- Awfully Wedded Strife
- ***Tales of a Dinosaur Prison World***
- Deities of a Dinosaur World
- ***Return to the Dinosaur Prison World***
- ***Nikolina Finch & the Dinosaur Utopia***
- Of Stags, Hens & Dinosaurs
- Dinosaur World Gladiator
- ***The Wounding Tooth***
- Dinosaur World Massacre
- Dino-Racers
- Dinosaur World Unscripted
- Lost Treasures of a Dinosaur World (gamebook)
- Christmas on a Dinosaur World
- Utara the Savage

Table of contents:

EXCAVATING
A
DINOSAUR WORLD

CHAPTER ONE

The great beast roared into the humid evening air, bellowing its rage that a tiny, near weightless creature lay beneath it, poking it with a screwdriver. The stupid thing could complain all it wanted, Garrel thought as she tightened the panel a little more; it was still going to be ready by morning. There were a lot of things Sara Garrel did not like about this place, but the constant dampness to the air had to be the worst. Of course, she had known before taking the assignment what conditions she would be working in, but the pay was too good for her to turn down. She had just come through a messy divorce and desperately needed as much money as she could get. At twenty-seven years old, Garrel was finding she had to pretty much start her life anew and while she felt an exhilarating freedom she was also terrified.

"You're doing great there, Sara. Anything I can help you with?"

Garrel closed her eyes and counted to five. She would have counted to ten but she had been doing that a lot these past couple of weeks and it never seemed to do any good. Lying on her back under the truck, she had completely no conception of what was going on in the outside world, but it seemed Allen had followed her out again just to ogle her. Tom Allen was not a bad person, far from it, but she could not seem to get through to him that she wasn't interested. And even if she was, she hadn't gone through a divorce just to involve herself with someone else. She needed to sort out her life before she even considered going down that path again.

Nor did she really see why he was even that interested. Garrel had never before considered herself anything special. She was of average height, average appearance, wore her long dark hair in a ponytail so it didn't get in the way of her work. She hadn't hit the gym in a while and knew she could have done with shedding a few pounds, but her work kept her physically fit. She actually had more impressive muscles in her arm than Allen – she knew because they'd compared them one time in an effort to get rid of him. She could only guess there were two reasons he was so obsessive about her; firstly because the temperature was so uncomfortable that she tended to wear as little as possible, especially when she was working; and secondly because aside from Professor Travers she was the only woman on the whole world.

"Sara?"

Knowing she could not put off the confrontation indefinitely, Garrel crawled out from under the buggy. She had stripped down to shorts and a sports bra and, suddenly wishing she hadn't left her shirt back in her room, grabbed a towel to mop the sweat from her face. Mopping up sweat was a lost cause on this world, and immediately her eyes were stinging again as her pores tried in vain to cool her.

Tom Allen stood by hopefully, going through her toolkit. He too was wearing shorts, his T-shirt all but plastered to his body, but still nowhere near as soppy as his grin. For no apparent reason he was holding up a hammer.

"What would I need a hammer for?" Garrel asked, tired in both body and mind.

"Uh, for bashing things?"

"That's an engine down there, Allen, not a coconut."

His face fell slightly and she knew she should have felt a little bad but didn't in the least. Allen was several years her junior, she guessed, but he was far from the love-struck teenager he made himself out to be. Apparently he was a good assistant to Professor Travers, but if that was the case Garrel couldn't see why he didn't hang around the Professor more. Garrel had been brought on this expedition as pilot, truck driver, odd-job-woman, engineer, navigator and survivalist. Among other things. She was the only member of the expedition not in the employ of the Jovian History Trust and was technically in charge of the entire thing. In reality of course she wasn't in charge of anything, but on paper any decision she made regarding the survival of their people was to be obeyed instantly. Such papers would be put to better use folded and thrown through the air as aeroplanes.

"Well if you need any help with anything else," Allen said, "I'm your guy. I don't have a lot to do at the moment, so I'm pretty much free all evening."

"If you don't have much to do," Garrel said tiredly, "it means you have something to do. So go do it."

Allen's face fell slightly and she could see him fighting for something interesting to tell her. "Professor Travers is having me clean up a portion of diceratops skull. You want to see it?"

"Why would I possibly want to see a dinosaur skull?"

Allen blinked, genuinely surprised. "Why wouldn't you?"

"I thought they were called triceratops anyway."

"Those are the ones with three horns. Diceratops had two. Want to guess what had five?"

"Could it possibly be pentaceratops?"

Allen's face lit up as though she had just set fire to his hair. "You fell for my trick question."

"Don't take that as a sign of affection," Garrel warned him. "I still don't care about your dinosaurs."

"Well, there's always time for that. We're going to be here at least another three months, so there's always hope."

Garrel had told him many times he didn't have a hope, but he had never got the message so she didn't bother this time. "Just go clean your skull, Allen, and let me get back to work."

He said something else, but Garrel had ceased to listen. Something about seeing her at dinner, which was ludicrous considering Garrel had eaten meals with the others probably three times in the month they had been out here. Except breakfast, of course, which Travers insisted they all share. She must have agreed to something because Allen left her to her buggy, and as she tossed the towel to one side Garrel gazed up into the sky and wondered not for the first time how her finances could ever fail so badly that she had been forced to take this contract.

As work went, it was far from bad. She got to do a little of everything, which was how she liked things. There was not even a specified end to the contract, nor was it renewed on a monthly basis. She had simply signed to say she would act in various capacities for the research team until they had finished up their work and decided to head home. Another three months, however, was not what she was looking forward to. Yes, it would give her a lot more money than she had believed she would get out of this, but the humidity coupled with daily doses of Tom Allen did not make the stay any more pleasant.

He could have been worse, she reflected as she worked out a kink in her shoulder. She supposed at least he was harmless, and quite sweet in his own way. Sometimes she would reflect what her reaction would have been to him were she not so annoyed over her divorce, but even then she very much doubted she would have been interested. Garrel was not a woman who ever really went by looks, but by how a man acted around her. It wasn't even really about their personality: she simply didn't like men who fawned over women or who pretended to be something they weren't. In Allen's defence, however, he most certainly was not trying to be something he wasn't.

Grabbing a bottle of water, Garrel sat against the truck, placing her back upon the warm metal and dreaming of an icy shower. As she took a swig of the bottle she cast her eyes about the area and wondered what was out there. They had made their camp in a spacious, rocky area, thankfully finding a flat space to keep their vehicles level. Beyond the rocks Garrel could see a line of trees, but then it was hard to come to Ceres and not see trees. Every schoolchild knew Ceres was nature's joke: that there were creatures roaming this world that had had their day and died out. For some reason that had not been sufficient for an unknown government, who had not only created this peculiar world but had populated it with all manner of oddities. Garrel had never really much cared for such things, and would be happy if, during her entire stay, she didn't see a single beast larger than the things she hunted for their food. She knew Allen was eager to see some of these creatures, but if he wanted to go wandering off into the jungle he was more than welcome.

Raising her hand to shield her eyes, Garrel could not believe even the evenings here could be so brutally hot. Dark clouds were moving in, promising some more bad weather, and Garrel would have welcomed the rain had last week's downpour not been so severe. The Professor had been unable to work for several days and was only now really getting back on track. If another storm hit them just as they were resuming work Garrel would likely have taken it to be an act of God. Human beings were not supposed to be on this world, and there was a reason it had been declared off-limits by the Jovian government. She felt uncomfortable even being here; their presence may have been legal in the eyes of the government, but there were far greater powers up there whose authority outweighed anything human beings could ever decide.

Lurking beyond the dark clouds was a colossal mass of churning gas Garrel had been trying to ignore staring down at her with its great red eye of judgement. It was normal for almost every world in the Jupiter system to see the massive gas giant looming in the skies above them at all times of the day, but here on Ceres was the only time Garrel had ever truly felt the great king of the gods was judging her. Born and raised in the French quarter or Io, Sara Garrel had seen this great planet almost every day of her life, and it had never frightened her. Since coming to Ceres she had lowered her eyes several times, feeling a deep sense of unworthiness whenever she met its unblinking gaze.

She had left the Jovian system only once, taking an assignment to ferry some businessmen to the Earth system. She had only spent a week on Earth, but it had felt strange, alien almost. She had been rather looking forward to spending some time on the world from which all life in the solar system had sprung, but having spent a week there she knew she would never return. She had not been able to get used to turning her eyes skyward and not seeing the face of God staring back at her. All they had on Earth was the smiling face of the Man in the Moon, and that had just been creepy.

Recapping her water, Garrel decided she would finish working on the buggy in the morning; it was only general maintenance anyway. She no longer felt comfortable under the intense scrutiny from above and wanted to go back to their camp and put a few walls and a ceiling between her and her god.

The camp was formed of solid walls and had taken a full day for Garrel and Allen to erect. Over the last fifty years or so companies had taken great advantage of the growing trend of exploration – which may well have resulted in the quarantine of Ceres temporarily lifted for Professor Travers and her expedition. Various makeshift camps had gone into production, with each company attempting to find the speediest, easiest methods for their customers to erect the unit once they got it to where they were going. The unit this expedition had brought with them had no flooring, so the rock of Ceres was the floor of their camp, but the walls were strong and durable and even did something to keep out the heat. There were several rooms to the unit they had brought with them, which included sleeping chambers for each of the expedition's members, storage rooms for food and equipment, and workshops. They had no bathroom and no running water, but there was a stream only ten minutes' walk from their camp and they had developed a system of going there in pairs. Any bather needed someone watching her back on Ceres. With only four members to the entire expedition – two men and two women – that had been something which had worked out rather well.

Returning to her chambers, Garrel struggled out of her sweat-laden clothes and hunted around for something clean. She found a loose T-shirt but it was too humid to be wearing trousers in her room. Digging through her private food-stores, she collapsed onto her bed with a book and a tin of cold beans. Her room was only about three by two metres, but she had brought nothing with her to Ceres save a couple of keepsakes she honestly felt she only kept for the sake of them. She had also plastered a film poster on her wall at the foot of her bed. It was advertising a romantic comedy she particularly enjoyed, and it never failed to bring a smile to her lips whenever the nights on this world were getting her down.

She tended to look at that poster often.

A knock sounded on her door and an ire rose in her which even at the time she knew was irrational. But on this world there were very few places of solitude and not being disturbed in her own sleeping chambers had to be one of them. She tore open the door with such vehemence that it nearly snapped off its hinges. Tom Allen jumped back a pace, a scream dying in his throat. The sight was so unexpectedly humorous that Garrel felt some of her anger drain from her.

"What?" she asked, barking a little less than she had intended. "This had best be something important."

Allen was staring, wide-eyed.

The expression on his face may have been comical, but Garrel was not cruel enough to laugh in his face. "Allen?"

"Uh ..."

Then she realised he was staring at her legs and she glanced down herself, as though by taking a look with her own eyes it would somehow change the fact she wasn't wearing any trousers. Her first instinct was to slam the door in his face and find something to cover herself, but she preferred to pretend she knew precisely what she was doing.

"Out with it," she snapped. "I'm in the middle of something."

Allen shook his head quickly, once, his eyes back to hers. "Professor Travers saw something outside. She wants you to take a look."

"Saw what?"

"I don't know. Something big though."

Garrel did not like being the only person in the entire encampment who ever went out to check on things. She had not been hired by Travers as a bodyguard, but as a workwoman. If she had wanted a job in security she would have become a police officer. However, she could not imagine any of the others being able to deal with whatever was out there.

"Fine," she sighed, half in anger, half in resignation. "Grab a pair of binoculars and let's go see."

"Right. Hold on ... me?"

"Well I'll need someone to watch my back won't I? That is, if you can tear your eyes away from my legs."

Allen looked away sharply, colour rising to his cheeks. "I'll go get some stuff together."

Garrel closed the door and dug out a pair of trousers Unfortunately she had yet to get around to cleaning most of her clothes and her only pair of clean trousers were a bright yellow which had been the fashion on Io last year. Going on a scouting mission wearing such things was hardly the best of options, but none of her other trousers were in her room and there was no way she was going anywhere with Allen only wearing shorts. She needed his mind as focused on their task as possible. Her T-shirt was already feeling moist, but changing her clothes every two minutes was not an option. Grabbing up a bandolier, Garrel made certain she had all the equipment she might need before heading out after Allen. This included a loaded pistol and several rounds of tranquilisers for her rifle. She wondered whether Allen had thought to bring any firearms, and whether he might have been more of a liability if he had. Allen may have been a bit of an annoyance sometimes, but he didn't mean any harm, she reflected. Maybe it was about time she started being a little nicer to him.

Or perhaps she would decide how she was going to treat him once she had seen how he handled this outing with her. Perhaps he would surprise her and actually come in use.

Moving back outside, Garrel felt instantly drenched, and it was a sensation she was unfortunately getting used to. Allen had indeed gathered together some things and was busily trying to cram them all in the backseat of the open-topped buggy she had been working on earlier.

"You don't need all of that," Garrel said as she passed him.

"You never know what you'll need until you need it. Recording equipment, binoculars, flares, hunting knife."

"You have a hunting knife?" Garrel asked, trying not to laugh.

Allen puffed out his chest. "I took a survivalist course in university, you know."

Garrel folded her arms. "Really? And did you perhaps learn how to take down a ten metre theropod with a hunting knife?"

"Uh ... no. But we need to take the rest of this equipment, just to make sure."

"If you insist. Just give me the blade before you hurt yourself." Taking the knife from him, she continued walking. "But we're leaving the buggy. Whatever Travers saw, we don't want to spook it by driving right up to it."

She could not see Allen behind her but was not surprised that when he caught up he was no longer carrying nearly as much equipment. The only thing she would have been happy for him to have brought along would have been a working radio, but communications equipment didn't want to work on Ceres. There were no artificial satellites off which to bounce signals, but even hardwearing radios only seemed to work temperamentally. It might have been something to do with magnetism, but Garrel could not say for certain. Since Ceres had been put together wrong it was hardly surprising its magnetic field was nothing to be happy about.

They moved to the edge of the dry, rocky area upon which they had camped. There was grassland about, and great clumps of trees which seemed to grow anywhere on this world, and it was to the trees that Allen was directing them. They moved without saying a word to each other, for they knew that if there was indeed something out there it could well prove hostile.

Hunkering down at the edges of the trees, Garrel unslung the rifle from her back. She seldom went anywhere on Ceres unarmed, although the rifle she favoured was generally only used to tranquilise the animals. Blowing holes in creatures seldom killed them, and even if she managed to kill one, the stench of blood would draw scavengers from miles away. Tranquiliser darts may have taken a short while for their effects to bring the animal down, but when the animal woke up again there was a good chance it would not be quite as angry as when she had shot it. At the very least it gave Garrel the opportunity to work out a more long-lasting solution.

She could see damage to the trees, and tracks indicating a large and heavy animal had moved through recently. Since coming to Ceres Garrel had become something of an expert of the local wildlife. She had done her research before arrival, of course, but there was only so much one could learn from books about animals which only lived on one world.

Keeping at a crouch, Garrel moved forward, listening for any change to the noises of the trees. There were forests on Ceres, but these trees only stretched for about a mile in any direction. The noises within each were not too dissimilar, however, and she knew precisely which birds would stop trilling when a predator was at large. She followed the tracks, noting one tree which had been torn from its roots and was now leaning against one of its neighbours. Something large had decided the tree was in its way, and if it could have done that to a tree Garrel shuddered to think what it might do to their camp.

Five minutes later Garrel could smell a freshness to the air which could only mean she was approaching the stream she knew flowed through the woodland. Keeping as low as she could, her rifle levelled ahead of her, Garrel peered through the trees to see she had indeed reached the stream. There was a creature standing there, drinking its fill from the water, and Garrel smiled as she lowered her rifle.

The beast stood at just over two metres from the ground and walked upon four powerful legs which still somehow managed to appear squat. Its bulky body looked cumbersome, flabby even, but this was mainly due to the armour spread across its back. A strange mixture of diamond-hard scutes and dulled protrusions, the creature's carapace resembled that of a tortoise, the legs extending below adding weight to the analogy. Unlike many of its kind, this specimen's armoured protrusions did not appear all that spiked, and she had seen some particularly vicious-looking denizens of this world clearly related to this beast. Its body length was probably around the six metre mark, its tail being at least two metres – longer even than Garrel's entire body. The tail was similarly armoured, consisting in part of fused vertebrae, the tip of which was clumped into what was likely either a mass of bone or compressed hair, like that of a rhinoceros's horn. She had never seen the tail in action but knew from her research that the creature was able to crush an animal's skull with a single swipe of that powerful weapon. At the culmination of its short, armoured neck, its head was protected by two large spikes, its sharp beak currently plunged into the water but its eyes ever alert for roving carnivores. An animal was always at its most vulnerable when lowering its head for a drink, and Garrel knew any creature would be wary at such a time. It was something human beings took far too much for granted.

The animal was called a talarurus, and was a part of the ankylosaurid group. These creatures had been so successful they had been there right up until the end of the dinosaurs.

Garrel smiled to herself as she had such thoughts, her eyes never leaving the wonderful creature. Every schoolchild knew of the dinosaur world Ceres, but no one understood it: some didn't even believe it. Ceres was a world so far away, and it was illegal for anyone to ever go there, so there was never any evidence the dinosaurs even existed. Many in the Jupiter system firmly believed it was all a government conspiracy, that they wanted people to think there were dinosaurs to deflect attention from other secrets they were hiding. Garrel had seen a few of the films they had made about Ceres, but none of them could ever compare to actually seeing one of these things in the flesh.

But she was also more than aware of the dangers these creatures posed. Whoever had put the dinosaurs here had not just brought about the return of the herbivores like talarurus. Ceres had far too many carnivores running loose, and Garrel would have been more than happy to have spent the rest of her days here avoiding them all.

It was sights such as this, watching a harmless wild animal drinking at a stream, that for Garrel made the entire trip worthwhile.

"Sara!"

Garrel's heart stopped as she recognised the voice as belonging to Tom Allen. Nor was it especially close. She watched in horror as he wandered out of the trees about thirty metres from her, walking backwards, looking all around him and shouting her name far too loudly. He stopped when he noticed the huge lumbering dinosaur not ten paces from him, and almost fell on his backside. The talarurus regarded him with agitation, and Garrel watched the mighty tail begin a swing designed to cow a rival. Garrel watched as Allen scrambled back to his feet. He would do the sensible thing and run, placing as much distance between him and the dinosaur as he could. He would do the sensible thing: he wasn't stupid.

Allen screamed at the top of his voice for help, falling and making such a mess of rising that he looked very much like a flailing swimmer fighting the rock tied to his feet.

The talarurus was turning towards him now, its tail swinging in wider arcs behind it as a warning. It opened its beak and shrieked at him: a challenge designed to test his reaction. Garrel knew whatever Allen did from this point on would be wrong but did not fancy having to explain to Professor Travers why her assistant was coming home in a body bag.

Bringing her rifle to her shoulder, Garrel sighted the animal but could not find a chink in its armour. She knew she could shoot one of the legs, but the armour seemed designed to protect these also, and she could imagine the creature being able to drop to the ground and bring its legs under the carapace. The animal was also agitated now, moving from side to side, and Garrel knew she would not be able to get in a clear shot. Shooting it and striking its armour would likely only annoy the thing.

Allen seemed to have entirely given up trying to get back to his feet and was staring in horror at the thing bearing down upon him. Whatever had to be done, Garrel knew she had to do it all herself.

Stepping out from the trees, Garrel swung her rifle back across her shoulder and pulled a pistol from a holster at her belt. Holding the gun away from her, she fired two shots into the ground. The explosive discharge from the gun proved enough to startle the animal, which had never before heard such an unnatural sound, and as it turned its head from Allen she shouted, "Go! Get out of here."

She felt only empty satisfaction as Allen scampered away, for by this time the talarurus was turning its entire body to face her. Behind its bulky form, the brutal tail swung mercilessly and Garrel knew it did not matter at all whether this animal intended to eat her. She knew full well that by necessity it was the herbivores which often grew the largest and were gifted with the most violent defences.

At the moment the great ankylosaurid was just looking at her with small, beady eyes. She considered running but had no idea the speed of this creature; nor was she willing to find out by simply running away from it. She struggled to think of what she had to hand, but aside from her pistol and her tranquiliser rifle her armament was pitiful. She still carried the knife she had confiscated from Allen, but all three weapons combined would not grant her a single hope against the thing before her.

The talarurus reared back its head and released a dull-pitched bellow which reverberated throughout the trees. Garrel felt her legs begin to lose their strength, but she knew this was the intention. It was an animal used to being wary while it watered, and today it had found a confrontation. It was reacting as she would have expected any animal to in a similar situation, and she fought furiously for the way out of this. She considered climbing a tree, but felt the talarurus might just smash the tree to toothpicks and her along with it.

Backing off a few paces, very slowly, Garrel hoped the thing would just go back to its drinking. However, the animal was far too agitated by everything that had happened and as it lowered its great head, raising itself on its rear legs, Garrel watched the tail go up into the air. She knew what was coming and that her chance of survival was diminishing rapidly.

Then she remembered that some large herbivores, like the elephant, had poor eyesight. She had no idea whether the same was true for ankylosaurids, but felt she had no other options. If she had something which would attract its attention, something bright and colourful, she might be able to deflect its charge.

Looking down, she suddenly remembered her bright yellow trousers and immediately tore at her belt and kicked off her boots. Unfortunately the talarurus chose that moment to bellow another challenge and charge.

Garrel fled, stumbling through the underbrush as she attempted to tear her trousers from her. Her legs were not designed for such multitasking, however, and she felt her foot twist in the material and she fell. The air exploded above her and she was showered by shards of wood as the lethal tail of the talarurus smashed through a tree and would have turned her head to paste had she not stumbled. Garrel looked back in horror as she ankylosaurid regained its balance after the assault and renewed its charge.

Tearing her trousers free at last, Garrel ran as fast as she could, holding them up to the side and waving them fiercely. She could feel the ground tremble behind her as the beast gave chase, but she was searching for something while she ran and knew that waving her trousers in the air was not sufficient to save her. Then she saw it approaching: precisely what she had been looking for. It was a natural ditch formed by the corrosion of excessive rain. They had been having terrible storms lately, and trees had been uprooted, rocks had been moved, and mudslides had formed ditches. Pouring as much speed into her legs as she could, Garrel ran for the ditch and leaped. As she left the ground she tossed her trousers and gained the relieving satisfaction to see them snag on the low branch of a tree. Then she was crashing into the ditch and pushing her back against the soil and mud, her breath catching in her throat.

Above she could hear the angry roars of the talarurus and the crashing of the woods as it tore into the offending trees. Branches struck Garrel like insane hail, and she gasped as she saw an entire tree slam into the ground where the animal had toppled it.

And then there was silence.

She waited a full minute before rising and risking a peek over the side. Of the talarurus there was no sign, but the woods had taken a terrible beating. Trees had been felled and the ground itself had great rents where the beast had slammed its armoured tail into the mud. Hoisting herself up the ditch, she wandered tentatively over to a splash of yellow in the foliage. Gingerly she lifted what was left of her trousers, but she was only holding one leg and could see no trace of the other. The material had been shorn through with the skill of a surgeon and she could only imagine that once it had attacked her garment with its tail the ankylosaurid had bitten through with its beak.

Tossing away the useless leg, Garrel wondered how she was ever going to find Allen in all this madness.

"Are you all right, Sara?"

She watched him scramble across the ground, almost tripping on several occasions, and felt like clobbering him. She was also extremely relieved to see him alive.

"I think we found out what the animal was," Garrel said. "Let's head back and tell Travers she doesn't have anything to worry ..." Her sentence drifted off when she realised Allen had stopped several metres from her, his eyes wide and staring once more. In all the terror she had almost forgotten why he would be doing that. "You really need to get a girlfriend, Allen."

"Sorry. I ... I wasn't staring."

At that moment Garrel did not even much care. She was too tired to argue, and motioned for him to precede her. They needed to get back to camp before the storms began anew, but there was no way she was going to have him gazing at her backside the entire journey.

CHAPTER TWO

It was raining. It was raining a lot. As Professor Diana Travers scribbled in her diary, she paused, scrubbing out what she had written. When she came to publish her discoveries she did not want to have to set it off with a boring description of the weather. Only begin a piece of prose with a description of the weather if it has some colossal impact to what would come later, she had been told. Staring out the window at the torrential downpour, she felt perhaps it might give her reason to begin her notes with a mention of the weather after all.

Travers set down her pen and reached for the flask of coffee which was keeping her going through the night. She was forty-two and married to a load of dead bones rotting in the ground. She had no children, no family to speak of, and aside from a love of Greek poetry very little in her life at all. She was a short woman with very little regard to her appearance. As such she always dressed in utilitarian attire, which usually meant anything hard-wearing, considering how much of her time she spent on digs. Her hair was short and flat, dark with hints of premature grey. Her glasses were hardy but not from any fashionable make, and she would not have been able to say who had produced any of her clothes.

She had always wanted to be an archaeologist, although it was something her parents had discouraged. Most of the archaeologists she had met in her time, especially during her student days, had gone into the profession because they held an obscene interest in history and in piecing together ancient societies. They had also held more than a passing interest in money, which was something Travers had never much cared for. So long as money got her to the next dig, she did not think of it at all. It was neither money nor history which drove Travers, however. It was not the ancient societies which inspired her passion. What Travers was interested in was Time.

Time was at the very heart of everything archaeologists did. They worked in the present so they could learn from the past and build a more knowledgeable future. Their work was slow, taking as long as it needed to, for the rock beneath a person's feet seldom agreed to give up its dead so easily.

Travers had become interested in time when her grandmother died. Young Travers had only been five at the time, yet while her family were grieving Travers had instead examined the situation and reached a conclusion. People were born, they lived and they died. Once the first had happened, nothing could prevent the final, but it was the middle that had sparked Travers's imagination. People lived, and it did not matter what they did while they lived, because they would still ultimately die.

Time was the most powerful force in the Universe. Time created and Time destroyed. And it did not care what happened between those two because there was nothing anyone could do against it. As she grew older Travers learned about the various religions of the solar system, most of which went back thousands of years to Earth. She had met so many people entirely devout in their beliefs of certain deities watching over their actions, and yet Travers had never heard a single tale of such a being more powerful than Time. Surely even the gods would be destroyed by Time, since at the death of the final human being those gods would be forgotten. And even an omnipotent being could not be considered a god if there was no one left alive to worship it. Gods needed to lord over the living, otherwise they were just ordinary.

Putting any of this into her diary would, of course, not be such a good idea. The animosity between religion and science stretched back farther than Travers could trace, and while she may have held strong opinions on both, neither was especially detrimental. Faith was all well and good, but Travers liked to examine the facts herself before reaching a decision. That was the thing she had always liked about science. In science there were no answers, merely speculation. Theories. And as soon as a theory was disproved, a new theory could be proposed and tested. After all, even gravity was in essence still a theory. If someone somewhere discovered a place where gravity did not operate, it would prove that gravity did not exist at all, and she could only imagine the scramble of scientists trying to work out what really drew smaller objects towards larger ones. Travers had long hoped to be able to make a similar discovery with Time.

There was one other important aspect Time had for Professor Travers. It was such an important factor because when the expedition to Ceres had been financed, it had been agreed that they would adhere to a strict schedule; a schedule she was no longer even certain she would be able to make work for her.

Presently, Travers was in her laboratory, running some tests on rocks she and her assistant had torn from the world. They had run all the initial tests upon the rocks of the surface, but these had been excavated from a quarter mile down. They were throwing up some interesting results, many of which Travers had not expected at all. It seemed Time was perhaps something equally as important to Ceres.

"Why are you looking at fossils when there are dinosaurs running around outside?"

Travers looked up from her microscope, knowing she wasn't getting any more work done tonight. Professor Albert Monroe was a few years older than Travers, thin, excitable and even when dressed in shorts and a T-shirt one could smell his wealth about his person. Being inside as they were, Monroe wore one of the many suits he had opted to bring with him. Travers was annoyed that she had been forced to leave important equipment behind for the sake of weight and space, yet Monroe had been given free rein to bring whatever he pleased. It was, however, his money which had financed the expedition, and Travers had found herself having to be far more pleasant to him lately than she had ever intended.

It wasn't as though Monroe was even a real professor. He had simply bought the title to add to the various others he had before his name, and the letters which followed. His titles were the beginning, his letters the end; Time did not care what happened to the man between.

"It's raining outside," Travers told him simply, hoping he would pick up on her mood and leave her to it. "They're not going to be running around in the rain."

"Dinosaurs don't care about the rain, Travers," he scoffed.

"Animals don't bask in thunderstorms."

"Ah, but these aren't animals, Travers. These are the gods of the animal kingdom."

The last thing Travers wanted was another discussion about science verses religion. "Would you like to help analyse some of these rocks perhaps? The sooner we get the rocks sorted, the sooner we can move onto deeper exploration."

Monroe snorted at the thought. He had come here to see the dinosaurs, even though their expedition had nothing to do with dinosaurs. Travers had been charged with discovering the secrets of Ceres. The dinosaurs were only helpful to her research if they were fossilised, and the excavation methods they were using had frightened off any local animals so it did not seem as though Monroe would get to see any of them at all.

"We've been here too long," Monroe complained, "and the biggest thing I've seen so far has been a bird."

"A prehistoric bird though."

"I didn't come here to look at birds, Travers."

"What about the rahonavis?"

"That doesn't count. We ate it. Besides, it wasn't a dinosaur either."

Travers had never really been interested in dinosaurs. She had of course always known about the fabled dinosaur world of Ceres, but had never had any inclination to ever want to visit the place. She could imagine that Monroe had grown up in his spoiled existence being given everything he so wished. As he reached adulthood he clearly wanted to see a living dinosaur, and the only place to do that would be Ceres. It was a pipedream for most, but since Monroe was rich it was a somewhat more plausible attainment for him. A part of Travers felt he only wanted to do it so he could rub everyone else's noses in his achievement. Especially considering it was illegal to ever visit Ceres. She still had no idea how he had wrangled their expedition, but was not about to question the results.

"If you want to wander in the rain looking for a wild triceratops, be my guest. But I guarantee they've all found somewhere dry to hide."

"Then you're certain there are triceratopses in the area?" he asked eagerly.

Travers had never mastered sarcasm, and had perhaps laced her words with too much of the truth. "There are a lot of ceratopsian species in this area," she said, indicating an especially large rock behind him. Within could be seen the unmistakable protrusion of fossilised bone, and it formed a crest which had belonged to what she believed to have been a diceratops. Indeed, she had identified at least six different ceratopsian species within a two mile radius of their camp. Whether any of them were still alive she could not say, for she was examining only what she had dug from the soil and stone. Garrel had reported several discoveries during their time here, but had never taken Monroe out with her to investigate any of them. Travers did not know much about Garrel but clearly the woman understood Monroe well enough.

Monroe seemed to mellow, his body was no longer fired by his intense eagerness to see some real live dinosaurs, and she could sense he was about to say something to make her feel as though they were friends. "How's the research going?" he asked. That would do.

"Well," she replied, "but slowly. I'm getting conflicting results, but then that's probably due to all the quakes." When she could see he did not understand, she added, "The rocks shift when the world does, so everything under the topsoil is a mess. We can't just dig down a quarter mile in one area and find detritus from the same time period as digging down a quarter mile in another."

"Oh."

She could see he still did not understand but did not much care. Ceres was an odd world and no one really knew where it had come from. Years ago some long-forgotten people had dragged some of the larger asteroids from the belt and fused them before hurling the resultant mess into orbit around Jupiter. There were various theories as to why someone would have done such a thing. The cost of terraforming a smaller world was always far less than terraforming a larger one, so that may have been one reason. Also, each moon of Jupiter had been claimed by various companies and countries as their own personal property, and short of waging war against an entire world the easiest way to get one was to form a new one. Neither of those theories made much sense to Travers, since by the time the world would have been ready for habitation generations would have gone by. In her experience people tended to care more for themselves than for future generations, unless of course it was currently politically fashionable to do so.

There were many other theories, and Travers had researched most of them prior to coming here. There were various religious orders which believed Ceres to be a holy land, and it was because of these that many believed the world was at last declared off-limits. Most were harmless enough, and featured Ceres as a show of their god's (or gods') divine intervention by creating a new world and populating it. Most vocal were the fanatics of the Church of Themisto, but they were from such a small moon that Travers was hardly concerned with their intervention.

And then of course there were the dinosaurs. Even after Ceres had been formed, it would have been many, many years before it would have been ready for population; and when it finally was ready someone had seen fit to introduce all manner of extinct species to the world. No one even understood how, since dinosaur cloning was obviously a ludicrous concept. That was why many believed Ceres to be a myth, or at least the dinosaurs living upon it. Ceres itself was rocked with constant quakes where the various asteroids tried to prise themselves apart; it was easily the most dangerous environment in the entire solar system. And that was even before one considered the dinosaurs.

Travers had been given the task of uncovering some of these answers. She intended at the very least to discover how long Ceres had been here. If she could figure out a date they might be able to work out who had formed the world, and if they could do that they may even be able to figure out why. Her mission, of course, had nothing to do with the dinosaurs, despite Monroe wanting to catalogue all the animal species. If they didn't meet a single animal between now and the time they left Ceres, Travers would have been exceptionally happy.

And Monroe would have been depressingly miserable.

She could foresee the religious people being especially annoyed at her discoveries, whatever they were.

The door opened then and Travers was grateful to see her assistant enter. Tom Allen may have been slightly annoying, but he was eager and knew his stuff. Thankfully he also knew a few things about dinosaurs, which meant Travers could often palm off Monroe onto him so she could get on with her work. She caught Allen's eye and tried to indicate that was just what she wanted right now, and they had gone through this so many times already that Allen knew the drill.

"Evening, professors," he said, dropping his pack on a table before turning his attention to the diceratops remains. "Man, what a specimen, huh, Professor?"

Monroe moved across to him, not looking all that pleased at Allen's intrusion, but Travers knew he quite liked the boy.

"Have you seen any ceratopsians out there, lad?" Monroe asked hopefully.

"No, sir. But Sara and I just came back from a fight with an angry ankylosaur."

Travers winced, having wished Allen hadn't mentioned that. Travers had noticed something and had sent Sara Garrel to investigate, but had not expected her to take Allen with her. The youth seemed to have returned none the worse for wear, however, so there was no harm done.

"Ankylosaur?" Monroe asked, eager to know more. "What kind?"

"Oh, uh ... I don't know. Sara did say, but I'm not sure I caught it. It ended in saurus if that helps any."

"Not really, no."

"Began with T. Talasaurus or something."

"Talarurus?" Monroe asked excitedly. "You actually saw a talarurus?"

"Nearly got eaten by one as well. You should have seen how Sara dealt with it."

"That, my boy, must have been a sight you'll never forget."

Allen's face took on a look of faraway happiness. "Yeah."

"I want you to take me out to where you saw it."

"I ... Huh? We barely escaped, sir. And it's raining."

"Why are you archaeologists so afraid of a little wet weather?"

Travers glanced to the window, not much liking where this conversation was turning. "That's not just a little wet weather, Albert. If it keeps up like this we could end up with flooding of the excavation site."

"Which would mean having to move to other sites?"

"Don't be getting any ideas."

Monroe seemed about to argue, although once more he relaxed and said, "You're absolutely right, Professor. Well, I've disturbed you enough. I should let you get back to your work."

Travers could not agree with him more, although did not like his sudden change of heart. Nor did she much like the way he placed his arm around Allen's shoulder and led him from the room. She could not think Allen would be stupid enough to take Monroe out during the storm, but there were so many things on Ceres which surprised her she was beginning to worry already.

Outside the window, thunder cracked loudly, the voice of the gods in their anger. Travers could not have said who had formed Ceres and why, but there was no mistaking that the king of the gods, Jupiter himself, watched over the strange world. Jupiter was one god with whom no science could ever hope to contend.

CHAPTER THREE

He may have been young, but Tom Allen was not stupid. He knew Garrel didn't think all that much of him, but Travers valued his work and complimented him often. Of course, he was her only assistant, and one of the conditions for this expedition to be green-lit was that Travers only brought the one assistant. That Allen had been chosen proved he was good at his job, and he would not let himself think otherwise. He would have been the first to admit, however, that his attention had begun to waver somewhat the more time they spent here. Sara Garrel wasn't just the only woman on the entire world aside from Travers, she was also incredibly fit. She knew how to handle herself, knew everything about the terrain and survival, could pull apart an engine and put it all back together with enough spare parts to create something else as well. She was, in short, amazing, and Allen wasn't just in love, he was infatuated.

Of course, Garrel didn't see it that way. She thought he was an annoyance, and perhaps he even was. He knew he was always underfoot, but then he was just so pleased to help her in anything that he would give the task one hundred and ten per cent. Not that that was possible, but the principle was there. He just wished he could think of a way to impress Garrel, to make her see that he wasn't just some gawky kid always trying to make her notice him. Besides, he was twenty-two: it was a long time since he had considered himself a kid and wished he could stop behaving like one.

"You're trying too hard, lad," Professor Monroe said as he poured some tea. The two had retired to Monroe's somewhat opulent chambers, and the Professor had insisted on brewing them some tea. Allen had always been fascinated by all the things cluttering Monroe's chambers and had no idea why he wanted half the stuff with him. The books he could understand, but there were at least five hundred of the things, and no one could read five hundred books in just the short time they would be here. He had also brought his collection of sticks. He did not know whether they actually were sticks, but they certainly looked like them. Each was around a metre in length. Some were polished, others rough, and Allen could not fathom what they could be used for. Walking sticks, he assumed, and could just imagine Monroe strolling through the civilised streets wearing his top hat, wielding a cane.

Right now all he was really concerned about was Garrel.

"Women are like dogs, my lad," Monroe continued.

"I'm sure she'd be ecstatic to hear you say that."

Monroe smiled. "Probably not the best analogy, but hear me out. When treated well they return affection, they roll over, fetch your slippers and play all the little games you love to play. But as soon as you kick one they'll tear your throat out."

Allen opened his mouth to say something, closed it, opened it, closed it and finally said, "Say what?"

"All right, a terrible analogy, but truer than you might realise. Have a digestive."

Allen took a digestive from the plate he was being offered. "How do I make a good impression on Sara though? I mean, she doesn't like me too much."

"She doesn't loathe you, lad. She's just going through a rough patch. Recently divorced, you know."

"Really?" Allen could not think of how anyone could divorce such a woman. "So that means she's single though?"

"It means she's wary of being stung again. When she falls for another man, it's going to have to be the right man."

"Right."

"Which brings us to the question. What are you after from her, lad?"

"Uh ..."

"I don't mean that. I meant long-term. Are you after a genuine lasting relationship or just a bit of rumpy-pumpy in the jungle."

"Does it matter?"

"To a woman? Yes."

"Oh." Allen had met many girls over the years, but had only ever known a handful intimately. All the girls he had ever been with had been fun-loving party-goers looking for a quick thrill. His longest relationship had lasted about three months, and that was only if he was being generous with his memories. In all honesty he had never given much thought to what Garrel may have wanted from their relationship. She was a woman, where all the others he had ever been with had been girls. It seemed such an obvious thing, and he felt somewhat embarrassed that it took someone else to point it out to him.

"She likes you," Monroe said. "You have to see that as a good start."

"She likes me?"

"Yes."

"How can you tell?"

"She took you with her today didn't she? And she risked her life to save yours. Sure, she might argue with you, but you only argue with people you feel something for. Otherwise she wouldn't care about your opinion."

"What if all she feels for me is ire?"

"Then she would have hit you by now. Hard. Has she ever hit you hard?"

"No, sir."

"Well then," he grinned, dunking a digestive, "she likes you."

Allen tried to think through this logic, for it was not entirely faultless. Still, Monroe was the only other man on this world and unless he was willing to talk with Professor Travers about it (which he wasn't), Monroe was all he had. "What can I do then?" Allen asked. "What impresses an actual woman?"

"Drinking six pints in two minutes won't do it for one thing."

Allen winced, wondering how he had been so transparent.

"Gestures," Monroe continued. "Nice gestures which don't seem like bribery. Pick her some flowers."

"Ceres is modelled after various prehistoric landscapes, sir. There are no flowers here."

"Then pick her some ferns."

"She's not an apatosaurus."

"A gem then. You're an archaeologist, you must be able to find something valuable from under the ground."

Allen considered that. There would only be anything of real interest if Ceres was at one time populated, but gemstones formed naturally and there was a chance he might be able to find something at least. And since Ceres was not a natural world there was a chance, however slight, that it might produce jewels unseen anywhere else in the entire solar system.

"That's the spirit," Monroe enthused, seeing his face brighten at the possibilities.

"There's nothing at our current dig-site though," Allen said.

"Then that's a shame. Couldn't you try digging somewhere else?"

"Professor Travers isn't keen on moving the operation too far out."

"What if she had to?"

"Sir?"

"Well, if she doesn't find what she's after here, we could always move the entire camp. It would be a pain, but it's certainly doable."

"And I could find my gems."

"Precisely."

Allen considered all of this. It was certainly worth a try, although he knew Travers would not like the idea one bit.

"There's an alternative," Monroe said, thinking aloud. "An alternative to moving the entire camp, that is. If we can avoid that, I think we should. Neither of the ladies would be too happy with all the extra work."

"What did you have in mind?"

"Well, the two of us could go together. Not far, but maybe a couple of miles out. We could take the buggy Garrel's been modifying."

"What could the two of us accomplish though? We can't take the excavation equipment, it's too heavy."

"No, but maybe there's better excavation equipment out there."

"You think there are more people on Ceres, sir?"

"No. And if there are, they're here illegally and would likely kill us to maintain our silence. But I didn't mean people," he quickly added. "The world itself could help us."

"Ceres?"

"Ceres is unstable. One thing I've noticed is that if you dig a quarter mile in one area you'll get different results than if you dug a quarter mile in another area."

Allen knew precisely what he meant and was impressed the man had come up with that. He knew Travers did not much favour Monroe because his title was honorary rather than earned, but Allen had always found the man charming and sincere. "The quakes could well have pulled all manner of things to the surface," Allen said.

"Remember, tectonic shifts make mountains."

Allen did not like to correct him, but there was no proof that Ceres even had tectonic plates. That was one of the things the expedition was out to prove, and the main reason Professor Travers was not willing to burrow too far through the rock. Ordinary worlds were formed of thick crusts, beneath which igneous rock flowed. Beneath this was the molten core of the world. Everyone assumed Ceres operated under the same principle, but since it was manmade no one was certain. Their machines could slam through the rock instantly: it wasn't as though they were digging with spades. As such they did not want to accidentally punch all the way through to the core and set off a chain reaction which would destroy the entire world. They knew Ceres suffered quakes, but beyond that there was only speculation at the moment.

"If we took the buggy," Allen said, "we could cover a lot more ground than just a couple of miles."

"If you think it best. Who knows, we might even see a couple of dinosaurs along the way."

Allen laughed. "Still after your dinosaurs, eh, sir?"

"We all want something from this world, lad. Just so long as Ms Garrel gets her pretty baubles, I think we can spare a few moments for me to watch some dinosaurs roam in the wild."

Allen knew it was not too much to ask, especially if Monroe was willing to accompany him. And if it was just a look Monroe was after, nor could Allen see any actual harm. In fact Allen was more than willing to scratch some backs if it got him those jewels.

"Are we going to have to steal the buggy?" Allen asked, not much liking the idea of having to lie to Travers or distract her in any way.

"Don't be silly, lad. My money's financed this dig. I own the buggy." He grinned and slapped Allen on the back. "You worry too much about silly things, boy. We're not planning murder or anything. And maybe we'll even bring a little something back for Travers herself, no?"

That made Allen feel a little better, and while he knew it was just a hollow justification it would perhaps even bring a smile to Travers's face.

There was nothing they could do about it while the storm raged outside, however, and so once the two men had finished their tea Allen retired to his own room. The camp may have been formed of solid walls, but the rain battered the structure with such ferocious intensity that he could almost imagine a cold sentience to the storm. With the carnivorous animals growing so large on this world he could well imagine why the weather itself was so violent.

Allen spent the night in a fitful slumber. The rain was not the only thing that kept him from doing more than dozing, for his thoughts turned always towards the image of Sara Garrel. Come morning, Allen was therefore far from rested, although his adrenalin and purpose drove him on and he knew he would be able to accomplish much throughout the day. He did not even understand why he was so infatuated with Garrel. It had to be more than just the fact that she was the first real woman he had even fallen for. He had often wondered lately whether he was even in love, but since he had never before been in love he could not say what it felt like. He had of course heard all the clichés about butterflies and not eating and whatever, but Allen had never been one for cliché. He realised as well that he did not know all that much about her, had not even known she was divorced until the day before. He found himself curious now as to what her ex-husband was like, and why they had become divorced. They were things he would likely never discover, unless Garrel herself told him, and that was hardly going to happen. Still, stranger things had likely happened on this quarantined world.

Come morning, the bad weather had subsided slightly. The ground was muddy from the storm, and there was still a light rain in the air, but not enough to hamper their journey. Allen packed some supplies: food, ammunition and some small pieces of equipment he felt they might need. He met Monroe by the buggy, and noted he did not appear to have brought much of anything aside from vigour and excitement. Allen shoved his back into the back of the buggy and noted Monroe was seating himself on the passenger side. The buggy

fearsome dinosaur hunting in their valleys would be nothing more than a speck against the smallest of those distant peaks.

"How far do you want to go?" Allen asked.

"Depends where the dinosaurs are."

Allen glowered at him and Monroe grinned once more, but did not verbally tell him he was just joking.

"There's hard ground up ahead, I hear," Monroe said. "Rocks with jagged edges. That's a likely place for the ground to have come apart during quakes, so we may find some interesting things there."

Allen could see where he was indicating and relaxed slightly when he realised Monroe did actually know what he was talking about. There was indeed an area of rough terrain and Allen estimated they could be there within the hour. They had taken an hour already to skirt the woodland, which meant if they could find the gems quickly they would not have been away from the encampment for too long at all. In fact, things seemed to be going in their favour.

Glancing in his wing mirror Allen did a double-take when he saw something behind them on the plains. It filled the mirror, dust churning beneath its feet even as it was being kicked up by the buggy. He recognised the huge bulbous shape, knew well the strong armoured spikes, and feared the animal was far larger than the tiny thing the mirror made it out to be.

"Uh, sir?" Allen stammered, his heart stopping, his wide eyes staring straight ahead. "You wanted to see a dinosaur? How about a triceratops?"

"A triceratops?" Monroe asked eagerly, straining at his seat belt. "Where?"

Allen could find no further words and shoved a thumb behind him. Monroe turned his head and his seemingly perpetual grin failed him at last. He sat back down in his chair, hard, and seemed to shrink visibly. "Put your foot down, lad."

Allen obeyed, and he glanced into the mirror to see that no distance at all had been gained. The triceratops seemed angrier than ever now that they had forced it to increase its speed, and Allen could not imagine what was driving it forward.

Monroe apparently sensed his thoughts. "We're a large body charging across its terrain," he explained as calmly as he could. Indeed Monroe seemed to have overcome the initial shock to be able to think straight once more. "It sees us as a rival. If we prove ourselves quicker than the triceratops, it will tear us apart."

"If we stop it'll tear us apart."

"No argument here. Watch out!"

Allen had not reckoned upon the sheer speed of the beast and it was upon the buggy before he could even think about reacting. Allen felt the entire buggy jolt and looked to the side to see the triceratops slamming the side of its head into the rear of the vehicle. The back of the buggy rose a metre from the ground but thankfully did not lose pace at all.

Allen could see the dinosaur in all its glory now. The huge bulbous body was like that of a rhinoceros, charging upon four thick, powerful legs. A weighty but relatively small tail would have been swaying back and forth at the rear of the beast, although Allen could not see that far back since the creature was so huge. At almost ten metres long and weighing in at something approach five tonnes, Allen knew it was a male – a T. prorsus – which gave value to the theory that it was protecting its territory against an assumed threat to its dominance. The great head of the beast was formed of a long, bulky snout, culminating in a beak perfectly designed to snap off delicious ferns but which would easily take off a human arm if one got in the way. From the rear of its head there erupted a massive frill, formed of reinforced bone. The frill offered protection to the animal's back and throat, although its main purpose was in attracting a mate, for tiny veins flew across the frill which burst crimson when blood was pumped through. Upon the end of its snout was a horn the size of Allen's forearm, while between the eyes there exploded two incredibly lengthy horns, far larger and thicker, which could offer the creature protection from predators but which were more often used in clashing against rivals, at least for the males.

Allen knew very little about dinosaurs, but he had learned a great deal about the various ceratopsian inhabitants of Ceres. The triceratops was the largest of them all and without a doubt the one he would have least chosen to face while driving desperately away in an unprotected vehicle.

The creature struck again and Allen heard something tear at the rear of the buggy. The triceratops roared – perhaps in triumph, perhaps in pain – and the buggy gave a sputter. Thick black smoke bellowed from the vehicle, hurtling into the dinosaur's face, making the creature slow its attack in confusion. Whatever ichor it had expected to erupt forth from the wound, this thick, oily mist certainly had not been it, and Allen hoped the momentary confusion would offer them some respite.

The buggy began to slow and he realised the triceratops must have torn through something vital. He knew nothing about the mechanics of a buggy, however, and could not say what had been shorn through; it could well have been anything from the engine to the fuel tank. The vehicle was still careening forward at immense speeds, but he knew it would not last long.

The two men slammed forward in their seats as they were struck once more from behind. Allen saw the ground coming towards him and braced himself as the vehicle overturned, striking grass and spinning in the air to hammer into the ground once more. He caught vague snippets of the image of the triceratops as it smashed into the buggy with its massive horns, tearing great chunks from the machine even as it careened to a stop, its wheels facing the air. Allen and Monroe were kept into their seats by their belts, their heads inches from the ground, and they gazed around them in fear. They had stopped moving, but the powerful odour of fuel was assaulting them and they knew they had to get away. Allen tested his limbs. He ached all over but could find nothing broken, and knew just how lucky he had been. Glancing across to Monroe he could see the man in a similar state of mind and could only imagine that he too had escaped relatively unscathed.

"That was lucky," Allen said.

Then the sound of twisting metal tore through their world as something large and heavy pounded atop the overturned vehicle. Allen felt the entire vehicle pushing down upon him, but the pressure eased and his heart began to beat once more.

The pounding repeated and Allen realised the triceratops was slamming its feet upon the base of the overturned buggy, trying to flatten the thing and kill them both. If they did not do something soon they would both be killed for certain.

He could no longer see Monroe. If he was dead he was dead and there was nothing Allen could do to help him, but even if he was still alive Allen had to get himself out of the ruined vehicle first. He had some vague idea about luring the colossus from the buggy and returning for Monroe, but quickly dismissed the thought as idiocy brought on by the adrenalin rush of being so close to death.

Again the feet crashed down upon the buggy and Allen felt the metal pressing dangerously hard upon his spine. The shock pushed him out of his state of fear and he fell forward with a jolt, his fingers having unconsciously been working to unstrap his seatbelt. He landed heavily, his forehead striking a metal bar which should not have been there. He was aware that his body was aching, that the wet stinging in his leg meant he had torn something, but the leg still moved so he could not afford to let it slow him. Working furiously, he saw daylight to his right and scrambled madly for it. The hole was tight, but Allen forced himself through regardless, thankful the buggy was formed of merely a skeletal metal structure and contained neither roof nor sides to speak of.

Here any thoughts of fleeing or luring the beast away died in his adolescent flight of fancy and he pressed his back against the buggy as he stared at the massive bulk of the monster. He knew from his reading and the digging up of bones that the beast would have been around ten metres in length, but seeing one whose body was filled out with flesh was vastly different to picking over the various bones which made up its carcass. He could only imagine how tall the thing was, but judging by his own cowering insignificance he would have said the creature was at least four metres from the ground. Just one of its legs was the same height and thickness of Allen himself.

Out in the open, Allen found he could not even move now. His heroism had deserted him and he simply stared in equal parts horror and awe at the mighty triceratops with its forelegs resting upon the overturned buggy. The animal appeared to have lost some of its ire now, and Allen could see it calming. Raising itself from the crushed vehicle, the triceratops dropped once more to the ground, snorted at the defeated adversary and wandered off. Its dominancy had been established and any females in the vicinity would have seen how the bull had dealt severely with the interloper. The buggy would not be mating with any of the herd's females now.

Allen stood for several moments, staring after the departing Goliath, until he finally remembered Monroe was still lying in the bottom of the buggy. Dropping to his knees, Allen peered through the wreckage and could just see Monroe stirring.

"You all right, sir?" he called.

Monroe grunted, holding his head and looking a little bleary-eyed. "I'm alive, so that's something."

"Hold on."

It took some time, but Allen found a metal bar which had been sheared off the buggy and he used it for a brace. Between the two of them they finally managed to get Monroe extracted from the dead machine, and they collapsed against it in exhaustion. Both men were covered in sweat and blood, their faces grimy through the mud and spilled fuel. The only bright aspect Allen could see was that it had stopped raining at some point, and he hadn't even realised.

"I prefer," Allen rasped, breathing hard, "studying their bones in the lab."

A change came across Monroe then as he remembered just what had placed them in such a predicament to begin with. "The triceratops, lad. Where is it?" He looked around as though he might still be able to catch more than a glimpse of the thing.

"Gone, sir. Thankfully."

Monroe sagged against the side of the vehicle and shook his head. "Almost killed by one and I still don't get a proper look."

Allen liked Monroe, he really did; he just wished sometimes the honorary professor could get his priorities straightened out.

CHAPTER FOUR

"Any sign of the boys, Prof?"

Travers had been going through her paperwork when Garrel entered the room. The group was so small they tried to maintain a semblance of a social order, so eating breakfast in the same room was encouraged. As Garrel helped herself to some cornflakes and opened every cupboard in search of a clean bowl, she had just been trying to make conversation. That Travers was too engrossed in her work to even offer a good morning annoyed Garrel sometimes; but she didn't much like Travers anyway so quickly got over it.

Locating her bowl, Garrel poured her cereal, drowned each flake in milk and purposefully sat at the same table as the professor, directly opposite, plopping her bowl upon the paperwork.

Travers looked up, mildly annoyed. "Good morning, Sara," she said tersely.

"There," Garrel smiled. "Wasn't so difficult. And a very good morning to you too, Professor."

Travers glanced at her bowl. "You sure you don't want any cereal with that milk?"

"Ah, funny lady. Where I come from we have a wonderful name for people like you."

"If it's not Professeur I don't think I want to know." Travers looked around. "Have you seen Monroe and Allen?"

"You know, for a professor you're really not very bright sometimes." She spooned in another mouthful of cornflakes, wishing she hadn't put quite so much milk on them after all. "They'd better not break my buggy, that's all I care about."

"Why would they break the buggy?"

Garrel chewed more cornflakes. "I get the feeling you didn't authorise their little excursion this morning."

"What excursion?"

"Are you going to repeat everything I say as a question?"

"What question?"

Garrel's spoon stopped halfway to her mouth and she studied the Professor's face, which was desperately trying not to break into a smile. "Funny," Garrel said, continuing with her breakfast.

"Seriously," Travers said, setting down her work. "You're saying Allen and Monroe took the buggy out, right? They're probably collecting samples or something. I wouldn't worry."

"I don't know; they've been gone a while."

"Well, let's not panic just yet. At least it's stopped raining."

"Yeah, but it's terrible out there. If they've lost my buggy in a muddy ditch I'm not going to be happy."

"Well if they only went this morning, I'm sure they're fine."

Garrel finished off her bowl. "Sure, but it's three in the afternoon now."

"It's what? Then ... why are you eating cornflakes?"

"I like cornflakes. And I had the feeling you were out of whack again on what time of the day it was. Figured I'd wind you up."

Travers narrowed her eyes. "You really are the most infuriating woman, Sara."

"I know. I really try."

"Well if you wouldn't mind taking a trip after them, I could get back to work," Travers said. She did not speak with imperious dismissal, although it was clear she thought her decision marked the end of the exchange.

"I'm not a bodyguard, Prof," Garrel said. "Nor am I a babysitter."

"I never said you were. But you're a human being and we have to look out for each other in this place."

"Then you go out after them."

"You're better suited for it. Besides, I need to finish my work before our time runs out. If I don't discover the secrets of Ceres before we leave my backers aren't going to be happy."

"I thought Monroe was your backer?"

"Financial backer, yes. But I don't report to him."

Garrel already knew some of this, and didn't much care about the rest. What Travers was saying was true, in part. They did have to look out for each other on Ceres, and it didn't matter what Garrel had been hired as: she could not let people face the wildlife alone if she could help it. That Travers simply wanted to carry on with her digging annoyed Garrel, but she was not stubborn enough to refuse to make sure Allen and Monroe were all right.

"Fine, I'll track them," Garrel said. "And if I fail and we all disappear, maybe you'll dig us up some day."

Travers properly looked at her for the first time since Garrel had sat down with her cornflakes. Her eyes were stern, her expression sour, and Garrel could sense she was about to start one of her lectures.

"You don't like me do you?" Travers asked.

Garrel thought hard for several moments. "No."

"Don't hold back or anything."

"Professor, you treat the bones of long-dead animals with more gentleness than you do those of us who are still breathing. I know you have targets and I know you're under pressure to find answers; but the secrets of Ceres have remained unexplained for generations. What makes you think you're going to solve all the riddles in just a few months?"

"You think we're wasting our time here?" She seemed genuinely shocked at the suggestion.

"Honestly? Yeah, I do. And even if you could find out all the answers, who says you should? There are some things we don't need all the answers to."

"I suppose you think Ceres was God's second stab at Creation then?"

"I don't know what to think. No, I don't necessarily believe that. But I don't not believe it either."

Travers shook her head. "You people are insane."

"What people would that be? I'm not a fanatic sent to sabotage your expedition. Just because I have different religious beliefs than you, you can't just label me as 'you people'. I thought science was all about asking questions and formulating theories. Sounds to me as though you're as narrow-minded as the religious fanatics you seem to hate so much."

Garrel had not meant to explode like that, nor had she ever wanted to get into a religious debate with Professor Travers. But they had been cooped up together for so long that every little thing was grating on one another's nerves and Garrel was suddenly looking forward to being away from her.

"You're right," Travers surprised her by saying. "I'm sorry. I'm just so frustrated with all of this. All I really have to date are rocks and fossils. If I can work out how long the fossils have been here, I can figure a rough age of Ceres. But I'm not a palaeontologist and I really don't care about dinosaurs anyway."

"What does that matter?"

"Ceres is the dinosaur world. I was chosen for this expedition because it was deemed I would be the one most likely to solve the riddle of Ceres. But my backers also want information about the dinosaurs, since no one living has officially even been here."

Garrel understood. "They're making you branch out into palaeontology when your specialist field is archaeology."

"And they're still expecting me to crack the case. Give me a vase any day, Sara. An ancient piece of pottery I can date to within fifty years. But dinosaur skeletons? That takes far more investigation and examination of the actual rock it came from."

"And they only let you bring one assistant," Garrel said. No wonder Professor Travers was frustrated all the time. Suddenly Garrel felt bad about baiting her the way she always did.

"You concentrate on your work, Prof. I'll go fetch the boys."

"My work," Travers said in exasperation. "I could actually do my work if it wasn't so wet outside. Half my equipment's not going to operate in all that wetness and my excavation sites are all flooded."

"I have a bucket."

Travers did not seem amused, so Garrel rose from the table. "I'll bring them back as soon as I find them. Might have to grab some heavy equipment to bring back the buggy if it's in a ditch though."

She hastened from the room and headed outside. The air was heavy with moisture and the ground was slick with mud, her boots squelching every step she took. It was still blisteringly warm though, and as Garrel looked up at the sun blazing in the sky she knew it was just one more thing about Ceres no one understood. Because that wasn't the sun. It was some form of artificial light which looked like one, and which was almost always in the sky. It would disappear at night, and night would always quickly set in, and would return come the morning; but there was no physical substance to the thing. Whoever had created Ceres had obviously decided the world was too far from the centre of the solar system to receive adequate lighting from the real sun so had created this artificial construct. But there was no artificial star orbiting Ceres. In fact, no one had even known how Ceres was heated, and had assumed it was either pale light from the sun or else geothermal in nature. When the expedition had landed, they were astounded to see an actual ball of hydrogen burning in the heavens.

For Garrel it was almost definitive proof that God's hand had been involved in the crafting of this world. She had never known what to think, and had always kept an open mind, but the very fact that she could stand there staring at a sun which was not actually there was the clincher for her.

Yet she could also see Travers's points of view. Before any decision was reached Travers wanted to examine everything and determine an answer. Garrel could understand that, and certainly if Travers did come up with some interesting results Garrel would be the first to examine them. But what if Travers came up with results which proved the world was indeed pieced together by some higher being? Garrel could not imagine Travers even then admitting the world was anything but artificial.

It was why Garrel was hoping Travers's research would prove inconclusive. She did not need to know, did not really want to know, and just wanted to get back home so she could tell her family about everything she had seen. It was ironic that before coming to Ceres Garrel had not even been especially religious. She had been born into a Catholic family and had gone to church every Sunday as a child. Since that time she had maintained her religiousness but had never been outspoken about it. Travers had in her obstinate manner torn all these thoughts and feelings from deep within her, which clearly had not been her intent.

Arriving at the transportation storage area, Garrel looked over the remaining vehicles. The actual craft which had brought them to Ceres stood off to one side. It wasn't much, but it had got them here. It did not belong to Garrel, but she had trained so many hours in craft of the same model that she could have flown the thing drunk and still have been able to crawl her way to the bathroom to throw up. Thankfully she had not used this for an answer during her interview.

The other vehicles were arranged undercover, although the rain had managed to seep through the thin wood of the prefabricated camp and covered each with a sheen of moisture. The buggy was the most useful vehicle, for it was designed to traverse all manner of terrain. But the buggy was gone, leaving only two other vehicles. One was a squat, box-like machine with a propeller. In this, two people could stand and rise into the air for a shaky flight. Garrel had always seen the thing as a cross between a helicopter and the basket of a hot-air balloon. It was a lightweight contraption and easily manoeuvred, but not a machine Garrel would have taken out by choice.

The final vehicle was a two-wheeled motorbike with room enough on the seat for a passenger if they clutched the rider very tightly. Mounting the bike, Garrel affixed the helmet in place and gunned the engine. The bike was faster than the buggy and she would be able to catch up to them fairly easily. However, she would not be able to bring both men back with her at the same time, so would have to make two trips if the buggy was stuck somewhere. She would need one of them to wait with the buggy anyway so she could return with some heavy equipment, so that worked out fine for her.

She liked to consider the vehicles her property, but the truth was they belonged to the expedition's financiers. However, she had signed a contract saying that she wasn't liable for any damages to the vehicles, but that if she failed to come back with one of them she would be charged for it out of her pay. And she needed all the money she could get.

The bike hit the muddy ground with a sputter and Garrel realised she would not have been able to achieve quite the speed she was after. A light rain was just starting up once more as she set off, but it was as nothing to the downpour of the previous night and she hoped to be back at the camp before it could repeat the deluge. The tracks of the buggy seemed easy to follow in the mud, although she could already see many of those tracks had been washed away. The initial path the tracks were taking seemed to be skirting the woodland, however, and that gave her somewhere to start. She was glad the men had not entered the woods, for after her last encounter there Garrel had no desire to return any time soon. She was not skittish about any animal, but knew rhinoceroses were purported to have excellent memories; and if one large herbivore could memorise people who had angered it in the past, she did not want to test the ankylosaur in case it held similar grudges.

She tried to think of what animals lived beyond the woods, although seldom did any of their team head out that way. There were herds of herbivores living on the plains, but she didn't know what types of animals they were. As for carnivores, she still hadn't seen any at all in the flesh, and wasn't really afraid of bumping into any. She would admit to a mild curiosity about them, for every child wanted to meet tyrannosaurus rex face-to-face, but she wasn't afraid to. Garrel had once been confronted by a lion and had survived. That had been something she *had* raised during her interview, and had embellished it as much as she could. In reality the beast had just feasted so she had been in very little danger. The lion had watched her with lazy eyes but as soon as it realised she was no threat to it, it had rolled over and gone to sleep, with one eye open. She could not imagine reptile predators being any different, especially since reptiles did not need to eat quite as often as mammals.

Thunder rumbled overhead and Garrel drew her bike to a halt, gazing out across the plains which came after the woodland. Much of the land around this area was rocky, and the tracks of the buggy would have been erased by the rain; but some of the land was covered with a grassy veranda and she felt she would be better off checking this area first. At least she would be able to better determine tracks from there, and return to the rocks if she had no luck with the grasses. She checked her watch and was surprised to find half an hour had already passed. Garrel enjoyed feeling the pressure of speed pushing against her while she rode against the storm and knew how easy it was for her to lose track of time in this place. She would have to be careful she didn't turn this rescue operation into a pleasure jaunt.

Starting the bike once more, Garrel had to admit to herself how nice it was to be alone on this world, riding around without a care, answerable to no one. It was intoxicating and addictive. She would have to be very careful indeed not to just ride away and leave her expedition and all its problems behind her.

She had often wondered what anyone would do about it, considering this world was quarantined, and not even soldiers could come in searching for her.

Garrel arrived at the grassy plains and found what she strongly believed were tyre tracks. That her search was going so well was uplifting, although Garrel had never been one to entrust too much to luck. She checked the fuel gauge on her bike and reasoned she was good for a few more hours yet. Even the time of day was working to her advantage, for the artificial sun would not flee for several hours yet. If the rain would stop she might even enjoy this excursion entirely.

Pressing on, Garrel passed a triceratops herd, but steered well clear of them. She knew full well the noise of her bike would spook the animals and the last thing she wanted was to be caught in the stampede of a frightened herd of five tonne monsters.

The grass began to peter out and Garrel slowed. The rain was intensifying and her visibility was decreasing incredibly. The ground gave way to rocks, made slippery by the rain, and so jagged did the terrain become that she decided if she continued much longer she was going to get herself killed. Bringing the bike to a stop, Garrel stepped off and located an overhang of rock which would offer the bike at least some protection from the downpour. With the rain came an overbearing chill and Garrel hugged herself tightly as she pressed her back against the rocks, wishing Ceres would make up its mind as to what the temperature was going to be. Shivering, trying desperately to still her chattering teeth, Garrel looked through the storm to try to work out where she was, and whether the buggy might have made it over this terrain. It seemed too haphazard for such a vehicle and she decided she had likely made a wrong turn somewhere along her journey.

The wind shifted and Garrel found herself being blasted with the worst of the deluge, so she headed away from her bike to try to find somewhere better to be hiding from the storm. Walking to the edge of the rocks, she gazed down and realised she was on some form of mountain range. Below she could see valleys and a torrential river which was tearing at the trees growing on the mountainside. Garrel could not be certain, but she got the impression that river had not been there only a week earlier.

She heard a terrible cracking and looked up to see a portion of the mountain give way under the pressure of the storm. Rock and filthy water careened down the side of the mountain, disappearing into the black depths of the river beneath her, and Garrel decided she needed to get away from the area as quickly as possible. Returning to her bike, she gunned the engine and headed back the way she had come. She was driving against the rain now, and it battered her as though some great god wanted to keep her where it could play with her. She moved slowly, fully aware she could at any moment lose her balance and topple over the mountainside, but if the mountain was giving way the worst place she could remain was beneath that overhang.

Garrel swore as something lunged before her. She swerved the bike as the creature, some form of deer, froze in fear at her approach. The bike twisted and she felt her fingers slip from the handlebar. The deer bolted, but Garrel was giving the animal no further thought as she felt herself tumbling away from her bike. Throwing up her arms, she felt the bike brush past her as it sailed over her head, but then she felt the ground give way beneath her and she knew her worst fears were realised. Frantically trying to grasp the slippery sides of the cliff, Garrel scrabbled in vain. She felt her foot tear through the crumbling rock and then she was falling like a plummet into the black depths of the raging river below.

Her final hope before she plunged into the freezing depths was that her crash helmet might somehow enable her to survive what was without doubt the worst crash of her life.

CHAPTER FIVE

The storm was strong, but Allen hoped the bad weather would keep the triceratops away. They had not seen the animal since it had crushed their buggy, but Allen was hardly taking any chances. He and Monroe had left the buggy and started back across the plains without any hope of reaching the camp before nightfall, even though they still had several hours. The rain and the animals would have likely proven enough to keep them back, although Monroe had suffered an injury to his leg and was hobbling. Allen knew he was himself fortunate to have come out of the wreck relatively unscathed, for his own injuries had turned out to be more panic than substance. But he was not a doctor and there was nothing he could do for Monroe. The Professor tried not to slow them too badly, but there was no denying they would not be getting very far.

And then a strange sight had appeared in the distance and Monroe had pointed it out eagerly, determining it to be a rampaging dinosaur. But it was moving too fast and causing too much noise to be a dinosaur, and Allen recognised the motorbike from the camp. Dropping Monroe, Allen had waved his arms frantically, shouting as loud as he could, but Garrel had not seen him and had all but avoided the plain, heading off towards a rockier area.

"We should head after her," Allen said, finding Monroe where he had dropped him. "We have a better chance of getting back to camp if we walk in the opposite direction."

"Chasing your girlfriend all across this wet world," Monroe said, teeth gritted through the pain, "is not a good reason to drag me around, lad."

"I thought you wanted to see dinosaurs, Professor."

"I do."

"Well do you see any on these plains?"

"No."

"Then maybe they've all taken shelter in the rocks."

Monroe laughed. "Ludicrous, of course. But at least you're thinking. Come on then, let's see how fast I can move when we're both properly motivated."

It took the two men far too long to cross the plain and evening was setting in by the time they made it to even the beginning of the rocks. Night always fell quickly on Ceres and they knew they would have to find somewhere to stop. They were exhausted and far from their camp, and they knew that night always brought out the worst predators. So far the expedition had managed to avoid being out at night, and if they ever went out to collect samples they were fastidious in making certain they were back before night fell entirely. Their video equipment had caught images of truly horrific monsters roaming the lands at night, and Allen did not ever want to meet any of them; although surmised Monroe would have been ecstatic to find himself in the hunting ground of such beasts. Allen was glad their monitoring of the lands were done purely for purposes of defence, for if their interest was in researching the dinosaurs rather than the fossils he could not imagine any of them walking away from this mission.

There had been a lot of speculation over the years as to why the dinosaurs acted erratically, although of course with no one legally travelling to Ceres there were only ever rumours as to how they behaved anyway. Information was supposedly gathered through long-range probes and really powerful telescopes, although Allen had a sneaking suspicion that the Jovian government knew far more about the dinosaurs here than they would ever say. Even since Allen and the others had arrived, they had noticed what could have been termed erratic behaviour for dinosaurs. Many of the old theories were being overturned when confronted with living specimens, although they had to remember that the dinosaurs on Ceres were unnatural. There were so many factors differentiating Ceres and prehistoric Earth – from the artificial sun, different gravity, smaller land mass, greater concentration of animals which had never existed together in nature; the list was endless. As such, what was true for Earth millions of years earlier was not necessarily true for Ceres today, and it was no surprise therefore that the animals had adapted, or had never been the same to begin with. Many of the predators on Ceres, for instance, were nocturnal. That may not have been the case on Earth, but with so many different predator species on Ceres it was sometimes as though they divvied up the day and night, each keeping to their own agreed parameters.

Which of course denoted a heightened intelligence Tom Allen really didn't want to even consider.

Allen carefully set Monroe down upon the wet rocks while he himself scouted the area. He had not thought to salvage any of the equipment from the buggy, but doubted any of it would have been in working order anyway. He did thankfully have a small torch in his pocket, which he presently cast about the ground to make sure he didn't take a wrong step. The terrain was jagged here, and he surmised it could have been the result of seismic activity. He suddenly remembered why they were out here at all, and shone his torch into the cracks in the rock and the crevasses of different sizes in the hope that something might shine back out at him. But he received no such sparkle and decided there were more important things to be worrying about right at that moment.

Shining his light further afield, Allen discovered they had arrived at a system of what he could have called mountains. Massive rock structures rose at every angle, blocking even the constant sight of Jupiter lording over them all in the sky. Allen could imagine if their entire camp was dropped into this system of mountains and valleys, it would never be heard from again, no matter how many search parties were sent in.

Returning to where he had left Monroe, he found the Professor had managed to move to an overhang of rock where he was keeping relatively dry. Allen was surprised he had made it so far in so short a period of time, and worried Monroe had aggravated the wound in his leg. Once more he wished he was a doctor.

"There's a cave here," Monroe told him. "No idea how far back it goes, but it has to be better than sitting out here in the rain."

"There are mountains and valleys everywhere around us," Allen said. The storm was worsening and he could barely hear himself speak by this point. "We'll have to wait until morning to move anywhere, so we may as well try this cave of yours. I have a torch. I'll go first."

"Don't worry about me, lad; I'm not an invalid." Monroe used the wall of rock to get to his feet and Allen noticed he had procured a stout branch from somewhere, likely broken off and washed to the rocks by the storm. By using it as a makeshift crutch he was able to walk reasonably well.

Knowing any further words would be drowned out by the storm, Allen set off for the cave, Monroe trailing only slightly behind.

The cave was dark, and Allen's light only penetrated so far into the gloom. He moved slowly, although the more steps he took the less the howling of the wind battered his eardrums. His boots began to squelch, indicating that the rock was now dry underfoot, although he would not be happy to settle down for the night until he had investigated the entire cave.

"You should rest here while I explore," Allen said. "Do you have a gun?"

"Why would I have brought a gun, lad?"

"Here," Allen said, wincing even as he produced the pistol he had himself brought. A creature could just as easily be lurking at the back of the cave as coming in from the entrance, but he did not feel right in leaving Monroe defenceless.

Monroe looked at the gun and appeared uncomfortable about something. It was the look of guilt. "You keep it, lad."

"I'll be fine. If I find something I'll come running and you shoot whatever's behind me. Besides, I've never fired a gun in my life." He did not know whether Monroe had either, but he was of the upper class and there was a chance he belonged to some rifle association or something. Allen knew he was probably being prejudice in his thoughts, but soaked through and lost in a cave he found he didn't much care about things like that.

"You're a good man, Allen," Monroe said, accepting the gun at last. "Hurry back, eh?"

"I'll try not to get eaten, sir."

There were no further words to say, and Allen knew if he stopped any longer he would likely lose the necessary courage to press on alone and unarmed. He could not see the feeble light of his torch doing much to deter an angry carnivore whose bedroom he was invading.

The cave was relatively smooth, the walls solid, and he knew it would come to an end shortly rather than opening out into a network. Allen knew little about caves, but being an archaeologist he knew perhaps more than most. He knew most caves were formed by water, for instance, and the general smoothness of this one indicated it was one of them. It was possible there had been a waterway running through this area at some point, perhaps even an ocean. He did not know whether there actually were any oceans on Ceres, but certainly there was water.

None of this mattered at present, however, and he knew it was just his nervous brain's way of dealing with the situation.

At last his torchlight pierced the blackness and found the end of the cave. There was a scattering of branches and a few bones to prove some animal had at one time called this cave its own, but there was nothing to indicate anything had been here recently. Allen kicked through what amounted to the nest, and it broke apart easily. Certainly there was nothing living here now, and he felt a little better knowing that any animal that might attack him would have to first get through Monroe and his pistol.

He was just about to return to Monroe when the light of his torch glinted off something. Crouching, Allen fished through the old detritus and found something which felt like metal. Picking it out of the mess, he rubbed the thing on his trousers to wipe away some of the dirt and examined what he had found. It was small, no larger than a penny, and seemed to be made of gold. There was a hook at the top to indicate it had at one time been attached to a chain, although such was long gone. He played his fingers around it and found a catch at the base. Pressing it, the small golden ornament split in two on a hinge and he realised what he was holding was a locket. There was a picture inside: an old, worn photograph of a young man's face. He appeared only around twenty, with dark hair and a pleasant smile. It was difficult to tell from such a small picture, but by the style of the image he would have expected this not to be recent.

Taking the locket with him, Allen worked his way quickly back to where Monroe was waiting. The Professor was glad to see him, and listened as Allen told him nothing had lived in the cave for a long while. Then Allen showed him the locket and he took it with intrigue.

"I wonder how it got here," Allen said.

"Someone dropped it."

"I guess. But Ceres is quarantined."

"Doesn't stop people coming here, lad."

"Really? But the law ..."

Monroe laughed, and Allen felt suddenly foolish. "Ceres is the most famous place in the whole Jovian system: in the whole solar system probably. For years there's been talk about sending people here for various reasons, Allen, but the recommendations have always been vetoed. It would be the ideal place for soldiers to train, or to send ex-wives and mother-in-laws. If you make something illegal it only makes people want to do it more."

"But there are patrols aren't there?"

Monroe shrugged. "There are also rumours of any incoming craft being vaporised, but we made it through. Ceres's airspace is apparently monitored, so the government knows who's coming and going, but even if someone lands here what then? No one is allowed on Ceres, so the government wouldn't be allowed to send someone here after them. If someone does manage to land on Ceres, there's nothing anyone can do about it."

Allen was not so sure, but then Monroe knew more about these things than he did.

"Picture this," Monroe said. "Let's say the government does a U-turn on our being here. They send us a message the instant we get back to camp, telling us we have to leave Ceres right now. And we say no. We even send a message back telling them where to stick it. What are they going to do about it?"

Allen had never thought of that before, but what Monroe was saying did make a certain kind of sense. Ceres was a political minefield, and there were more governments trying to claim the world than any other piece of land in the history of the human race. Even within the Jupiter system there were various governments which thought Ceres should belong to them, and that was before Earth even put their oar in. Their own government sending in an extraction team would likely spark a system-wide cold war.

"So how many people," Allen asked slowly, "do you think have been here over the years?"

"I wouldn't care to guess. How many fleas on a dog?"

"You really think it's that many?"

"Allen, there aren't any records kept about Ceres, no official records anyway. No one's supposed to know anything about this place for the simple reason that no one's ever been here before."

"I think the government must have been then," Allen said, although not liking to admit it aloud. "I agree they've probably been here more than once without telling anyone. But they wouldn't leave a locket behind."

"Then it could be anyone," Monroe said. "Young lovers looking for solace, teenagers on a dare, religious nuts who seem to think the world evidence of the Second Coming. Or just unfortunates who crashed here. You can't stop people coming to Ceres, Allen: especially not by putting up a 'do not enter' sign."

Allen clutched the locket tightly, imagining which of those the owner could have been. Young lovers seemed the most appropriate. He could only imagine the horror they had gone through for that locket to have ended where it had.

"How old do you reckon the locket to be?" Monroe asked.

"I don't know."

"Give it here."

Allen complied and Monroe turned it over in his hand, curious. But Allen knew Monroe knew next to nothing about archaeology, and curiosity alone did not solve riddles.

"I'll get Professor Travers to look it over," Allen said, taking it back and dropping it into a pocket. "Maybe we can even try to return it to the boy's family."

"What boy?"

Allen wondered whether Monroe was being intentionally stupid. "We should camp down for the night," he said instead. "In the morning we can start looking for Sara again. With any luck the storm might have stopped by then."

Monroe nodded and struggled to his feet, but Allen made him rest.

"Stay and watch the cave entrance," Allen said. "I'll fetch some of the wood from the back of the cave and start a fire. I don't have any food, but maybe we could dry out our clothes."

It was not ideal, but it was all they had. Things would look better in the morning.

CHAPTER SIX

Jeannie looked up at her with wide, expectant eyes, clutching the swirling lollipop which was almost as large as her head. She knew the lolly had been a bribe, because Jeannie was the smartest five-year-old Sara Garrel had ever known. Of course, being her mother, she was slightly biased.

"The clown show starts in ten minutes," Garrel told her with a broad grin. "If we don't hurry we're going to miss getting a good seat."

"Mummy, why is Daddy leaving?"

It was a question Garrel had been hoping Jeannie wouldn't have asked aloud, or at least not quite so bluntly. It was of course all the girl cared about at that moment. The visit to the circus at the seaside was supposed to take her mind off things, take both their minds off things, but it seemed Jeannie was so smart she was going to take the bribe and still ask the awkward questions anyway. Garrel was beginning to feel the upcoming mad sugar-rushing five-year-old was something she could have done without if she was going to be answering these questions anyway.

"Daddy loves you, sweetheart," Garrel said, falling to one knee so she could talk with her daughter at eye level. Hundreds of people were walking or running past them, so many other families with candy floss and ice cream tucked into the children's tiny hands, but none of them paid any attention to Garrel and Jeannie. "Daddy just ... needs some time away."

"Is it because of that floozy?" Jeannie asked, licking her lollipop.

Garrel started. "Jeannie, where did you pick up a nasty word like that?"

"I heard you talking on the phone to Grandma. You were crying. You said you hoped that floozy was already cheating on him so he'd know what it was like."

Garrel did not know what to say, or perhaps had said too much. She ruffled her daughter's hair and said, "Mummy's going to take good care of you, OK, sweetheart? Daddy's not going to be around so much any more."

"Is that because his floozy told him not to be?"

That was precisely why, but Garrel could think of no way to explain that to a five-year-old girl. Then she realised she didn't have to, considering Jeannie had just explained it to her own mother. Garrel caught her daughter up in a tight embrace and tried to hold back her tears. "You're a special girl, Jeannie. Don't ever forget that."

Jeannie hugged her back and Garrel felt warmth flowing through her. Then she felt something tugging at her finger, and with each tug she felt colder and colder, an uncomfortable wetness seeping through her very being.

Sara Garrel opened her eyes to find herself lying on her back, staring up at a thin strip of light formed by two almost joining sides of a steep crevasse. She could feel water soaking through her back and knew if she was lying on her belly she would have drowned. The steady slosh of the water told her she was close to a body of it, and as she turned her head to the right she could see where the artificial river was funnelling away. The sky above did not appear to be showing any further rain, but there was still a steady trickle leading into whatever rocky pit within which she had found herself entrapped. She doubted there was a way out, and that was even before she had stood up. Her body ached from exertion and near-drowning, while her stomach rumbled in hunger. It may well have been many hours since she had plunged into the river and she knew she was lucky to be alive at all.

She felt something tugging her finger again and looked to the left; and suddenly jerked her hand in revulsion.

The two-foot-long beast jumped in fright and began hissing at her.

What the thing was, Garrel could not say. It looked part bird, part dinosaur, but might well have been neither. Its arms and legs were entirely feathered, much as a bird's, and even as it hopped backwards in alarm she could see it likely used them for gliding rather than flying; which meant it was as trapped as she was down here. It had a short body with what appeared to be very feeble bone structure, while its head was formed of a snout filled with small, sharp teeth.

The creature looked more scared than dangerous, and Garrel assumed it usually ate fish and insects. She saw her fingers were bloody where it had tried to tear into them, although thankfully she had worn gloves with her bike and aside from tearing through the material the dinosaur bird thing had done her very little damage at all.

Rising into a sitting position, Garrel groaned and realised she had lost her helmet somewhere along the fall. That may well have been a good thing, considering the glass of the visor might well have blinded her otherwise.

The creature cawed and hissed at the same time now and Garrel felt like wringing its neck and eating it just to shut the stupid thing up.

Getting to her feet, Garrel went through a systematic arrangement of her daily exercises and determined the worst part of her condition was that she was hungry. Performing a brief visual search of her surroundings, she decided she was in a strange place indeed. Some of the rocks were smooth, and there were marks upon the walls indicating the rising of the tide. Yet the water sloshing around before her was only there because of the flood. She was standing upon a wide ledge of rock, and could see the river was only focused upon the one side of the valley because of the depression in the ground. By all she could see, water flowing through here was a common process, which meant this area of Ceres was prone to flooding. It might well be seasonal, since they had not known any truly bad weather until a week or so earlier.

However, the valley was not all smooth. Sharp, jagged rocks rose at all angles, indicating it had been formed by seismic activity. She could only imagine what destruction the two combined could accomplish. Quakes and floods together had formed this valley, but if both were to strike at the same time it would be as though Ceres itself was exploding in anger.

But Garrel was not an archaeologist and understood very little of such things. If Travers or even Allen was with her she might have some better answers.

Thoughts of Allen brought a sharp stab to her mind. She had set out initially after Allen and Monroe and thus far had seen no sign of them. That she had fallen foul of the weather likely meant they had fared far worse, for she had been hired as a survivalist. That they could both be dead was not something she wanted to consider, yet it was the most likely possibility: unless they had taken shelter somewhere. Still, there was nothing she could do to help them until she got herself out of this mess, so she concentrated on her own predicament.

Light was still pouring in from above, although she knew once it began to get dark she would lose light very quickly, what with the small aperture through which the sun's rays were filtering. Tufts of vegetation grew by the side of the river, struggling for survival in even the worst of conditions. Garrel decided she would not be outdone by a weed.

She moved across to see where the water was going. She could see how it was coming in, by flowing down the valley's side and running through the enclosed area. It only ran for twenty metres or so before crashing against the far wall and disappearing, and it was to this that Garrel headed. It did not look especially pleasant as the dirty river water slammed into the wall and disappeared down a crack in the haphazard formation of the valley. The hole did not appear very large, but she felt she would be able to squeeze through. However, she could not see anything beneath her. For all she knew the water dropped for a thousand metres, or else crashed into jagged rocks. The one thing she had in her favour was that there was so much water going down that hole that it had to lead somewhere: it could not simply hit solid rock and trickle through cracks smaller than Garrel's body. If she went down that hole she was certain she would not become trapped, with tonnes of water hammering at her head.

But leaping into the unknown did not seem like the best of ideas either.

The dinosaur bird snapped at her once more where she was crouching, trying to nip her backside. She looked at it, wishing she had some fancy green and yellow feathers so she could fly out of the valley, but even if she plucked the beast it would not help her any. That the creature was trapped just as badly as she suddenly occurred to her, for the creature could glide but not fly. It was frightened and nipping at her because it perhaps felt she was either a threat or even the reason it was trapped here at all. She could hardly blame it for its panic, but tying it to a rock and dropping it through the hole was appealing to her. If she listened to its shriek as it fell she might be able to get a fair idea of what was down there.

Then she disregarded the idea as cruel and wondered what Jeannie would have to say had she heard such thoughts.

Jeannie.

She was so far away now, worlds away, and Garrel felt a stab in her heart as she thought of her. She didn't want to be here, she wanted to be with her daughter. But that wasn't possible, and if she wanted Jeannie she needed money. Money was what kept life going, and as much as Garrel hated it, it was the only reason she was here. It was strange being on Ceres, a world which had never even countenanced a monetary system, and she wished she could just take Jeannie and bring her here. At least she would be safe, and away from her father.

She shook such thoughts from her mind. Jeannie was a long way away and she needed to focus on where she was, else she would never get to see her again.

Standing upon the edge of the hole, water sluicing through and frothing dark murky slush, she could see nothing of her fate and tried to still the sudden tremble to her body. She had convinced herself she would not be crushed to death should she make this leap of faith, but that was because she had no other choice. She could not ascend the smooth valley walls which sloped inwards to the summit, and could not stand around waiting for a rescue when there were only three other people on the world, two of them lost.

Beside her the strange dinosaur bird cawed once more, and she realised the major difference between her and it. They were both panicked and afraid, but the creature would do nothing about it. It would leap around frantically but ever remain trapped. Eventually it would die from lack of food. It was not willing to take a risk and potentially save its life. As much as she was jealous of its beautiful plumage, Sara Garrel was not a dinosaur bird. She would shape her own future.

Taking a deep breath, Garrel closed her eyes, took one step forward and disappeared into the raging maelstrom.

Her world exploded as she was physically battered by the massive assault of water. The thunder slammed through her ears, the savage chill freezing her to the marrow. Garrel had never been one to underestimate any force of nature, and water had always been the thing she respected most. Even a simple stream which looked so calm could hold a hidden current to snap away a human life in moments. Water knew it was necessary to the continued existence of all life, and lorded over all species in its arrogance.

Her back slammed into a particularly sharp rock and she could feel the sting of an open wound. Her body was being battered from all directions as she was swept through the rock structures, and she felt her lungs screaming at her for release. But she kept her eyes closed, her breath inside her, and just allowed the current to take her, playing with her as it saw fit.

Something struck her in the stomach and Garrel felt the air explode from her lungs. She gasped, stale air filling her chest, and she opened her eyes to find she was in some form of lake. The water cascaded from above, creating a dark and terrible waterfall which fed the lake constantly. Garrel trod water and turned to survey the area into which she had fallen. She estimated the lake stretched for perhaps fifty metres, yet the massive cavern in which she found herself was so dark she could not be certain of anything. She could see light reflecting off the cavern walls and sought out the source of illumination, but could find nothing. She had floated clear of the falling water and found the lake calmer now, more relaxing. It was even warmer than it had been in the river above, and she guessed it was being radiated with geothermal energy from below. She could see no sign of the water running off anywhere but hoped it was not all collecting in this lake; otherwise it would eventually fill the entire cavern and she would drown.

She could not see any sign of a shore, but the cavern was terribly dark, even with the strange illumination, and she had to hope there was one. Otherwise her already haggard body would tire and she would fall unconscious in the water.

Something brushed her leg then and she remembered the contact with her stomach which had expelled her breath. That there were fish in this lake was unlikely considering it had been mainly formed of rainwater, but she had no idea how long the actual lake had been here. She could not think that there would be anything actually living in the lake, but nor could she chance her life upon it.

Pushing her body into motion, Garrel gently began to swim in a direction away from the cascading waterfall. She knew a massive amount of splashing would alert anything in the lake, and in her exhaustion she knew she would not be able to fight against whatever was there.

She had made only several strokes before something once more touched her leg. She had no idea what it might have been, and was not about to craft terrible images within her mind. The only possibility she could entertain was that she was in a dark lake with a potential creature feeling her out as prey.

She continued swimming, not stopping even when the thing had touched her. She paddled for several minutes and slowly she could see the waves lapping ahead and drawing back as though they were caressing a shoreline. The farther she travelled, the more she became convinced it was indeed a shore. The thing in the water had not troubled her for some time and she had even managed to convince herself that it was nothing but a harmless fish. Perhaps there were so many of them in the lake that she had connected with different ones each time. If so, once she was on dry land she could cast in a hook or a net and catch something to eat.

She could make out shapes ahead of her now as well, in the gloom. There were a lot of rocks, some of them seeming to be piled in some form of structure, but she knew she might well have been mistaken. There were strange-looking boulders lining the shore, and Garrel wondered what they were and whether they had been placed there on purpose.

Then one of the boulders moved, waddling towards the water's edge, and Garrel froze. She watched as the boulder slipped into the lake, disappearing beneath the surface, and she knew that whatever had been touching her under the water was the least of her concerns now. In fact, she would almost welcome the simple fish as company.

Changing direction, Garrel swam as hard as she could for what she hoped was another section of shore. She no longer cared what was in the water noticing her splashing, for she could see the tell-tale sign of a wake ahead of her; a wake suggesting there was something heading straight towards her.

Pouring all her strength into her already tired limbs, Garrel knew her adrenalin could only take her so far.

And then something rose behind her and she spun in the water as a great form came down towards her. She could see very little of it, but the flash of its eye and teeth was unmistakable. Thrusting out with her arms, Garrel attempted to fend off the beast, but it was too late. As it landed upon her the two of them vanished beneath the surface of the lake and her world once more descended into the murky watery depths.

CHAPTER SEVEN

The rain had ceased by morning and as Allen awoke it was with a real sense that he might be able to find Sara Garrel. Without doubt she had done the same thing as had he and Monroe: taken shelter for the night in a cave. It was possible she had headed back to the camp, which meant she would be setting out again to look for them at any moment. Either way she would likely be in the rocky terrain, unless of course she had doubled back to locate their demolished buggy. He could only imagine how she would react to that, thinking they had both been devoured by some terrible lizard. He knew how he would react were he to even suspect that Garrel had been killed in such a fashion and liked to think she would be at least slightly saddened at his loss.

As he kicked to death the remnants of their fire, he forced himself to face the terrible reality that Garrel did not care for him quite that much. He had been hoping he might grow on her, that he might be able to help her forget all her problems, but he had been thinking all night about what Monroe had said about trying to hook the woman and had come to one fatal conclusion; all he did was annoy her. He wanted something special with her and she saw him as an irritation, like a swarm of gnats by the riverside at night. It was not an analogy he liked to consider, yet he had to be truthful. And if he was that much of an annoyance perhaps he could make it up to her.

Make it up to her by having to be rescued. Allen knew his courtship had started off very badly and only promised to get worse the more time passed.

Monroe was outside, scanning the landscape with a small pair of binoculars Allen did not know he had. Emerging into the vast outside world, Allen was taken aback and could not imagine how anyone would want to lessen the greatness of what was spread before them by focusing on something so small. The mountains rose darkly like giant stone sentinels, watching over the twisting, meandering valleys flowing below. There was a sticky mist to the air following the storm, and the humidity of the air was returning now the chill mixture of the storm and night was over. Allen could see where water had torn down massive chunks of the mountains, and he could see where a slurry of dirt and rock, even a scattering of trees, had brought down the mountainside in a sludgy mess. He could hear the distant roar of waves crashing on rock, and knew the storm itself had been strong enough of late to have formed those rivers.

"Morning," Allen said, taking a deep breath of the fresh mountain air.

Monroe made a noncommittal sound and Allen began working through some stretches, noticing that Monroe was no longer using his makeshift cane. Last night Monroe had insisted on bandaging his own wound, although as Allen looked it over from behind he could see no sign of blood saturating it. That was good, considering they didn't have any bandages and were just using strips of cloth, but it also made Allen pause with a frown.

"This isn't good," Monroe said, lowering the binoculars and turning to Allen at last.

Deciding to test a theory, Allen reached into a pocket and accidentally dropped the locket he had found the night before. It skittered close to Monroe's feet and the Professor bent to collect it for him.

Easily bent the knee which had caused him to hobble all yesterday afternoon.

Monroe handed the trinket back and as Allen took it he accidentally banged his knee into Monroe's. There were a lot of accidents this morning. Monroe did not even flinch.

"How's the leg?" Allen asked acidly.

Confusion flashed across the Professor's face; then he realised what Allen meant. Allen could see the older man was considering putting the limp back on, but said instead, "All right, you caught me. I wanted to see the dinosaurs and didn't fancy returning to camp straight away."

"Why you ..."

"And it's a good thing I did. Look."

Allen's anger turned to confusion when he realised he was being offered the binoculars. He looked from them to Monroe, and back to the binoculars. Then he snatched them and concentrated his gaze across the mountains.

"Here," Monroe said, lowering them slightly. Allen bit back his retort, but all his anger drained from him as he recognised what he was seeing. It was a streak of unnatural blue on the otherwise red/brown rocky landscape.

Removing the binoculars, he could just make out the blot of colour with his naked eye.

"That's our motorbike," he said.

"Yes. And since neither of us brought it out here, I think we know what that means."

Allen's heart thundered. "Sara."

"She came after us, lad. And the storm got her last night."

Allen rounded on him sharply. Monroe looked guilty, and he had every reason to. Allen felt like shouting, kicking his leg to make it really limp, pushing the man down the cliff; but none of it would accomplish anything. Monroe had lied and now Sara Garrel may well have paid the price. Attacking Monroe would not bring her back, and if there was a chance of saving her Allen would need him.

"I'm going down there after Sara," Allen said, his tone brooking no argument. "I want you to head back to the camp and tell Professor Travers what's happened."

"Allen, I ..."

"Save it, Professor. Sara could be dead because you were playing the wide-eyed boy searching for his dinosaurs. Do the decent thing for once."

Monroe hung his head and Allen could see he genuinely did regret his actions. It did nothing to bring Sara back, however, and Allen could not forgive him until he had found her alive and well. "I'll gather some proper equipment," he told Allen, "and return to help find her. If she's still alive, we'll rescue her."

Allen felt like keeping the binoculars just to spite him, but they would be extra weight and he needed to travel as light as possible. He did not see whether Monroe left in the direction of the camp, but had to assume the man had some decency left to him. His attention had to focus exclusively on Sara Garrel if he was to save her, and as he set off down to where the motorbike lay he felt his own pang of guilt tug at his heart. He had desired a way to prove himself to Garrel, had not wanted her to have to rescue him. That she might herself have fallen into danger, might be lying bleeding to death at the bottom of a ravine or drowned by the torrential rains ... It was not what he had wanted, yet at the back of his mind he knew it was just what he had been wishing for.

The journey down the mountainside was difficult. He knew if he followed the path back to the plains he would be able to find the route Garrel had taken, but there were so many ways to go he knew he could well be searching for days and still not find the correct path. While he had the bike in sight he was going to take as direct a route as he possibly could, and if that meant scaling treacherous declines then so be it. Climbing equipment would have been nice, but, to consider things in a positive light, it wasn't as though he was actually climbing anywhere.

He had been descending for perhaps ten minutes before his foot slipped on the mud, the root he had balanced himself upon giving way. Allen clutched frantically at the sides of the incline but there was nothing he could do to stop himself from tumbling. His body scraped along the sides and he felt a dozen rocks slam into him as he careened down the mountainside. He ended in an explosion of pain which winded him with an audible gasp as his back struck against a particularly sharp rock. But he had stopped moving, even though his brain was still sloshing in his skull. Closing his eyes, he focused his attention and tried to recapture his breathing.

Opening his eyes once more, he tested his limbs and found them sore but not broken. Assessing his injuries, he found various scrapes and cuts, great tears in his clothes, but nothing which would not heal. Slowly he returned to his feet and looked about himself. He could see how far he had fallen and counted himself extremely fortunate not to have killed himself, so to have walked away without even a broken bone amazed him. At the rise of the mountain down which he had tumbled Allen could just see the swirling gas of Jupiter peering down at him, as though taking the credit for his miraculous escape.

On the plus side, he had descended another half hour's journey in just a few minutes.

He could see he was closer to the bike now, but still some way from it. Taking a moment to rest, Allen looked over what he could make out of the bike, trying from his aerial viewpoint to piece together what had happened. The bike lay on its side and there was a massive blue smear across the ground to indicate where it had fallen and scraped along the floor. The handlebars were dangerously close to the edge of the cliff, which would indicate Garrel had fallen into the torrent below. If that had indeed been what happened, Allen knew her chances of survival were slim, but he would not give up hope until he had exhausted all possibilities.

Unfortunately he knew there was little chance of ever finding her body. Even if it had not been consumed by some prehistoric beast, it would be buried under tonnes of silt and mud. However, he did not stop to think about how long he was going to search for her. The instant he even considered giving up the search was the moment she was lost forever, and he was not about to accept that as a possibility.

He worked his way down to the bike as quickly as he could, but after his last slip was warier in every step he took. He knew Garrel's best chance of surviving was if he hurried, but if he slipped and broke his neck he would not be doing her any good at all. After a painful eternity he finally set foot on the rocky path which also contained the bike, and moved across to assess the situation.

There was no blood on the bike that he could see, which meant Garrel had not been torn from the vehicle by any of the local animals. That was something at least, but he knew the storm was far more powerful than any of the animals could ever hope to be. He tested the bike and found it was still in good working order. The fuel line was not severed, and he tried the engine and found it grunted into life in a satisfactory manner. There was no sign of the helmet, which meant Garrel would have been wearing it at the time of her plummet, which was small consolation for him, but he was willing to take every small victory as it came.

Peering down into the thick, dirty water of the river, Allen could see no hope for Garrel at all.

"Sara!"

His voice echoed throughout the valley, yet as he listened to it die away he received no answering cry. Wherever Sara Garrel was, she was gone.

Climbing onto the bike, Allen decided the only thing he could do was follow the direction of the river. With any luck it might have spewed her out somewhere along the way and he would find her lying on the rocks somewhere. It was all he had to work with, and so he rode slowly, one eye always upon the river.

The river continued in more or less a straight line and Allen followed it relentlessly. While he was moving he was content, yet he knew he would not be happy until he found Garrel alive and well.

He continued driving until he lost the river from sight. It continued to rage, but passed through the very rock and likely continued underground. That the water was going somewhere meant it had to lead to a cavern of some form, so there was at least a chance for Garrel to still be alive. Short of leaping into the river after her, however, he could think of no means by which to find her.

Then he noticed a huge crack in the ground a little further along and he sped towards it with hope surging through his breast. Dismounting, he worked his way carefully to the crack and peered down. He could see very little, but the light of the river glinted back up to him and he knew he had found at least a portion of where it had come out. He called Garrel's name once more, although again was met only with silence. If she was down there, she was unconscious; and if she was wasn't conscious she was most likely dead.

Unable to continue his search, Allen realised his self-claimed mission of not stopping until he found her was flawed by the fact that he could do nothing about rescuing her. Heroics were a fine thing, but if he lacked the equipment to proceed it did not matter what he would risk to save her life. Only climbing equipment would help him here, and he had to be man enough to admit he could not search indefinitely without it.

He thought about the camp, about what they had stored there. Garrel had insisted on bringing all manner of equipment, and there was even more on their craft they had never even unpacked. Garrel liked to plan for every eventuality, and he could not see that she would have omitted something as simple as a rope.

Getting back on his bike, Allen headed back for the camp, hoping his selfish machismo had not endangered Garrel's life.

Hitting the open fields, Allen coaxed as much speed as he could from the bike. Before coming to Ceres he had never ridden a motorbike, but Garrel had insisted he learn how to properly use all the equipment, and this included all the vehicles. At the time he could not think how he would ever get the opportunity to ride the bike anywhere, considering Professor Travers had him examining all their finds at every opportunity; but now Garrel's life was at stake he was glad he had listened to her training.

Shooting across the plains, he was pleased to see the woodland coming into view. Thus far he had seen no sign of Monroe and had expected to catch up to him along the way, but felt perhaps he had spent more time searching for Garrel than he had realised. It was the equipment he needed anyway, not Monroe, and while his anger for the faux-archaeologist had staved off somewhat he was still more than willing to have a few cross words with the man.

Allen caught sight of movement at the edge of the woodland and feared it was another ankylosaur. But as he neared it he could see this was nothing like it at all. The long, lithe predator was eight metres long and stood twice the height of a human being. As with most large dinosaur carnivores, its body was a horizontal bullet supported by two incredibly powerful legs. Two strangely lengthy arms protruded from the fore of the creature, and indeed he could see that all four of its limbs were oddly long and thin. He was under no illusions that this made the creature less of a threat: what it might lack in raw strength he knew it would make up for in speed.

The creature seemed to be sniffing around something on the ground, a carcass perhaps, and upon seeing Allen approaching on his motorbike it raised its great razor-filled snout in the air on a thick and sinewy neck. Its tail, again quite thin for a theropod of its size, whipped lazily behind it, and Allen noted it made up for over half the creature's length.

He knew what this creature was, but only because Garrel had made him study some of the animals she knew were definitely in the vicinity of their encampment; just the carnivores – she didn't care anything for the herbivores. The dinosaur was known as a deltadromeus, and while not as large or as powerful as some of its kin, it was certainly one of the fastest. He remembered Garrel impressing upon him that the jaws of the deltadromeus were not built for snapping through bone, yet as he drew near to the creature he knew he had no desire at all to put that knowledge to the test.

Allen drew his bike to a stop around fifty metres from the beast. The pathway skirting the woodland was not very wide, perhaps only thirty metres or so, and if he went too far out it would mean taking the bike over terrain they knew was uncertain and unstable. It would not do for him to lose the bike in a pothole or a hidden bog. But riding straight past the dinosaur was also not a very clever option. Desperately Allen tried to think of an alternative, and the only other thing he could think of doing was waiting until the carnivore had moved off. But, if that was indeed a kill it had its snout in, the beast could well stay here for hours.

Sara Garrel did not have hours.

Taking a deep breath to steady his nerves, Allen gunned the engine and focused his full attention upon the deltadromeus. All he had to do was get past it and not look back. He had bad memories of the triceratops overturning the buggy, but that had been a buggy: the bike was much faster. But then so was the deltadromeus.

Before he could talk himself out of it, Allen revved the engine and shot forward. He would not attack the dinosaur directly, but pass by it within ten metres or so. Hopefully it would watch him but not give chase. As he neared the creature he noticed it watching him curiously, but making no move to intercept him. He felt if he could just pass the animal he would be back at the camp within half an hour.

And then he was passing the creature, so close he could see the blood upon its snout and teeth where it was devouring its kill. He held his breath as the bike passed the animal, and he watched that maw part slightly as though to shout obscenities after him.

"Allen!" the dinosaur shouted in the voice of Sara Garrel. "Allen, you hear me?"

His heart thumped, his hand jerked in shock, and the bike tore away from under him. It shot ahead, bouncing several times before sliding to a halt, and Allen felt the ground strike him several times as he bounded along, collecting bruises and scrapes all the way. He at last stopped rolling and struggled to rise. Pain was shooting down his leg, but he knew even if it was broken he could not afford to lie there. The deltadromeus was watching him now, its attention no longer upon its kill. It had even taken two steps towards him. The distance between Allen and the dinosaur was around forty metres now, but he knew the creature could close that gap within seconds.

He heard no more of Garrel's plaintive voice.

CHAPTER EIGHT

Tom Allen saved her life.

It was not something Garrel had ever thought she would admit, yet it was also true. As she dragged herself onto the dark shore she collapsed upon her back and regained her breath. Since coming to Ceres she had encountered all manner of creatures, although the thing in the water had been by far the most frightening. Even when she had faced that ankylosaur in the woodland she had not been so terrified; but then the water was the natural element for whatever the beast was she had just killed. And she had managed to kill it solely because of Tom Allen.

When she had taken his hunting knife from him in the woodland she had tucked it into her own belt and given it no further thought. But as the great blubbery mass of scale and flesh descended upon her she had instinctively lashed out with whatever came to hand, and that just happened to be the young man's knife. The creature had likely been used to preying on fish which did not bite back, so its attack upon Garrel had been somewhat lazy. As she sunk her knife into its head, however, the creature had thrashed in unknown pain, allowing Garrel the opportunity to stab it in what likely passed for its gut. The creature had ceased trying to kill her at that point and Garrel had kicked away, clambering onto the shore where she now lay.

Her breathing quickly returned to something approaching normal, although while she was trapped in this underground cavern she would not consider anything normal. She forced herself to think, though, for she knew that there was no problem which could not be solved without setting enough mental energy to the task. She knew she was trapped here for the moment, but she knew also that was not necessarily a death sentence. There were fish in the lake and other things preying upon them. She had seen more than one of the things on the shore, even though she could see nothing of them now through the darkness, and so much life had to endure somehow.

Having survived the water, Garrel's priority now was assessing her surroundings. From there she could try to find a way back to the surface, but not before she had taken into account everything of potential use. What she needed was light, but if she had brought a torch along with her it was long gone. Now she had the time, she tried to work out why she could see at all. She could see nothing of the ceiling so there could not have been any cracks in it, yet she could see the black shimmering surface of the lake, and also her hand if she held it before her face. She had heard of bioluminescent moss or lichen, but never outside of fiction. There was so much about Ceres no one understood, and perhaps such things did exist down here. Whatever the cause, she could see, and that was all she should have cared about. If she began analysing everything she happened upon she would turn into Professor Travers.

Moving away from the shore, Garrel held her hands out before her in case she bumped into a wall, and after only half a minute of walking did she come across something. By the feel of it, it was certainly rock, although there were grooves upon it which denoted that it had been hewn by something other than water. Crouching, Garrel stared at it as much as she could, slowly running her hands across its surface. It seemed to be formed of three separate rocks, all cut evenly and piled atop one another to stand a metre from the ground. It was likely a marker of some form, although what it could be marking she had no idea.

Moving around the stone, she felt her foot come into contact with something strange, and holding onto the marker for balance she used her foot to test the area ahead. It was formed of stone, and raised every ten centimetres or so. There was no doubt it was a narrow staircase, and as her foot found the fourth stair she decided she would lose nothing by ascending. Removing her hand from the marker, she therefore started upward, moving slowly lest her foot pass through suddenly. After fifteen steps she began to see something take shape ahead of her. A wall perhaps, and an intense blackness which might have been a doorway. The stairs ended at the blackness and she carefully walked forward, her steps slow and small, her hands outstretched. The floor was formed of flat stone, and she could smell a mustiness to the air which indicated no one had been this way for a long time. The farther she walked the more the mustiness increased, and she could only wonder at what she had stumbled upon.

Her fingers brushed against another wall; and something else. Frowning, Garrel felt around the edges of the thing she had found. It was cold, and as she flicked it, a flat, empty sound was given off. It was certainly not stone, and felt remarkably like plastic. In the centre there was a smooth, flat surface lying at an angle.

Garrel paused several moments in thought, then flicked the switch.

The entire place exploded into light and Garrel winced, closing her eyes to avoid irreparable damage. No sounds came to her, so she knew she had not disturbed any animals which might have chosen to nest in this place. Carefully she opened her eyes, staring first solely at the floor. It was indeed of stone, and formed of large, even slabs. As she raised her eyes, it was for them to widen at what was arrayed before her.

The chamber was large, with doors leading from it to places which were likely of equal interest. There were chairs in the room, and tables overflowing with various forms of equipment. She recognised some, but could not say any of it was especially modern, and none of it appeared to be turned on. She recognised a heating unit and a cooling unit side by side, which indicated the temperature fluctuated down here. As soaked through as she was, Garrel could only at the moment feel the cold, but she suspected that would change when there wasn't floodwater overfilling the lake outside.

She could see other things also: a device to play music, a scanner and various forms of information-collecting equipment. There was a generator also, which when turned on would provide enough power to light the entire structure. Overhead she could see a row of bulbs, some blown, which had come on when she had flicked the switch. There were likely other generators scattered around the structure, and perhaps somewhere there was a light left on. It would explain the diffuse light outside, and was a far better explanation than bio-luminescent moss.

However, the doorway was without a barrier and there was no indication that any of the animals outside had ever wandered inside. Why that could be she had no idea, for even if there was any deterring equipment in here it would have been shut off.

Garrel looked over the equipment without touching any of it. It all looked old, and some of the models had not been used for at least fifty years, even second-hand. She could not even believe it would still work were she to try to activate it all. There was no indication as to how long it had actually been here, but the chamber seemed to have been abandoned a long time.

Knowing there was likely more to gain from the rest of the structure, and wondering just how great it was, Garrel opened a door at random and found a storage cupboard lined with boxes of wiring and spare electrical equipment. There were also boxes of rivets and tools, so clearly this place was meant to be self-contained.

Closing the door, she tried another and found a short corridor which ended in a narrow stairwell. Deciding to climb this, she noted it too was built of stone. Indeed the entire building was well constructed and hardy. It would have taken some time to build this place, and certainly it had been meant to last. But for what purpose had it been built? Why would anyone want to build such a structure down here?

Perhaps it was not down here initially, and had only submerged through quakes. But then, if such was the case it would be a partial ruin, where in actuality there was nothing wrong with anything of what she was seeing. For someone to have constructed an underground lair like this seemed strange, considering the entire world was off-limits. Hiding on the surface would have been just as effective as hiding underground if there was no one looking for you.

The stairs ended at a landing and she could see several bulbs were glowing on a low setting. How long they had been doing that for, again, she could not say, but bulbs nowadays were designed to keep powered indefinitely unless switched off. Flicking a switch, she cast greater light through the landing and discovered yet further doors. She checked the first and it revealed a sleeping chamber, and she hoped it might reveal some indication as to who might have been living here, and why.

It was a small chamber, but homely, with several personal possessions scattered about. There were books lining one shelf, various small ornaments atop a cupboard, and a teddy bear lying on its side on the bed. Garrel checked the books and found they were editions published ten years earlier. That gave her a date to work with, and also meant there was a chance whoever was living here might still be alive. It also meant the equipment downstairs, which she had dated as fifty years old, was outdated even when it was being used. But if it worked, perhaps whoever worked here was not particular about having state-of-the-art technology.

There was little else of interest in the room, and no sign of a diary. She did however find a well-worn Bible and wondered whether this place was a research base for one of the various religions in the Jovian system. Perhaps someone had been conducting research similar to that of Professor Travers, but had approached it from an entirely religious point of view. Reaching the truth was always the goal, and Garrel was beginning to think that it did not matter the path one took to reach it, since there was only ever one truth.

Putting aside her own philosophical speculations, Garrel left the bedchamber, taking care to close the door behind her, and continued down the corridor. If there were answers to be found here she would find them, no matter whether they came from a scientific or religious background.

She continued her exploration of the building, finding several more bedchambers but very little of interest in them. She came at last to another stairwell, and followed this to emerge in the centre of a large room. It was domed, and as she flicked on the light was amazed to see that the roof was formed of rectangular panes of glass, each an amazing work of stained glass. She could see depictions of Biblical scenes and various saints throughout the ages, with a scattering of mermaid iconography which had decorated church carvings for centuries. There were candles standing in rows, unlit, leading to an altar, and Bibles set out upon individual chairs. She surmised there may have been pews set up here if they could have been brought up the narrow stairwell.

Any doubt Garrel had held about the occupants being religious were thrown to the winds in that moment, but it still told her nothing of their purpose for being there. It was possible they had arrived only ten years ago, if the date on the books was anything to go by, but it was also possible that this temple had been erected at the construction of the world and that over the generations new occupants had arrived. But where had they come from? Or had people stayed here for generations and there were now officially people born of Ceres descent?

It was frustrating not to have answers to any of these questions, yet she was not here to study anything. Now that she had surmised at least some of her surroundings she needed to find a way back to the surface.

Moving to the stairwell, she ignored the upper floor, since it consisted only of bedrooms, and headed back downstairs. She noted there were still no animals wandering through the open doorway and could only assume there had been some repelling force built into the building itself, since the machines were all turned off. Either that or faith was keeping them back, which was a little bit of a stretch of the imagination.

Checking the remaining doors, Garrel eventually happened upon something which really interested her. It held several pieces of machinery she recognised as a communications system. There were no artificial satellites orbiting Ceres, so signals could not be bounced from orbit, and there was something in the atmosphere which jammed most attempts at radio communications. However, they would not have kept this equipment here if it did not work, so Garrel sank into a chair and cracked her fingers. She had tinkered before with equipment very similar to this and with any luck could get it working.

She was just thinking about what she could do when she noticed a disc sitting beside the communications system. She picked it up, turning it over and seeing there were some numbers scrawled on one side. She had no idea what might be on it but shoved it into her belt and gave it no mind.

Returning to the tool cupboard she fetched some screwdrivers and set to work on the equipment. First she tore apart almost everything before her, but as she began to put it all back together, she was able to cannibalise enough parts to produce something of what she hoped was a working device.

At last she felt she was ready and, saying a quick and silent prayer, she thumbed on the machine and listened to its sweet hum. She had even built a handheld crank into the machine in case it began to lose power. The crank was fortunately not needed at present, but since she did not know the energy source this device used she could not say how long it would be before it conked out on her.

Garrel scanned through the frequencies until she found the one they used for their radios. Hoping there was someone out there to hear her, she depressed the transmission button and said, "Allen!" Releasing the button, she listened for a response. She heard something rather odd. It sounded as though his radio was transmitting, but she heard an immense crash, as though the system had collapsed. It sounded oddly familiar to her. "Allen, you hear me?" she said, but there was no response now at all.

She did not know why she had contacted Allen before anyone else. Travers would have been a better choice considering the Professor was still back at the camp. But Allen had been foremost on her mind, and she did not like to think what he would have said to that were she ever to tell him. She smiled at the thought, just hoping she would have that opportunity. There were worse people in life than Tom Allen, she had to relent.

Next she tried to contact the radio in the buggy, but received only a dead line from that. That was not a good sign, although she did not lose hope and contacted the camp directly.

"Garrel to camp. Professor Travers, do you copy?"

There was a moment of static as Garrel released the button.

"Garrel?"

Garrel's heart leaped. "Travers. Are the boys back yet?"

"Monroe's back," Travers said, concerned. "How are you getting this signal through?"

"Powerful equipment."

"Where are you?"

"In a temple, I think."

"Come again?"

"Where's Allen?"

"Looking for you. He found your bike."

Garrel's grin faded as she realised where she had heard the sound before: the explosion-like sound which had come from Allen's radio. It was identical to the sound of her bike crashing when she had come off it only a short while earlier. Allen had been riding and she had brought him off the bike with her sudden voice.

Travers tried to say something else but the transmission began to die. Garrel frantically grabbed the crank and savagely yanked it again and again to get the power flowing once more.

"Say again," Garrel said.

"... said we should go looking for him, but all we have left is the copter."

"Stay where you are," Garrel said. "The floods are bad enough, and that's even without the dinosaurs. I'll get out of here and go after him myself."

"All right. We'll wait for you to contact us again then."

"Good. I'll be in touch."

She cut the transmission before the power could fail once more. The thought of going after Allen herself was only hampered by the fact that she was trapped underground, but whoever had lived in this temple would have had a means in and out, and Garrel knew she only had to find it. She could not understand why she felt so anxious about Allen and reasoned it was because she had been the cause of his crash. If not for her, he would have been happily riding around on his motorbike; and he was only out there to begin with because he was searching for her.

Even if she hated him, she was responsible for him and would rescue him.

And she did not hate him at all.

CHAPTER NINE

"We're not really going to sit here doing nothing are we?"

Travers looked up from her work. After Garrel had contacted them she had just gone back to work since she had such tight deadlines. Monroe had taken to pacing the room, which was proving somewhat irritating.

"You heard her," Travers said. "She wants to go after Allen herself. Besides, we're not doing nothing. We're working. Now make yourself useful and pass me a tongue depressor."

Monroe looked blankly at a row of equipment and tools and Travers shook her head, fetching it herself.

"You really don't know anything about archaeology, do you?"

Monroe shrugged, still looking very uncomfortable. "I feel responsible for the lad."

"Good. You should, considering you took him out under false pretences. Hand me the ... Never mind."

She brushed past Monroe, fetching what she needed and making sure he knew she thought he was useless. Travers needed to focus on her work, for she was now more than ever fighting her deadlines. She did not know Allen too well, but he was a bright lad and the most eager of her students. That he was infatuated with Sara Garrel would have been obvious to a dead turkey, but it had never done any harm. Garrel was not interested, and so long as Allen didn't annoy her too much the young woman was willing to simply ignore it. Travers herself had paid no more mind to the infatuation, harmless as it was. But then Monroe had taken the boy off on some grand adventure. Travers did not know the specifics, but without a doubt had Monroe promised him something. Maybe they were hunting the claw of a tyrannosaurus rex or something. Whatever the specifics, Monroe had deceived the boy into accompanying him, and now Allen was lost.

There was no way all of this wasn't Monroe's fault.

"I'm going out after him," Monroe said with stern resolution.

Travers laughed dryly. "And take the only remaining vehicle, since you've lost the other two?"

"What can I do then to make amends?"

"Nothing." She set down her tools so she would not ruin her work, looking him square in the eyes. "There's nothing you can do, Albert. You screwed up, and now we just have to wait around until Garrel contacts us again with some news. Now, either make yourself useful or get out of here, because I have a lot of work to do."

By the look on his face it seemed Monroe intended to offer his services, but they both knew he would be more of a hindrance than anything. He hung his head. "I'll get out of your way then."

"Sensible."

She heard the door close quietly and returned to her work, but her mind refused to focus, her hands were shaking, and she set down her tools once more and sank her head into her hands. Before coming out here there had been concerns about the threat from the dinosaurs, but it was turning out that they should have been more concerned with the way they intended to treat each other.

Throughout his life Monroe had never had to work for anything. It had been so good knowing he would never have to worry about money or what people thought about him. His family were wealthy enough to socialise in the circles wherein he could be put in contact with all the right people, whatever he wanted to achieve. Nor had there been any shortage of servile yes-men willing to accede to his every demand and forever tell him he was right. It had allowed him to rise to adulthood thinking he was indestructible, both in spirit and in morals.

But now he found himself on a world with only three other people, none of whom were going to suck up to him, none of whom regarded his position as anything other than the sham it was. He had continued to act as though he was going to have people falling over themselves to please him, and none of his companions had taken to it very well. They had, however, done the worst thing; and that was ignore him. They knew his money was funding this venture and likely thought it gained him a little leeway. But he had taken advantage of his position and now a young man was paying the price.

Monroe had been told to do nothing about the situation he had created, but he had never been very good at doing what he was told. He had placed his own selfish desires to see some dinosaurs ahead of the welfare of his companions, and that was something he was going to have to correct. He may not have been good at archaeology, may not have been good for much of anything in fact, but he knew the route Allen would have taken on his way back and if he had to follow it on foot then that was just what he was going to do.

But he did not have to go on foot. As he walked into the outside air he thought about that copter they still had left. It was indeed their final vehicle and for him to lose that on top of all the others would have been terrible; but if he could rescue Allen it did not matter how many vehicles they lost. Besides, they still had their space-faring craft to get them off Ceres, and if he could bring both Allen and Garrel back to the camp they could always send for more land transport. Whether they would be allowed to receive any more was another matter, for that would entail allowing someone else to land upon Ceres; but that was something they could deal with once everyone was safe and secure.

No longer thinking along the lines of his having paid for all this equipment, all Monroe cared about was locating young Allen, and with this thought in mind he approached the copter. It was indeed a strange-looking contraption. There was a basket reminiscent of that which a hot-air balloon would utilise, while above there hung a powerful lightweight engine, attached to which was a propeller. There were metal supports either side of the basket, although as with the buggy these were skeletal and designed to be entirely utilitarian. He had never before flown one of these things, although when they had initially landed upon Ceres Garrel had insisted they run through various aspects of survival training, which included basic instruction for each of their vehicles. Reluctantly Garrel had even shown them how to operate the main craft, as though she feared one of them would take the thing and flee, abandoning the others to a life without hope of escape.

Stepping into the basket, Monroe found the control panel and flicked the appropriate switches to run power through the contraption. A steady hum built within the engine and he pulled the lever which would take him into the air. The basket shook as the engine began to vibrate and he watched as slowly the propellers powered up. Within moments they were spinning so fast it appeared the four blades were actually two dozen, and shakily the basket rose. It jolted, pitching Monroe forward, but he recalibrated the controls and was once more rising. The downdraft from the rotors was not quite as bad as he had expected, and he could imagine the engineers designing such a thing growing with excitement as they worked out ways of making the copter as aerodynamic as they could, while not sacrificing any of the necessities. Nor did the blades make too much noise, and he could imagine Travers still intent upon her work, not even realising Monroe was taking the thing out. With any luck he would even be back before she noticed he had gone against all orders, and perhaps he might even be forgiven some of his faults.

The copter rose to a height of around fifty metres. He could easily have gone higher, but if Allen was lying wounded somewhere he did not want to miss sight of him. Flying towards the woodland, Monroe knew he would not be able to see anything through the trees, so veered off for the route Allen would have taken were he able to get the motorbike working. From what Monroe had seen of it prior to leaving Allen, the bike had not appeared irreparably damaged, but he was no engineer; all he had really seen was that the wheels were still attached, and to his non-mechanical mind that was surely all that was needed for a motorbike to be stood upright and mounted.

A flurry of animals took flight beneath him, and immediately he watched them, but could not tell what they were, let alone whether they were dinosaurs. His heart was racing at the prospect of seeing something that wasn't a prehistoric mammal or bird, but the things disappeared into the woods before he could properly identify them.

But he was not up here to compound his mistakes by seeking out further dinosaurs. Slowly, painfully, he forced himself not to look at the trees to glimpse the animals, but concentrated his efforts on locating young Allen.

He drifted on, although in reality was moving under his own power. The juddering, jerking movements of the basket gave the impression that he had no control over his own direction, as though the wind was his master and tormentor. In reality the copter was a sturdy, trustable companion, only disguised as a ramshackle mess. From above and looking down it appeared as though the land was moving slowly, as though he was nothing but an extension of Jupiter's army of clouds sent to watch over the unnatural denizens of Ceres. He knew the view was deceptive, that he was in fact travelling across the lands far faster in fact than if he had taken the buggy or perhaps even the motorbike.

Something caught his eye: a familiar blue which seemed to enjoy being abandoned. He frantically tried to remember how to cut the power and slowly eased the copter down to land. The sight of such a large raptor descending would keep the animals at bay, as would the sight of the whirring propeller and the dull hum of the motor. The basket set gently to the ground and Monroe secured the vehicle before throwing his leg over the side and setting foot gingerly back upon solid ground. His legs were slightly shaky, which was to be expected apparently, although he ignored the sensation as he approached the bike.

It was in a terrible state. The wheels were still attached, yet the paintwork had great rents, as though torn by the claws of some mighty beast. The metal was twisted and bent, an entire plate had been torn and crumpled, still hanging loosely and resembling scrunched paper. One of the wing mirrors was shattered, its plastic covering twisted by powerful jaws or hands, while padding had exploded from the seat as though in a valiant attempt to escape its manic assailant.

Monroe could not help but take especial note of the state of the wheels, for neither was punctured. He had thought before that so long as the wheels were attached the bike would still function, but now he was not so certain. When a large theropod tore something apart, he could not say it would ever run again.

There was no sign of Allen, nor was there any blood. He could see the skid-marks where the bike had veered off and surmised that Allen had been surprised by something. Since there was no evidence of the theropod either he could only assume Allen had fled the beast or been devoured.

The thought was not a pleasant one, yet he could not sugar-coat his suppositions. Pretending everything would be all right was not going to do anyone any good, and Allen deserved better than that.

He noticed something else then, a scent upon the wind, and walked slowly towards the mighty woodland. There was something there: an animal lying with its body open to the world. Flies festered the corpse, and he could see tooth- and claw-marks indicative of a carnivore having fed upon it. He could not make out the species of the animal, nor did he want to get close enough to be able to. That it was not Tom Allen was all he cared about.

There was nothing he could accomplish from the ground, so Monroe clambered back into his basket and took to the air once more. It was only as he climbed back to fifty metres that he realised he really had no idea what he was doing. Searching for Allen was all well and good, but he no longer had any clue as to where to search. All he could do was continue and hope he struck lucky, because if there was one thing he had decided it was that he was not about to head back to camp without him.

Allen ran. He had never been an especially fit young man, had never bothered with things like gymnasia, but nor had he ever been chased into the woods by a hungry dinosaur. The deltadromeus had come at him in a rage when Allen had fallen from his bike, and he still did not entirely know why. The carnivore had been feasting when it had sighted Allen, which meant it could not see him exclusively as a food source. That it saw him as a threat was a possibility, for he had been fast-moving and noisome, especially once he had crashed, and the fact he had stopped so close to the dinosaur could have been received as a challenge. Having chased him off, however, Allen could not see that the deltadromeus would not have simply returned to its hard-won meal: unlike the triceratops earlier it was not establishing its dominancy or attempting to impress the females of the herd. The only conclusion Allen could really come up with which made any sense at all was that the deltadromeus was curious about him. This strange two-legged creature walking with an upright back had come off a faster-moving body like some high-spirited remora. That a dinosaur could be curious enough to chase him into the woods and still be seeking him out was not something he had ever considered about the creatures; but then perhaps the dinosaurs of Ceres were far more intelligent than anyone had ever believed.

Whatever the reason, all Allen actually cared about was the fact he was still being hounded, and that his pursuer really did not seem to want to surrender.

Initially he had run into the woods because he had not expected such a large creature to be able to give proper chase with all the trees in the way. He was horribly surprised at how swift the thing could be even with the trees hampering its movements, and if Allen had not somehow been able to pour on more speed than he had ever thought himself capable, he could not imagine that he would have survived even this long.

Presently he was hiding behind a tree, desperately trying to catch his breath. He could hear the tread of the deltadromeus close by and could feel its nearness. Its strong lungs released its exhalations as deep sighs, but they were far from mournful wails at its lost prey. The deltadromeus did not for one moment believe it had lost Allen: it knew it just needed to find him. Allen could not help but feel he was attached to the animal by an invisible cord, and that it was sheer impossibility for him to make his break from the creature, no matter how hard he ran.

He felt something brush against the tree behind which he was hiding. He did not know precisely what it was, for he could not bring himself to turn even his eyes in case the great beast recognised the movement. He thought it was the creature's tail, and feared it was long enough to probe the nearby trees like the feelers of a growing cucumber plant. He wished the creature was only a giant cucumber, for that would solve all his problems, but, closing his eyes and forcing the imagery away, he realised how ludicrous he was being.

If he was going to survive this he needed to focus.

The trees shook fearfully at the sudden bellow of the monster, leaves falling from trembling branches and littering the ground. Small animals exploded from the underbrush and Allen could hear the snapping of mighty jaws and knew the deltadromeus was making only half-hearted attempts to catch them. It was trying to frighten him out of hiding, and Allen wondered what it would do now that it had discovered he was not some scared rabbit willing to leap out of concealment the moment a predator told him to. Perhaps it would think he had escaped already, that he was halfway through the woodland and still running. Perhaps it would just give up and go back to whatever it was it had been eating.

The tree behind him shattered and Allen was thrown forwards, his cover no longer there. He raised an arm as he fell to the floor, but the splintered wood missed him, the heavy branches and leaves thankfully falling at an angle not to pin him. The deltadromeus was revealed behind, standing free and angry, and smugly pleased that it had found its prey with so little effort.

Allen scrabbled to his feet, his boots finding little purchase in the fallen wet leaves, and the deltadromeus lunged for him. Allen rolled to the side, barely evading the serrated teeth, the stench of raw meat washing over his face as he came face to tooth with those bloody jaws. The huge dinosaur snapped at him once more, but Allen scrambled backwards, at last regaining his footing. But he knew that to run would be to die, for he would not be able outrun the creature.

Standing before the thing, he suddenly realised why the creature had been chasing him all this time. It had not been hungry or asserting its authority, or even curious. It was simply playing with him. This was all a game to the animal, for it could have caught him at any time. It was honing its skills, testing this unknown animal to determine whether it could learn anything from it. It was a clever, adaptable animal, and it had just proven its superiority over him.

The deltadromeus yawned wide and roared once more, informing the entire woodland that it was the king here, that this small unknown creature was nothing beside its glory. Allen could not find it in his heart to disagree with such a statement. He had never in his life faced such a situation. He was terrified, his body was petrified, his mind shutting down; but it was more than that. As he stood before the amazing killing machine that was the deltadromeus, he could only marvel at the wonder of such a beast, that nature could have crafted this vision of pure beauty and sent it forth into the world to see what it might accomplish. That millions of years later mankind had taken that creature and brought it back made the wonder no less, for life was amazing no matter what form it took.

That was the problem he had always found with archaeology. It dealt with things long dead, while the true beauty was in life. He thought of Sara Garrel then, in his final moments. She was an equally amazing creature of beauty, sent forth into the world, and all people like Allen concentrated on was the dirt around her feet, digging and looking for clues of civilisations long gone. It was a necessary study, he had always known that, but Allen knew he was someone who needed to keep his eyes firmly on the present. It had taken him this long to realise this, and he was only upset it had come all too late.

He vowed if he somehow managed to make it out of this, he would change his life. He would leave the field of archaeology and move into something where his vision could encompass the present and future, and leave the past to the Professor Traverses of the solar system.

And then he had something in his hand. His eyes may have been focused upon the creature, his body may have been frozen in fear, but his fingers had been working the entire time, and had retrieved something from a pocket. The deltadromeus may have been his physical superior, but there was nothing which could ever compare to the human mind.

He held the torch up and flicked it on. The deltadromeus paused as the light shone directly in its eye. It shook its head, trying to avoid the glint, but Allen kept the beam focused. The creature grew angry, snapping down at him, but Allen leapt aside and shone the light in its other eye. He was under no illusion that the thing was now blinded, but it would certainly be blinking spots from its eyes for at least a second, and that enabled him to turn and beat a hasty retreat into the trees.

Behind him he heard the raging bellow of the monster, and the steady thump of its powerful feet giving chase. Allen knew the game was over, that the creature was through training itself and was now moving in for the kill.

It seemed the deltadromeus disagreed with his new philosophy: it was far more interested in Allen being dead than alive.

CHAPTER TEN

She had a desperate urge to explore the remainder of the temple, yet Garrel knew she had placed Allen in danger by contacting him. He took precedence, there was no question of that. Why she was lingering then, she could not say, or did not want to. She liked to think she was searching the temple for something she might be able to use, for she still had no means back to the surface, yet the truth was plainer. She had never become involved in the Ceres debate, yet here was concrete evidence that people had been here before, and recently. She could only imagine what secrets they had uncovered, and if they approached it from a religious perspective they may have found some answers Travers could not.

The answers, however, were not worth Allen's life. She knew it was guilt that kept her at the temple. She had been born to a religious family and had been raised to respect her deity, but she had never been active in her religion. It had always been something in the back of her mind, yet nothing she had ever acted upon. And here was her chance to atone for that, to find her answers and make up for all that lost time.

But Tom Allen was still on the surface, needing her help.

Resolving herself to a decision, Garrel ignored all the equipment, all the potential clues, and instead pulled open every door she came to as quickly as she could, ignoring anything which would not get her to the surface.

Then she opened one door and found she was in a large circular chamber without any form of ceiling. Within the centre of the chamber there was a strange tube-like contraption, around two metres tall and half a metre wide. What it could have been was not obvious, although as she turned her gaze skyward she could see a pinprick of light in the rocky ceiling high above. Now some of the temple's lights were on she found she could see a portion of the surrounding rocks, and they rose to perhaps sixty metres. But she could still see that pinprick and knew it led to the surface.

Garrel walked to the tube, running her hand along its surface. It was transparent and empty, but she was not surprised when she found a catch which released a door. Looking skyward once more, she could not say the light from the surface was entirely aligned with the tube, but she had a pretty good idea of what would happen were she to get inside. It was a risk, but it was her only chance of getting to the surface in a hurry. If she explored the temple fully she might be able to find another means to the surface, but by then she would have lost too much time.

Taking a deep breath to calm her nerves, Garrel stepped inside the tube and closed the door behind her. It was confining in such a tight space, and the air was staler than that of the building, but Garrel knew she would not be in there long, whatever happened. She could find no controls, although as she looked down realised there were pressure points upon the floor. Placing her foot upon one, she pressed and prayed.

The tube shot upwards and she could see the temple blurring past her. Her entire body tensed, knowing if it was not properly aligned she would slam straight into the rock and obliterate herself. She looked up, watching the rock streaking towards her, and the hole, so small above, blazed into life as she slammed into the rock, shooting through and exploding into the light of the outside world.

The tube stopped and Garrel collapsed against the door, forcing it open and stumbling out. She landed upon rocky ground, breathing heavily and feeling her entire body shake. When she was able to control herself she looked back to see the tube still there, and carefully she closed the door. With any luck it would stay there until the pressure pad was activated once more and it would descend. She could not see it would have been the only means to get to the temple, for the tube would only take one person at a time, and there was no way to send it back up empty to fetch someone else. Unless the temple was used by only one person, there had to have been another way in.

Now she was back in the real world she began to question why she kept referring to it as a temple. It was a research centre which held religious iconography, but that did not necessarily make it a temple. Perhaps she was just placing too much faith in what she had found, or perhaps she wanted to make amends far more than she realised.

But all that could wait. She was back on the surface and needed to find Allen. Of course, she had no idea where he might have been, so clambered up the rocks for a better view. She could see the edge of the woodland and from this worked out where the camp would lie. Assuming Allen was anywhere near the camp was ludicrous, yet she had to begin somewhere and if she was headed back to camp she could liaise with Travers and Monroe and be filled in on anything she had missed. Then she would take the copter and perform a detailed search of the local land.

It was only half a plan, for she would much rather have been able to head straight for Allen, but it was all she had to work with. So Garrel started walking.

Ten minutes passed before she saw something in the air and wished she wasn't wandering over such rocky ground. Exposed as she was, if some aerial predator had labelled her for dinner, she would have no choice but to fight the thing. She did not know much about prehistoric air monsters but could not simply assume they only ate fish. The more she stared, however, the stranger the image became to her eyes, and at last she recognised the familiar shape and knew nature could never have crafted something so bizarre.

Leaping, waving her arms, Garrel attempted to gain the attention of the thing, but she knew from past experience in flying vehicles how difficult it was to spot something on the ground. Everyone could see the thing in the air, but even an eagle-eyed pilot could well miss someone on the ground if they were looking in the other direction.

Wishing she had managed to find something useful in the temple, or that she had not lost her gun, Garrel patted herself down in search of something she might be able to use. She needed to signal the copter and a flare would have been nice, but she had as much chance of producing a flare as she had sprouting a pair of wings. Her fingers closed about her radio, which was about all she had left on her. Radios of course were generally useless on Ceres, but since the copter was in the air there was a possibility she might get through. It was not likely, but as she watched the copter moving away from her she knew she had no other option.

Thumbing the radio, she called into it, depressing the button which would allow the other party to speak. All she received was static, but she tried again, her eyes locked upon the copter. It was not receding any more, seemed to be sweeping the land, and she tried the radio once more, waving her arms as she did so.

The copter turned and headed her way. Garrel yelped with glee, leaping and exhausting herself to make sure the pilot could see her. The vehicle grew as it approached, and she waited eagerly while it landed. She was somewhat surprised to find Professor Monroe turning off the engine and leaning over the basket.

"I was wondering why my radio was suddenly spouting out static," he said. "I figured it had to mean someone was trying to contact me."

It seemed, Garrel thought, that even a lack of communication could also be used for communication, but there was a more pressing lack of communication she had to deal with.

"I thought I told you to stay at the camp," she said.

"You're welcome."

"Where's Tom?"

"I don't know." Monroe became at once concerned. "I found the wreck of the bike. It had been clawed and bitten by something large."

Garrel's heart sank. "Was there much blood?"

"None."

That did not mean much. If the carnivore was large enough it could have taken Allen in one bite. Or maybe he had managed to run for a while before it had caught up to him and torn him apart.

"The bike was close to the woods," Monroe continued. "There was a carcass close by."

"Dinosaur?"

"I think so. Something large anyway."

"So you got to see your dinosaur at last, Prof. Hope it was worth it."

She regretted the snide comment as soon as she had made it, for she could see how guilty he felt. But she was tired, irritable and concerned for her friend, and did not much care what Monroe felt like at that moment in time.

"We need to get back in the air," she said. "Have you been sweeping the land properly?"

"I don't know. I've just been looking."

Which meant she might have to begin the search again. But she would do that once she had had a chance to check the scene of attack. "Take me back to the bike."

"I checked that area."

"And I'm going to check again."

To his credit, Monroe did not argue. The two climbed aboard and took to the air.

They did not speak as they travelled. Garrel stood at the edge of the basket, her hands grasping the side as she peered down at the world raging below. There were vast tracts of plains, ragged rocky mountainous regions and of course the scattering of trees and the great woodland. It amazed her how very little there was of anything else, although now there were patches of water, even unnatural streams, added to the landscape. She could imagine Ceres being like any other world, and wondered what else they would discover were they to set the copter on a straight course of exploration.

A pack of small carnivores scavenging through the rocks gave her pause for thought regarding this, and she knew she could not afford to concentrate on such things.

"We destroyed the buggy," Monroe said behind her. "I'm sorry."

"I don't care about the buggy."

"I'll pay for it. I know it comes out of your pay if it ..."

"I don't care about the damn buggy." Garrel tightened her grip on the basket, trying to keep her anger in check. She liked to feel as though she blamed Monroe for what had happened, but the truth was he was not to blame. She had worked for people like Monroe before and had always known what they were like. You didn't trust them with anything and steered clear of them whenever possible. It was not Monroe who was to blame here, but her. She had been the one in charge of security and she had let Monroe talk Allen into going out with him. She should have warned Allen about him, should have taken the time to explain just what people like Monroe were like.

The shepherd cannot blame the wolf for eating the sheep if the shepherd hasn't bothered setting up a wire fence.

The surprising thing was that Monroe seemed remorseful, seemed to genuinely realise he had done the wrong thing and wanted to make up for it. Otherwise he would not have disregarded her orders and stolen the copter.

She should have perhaps granted him some leeway because of this, although it only made her warier.

They made it back to the bike within ten minutes, the copter able to take the direct route between the two points. Their landing was smoother this time, for Garrel had taken the controls. She could see even before disembarking that the bike was in bad shape, but as she looked it over she could find no sign that Allen had been on the bike when it had been damaged. Most likely her unexpected communication had startled him into crashing, and a dinosaur had taken umbrage at the running engine and had attacked it, thinking it was issuing a challenge.

Monroe showed her where he had found the carcass of an animal and as they approached several scavengers fled with whatever they could carry. Garrel tried to breathe through her mouth as she bent to examine the bite marks and tears made upon the animal's corpse. Whatever had made the kill had been large, probably a small tyrannosaurid. She knew of at least two species of tyrannosaurid in this area, which was what had made her so wary of what Travers had seen in the woodland so long ago.

She looked to the woodland now, wondering whether Allen could have been chased in there. It would be a logical place for him to run, although she doubted it would have done much to save his life.

"You're thinking he's in the woods," Monroe said.

"I'm thinking you need to go back to the camp while I go off looking for him. Take the copter and give me your gun."

"What gun?"

"Don't kid me, Professor. You wouldn't have come out here unarmed, so hand it over and get out of here."

Monroe seemed about to argue further, although lowering his head he withdrew a pistol from where he had it tucked into the back of his trousers. Garrel accepted it and checked its ammunition. There were several shots remaining in the clip, and if they weren't enough to bring down a small tyrannosaurid she doubted extra bullets would have done her much good. She suddenly remembered the disc she had taken from the temple and decided she had no need to take it any farther with her so handed it over to the Professor. "Make yourself useful and see what's on here."

"What is it?"

"If I knew that, I wouldn't be asking you to check."

Monroe turned the disc slowly over in his hands and Garrel could see he was trying to form words he was not used to saying. "I feel bad just leaving," he said at last.

"To be honest you'd just get in my way."

"But it's my fault Allen's in this mess."

"Allen's probably dead. There's likely not even a body left. But I'm going to see what I can find. You need to get out of my way." She could see he was upset by everything that had happened and felt a pang of remorse for him. "Professor Travers is all alone back at camp," she said gently. "Watch over her until I get back."

"You think the dinosaur will attack the camp?"

"No. Our repelling devices have kept them at bay so far, I can't see why they would fail now. But she might be a little scared."

"I doubt she's even noticed I'm missing."

If he was going to fall back into his old self-absorbed pity Garrel suddenly lost all willingness to pander to his ego. "Just go," she told him and headed off into the woods. She did not wait to find out whether he obeyed her orders, but Monroe was an adult and could do whatever he wanted.

Swallowed by the trees, Garrel cast her senses around her, listening especially for any signs there was anything amiss. The birdsong was as it should have been, and there were no strange scents to the air. She walked slowly at first, but built up speed quickly. There was an obvious spoor of a large animal that had come this way, and there were more than just a few trees either with gouges or else entirely uprooted. It was not promising, but it gave her something to track, and clutching her pistol that was just what she did.

After a few minutes she found evidence of what appeared to have been an angry explosion from the monster, for trees were splintered and leaves were strewn up as though there had been a scuffle. There were no blood that she could see, yet she knew she could search for hours and still find nothing. If the creature had been large enough to swallow Allen in one or two bites there might well not be any blood at all.

She bent to examine the ground, feeling the imprint of the tracks and discerning a direction of travel. She froze in her crouch, her body experiencing a sudden shiver. She could hear something behind her, something moving in a slow shuffle, accompanied by a low and dull moan.

She desperately hoped it was Monroe.

Turning her head very slightly she could see something standing only twenty metres away, locking eyes with her as its prey. It was large, with powerful rear legs and short forearms. Its bulky body was muscle, not fat, and with its counterbalancing tail and great head atop its long, horizontal neck, the thing was unmistakably carnivorous.

The creature opened its serrated maw and issued a challenge.

Garrel levelled the gun she had taken from Monroe. She cursed the shaking of her hand and used the other to steady it, but it still did little good. She cracked off a shot, but wherever the bullet went it certainly didn't go anywhere near the dinosaur. The beast grew angry at the sound and she fired again, once more missing her target. She had been hoping the sound alone would have been enough to scare the dinosaur away, but it treated the sound as though it was not an unknown noise.

It took a single step forward and Garrel knew her pistol would do nothing to deter the thing. She bolted into the trees before it could even begin its charge. She heard its light pad behind her as this expert, swift hunter gave chase through the trees. If this was the thing which had killed Tom Allen, she could only surmise it had developed a strong taste for human meat.

CHAPTER ELEVEN

Professor Travers could not abide all these constant interruptions. First Allen had gone out to impress the girl who was clearly not interested in the slightest, then Monroe had gone out after him and in the process taken the last of their vehicles. Now Monroe was back, and while he may have brought the copter with him, Travers was beginning to wish he had just stayed outside and gone after Allen with Garrel. In fact, of all of them, it was Garrel for whom Travers held the most respect. She knew her job and just got on with it. Allen had been fine until they had got here. She had chosen to bring him because he was young and obedient, but since coming to Ceres he seemed to have developed a restless streak and followed Garrel around like a lovelorn teenager. It was not what Travers had expected of him, but if that was the way he was going to behave she could have done without him as well. Travers may have been given tight deadlines, but if Allen had his mind elsewhere he was going to make mistakes.

Once Monroe had left the camp, believing he had sneaked out, Travers had been able to get on with her work. It had been a blissful time without any of them. Now he was back and pacing again, she was working much more slowly than she had been.

"Why did you come back?" she asked at last, trying not to bark.

"Garrel told me to."

"And when was the last time you did something someone told you to?"

Monroe paused in his pacing. She could see him thinking, but he still wasn't leaving her alone. "I keep doing the wrong thing, Travers. I'm not used to dealing with people in this way, and I'm doing it all wrong."

"You're winding people up without even realising?"

"Yes," he said hopefully. "You understand."

Travers wondered how anyone could be so dense. She made a point of setting down her tools, showing him that she was unable to work with him hovering over her like he was. "This world," she began, not even knowing where she was going with this but feeling she had to tell him something to get rid of him. "This world is amazing. It's not just prehistoric, it's primal. There are no inhibitions here, no laws. And there are only four people on the entire world. You can do whatever you like here, say whatever you want. The social rules you've lived by your whole life ... none of them count any more. While we're here on Ceres no one can tell us what to do, no one can tell us how to behave. But," she added sternly, "that's all going to change when we get home. And when that happens I'm going to have to produce results. Allen and Garrel can go off into the woods playing Tarzan all they like, but they're not going to have to answer for anything when they get home. And you ... Well, you have enough money not to care what anyone thinks."

"You think they'll fire you?"

"I think this is the human race's one chance to find out precisely what's going on here, just where Ceres came from and why. I have the responsibility to provide some answers about it, and I can't do that with people hanging around me who are too busy delving into their souls to concentrate on what they're doing."

Monroe looked at her a moment in silence. "Are you telling me I'm in the way?"

Travers sighed, exasperated. "You're always in the way. Your money's not, but you, physically, have never been anything else." She rubbed at the bridge of her nose with thumb and forefinger. "What I'm saying is that this is a free world, Monroe. Freer than anything we've ever known. Just because Garrel tells you to do something, it doesn't mean you have to do it. You want to stay here and pace? Stay here and pace. You want to go back out there and see if you can help? Go out there and help. You want to see a dinosaur, right? Have you seen one yet?"

"No."

"Then go find a dinosaur. Find a dinosaur and make yourself happy."

Monroe thought about her words and Travers was delighted to see she seemed to be getting through to him. "You're right," he said, something breaking in him, something being released. He stood taller, stronger, and perhaps he had become a new man: Travers did not care, so long as he left her in peace. "I'll be back with Garrel *and* Allen," he told her and walked out once more.

Travers returned to her work. So long as he returned with them slowly, that would suit her just fine.

She tore through the woods knowing she would not be able to outrun the creature giving chase. Garrel did not stop, did not pause, did not so much as even think about slowing down. In her research of dinosaurs prior to coming to Ceres she had focused upon the carnivores, knowing they had the potential to cause the most damage. There were two types of carnivorous dinosaur she was most concerned with, and she did not care for the technical terms. She had labelled them small carnivores and big carnivores, and all of them were what were known as theropods. It did not matter how big or small the creatures were, they all looked pretty much the same; thick, powerful legs, smaller arms, lithe, well-muscled body, counterbalancing tail and neck and vicious head. There were differences between each animal, but all dinosaur carnivores shared this appearance. The smaller dinosaurs were more likely to hunt in packs, and were an even distribution of scavengers and hunters. They were dangerous, and just because they were small it did not make them any less lethal. She could not help but imagine piranhas tearing apart their prey with equal ferocity. The larger carnivores were more likely to be loners, and hunters. There had been many debates regarding this over the years, but modern research seemed to agree that this was the case. Before coming to Ceres, Garrel had known to fear the smaller pack animals, but that it only took one shark to rip her to shreds.

The creature chasing her tore through the woods on massive hind legs, and she knew the trees would not slow it indefinitely. She was not entirely certain of her dinosaur classification, but she believed the creature was called an albertosaurus. It was difficult to tell, considering she had of course never seen a live albertosaurus, let alone knew how to differentiate between one and any other large theropod with only a momentary glance. It was strange how much

Garrel was even thinking about such things as she ran for her life, for ultimately it did not matter at all the name of the thing. The bottom line was that it could kill her with a single snap of its massive jaws.

Garrel could see a cluster of trees ahead which was denser than any through which she had thus far passed, and her hope was that the dinosaur would be slowed by it. The best result she could hope for would be for the creature to lose sight of her, but there were so many conflicting theories on which sense dinosaurs used for hunting that she did not want to place her fate to chance. Throwing her arms ahead of her, she charged through the thick brush, deciding she would have to take things as she came to them and focus on her prayer getting her through this alive.

Breaking out the other side, Garrel saw what looked like a slope leading to lower ground, and leaping for this she poured on as much speed as she could.

Her foot passed through the loose brush and she felt herself bodily falling down the slope, tumbling end over end, the world exploding around her in panic and frustration. Then an intense coldness shot through her and she felt incredibly heavy as she was dragged away from the air. Garrel broke the surface of the muddy pool, formed by the intense rains of the previous few days, and looked about. Her feet touched the bottom of the pool, and it only stretched around ten metres in any direction. The water was thick and muddy, and as she slogged her way to the far side she became well aware that at the top of the rise the carnivore had paused to gaze down upon her. Glancing back towards it, she could see she had fallen farther than she had thought: around three times the height of the dinosaur. She could see it was apprehensive about giving pursuit, and wished she could move a little faster through the muddy water.

"Sara!"

"Tom!"

Tom Allen was at the side of the filthy pool. He took two steps in and reached for her hand, pulling her to dry land. Garrel threw her arms about him, her soiled, wet hair slapping into his face. She laughed with pure joy, felt relief flood through her along with an intense heat which warmed her even through the chill waters clinging to her clothes. Breaking away, she could see his grin was equal to her own, although as she spoke he shushed her gently.

"It's good to see you," he said quietly.

"You put the loose leaves at the top," Garrel said, realising suddenly that Allen was not as useless as he had always seemed.

"Well, it was supposed to give the deltadromeus a tumble, maybe even break a few bones, but if it saved you from being eaten I'll go with that."

"I'm impressed," she said, and meant it. Looking upon him now she could see nothing of the gung-ho annoyance that had always hung around Allen. His face was dirty, his clothes torn, and there was a stern realism to his expression. He had survived through his wits, by using his mind against the monsters of this world, and it was something she never thought she would have thought about him. Even if asked yesterday she would not have said it was possible.

"Where'd you learn all these survival skills?" she asked.

"From you, silly."

"Me?"

"Some of the things you ran through with us. Others I just picked up from watching you."

"Seems stalking does have its advantages after all then."

He smiled at that, and she could see some of the old Tom Allen still there. He seemed sorry for the way he had treated her, and she did not think she could handle both men in her life having a sudden epiphany of character.

"We should leave," she said, "before that thing works its way down. Oh, I don't think it's a deltadromeus, by the way. It's slightly larger: I'd place it as an albertosaurus."

"I'll take your word for it," Allen said, only glancing up at the creature still loitering at the top of the rise. "But that's not the one that chased me."

Garrel's heart sank at the news. To be hunted by one behemoth was bad enough, but that there was a second lurking around the woods was unthinkable. She looked back up the slope to see the albertosaurus disappearing into the woodland. Perhaps it was giving up the chase, perhaps it had decided to work its way around and find an easier way down. Garrel could not say, but she did not want to hang around the pool waiting to find out.

"We need to go," she told Allen urgently. "What happened to your deltadromeus?"

"I don't know. I lost track of it, but I don't know the way out of the woods. So I figured I'd lay the trap and hang around here."

"Well I've sprung the trap now. Out of interest, what were you going to do if your deltadromeus came at you from ground level, instead of from up that slope?"

Allen's face fell slightly. "Oh. Hadn't thought of that."

Garrel sighed, punching him playfully on the arm. "That's why you need me, Tom."

It was such a small gesture, yet Garrel realised she did not feel odd at all in it. They had known one another for a while now, although had never really *known* one another. This was the first time Garrel felt as though she was actually seeing the real Tom Allen, and she was pleasantly surprised by what she saw. The fact he wasn't using corny lines or trying to stare down her top showed her he had matured. Tom Allen had at last become a man.

She wondered what she would have thought of him were this their first meeting.

But there was time enough for that later.

"You realise," Allen said, "this is two of us against two of them."

"Sure it is. But we're humans, with human minds. I think you've already demonstrated we're more than a match for them, Tom."

They moved further into the woods, uncertain as to the location of either of the beasts which were stalking them, and which they would themselves have to stalk if they stood any chance of survival. Allen did not speak as they moved, was listening intently to every slight sound around him, taking note of any sudden change in their surroundings. This allowed Garrel to focus half her attention on devising a plan of attack. She thought back to the encounter with the ankylosaur and how badly they had both dealt with that. The ankylosaur had been a herbivore and not actively trying to kill them for food. Facing predators would be a whole different matter, and she wished she had looked more into the hunting habits of large theropods. For all she knew they would both be hiding in bushes waiting to leap out at her. Their sheer size indicated this was not feasible, but Garrel was quickly discovering that there was far more about dinosaurs that she didn't know than that which she did.

"Have you had any contact with the camp?" Allen asked at last while they walked.

It seemed a bad idea to break the silence with idle talk, but perhaps it was what they needed. They were both so tense that Garrel knew if familiarity would relax them then it was something they needed to engage in.

"They're both fine," Garrel said. "They're staying put."

Allen accepted this without comment. "You contacted me through my radio. How did you manage that?"

It was surprising that Garrel had almost forgotten about the massive building she had found hidden underground, but she filled Allen in on some of what she had encountered down there. He listened carefully, and she could see his brief time in the woods had certainly made him more cautious.

"So who were they?" he asked when she was done.

"No idea. They didn't leave many clues. But even if the building was old, it had certainly been revisited at some point in the last ten years or so."

"So the government may well have already sent people here ahead of us. They may have made a big thing about our being allowed out here so they could cover up what they were really doing."

Garrel had never thought about that possibility, although now that it had been spoken aloud it certainly made a lot more sense than anything she had come up with. "It could be a religious order, Tom. People sneaking in against the law to research this place. The world may be quarantined, but I guess people could come and go if they didn't do it too often."

"I thought Ceres was monitored."

"But not patrolled. And I'm not sure how well the monitoring is either. We certainly didn't have to pass any checkpoints on our entry, and I couldn't see any satellites or buoys. Maybe the government just likes people to think they're doing something they're not. Saves them some work. If the right people say the right thing, everyone believes it. Look at the April fool's jokes they've done in the past, like the spaghetti tree and the neo-Nazi dinosaur project. Get people of importance to say something's true and everyone believes it. And that's not even mentioning things like the puffer fish."

"What about the puffer fish?"

112

"Well it's poisonous if you eat it, right?"

"Sure. Everyone knows that."

"And how many people have you actually seen die from eating a puffer fish?"

Allen's smile was very tight. "You're more paranoid than I ever realised, Sara."

"More cynical than anything. Bad marriages tend to do that to you."

"You all right? If you want to talk about it ..."

"No," Garrel said, too quickly, then realised she had snapped and tried a smile to placate him, but the smile would not come. "No, I'm fine. We should just get on with what we're doing and get out of here."

The last thing she wanted to talk about was her marriage, or lack thereof. She had thought her divorce would have been the end of all her problems, had expected she would have been able to start a new life with Jeannie once the awkward mess was out of the way. But life didn't work out quite like that, and when one party could afford a much better lawyer than the other it was hardly ever predictable. If she wanted any shot at seeing Jeannie again she would need as much money as she could get. She would need to hire the best lawyer and beat her ex at his own game.

Which meant she would have to retrieve both the buggy and bike before they left Ceres, else she was going to be a great deal out of pocket when she was paid for this venture. She hoped for Jeannie's sake Monroe had taken the copter back to the camp safely.

They reached the river which flowed through the forest and Garrel relaxed slightly. It was not the same point at which they had encountered the ankylosaur, but the river only flowed in two directions and she knew if they followed its flow they would emerge from the trees close to their camp. It was the best news they had discovered since meeting up at the muddy pool and at last Garrel felt they might get out of this alive. Thus far there had been no sign of either predator, not even a single sound, and if they could just make it out of the trees without immediate pursuit she felt they stood a reasonable chance of getting back alive.

It was strange how she was considering a reasonable chance for survival a good thing. Ceres was a dangerous place and until coming here she had never really understood just how dangerous. Keeping this expedition alive had never seemed such a difficult thing, but now that she thought about it she decided she was not being paid enough.

Asking Allen to keep a watch out, Garrel crouched beside the river to examine whatever spoors she could find.

"There's a lot of activity here," she said, working through things aloud since that had always been the best way she had found to get her thoughts into order. "Mostly small animals, probably herbivores. A couple of heavier animals, walking on four legs though, so nothing to be afraid of."

"There's something across the river."

Garrel looked up, but was relieved to see it was just a small creature. It wasn't even a dinosaur, but some form of vole by the looks of it. It was about the size of a small dog, and Garrel wondered whether all prehistoric animals were much larger than their later counterparts. It did not much matter, however, for so long as the vole was happy to sit there drinking from the river it meant there could not be any predators around.

It gave the two of them the opportunity to take stock of their situation.

"I'm sorry if I ever made you uncomfortable," Allen said when they were seated on the damp ground. Allen had fetched water while Garrel identified some berries which were safe to eat. A fish would have been nice, but they did not have the time to catch one, and if the fish here were larger than those back home she knew their dinner would have an equal chance of eating the two of them.

Garrel popped another couple of berries in her mouth and chewed thoughtfully as she regarded the young man. "It wasn't so much that you made me uncomfortable," she said. "It was just annoying."

"I know. But you still came back for me."

"I couldn't let you die. I wouldn't be paid."

She had meant it as a joke, although as she spoke the words she realised they sounded genuine. She said nothing more, knowing if she tried to defend her statement she would only make things worse.

"If you need to talk about it, Sara, you know I'll listen."

"That's kind of you, but there's nothing to talk about. Unless you have a fortune in your bank account you don't mind parting with."

"I don't, no. But I know a man who does."

Garrel narrowed her eyes slightly. "Monroe?" She paused. Even with Monroe's change of character she still couldn't see him handing her the money she needed.

"What do you need the money for?" Allen asked.

She thought about putting him off again, although could not see the harm in telling him. "My ex-husband, Jonathan. He's ... he's a nasty piece of work. He got custody of my daughter, Jeannie, by presenting a damning case to the court. According to his lawyer, I cheated on him and was involved in a plot to steal Jeannie and run away with her and my new lover to Ganymede. He also provided them with evidence that I was a violent person, and got statements from Jeannie to say that I'd hit her when she was bad. I don't know how he managed that, but Jeannie loves her father, trusts him. And he's always had a way with words."

The memories brought back pain, but it was not a pain she could ignore. If she did not work through her problems they would not simply go away. The worst part of it was her ex had sprinkled some truth to his case, for indeed she had had an affair. It wasn't something she was especially proud of, and it certainly wasn't either planned or prolonged. But she had lost faith in her marriage and had hit about as low as she could. It was no wonder she had found comfort elsewhere, although of course she regretted it now it had lost her Jeannie.

"So you need money to fight your case," Allen surmised.

"I've never hit my child," Garrel hissed without meaning to. "I don't care what Jonathan says about me in court, I don't care what the worlds think of me. I just want my daughter back, and at the rate he's going he's making sure I never see her again."

"And you accepted this assignment because it would give you enough money to help fight your case."

"Not enough to win it, I'm afraid. But it's a start." She glanced back to the vole, pretending it was to make sure the thing was still there, but really it was because she didn't want to cry in front of Allen. "All these months away from my baby, Tom. I ... I needed to do it so I could afford to fight for her, but it's killing me."

"I'll talk to Monroe. He kind of owes me for nearly getting me killed, and we both know him. If there's a problem he can solve by chucking money at it, he'll do so willingly."

Garrel looked back at Allen, expecting his eyes to shine with the promise of hopeful gratitude, but he was not doing this for himself. He was doing it for her, and she felt bad about any of the derogatory things she had ever thought or said about him.

"You're a nice guy, Tom."

"I wouldn't go that far."

Something exploded from the trees on the other side of the river and they both all but fell over as they heard the squeal of the vole. The deltadromeus grabbed the animal in its powerful jaws and crunched down with a sickly crack of bones. It dropped the carcass and pawed it with the claws upon its toes, before dipping its maw into the kill and tearing off a great chunk of stringy, wet meat.

Garrel and Allen were backing away slowly, their water spilled, their berries trodden into the mud. The mighty carnivore kept one eye upon them as it ate, and while Garrel knew the kill should have satisfied it she was under the impression this hunt was personal. As with the albertosaurus which had chased her, she could see in the thing's eyes that it would not be content until it had made the kill it truly wanted. She checked for her gun, but could not find it. She had likely lost it during her tumble down the ditch and into the muddy pool, and there was no chance of her going back for it now.

Thankfully the river was a good ten metres wide in this area. However, that was not much longer than the dinosaur itself and Garrel had the horrible sensation that even should the dinosaur prove unable to leap the gap, it would have no trouble at all in wading straight through.

They hastened away downriver while the monster ate, knowing they would have to place as much distance between them as they could. Because they knew that as soon as the deltadromeus had finished its meal it would be coming straight for them once more.

CHAPTER TWELVE

There were dinosaurs in the woods and Monroe had gone prepared. The copter had taken him to the edge of the wood, where the river broke the trees, and he had gone in on foot. Slung across his shoulder was a rifle, while at his hips there rested two revolvers as though he was a cowboy entering a duel. Straps of ammunition crossed his chest at both angles, while in his hands he carried a gun fashioned in the style of a blunderbuss. He had been guaranteed that the thing would bring down an elephant, although had no intention of going after such creatures. It was the carnivores he knew he would have to fight, and while no one had ever guaranteed him it would bring down a fully grown tyrannosaurus rex he knew he would have to take his chances.

Striding boldly into the woods, Monroe felt more at peace with himself than ever he had before in life. He had never done anything like this, had never so much as considered doing something so dangerous, especially on someone else's behalf. If he was at home he would have had a dozen sycophants leap to carry his weapons for him, to go on ahead to make sure the path was clear. But his blunderbuss was designed with elephants in mind, not sycophants, and it was all his.

It was oddly refreshing to actually do something selfless for a change, and as he walked he smiled.

Keeping the river to his right, he headed deeper into the woods, knowing all the while he had an easy route out once he found the two for whom he searched alone.

Allen and Garrel had broken into a run the instant they had been out of sight of the deltadromeus, although now they stopped, breathless, haggard, collapsing against a tree. Allen had never seen Garrel so frightened, although after everything she had told him he knew she was scared more for her daughter than she was for herself. It was no wonder she never spoke about her daughter, that Allen had not even known about her until recently. It must have been torture for Garrel to spend all this time on Ceres, knowing her ex-husband was likely cementing his case against her. Even if she did manage to get enough money together, she could return home only to find her daughter permanently in the man's custody. Perhaps he would even have fled with her, disappearing to some distant world where Garrel would never find him.

Allen could not imagine what she was going through. He had never had any children of his own, had never thought about such things, and whatever Garrel was going through, it was certainly not something he could ever hope to understand. He knew there was nothing he could do to help her, since his own financial situation was that of any archaeology student; but constantly did he think of Monroe, of how he could be made to help her. If nothing else, Monroe had known Garrel for all this time and had to have begun to feel something for her. At the very least she had provided security for the camp and therefore had saved his life with her safety measures, likely time and again, without him even knowing.

By this point they had both managed to regain their breaths. Allen looked at Garrel with her muddy, soiled clothes, her hair wet with sweat and black with dirt, and could see a soul alive with possibilities. Garrel did not intend to die here in the woods, torn apart by some long-extinct reptile; and if she had already determined to survive this, Allen could not see how she would have any trouble fighting the courts when she got home.

Looking upon her now he also realised his feelings for her had changed. She was still incredibly fit and he fancied the pants off her, but now he could see something of who she really was. Before he had seen her as he would a model in a magazine, but the more he came to know her, the more he could see she did not need him fawning over her. She had far too many problems without him adding to them, and if he could be her friend then he would be of far more use to her.

It meant he would have to curb his flirting, but the more he thought about how he had been, the more he was ashamed anyway, so that wasn't such a big deal.

"This is a high-profile mission," Allen said. "No one's ever been allowed to legally come to Ceres. It was all over the papers before we left, and when we return we're all going to become celebrities, at least for a while."

"What's your point?"

"You're entering the public eye, Sara. It gives you ammunition against your ex. You may not have the money, but you get the next best thing. Public support."

"Could we drop it until we're safely back at the camp?"

"Sure." He could sense she was upset more than angry. She did not like to talk about her situation because thoughts of her daughter brought tears to her eyes. But he could also see that his words had hit their mark and that she was thinking them through. They were the first known people to land on Ceres: their names would be remembered along with the likes of Neil Armstrong, Buzz Aldrin and Michael Collins.

It was something which certainly could not hurt her case.

A roar shuddered through the trees then and a great mass appeared on their side of the river. Allen watched as the albertosaurus thundered through the trees, bearing down angrily upon them both. Allen and Garrel sprinted once more, keeping to the river, although the creature was too fast, the cover too sparse, and Allen knew in seconds its jaws would snap down upon them. A million thoughts rushed through his mind. He had made the decision to concentrate upon the living, not the dead, and so far as he was concerned Garrel was the epitome of living passion. She had a daughter she was fighting for, and she had to return home to win her back. Garrel was alive and knew how to live her life, while Allen had only just rediscovered what life was. When compared to Sara Garrel he had nothing, only promise, and that was not a good enough reason to lose Garrel to a dinosaur's jaws.

He stopped running and turned around, standing his ground against the monster. It slowed as it reached him, perhaps expecting a trap, and stopped, staring down at its chosen prey. A moment later Allen heard Garrel screaming at him to move, although he could sense she was still hanging back out of the beast's reach. He looked back to her and smiled.

"Just go," he told her. "I got this one."

Garrel stared back with tears to her eyes, her chest heaving in panic, her gaze darting between Allen and the dinosaur. She went to say something, but her words died in her throat.

Allen looked back to the albertosaurus and felt a strange sensation of having done the right thing. Then he balled his fists as though he was going to box the animal, and dropped into a crouch.

The mighty Titan had hesitated long enough and widening its massive jaws did it snap down upon its hapless prey.

The woods exploded, birds hurled in every direction from the trees, and the albertosaurus staggered back, blood arcing from its nose. Allen blinked, not understanding why he was still alive, and then heard the booming laughter behind him.

"Right on the chops!" Monroe enthused as he levelled a massive cannon in his grip. "Take that, you magnificent beast, you."

For a moment Allen thought he had indeed died and gone straight to hell. Then he remembered Garrel was still nearby and that no matter what he needed to save her.

Running for her, he grabbed her by the arm and made to flee downriver, and she looked at him with confused, panicked eyes which revealed something of her he had never seen before. Respect, admiration even. He pulled her arm again, more forcefully, and she ran with him several paces just as Monroe moved ahead of them, between them and the dinosaur. The albertosaurus roared in pain and anger, not having understood the attack, and Monroe laughed, ramming another shot into his gun and shoving it down with a stick and a mixture of powder. Allen knew nothing about loading a gun but was sure that wasn't the right way to go about things.

"Go on," Monroe urged. "I've finally met a dinosaur and I'm not about to run away from it." He fired again, the shot striking the dinosaur in the thigh and sending up an explosion of blood. It took a step backwards, uncertain what was happening, but Allen could see the rage building within it.

"Come on," Allen urged. "That albertosaurus is about to explode."

"Albertosaurus?" Monroe laughed. "Well, I never. Albert Monroe verses an albertosaurus. Extraordinary." Even while he spoke he was shoving in another shot. "You two still here? Toddle off and let me have my fun. Go make beautiful babies or something. Miss Garrel: I'm not sure you've noticed, but the lad's a mite sweet on you."

Allen shook his head in wonder at this man. He was the same old Professor Monroe, yet in a bizarrely different fashion. He went to say something, to argue with Monroe, but Garrel grabbed Allen's arm this time and tried to drag him from the area. "Come on, Tom."

Allen ran. He did not know why, but he ran with Garrel, leaving Monroe to whatever he thought he was doing. He could hear the man laughing still, and another shot tore through the woods. It was all intermingled with roars from the dinosaur, although Allen could no longer tell what was happening.

He pulled his arm back, feeling suddenly guilty for having abandoned him. He and Garrel were exhausted, dripping with sweat and mire, and his mind was racing with what they had just done.

"Monroe's going to get himself killed."

"We don't have any weapons," Garrel said, her breathing ragged, her eyes wild. "What do you expect us to do? Wave our arms in the air?"

"We didn't have any weapons before and still managed to outfox both creatures. I'm going back."

"If you do you'll die too."

"At least I'll die with a clear conscience."

"Tom." She grabbed his arm then, and he tried to shake it off, but her grip was too strong. Their faces were close enough now that he could see the genuine terror in her trembling eyes. He could also smell her natural odour, her body washed clean of perfumes and scent, and found it oddly pleasing. "Tom, I don't want you to die."

"Well, nor do I, oddly enough. But I'm not leaving a man behind in the woods."

She released him, her back held straight, and he could see she was reaching a decision, could see he had touched her in a way he had never meant to. "You're right," she said. "God, you're right. I never thought I'd learn anything from you, Tom, but ... You're not the man I always took you for."

He smiled, waited for more, although she made no move towards him. His grin faltered slightly. "You're not going to kiss me are you?"

"No."

"Oh."

Garrel punched him playfully on the arm, which seemed to be her odd way of showing affection, and Allen watched as she headed back the way they had come. She had only taken two steps, however, before the trees parted and the albertosaurus lunged through. Its skin was pockmarked with injuries, and as it opened it jaws it was to reveal a sticky wet mess of torn flesh. There was intense hatred in its eyes now, for it had long passed the curious or even wary stages and had fallen into pain and rage. Allen hurled a rock at the thing, but the albertosaurus did not notice, mainly because the rock missed and fell in the river to hide from the monster. Garrel drew to a halt before it, indecision flashing in her eyes.

Allen froze, with no idea what to do. He watched as Garrel backpedalled, narrowly evading the first lunge of the beast. It was moving with a slight limp now, and Allen knew the pain was the only thing which had caused it to miss its first attempt upon her. He fought to think of something which might help her, but he had nothing upon him aside from his torch and very much doubted that would prove a potent weapon against the behemoth. His mind shot back to something Garrel had said earlier and realised it was the only thing he could do.

He began waving his arms and shouting.

The albertosaurus glanced his way in irritation, but it was only a momentary pause. It proved enough for Garrel to clamber another few metres away, although Allen could see she wasn't going to make it. He needed something else and he needed it now.

An infuriated screech filled the air then and Allen saw something crashing through the river from the other side. The deltadromeus was marginally smaller than the albertosaurus, but it was not wounded and just as angry. This section of the river was narrower, only perhaps seven metres in width, and the deltadromeus tore through it as though it was a puddle. The water rose only to its thighs, splashing against the mighty creature in a vain attack which could cause no harm, and within moments the deltadromeus was across the river and snapping at the albertosaurus.

Allen was shocked, staring at the twisted scene as the deltadromeus roared with razor fangs at its wounded rival. The albertosaurus lost all interest in Garrel at this point and snapped back at its assailant. Garrel dropped low, throwing her hands over her head as the two Goliaths danced about her, their attention focused solely on the fray.

The deltadromeus was the first to make a lunge, tearing its teeth across the already wounded thigh of its foe. The albertosaurus made a lunge for its opponent's exposed throat, but the deltadromeus pulled back, its statement made. Bellowing in indignation, the albertosaurus took a step forward, its claws almost tearing through Garrel where she desperately tried to regain her footing.

Taking a deep breath, Allen threw himself forward and ran until he reached her side. She stumbled and he could see she had twisted her ankle, so he threw her arm over his shoulders and hobbled with her as best he could. Allen had never won any prizes for his strength, but when the world about him was afire with furiously combatting monsters it was certainly an incentive which could get him moving.

"We're not going to make it," Garrel said through gritted teeth.

"I'm not leaving you."

"Wasn't asking you to. Go left."

Allen looked to the left, but all he could see was the river. Then he jolted as Garrel pushed him and the two fell into the water. Allen gasped as the surprisingly strong current seized him. He glanced back at the two enraged animals tearing chunks out of each other, and realised they had not even noticed the departure of their prey. And then water sprayed in his face he felt himself go under. He came up spluttering, floundering with his arms, and was aware of something coiling around his chest. He strained to look behind him and saw Garrel was clinging to him. It increased their weight but he doubted it would slow them any.

Just as he was fearing they were going to drown it was all over and they were rolling in the grass, sputtering and coughing. Garrel had seen a bend in the river and had thrown the both of them free.

There were no trees ahead, for the woodland rose menacingly behind them. There was something there, however, and Allen looked upon it with a heavy heart. The copter which had brought Monroe to their rescue.

"We should still go back for him, you know," Allen said.

"I know. But you also realise he's dead, right?"

Allen did not like to think that, even though he knew it was true. "What he did for us was a good thing," he told her.

"I never really liked him, but he made good in the end, Tom."

Allen knew what had happened was terrible, but whenever Garrel used his first name it still sent a thrill running through him. He looked at her freezing body in her dripping, torn clothes, some of the mud washed from her face and hair now, and he was at once reminded why he had become so infatuated with her to begin with.

"Before we leave," he said, "I just want you to know I love you."

"I know you do, sweetie. But I have enough problems to worry about without adding you to them."

Allen would have preferred it had she just slapped him in the face: at least it would have made physical contact between the two of them.

Garrel boarded the copter and started the engine. Allen followed, glancing back but once to the woodland. He heard a terrible cry resound from somewhere lost within the trees and wondered whether a victor had emerged from the horrific duel. It did not matter which survived, though, for they had lost Monroe regardless.

The copter rose into the air and Allen watched the woods recede. He could not help but feel a chapter in his life had ended and from hereon in things would be different for them all.

CHAPTER THIRTEEN

It was with a heavy heart that Garrel and Allen walked back into the camp. Together they explained to Professor Travers everything that had happened. She seemed agitated even before they had told her about Monroe being killed, and that was news which she took with a twinge of uncharacteristic sadness. Garrel did not think much of Travers, did not think anything of her in all honesty, but she could not fault her for the way she was. Travers held a strong work ethic, and if not for people like Travers no one would ever discover anything. It came as something of a shock, therefore, when Travers listened to all they had to say and said, "I think we need to leave Ceres. Right now."

Garrel exchanged a surprised look with Allen. "But we still have a while left on the excavation, Professor," she said. "Unless you've found something really bad in the ground?"

"It's not what I've found, it's what you found."

For a moment Garrel did not understand; then she remembered the disc she had handed to Monroe. "You looked at the information I took from the temple. What was it?"

"Nothing good," Travers said. "I don't know who those people were, whether they were government sanctioned or not, but they weren't researchers in the way we are."

"How do you mean?"

"They were experimenting on the dinosaurs. It was research, yes, but nothing humane."

"I want to see."

"I don't think you do."

"I need to."

Travers slowly nodded and indicated the console behind her. Garrel approached and sat before the monitor, keying in the necessary sequence to get the video started. She had found her faith in that temple, had discovered something about herself she had thought long buried. She did not like to think that by pressing just one more button she would be destroying everything she had regained since coming to this world.

But there were some things she simply could not take on faith. Whatever was going on in that underground temple, she had to know.

Images appeared on the screen then. There was a display in the corner, showing her a time and date from only five years earlier. The video was shaky, held by a manual operative, and there was a female voiceover detailing processes which Garrel did not understand at all. But she could see an albertosaurus on the screen, a heavy chain bound to its leg. It fought to move, but was too tightly packed into the room to be able to do much of anything. Garrel physically jumped as the dinosaur screamed, a visible electric charge flowing through its body suddenly.

"Test subject albertosaurus," the voice said, "still shows resistance to electric current. Increasing voltage by two per cent." A few moments thereafter the creature cried again, and Garrel cut off the image entirely.

"Good lord," Allen said behind her, his eyes wide with fear and shock. "No wonder those carnivores were so determined to chase us."

Garrel had heard tales of rhinoceroses seeking revenge on people who had harmed them years earlier. Nor was it exclusive to mammals. It seemed dinosaurs had more in common with non-extinct animals than anyone had ever thought.

"Mankind has to exploit everything," Travers said evenly. "Every animal they can find."

"But what are they doing?" Allen asked rhetorically. "I mean, why run a charge through a dinosaur?"

"Maybe someone's looking to colonise Ceres," Travers said. "Maybe our government has always been here, underground."

"And they didn't think sending in a team to dig around in the dirt wouldn't uncover their secrets?"

Travers said nothing. Garrel could see she had nothing else to say. Allen was angry, but more than anything he was confused. She could not blame him that. As for Garrel herself, she felt nothing. There was nothing to feel in situations like this. But Travers was right. They could hardly stay on Ceres with what they knew. If anyone came back to that outpost and found out Garrel had taken the disc they would come to silence them. But what would they do if they were to leave Ceres? They could claim they had cut short their mission because Monroe had been killed, and none of them could ever mention what they had discovered. It was the only way to safeguard their lives.

She could see Travers already understood this, so it would just be a case of explaining it to Allen, to make him see that if he spoke a single word they were all doomed.

"Pack up your things, Professor," Garrel said. "Tom, why don't you give me a hand gathering up all our stuff?"

Allen nodded, his mind elsewhere, and as they departed the room Garrel could see Travers offering her a silent wish of good luck.

They went first to clear out Garrel's room since she hoped it would give Allen a sense of achievement that he was even there at all. She had only a scattering of possessions and knew it would only take a few minutes, and as she removed her poster from the wall and rolled it up, she asked if Allen could grab her suitcase from the wardrobe and fold up some of her clothes. She watched him while he worked, absently folding all her shirts while his mind was awash with the horrors they had just witnessed on the screen. There was a time when he would have gone straight to her underwear drawer, and she wasn't all that certain any more the change was necessarily good. She had always found Allen annoying, but at least she knew who he was and what he was capable of. Just as she had always known the parameters of her religion.

"We can't tell anyone," she said, deciding to just be blunt about it. "If one of us does, we're all dead."

"Monroe already is."

"I know. And I'm sorry. But I have to think of Jeannie here. You do understand that, don't you?"

Allen looked at her with a soulless expression. She had never before seen him so despondent and a part of her heart wanted to take him in her arms and hold him close. But this was important and she could not afford to let the moment pass.

"We don't know who those people in the video were," she continued, "and we can't afford to make assumptions, but nor can we take risks. They were running experiments for a reason, Tom. If we talk, we'll just disappear."

"I know. I don't like it, but I know we can't say anything."

Garrel felt her body relax slightly, although she could see in his eyes there was something he was not saying, some plan he had. "What are you thinking?"

"That I need to find out what they're doing. I'm staying here on Ceres, Sara. I'm staying until I've found out what's going on."

Garrel was momentarily speechless. Whatever she had expected to hear from him, that most certainly had not been it. It was a good and decent thing to do, yet all Garrel could picture was the face of her daughter. The dinosaur being electrocuted had been horrific, but the thought of not seeing Jeannie again was a constant nightmare.

"I can't stay with you," she said in a small voice.

"I'm not asking you to. You need to go home, fight for your daughter. Think of me every now and again, but aside from that forget you ever came to Ceres."

"And what are you going to do here? If we leave, you won't even have a craft to get off this world."

"Sooner or later someone will come back to that temple."

Garrel cringed at the word. "It's not a temple. It's a torture chamber."

Allen accepted the correction. "Someone will go back there. When they do, I'll be waiting for them."

"And you'll what? Attack them? Run electricity through *them* for a change?"

"I don't know. Maybe. Maybe I can redirect the angriest dinosaurs towards that place and have them deal with the problem for us."

Garrel smiled at the new image forming. "I can just imagine you riding to the rescue on top of a triceratops, Tom."

"If all goes to plan, I can take their ship and get off-world before reinforcements arrive. With their building destroyed, their personnel devoured, maybe they'll think twice about sending anyone else. Either way I can take back proof of who they were. Whether they work for our government, someone else's government, or are a private enterprise, I'll have that proof."

"And what will you do with it?"

"That depends on who's behind it. Try to publish it perhaps. Take it to the cops, I don't know." He focused on her with such an intense gaze that it almost frightened her. "But I'll not bring it to you. I won't come asking you to hide me, and I'll never mention your name. I'll keep you and Jeannie out of it, Sara. I'll keep you both safe."

Garrel felt ashamed that she could not have been so selfless, that even faced with the decision she knew she could never do what he was doing. Even if Jeannie was not waiting for her back home, she would never have had the strength of character to have committed herself to such a thing. She placed a hand upon his shoulder and felt her heart race at how good this man was. "I'm proud of you, Tom."

"Sure." And then he grinned like the old Tom Allen. "Do I get that kiss yet?"

Garrel drew him towards her and pressed her lips to his. He seemed surprised at first, as though he had only ever been joking about it because he had known there was never any chance she would have wanted him. But within moments he seemed to realise she was genuine and he surrendered to her embrace. She tasted salt upon her lips and knew she was crying, and as she pulled away it was to see the intense joy in the young man's face which she knew only mirrored her own.

"Did I tell you I loved you?" Allen asked with narrowing eyes.

"You did with words, Tom. Now show me you mean it." In one swift motion she removed her shirt and tossed it crumpled onto the neatly-folded pile Allen had been making. They sank onto the bed as one and for a while at least were able to put all the strains and stresses of Ceres behind them.

The craft was loaded. Garrel had insisted on leaving Allen enough equipment to see him through. He wanted to keep moving, so only wanted a few things, and the more that was left behind the more chance there was of the torturers discovering him. To this end Garrel had reluctantly agreed to take back the copter and all the prefabricated walls which formed the encampment. But she had left a few crates of equipment and batteries, weapons and ammunition. And food, since Allen would never say no to extra food. Together they had buried the crates in shallow holes so he could remove the lids and reveal their contents, covering the lids with a thin layer of sand to keep them hidden.

They had left the wreck of the buggy where it had fallen. Garrel knew she would lose money because of it, but did not want to go back out to retrieve the thing. The dinosaurs were too angry for her to feel safe doing that, and she would not add to the body count just to retrieve a hunk of twisted metal. The motorbike had been a different matter, and she and Allen had taken the copter out to find it still in barely working order. One had taken the copter back to camp, the other the bike, and Garrel had spent a few hours tinkering with it and beating the metal back into shape. Allen would need the bike if he was going to survive on this inhospitable world, and she needed to provide him every opportunity.

Allen had stayed with her while she worked, picking up pointers on mechanics. By the end she doubted he would have learned enough to fix any major fault in the bike, but if he only ran into small problems he might have gleaned enough.

At last there was nothing more to do about the camp. Travers had carefully packed away all her research materials, soil samples and unearthed bones. There were no fossils on Ceres, since the world was not old enough to have formed them, but Travers was hoping she had gathered enough to be able to placate her employers, even if she could not provide them with all the answers they sought.

Garrel kept her distance from the Professor, disgusted by her attitude. She knew Travers had spoken a brief farewell with her student, although could not see there had been any emotion in the parting. She understood how Travers could be concerned with her research, but this was the final time either of them would ever see Allen.

Leaving the Professor in the craft, Garrel moved to the ramp to find Allen checking the exterior of the craft for signs of wear or damage. It was something Garrel had intended to do herself, although she trusted Allen's judgements. She could tell from his demeanour that he was just trying to keep busy so he would not have to say goodbye, but there was no chance she was going to leave without seeing him.

"You're sure about this?" she asked as she reached the ground. She encircled his shoulders with her arms and waited for him to look at her.

"If I wasn't, that was a dirty trick I played on you in your chambers."

Garrel smiled. Despite everything that had happened and everything that would happen, there was still room for a little humour. "I won't think any less of you if you change your mind, Tom."

"I owe it to Professor Monroe at the very least. These people ... their experiments got him killed. Someone has to put that right."

"Then look after yourself. If it turns out not to be any government, if it turns out to be criminals the law can deal with ... maybe you could look me up sometime."

"If it's safe I will."

She could see in his eyes he was lying. Or at least that he wasn't telling the truth. He wanted to see her again, wanted to be with her, but above all else he wanted to protect her. And the only way he could do that would be if he never saw her again.

She kissed him once more, a final farewell. Afterwards she could not say how long they stood there, nor did she much care. Ceres was a dangerous place, but so long as she was held in Allen's arms she knew she was in the safest place she could be.

When finally she broke away it was to see a sadness to Allen's eyes, and she could feel her own cheeks wet with tears. Whether they were hers or his, or even a mixture of the two, she did not care. Garrel did not care for much at all at that moment.

"I have a leaving present for you," she said.

Allen looked at her quizzically and Garrel hung something about his neck. Allen looked down to the locket he had found in the cave when he had been searching for Garrel. She knew he had been looking for something nice for her, a gem or something of equal value. Instead he had found a locket containing the photograph of a man who, perhaps, had turned out to be an inhumane monster. Allen had not even noticed that Garrel had taken the locket from him earlier, but then he had had other things to keep his mind occupied while he had dressed. He flicked the locket open now and saw she had replaced the image of the stranger with a smiling image of Sara herself. She could see he was moved by the gift, but she placed a finger to his lips. There was no need at all for him to say anything, least of all to thank her.

"I love you, Tom," she said. "I just wanted you to know that before the end."

"Better late than never. You should go, Sara. You have someone waiting."

"Travers can go screw herself."

"I wasn't talking about Travers."

Garrel's mind turned back to Jeannie and she felt an immense weight bearing down upon her once more.

Allen seemed to sense her sudden change in mood and raised her chin with his finger. "Money isn't everything, Sara. You'll think of something."

"I wish I had your confidence."

"You should. You're a strong woman, Sara. We wouldn't have lasted this long without you. Now go home. Go save your daughter."

Garrel walked back onto the craft and pulled the door shut. The ramp retracted automatically, leaving Allen stranded on an alien world with no way out. Garrel hung her head all the way back to the pilot's seat. The craft was formed of only three rooms, and their equipment was all tied down in the main chamber, behind the pilot's seat. As she flipped on the controls Garrel looked out the window and saw Allen standing on the desert which had at one point been their camp. Once the craft departed Allen would brush away the marks left by the craft's landing gear. Within a few minutes it would look as though they had never even been there.

But they had been there, and Sara Garrel would never forget.

She tried not to cast her eyes behind her to where Travers was fumbling with something, probably making sure her precious research was secured.

"It's not that I don't care," Travers said, sensing the animosity thick in the air. "I respect him now more than I ever have. But my work is important, and I need to get it back to my employers."

"I wish I could be half the person Tom is."

Travers said noting, and Garrel could see this was the way the Professor was dealing with everything. She was upset about things, had been moved at the very least, but all she knew was her work. To throw herself into her archaeology was the only way she could cope. Garrel knew she should not judge the woman, but did so anyway. Garrel was upset, angry and afraid for Tom Allen. If Travers didn't want to bear the brunt of that grief she should have stayed on the world with him.

Which was precisely what Garrel herself would have done if not for Jeannie.

"Where did these come from?"

Garrel had not expected the question, and stared silently as Travers drew forth some kind of long stick. There seemed to be a whole case full of them. Garrel remembered seeing them once in Monroe's chambers. She had not known what they were for, but assumed them to be a slice of home for him. The way Travers was looking at them, however, made Garrel want to lie.

"They're mine," she therefore said. "I collect them. What of it?"

"Nothing." Travers put it back reverently. "Just never took you for someone with such expensive hobbies."

Garrel narrowed her eyes. "It's why I take assignments like this," she continued to lie. "So I can add sticks to my collection. You like them?"

"My bank account would like them. Genuine Nineteenth-Century English walking sticks are hard to come by. They're massively sought after by upper class people who like to show off their money. People like Albert Monroe actually."

Garrel could feel Travers watching her, probing, questing. But Garrel had faced down a raging deltadromeus: she could handle a curious expression from an ageing archaeologist.

"He did seem interested in my collection, yes," Garrel said. "In fact, he knew more about them than I did. I was hoping to maybe sell him a couple of my least favourite ones, but it looks like I'm going to have to keep them all now."

Travers held her gaze for just a few more moments, then broke away. She could sense Travers wasn't going to pose any further problem over this. Garrel's heart was racing. She had it at last: the means to fund her fight to regain her daughter. She had everything she needed to rebuild her life. Her heart ached to tell Allen, but she knew he would never discover her fortune. As she returned her attention to raising the ship, however, she looked through the window to see a motorbike tearing across the lands below and smiled. Allen always knew, always had faith in her. He didn't need to see the money to know she was going to find it somewhere. He had faith in her, and now she knew she had faith in him.

Somewhere below a terrible carnivore sent a roar bellowing through the land and Garrel thought about Allen, alone in a world of madness. Hitting the atmosphere, Garrel took the craft into space, leaving her heart behind forever.

DINOSAUR FALL-GIRL

CHAPTER ONE

Apparently you shouldn't wear green because it offends the faeries. It's why no one ever wears green at weddings, why we're psychologically conditioned to never buy green cars or stereo systems (although since faeries can't stand noise, having a green car or stereo system is surely rubbing their noses in it). Presently I'm crouched low in the bulrushes, unnaturally tall grass the size of corn stalks growing all about me, the sun beating mercilessly upon my unprotected face, an unknown quantity of unknowable creatures potentially surrounding me.

Screw the faeries.

The material I'm wearing is poly-something-fibre; I don't know what it means but not knowing has never bothered me before. It looks like metal, feels like plastic and is as hard as diamond. Not that any guy's ever given me a diamond to compare it to, but I had one married friend who even tried to cut her suit with her ring. Pretentious cow. The poly-whatever-fibre is a very deep green, almost a browny-black, and blends me nicely into the grass and mud and what limited shade the trees offer. It's actually quite flattering, now that I'm thinking about it. It hugs the body, not allowing excess movement beneath so an impact is absorbed by the material. Most days I wouldn't want a material clinging to me so tightly, since I've always been self-conscious about my less than impressive chest; but I'm making no argument this time around.

Of course I'm not relying on just my suit to keep me alive. Before coming out here I was put through the most invasive spa treatment I've ever not paid for; but then I knew I wanted every part of my body smeared with the oddly-smelling paste. Once it soaked into the skin it did not even appear visible, and left only a faint odour of lilac. I'm told it's enough to keep the animals at bay, to mask my natural odour from them for short periods at least. I didn't even get into an argument about whether I actually had a natural odour: I'd seen footage of what those animals could do.

Lastly I smeared my face with some of the local mud once I'd set down. It wasn't necessary, I was told, but I've always liked to think no precaution was ever wasted. Remembering the footage of these things, I didn't actually care what a mess I looked.

Peering through the grass I can barely make out my target, but it's difficult with this wind kicking up the grass like this. It's as though the individual blades are laughing at me, taunting me, knowing I'm not going to make it out of this alive.

I check my own blades: two knives in my belt, one in a boot. They're secure, as are the guns attached to my hips and the rifle at my back. Everything is tied down, nothing clatters. Like I said: precaution can never be overrated.

Flicking my dark fringe out of my eyes and thankful I opted to tie my hair back for this mission, I hold steady a pair of goggles so I might be able to at least determine direction. A thousand heat sources erupt into focus and for an instant my heart leaps and every pore on my body opens, a thin layer of sweat trickling out. Insects, I scold myself, and adjust the scanner. The heat source count drops to a more manageable score, and determining from the size it seems the majority of these are small mammals foraging in the grass. I focus on anything larger than a vole and start breathing again when I'm shown only one result. That means there's none of the native wildlife out here stalking me.

Moving at last, I make my way swiftly through the grass without properly rising to my feet. I draw my pistols; I prefer my rifle, but it's easier to move quickly with the smaller guns in hand. I don't expect to need any weapons at all; yet again my mind is drawn back to that terrible footage.

I stop to check my position only once, and slow as I approach my target. My anxiety is pressing me forward, but my common sense is telling me not to spook my target. The last thing I need is for a loud scream to bring the wildlife running.

I can see movement through the grass ahead of me and realise now I'm only a few metres away from my quarry. I slow considerably and tiptoe through the grass until I part the fronds before me with one pistol and see the woman for whom I've been searching.

Professor Marigold Harper is twenty years old, the daughter of two noted physicians and heiress to a considerable fortune. Her life is constructed around botany experiments and she has apparently proposed some revolutionary theories over the past few years. I have of course never read any of her papers: I just read the profile I was given in my mission overview. My impression of Harper is that she's a spoiled rich kid, too much money and not enough sense. And no experience in the real world. If she had any of that, she wouldn't be here now looking for extinct plants to prove some useless theory. It long ago stopped amazing me what money can do. Even at just twenty, Harper has a title and a string of achievements to go with it.

She has her back turned to me, entirely unaware I'm even here. If I was a predator she would be dead already. This is of course my first look at her, and I pause to set her to memory should we somehow become separated. Even crouched I can tell she's short, dressed in stupidly bright blue and yellow. Her long blonde hair is tied back, and she's wearing trousers and a tunic, so at least she's had the sense not to come here in her best dress. But there my respect dwindles.

Replacing one of my pistols at my belt I decide the only way to introduce myself without making her shriek is not one she's going to like. But she's coming off this rock alive and if she complains to daddy about her rough treatment it's something I'm just going to have to handle later.

I encircle my free hand about her head and clamp it across her mouth, drawing her bodily back to press against my chest. She struggles, tries to scream, and beneath the thin glasses I can now see she wears her eyes bulge in terror.

"Shh," I say gently, quietly. "Calm down." She doesn't calm down, her body shuddering violently, her arms flailing even though I'm keeping all her limbs against me to prevent too much movement. "Calm down," I repeat just as quietly but this time with some ice. "You're going to attract the predators."

She stops thrashing at this point, although her body does not relax at all. It's a start, but I can almost feel her cold, imperious eyes boring into me.

"I'm going to let you go now," I tell her. "I don't want you to run, I don't want you to shout. If you have to speak, whisper.

Understood?" She does not reply, so I repeat my question and she nods slowly.

I release her and she wheels from me the instant she's free, fire blazing in her eyes, a fierce hatred of anything which isn't a plant evident upon her brow. Standing there flustering, she affords me my first actual look at her. Her file said she was twenty, but I would have placed her even younger than that. She has soft features, naïve and innocent. Her face is rounded, but her eyes are pinched and alert, lending her an almost elfin appearance, and I wonder whether she's offended I'm wearing green.

"Who are you?" she blurts. "What's the meaning ..."

"My code-name's Autumn, you don't need to know more than that. This is a military extraction, Professor. You're not supposed to be here and you know it. Ceres is off-limits for a reason, and it's a damn good one."

"I'm not afraid of animals, and I'm not afraid of soldiers."

"You don't have to be afraid of me, ma'am. I'm here to save your life, that's all. Now come with me, I have a craft waiting."

"I'm here collecting flora samples, and I'm not going until I've ..."

"You're going when I tell you, and that would be now." I cast my eyes about her basket of plants and a small amount of electronic equipment. "Now gather your stuff, we're leaving."

"I haven't finished my studies."

"What's to study? There aren't even any flowers on Ceres."

"I'm looking into the effects plants may have on the reversal of cancer. You *would* like to see a cure for cancer wouldn't you?"

She's not going to hook me with that. But as she stares so imperiously into my eyes it's almost as though she knows about my mother. About how I didn't make it to her bedside in time because of my work. About how my dad and my brother shut me out of their lives, about how everything I ever knew was screwed over because of that one word.

But she doesn't know – she can't – so I say, "People better than you have been searching for the cure for cancer for centuries, ma'am. You're not going to find it on Ceres."

"But on Ceres we have extinct plants, soldier." She's actually trying to reason with me. "Plants whose properties need to be studied." And I'm actually listening. "Plants which may well not only cure cancer, but headaches, the common cold and world hunger to boot."

"And which world would that be?" I snap, taking any opportunity now. The plan was to find her, take her back to the ship and get out. Instead I find myself losing control by falling into a conversation with the girl. "We can discuss this back at the ship," I tell her and grab her roughly by the wrist. "Now come on."

She shakes her arm, but there's no way she can dislodge my hand and she knows it. Her eyes narrow angrily at me. "I have work to do, soldier."

"Illegal work. This world is quarantined."

"So what are you doing here?"

"Special permission for extraction. It happens when we get idiots like you deciding to take a wander."

I thought she might take a shot at me for the idiot comment. After all, she probably has a dozen degrees and can comfortably hold a conversation regarding the relationship between different molecules and how best to split an atom. I'm several years her elder and don't know any of that stuff. But take away my weapons and my clothes and I can go four or five rounds with a polar bear.

Suddenly the world turns dark and I grab hold of the professor, throwing us both to the ground. The sunlight returns and I peer upwards, pressing Harper into the ground, holding my own body against her to prevent her moving, my hand still firmly pressing into the small of her back. I can see the pale blue sky beyond the tips of the waving grass and cannot help but believe the grass is signalling something as to our position.

I do not want to meet anything which has the sheer mass to block out the sun in that way, and having read up on the various creatures which inhabit this place I'm fighting down panic. Fear is the greatest killer in a professional soldier; ineptitude is the greatest killer in battle, but a soldier should not suffer from such, which leaves only fear. Because no one, I don't care who they are, can fully banish fear. Everyone's afraid of something.

Whatever that thing was, however, it seems to have gone for now.

"We're moving," I whisper in a voice barely above the soughing of the wind through the grasses. Harper can see my lips moving though and doesn't need the words to know what I want. "Go slowly."

I rise back to a crouch and drag Harper to her feet also. Being shorter than me she does not have to crouch quite as much, although nor is she stupid enough to walk brazenly tall. It seems even posh botanists understand when there are predators watching them.

We move as quickly as we can, but I'm not willing to sacrifice silence for speed. I think about my goggles and how I foolishly trained them all about the grass, but did not think to consider anything in the sky.

Again the world is plunged into darkness and again I shove the professor to the ground. Light returns momentarily, but I can't imagine anything of a size to block out the sun for even the second it had. I run a few calculations through my head, trying to work out whether I can make it back to my craft. That's a definite no, but there's tree cover at the end of the field, beyond which is the ship. If we can make it to the trees I'm certain we could lose our pursuer. Ordinarily I would not automatically assume the thing was after us, yet with two passes I'm willing to take no chances. Even if it doesn't intend to attack, we've clearly piqued its interest, and that's the worst thing to achieve on Ceres.

Harper shrieks, and the sun is once more blacked out. I do not berate the professor, but nor do I release her arm, for I don't want her running off in the wrong direction. The grass almost flattens in the wind and as I rise once more to a crouch I feel myself almost blown over by the sudden gale. A sliver of sunlight emerges, and is gone in an instant, and I look up to see the grass parting, attempting to flee from the menacing sight hovering directly above.

The winged beast is huge, and from the files I read it was the airborne menace on top of my list of ones I really didn't want to meet. Its length from head to feet is eight metres, but its wingspan, like some gigantic bat, stretches to over twelve. It would take three human beings lined head to toe to equal even one of its mighty wings. What those wings are made of I have no idea, but I know they put my military attire to shame. A dull grey, they at once appear translucent and opaque, like wet leather catching the sun and glinting the light into my eyes. A strong bony ridge forms the very outskirt of each wing, the remainder being flexible material strong enough to keep this monster in the air.

Its body is long and bullet-shaped, with lengthy yellowing feet trailing behind. The body itself reminds me of the sleekness of a fish, and I can imagine this thing diving into the waves to retrieve whatever monstrous sea-life it would call a morsel. Its neck is long and hardly distinguishable from the main body, ending in a yellowing head which is formed almost primarily of beak: a large wide maw which ends in two beady eyes affixed one either side of the head, culminating in a small bony crest which may well offer defence against natural predators.

I cannot imagine a natural predator for this monstrosity so large it could comfortably fit three or four people upon its neck in flight.

It hovers above us, examining us carefully, and I notice that it does not seem able to move its long neck too easily. That would be an advantage if it came to a fight, for fleeing the thing would mean it would not be able to accurately track us. It opens its beak to screech at us, and I'm forced to cover my ears as the grass about us vibrates in fear, Harper releasing a yelp as pain explodes through her brain.

I do not release my hold upon the professor. The quetzalcoatlus, as with all winged creatures of its time, had a diet which consisted of fish and insects. This beast is large enough to scavenge upon the dead of large animals, however, and there were theories put forth years ago which suspected this beast of being the vulture of its day. Still, even vultures would not attack a living prey with a sting. The quetzalcoatlus will not attack, I feel myself lying silently. It will not attack; it was not biologically programmed to attack.

I can see in its eyes it's at any moment going to attack.

"Move!" I shove the professor through the grass, releasing her so she can run without stumbling, my eyes ever upon the great winged beast above us. Its downdraft is immense and my feet catch upon one another, threatening to smack me into the ground where the prehistoric vulture could gain an easy meal. It raises its head in what amounts to a primal glee, altering the angle of its wings that it might gain a better view of me. From what I've read about these things I was under the impression they glided by catching updrafts and winds. That doesn't amount to a lot of wing-flapping, which means it shouldn't be able to just hover there like that.

I'm beginning to feel there's a lot about Ceres which isn't natural, and when one's faced with a twelve metre prehistoric vulture that's no mean statement.

Its beak snaps towards me through the grass and I level my pistol and squeeze the trigger. The air is suddenly filled with an exploding thunder, adding to the wind-tossed storm the quetzalcoatlus is already drawing up. For all its sheer size and width, however, my bullet goes entirely wide, but the sound is enough to send the monster reeling in shock. I can literally feel the grass sigh with relief that the thing is leaving as slowly the tall blades return to some semblance of normality.

I'm just through congratulating myself when I suddenly remember I told the professor to run.

Damn rookie mistake, that's what it was, but I waste no time in self-recrimination and instead activate my goggles to track her movement. There's a heat signature roughly the size of my wayward professor moving in an easterly direction. Fear may be the greatest killer in a professional, but it can certainly be a great motivator: somehow the prof's managed to put almost fifty metres between us.

Breaking into a run, I charge after her, keeping the goggles affixed to my eyes so I can see if she changes direction. It's odd running with the goggles, especially since I've never really liked even walking with them. I can register heat sources, but little else, so the blades of grass aren't even showing up. It's as though I'm running through an empty field instead of a forest of grass.

My heart catches in my throat as I see another heat source ahead, circling the professor, and I tear the goggles from my eyes. The quetzalcoatlus is circling once more, training its beady eyes upon Professor Harper. I can't see the prof any more, but I know precisely where she is and I can travel faster without the prohibiting goggles. Holstering my pistols I draw the rifle from my back. Without the goggles I can certainly shoot better, too.

The quetzalcoatlus makes a lunge into the grass, but comes up empty, and I realise I can't afford for it to make another pass. It's circling again, almost lazily, but I know it's just trying to catch the wind as best it can while it sizes up its prey and assures itself of the best angle of descent. I'm somewhere within twenty metres of the prof now, assuming she's stopped, and can't afford to get any closer because the quetzalcoatlus is dropping again.

Throwing the rifle to my shoulder, I stare at the thing down the sight and lead it for an instant before cracking off a shot. The rifle releases a single dull explosion and I watch in a panic far surpassing satisfaction as the beast reels off, a bloody arc trailing from its throat. It veers out of range, putting itself between me and the sun, and I decide I'm not going to get another shot at the thing until it comes back down.

Hurtling through the grass, I find Harper lying on the floor, trembling and attempting vainly to get to her feet. She turns terror-stricken eyes upon me and I can see her face and lips have paled as though she's already dead. Grabbing her by the arm I haul her to her feet and stare directly into her eyes and just pray there's some small semblance of calm remaining in my own.

"There are trees to the north. A minute's run. Go."

"I ..." She can barely speak, and I know if she doesn't do what I tell her neither of us is getting out of this mess.

"You can do it," I promise. "Run. Believe me, I'm right behind you."

A screech fills the air again and the grass trembles as the quetzalcoatlus swoops down once more. All sense of curiosity has fled its system now as it attacks, its beak snapping open, its eyes small and intensely cruel. I bring my rifle to my shoulder and fire, my shot taking it through the wing and tearing a hole which doesn't slow it at all. I don't know whether it's the wind or my own fear, but I can't seem to hit anything today.

"Go!" I shout at Harper, the one thing I at least have some semblance of control over, and I can hear by the pounding of her boots that she's actually done as she's told.

An instant later I gasp at the impact as the massive head, easily the length of my entire body, slams into me. I've narrowly managed to avoid its jaws, yet the impact of being butted by such a great force sends me flying through the grass. I slam into the ground, rolling, unable to determine even my direction, and as I grind to a halt, my face pressed into the mud, I can feel my ribs screaming in pain and I'm suddenly very grateful for whatever materials the military uses to make this armour of mine.

Unable to repress a groan, I drag myself to one knee, hacking blood and fighting the dizziness my sudden intense nausea is bringing on. My head's pounding and I know the only way I'm getting out of this is if I allow my adrenalin to take charge.

Suddenly my leg goes in the air and my face slams into the mud once more. I can feel something yanking at me and I can't find my rifle. Panicking, I draw my pistols and without even looking I point them both behind me and fire two shots from each. My leg is released in an instant and I'm back in the mud, floundering in my vain effort to get anywhere. Oblivious to the location of my enemy, I roll onto my back, pistols raised to see the quetzalcoatlus coming at me once more. Screaming in rage and pain and fear and panic I squeeze off far too many shots for me to be able to afford to lose, and the air above me explodes in a crimson cloud, foul rain spattering my body and face, a coppery almost acidic taste splashing my tongue and stinging my eyes.

The quetzalcoatlus attempts to rise, flaps its wings to escape, but to allow it such freedom would only be to have it return and that's something my fear won't allow. Taking careful aim, I release one final pistol shot and watch as the bony skull between its eyes erupts in a mass of blood and cartilage, and the great beast collapses one final time, jerking as it settles into the grass.

My body tingling with energy, my chest ready to burst, I struggle to my feet, slipping once, twice, but ultimately forcing myself back to my feet. Breathing heavily, I take one final look at the great monster now lying dead before me, and realise even in death this creature is the most majestic thing I've ever seen.

Then I remember the professor and start off after her, grabbing up my rifle as I run.

Thankfully Harper for once did as she was told, and as I leave the grass behind and reach the trees, I find her leaning against one, shivering. She's pale and weak and I can see she's vomited whatever she had for breakfast. She's also lost any equipment or samples she had had out in the grass. As I stand there, body and hair caked in mud and blood, but with all my equipment as intact as my bodily functions I can't help but feel I've won something over the professor already.

"Why did it attack?" Harper asks in a tight, trembling voice. "They feed on fish and insects. I read up on them!" Her anger is momentary and I know it's just her brain's way of trying to cope with this. She's not crying, so that's one thing at least.

"Maybe it was hungry," I suggest. Maybe there's not a lot to eat here on Ceres, maybe the things living here aren't quite what we expected. Studying the fossils of extinct animals, it would seem, doesn't do much to prepare one for the real experience. "I think maybe Ceres doesn't play by the rules, Professor." I'm trying to reassure her, trying to be kind. Not because I much care what she thinks of me, but because I have to travel with this woman and would like her to do what I tell her. Besides which, my ship's back in the other direction, which means circling the grass the long way around.

I notice she hasn't thanked me yet, and don't hold my breath on that.

Behind me I hear the sudden squawk of predators and watch as three further quetzalcoatli descend upon the grass, presumably upon the corpse of their fallen. There are theories about them being scavengers, but nothing in the files about them being cannibals. But then I guess no one's ever spent enough time down here to actually catalogue their behaviour.

"We should get out of here," I say, and realise Harper's staring distantly at the scene which we thankfully cannot see in its gory entirety. "Harper?" I ask, stepping between her and the sight. "We need to go."

She shakes her head, blinking rapidly, but no colour returns to her face. "Yes, of course." And she starts walking off through the trees, no course in mind, no heed being paid to her movements. I'd have a better companion if I'd brought my son's dog with me.

Starting off after her, I cast one final glance at the rise and fall off wings in the grass, knowing full well how close that came to being me out there. There's a reason this place is out of bounds, and whatever it is I'm fine with it. It's one time where I think politics actually got something right.

The sooner I'm off Ceres the better.

CHAPTER TWO

Call me cruel but I can't help feeling Professor Marigold Harper deserves a good slapping. I'd certainly be willing to slap her simply for having a silly name, but then upper class tossers always give their kids stupid names so that's hardly her own fault. Her running off into the woods would hurt her a lot more than it would me should some stalking carnivore get hold of her, but then it would be my neck in the noose when the lieutenant had to explain to Mummy and Daddy dearest why their delicate, fragrant little one never made it back.

I meant the fragrant thing as a joke, a play on words of her name, but now that I think about it she does smell quite nice, like apple blossoms in a summer wind. Entirely inappropriate for out here, and utterly destroying my camouflaging smell and even the mud caking my face I haven't quite managed to wipe entirely off.

Catching up to her was easy, and thankfully she's given my no trouble in my steering her in the right direction. She's still somewhat in a daze, which means her upper-class imperiousness has yet to settle fully into her character, which is of course a good thing. If I can get us even halfway to the ship before her confidence reasserts itself I'm going to be one happy girl.

Still, for all the trouble the little madam's already caused me I really, really want to pull down her 100% silk panties and give her a free four-fingered tan.

I can just imagine what would be said when she got back home. That'd be my career in shreds, but sure it'd be worth it.

I must have sniggered aloud at the thought because Harper is looking at me curiously, her heart still racing too fast for her to actually put into words whatever question she has. I choose not to elaborate but nor do I lose the smile. It's best to keep her afraid, or at least wary of me if at all possible.

"You know I should be collecting samples while we walk," she says, and I can detect some of her superior character coming out at last. There's still fear to her voice, but it's quickly being replaced. I don't give a whit about her samples, and try my radio again. "That won't work," Ms. Supercilious decides haughtily, as though she knows something I don't. "There aren't any satellites around Ceres, and the world's magnetic field's all screwy with signals anyway."

"Nice to see your Daddy's money hasn't been completely wasted in your education, Goldie," I say as sardonically as possible. "The field's all screwy the best you can come up with?"

She raises her nose and I desperately want to make it bleed. "Everyone knows it's almost impossible to get a signal on Ceres."

"And since I'm someone I must fit in the definition of everyone. But it doesn't do any harm to try, does it?"

She relents this point and continues walking in silence, which is fine by me. And yes, I knew I wouldn't get a signal through. But there are receivers on my ship and sometimes they're enough to boost signals, especially if I'm only trying to send a message into low orbit, and especially if my guys are monitoring the radio waves, which I know they are. Once I get back to the shuttle I should be able to get a powerful enough signal through the atmosphere, but until then I'm cut off, with only Harper for company.

In all honesty I'd prefer the flying lizards.

"So," Harper asks as we walk, as though extending an olive branch I'd simply like to set alight, "where's Autumn come from? You say it's not your actual name?"

"No. My name's not up for discussion. Autumn's my call-sign. Corporal Autumn."

"Early thirties and still only a corporal?" she asks sympathetically.

I don't bother answering the obvious jibe. She has no idea how old I am, and there's no way I look early thirties. Shove her face into some brambles, see how she looks then. "Do you like games, Prof?"

"No."

"Well it's a good thing this is a real easy one then. Can you guess the call-signs of everyone else in my unit? Here's a massive clue: there are four of us."

She stares at me, half in mute horror, half in silent amusement. I smile, realising she's got it already. "You have to be kidding me," she says. "What, really? No, that's just stupid."

"Tell that to Lieutenant Winter. She made up the call-signs. In fact I dare you to tell that to the lieutenant. She'd break your face, sister." I broaden my smile at the very possibility and Harper shudders. God, sometimes I'm cruel.

We walk in silence for a while longer. The trees aren't very dense where we are, which means I should be able to see any predator activity even if they're stalking us. Besides, with Harper out in front there's a fifty/fifty chance they'd go for her first and I could just shoot anything which attacked.

"What's it like being a soldier, Fall-girl?"

Fall-girl? Forget the lizards, I'm more tempted than ever to just put a bullet in the back of her skull and claim the wildlife have developed firearms. "Oh, being a soldier's dandy," I tell her simply. "The pay's always late, they need a certain amount of us to die so the rest of us have enough to eat, we gamble and whore all our money away and we live life as though each day's the final one. Which means we get into a lot of unnecessary fights and screw anything that moves."

She stops walking and glances at me, more than half believing my sarcasm.

"Why," I ask, "what's it like being a rich cow?"

The back straightens and I know I've got to her even as she storms off ahead of me. At last I'm actually beginning to enjoy this little romp.

Not surprisingly we don't talk for a while. The trees are really thinning out now, and I cast a glance to the sky but there's no sign of any more of those flying beasts. There is one thing I can see, and I'm carefully keeping it in view while we walk parallel to it. The creature stands about a metre from the ground, maybe a little more, and is about three in length. Its rear legs are slightly more muscular than the forelegs, although none are long or suitable for long-distance running. The head is a neckless extension of the bulky body, the thick fat tail falling from its back and presently dragging the ground as though it was some form of snake. The body itself is covered with an armour-plated carapace, bearing a scute-like texture. From its plated back there protrude several series of blunt bony spikes whose purpose I have no idea, but it does make the thing look a little weird and at the same time beautiful. That the creature is aware of us is not in question, for it's stopped several times now to stare at me with its small curious eye.

"You really don't know much about Ceres, do you?" Harper laughs like a toff.

"What are you whining about now?"

"That's a minmi. An ankylosaur."

"Yeah, I know. What of it?"

"Well can't you see it's eating the grass? It's not going to attack us, soldier girl."

"Like those fish-eating quetzalcoatli didn't?" That shuts her up, even though we both know the creature must have either been starving or injured to have attacked us at all. Or simply batty, which would be my personal choice. "Anyway," I continue, "can't your Oxford education maybe think of a reason I'm keeping so close an eye on the minmi?" I leave her to think through that one, to ponder that maybe I actually know a thing or two about survival.

After I can all but hear not only the cogs grinding but the cuckoo screeching as well, she just shrugs in that teenage way which means she no longer cares, but which translates to that she doesn't know the answer. I have to get it out of my head that she's a teenager. She's twenty and playing all the right cards to annoy me, that's all.

"That dinosaur may weigh a tonne and it may be protected by that hard shell," I tell her, purposefully sounding as much like a teacher as I can, "but its soft underbelly is precisely what a carnivore would go for. And believe me, a carnivore could get to that underbelly if it wanted."

"And your point?" she asks petulantly.

"That if the minmi suddenly spooks it likely means there's a predator nearby. So long as we keep pace with it and it's happy, I'm happy."

Harper is silent for some moments as she digests this. Unlike a petulant child she's actually taking into account what I've said. I can see she even agrees with it, although I doubt she'd ever say as much aloud. She is a scientist after all.

"You researched the wildlife before coming here," Harper says. I'm not sure whether it's an accusation or praise.

"I know jack squat about plants," I admit, "but I've never had a plant charge me with its fangs. So yes, I learn what I need to survive."

"But surely you'd need to know something about plants if you wanted to survive on Ceres. If only so you know which berries are safe to eat. The wrong kind of berry can kill you just as painfully as an alligator's jaws."

"All right, maybe I do know a little something about plants, Prof."

Harper nods, her features softening a little. "I think we got off on the wrong foot, Corporal Autumn."

"Well we'll be off Ceres entirely soon enough, so we won't have to put up with each other much longer." She may have been trying to make peace, but I'm not really bothered about that. I wouldn't even be down here on Ceres if it wasn't for Professor Harper and the last thing I'm going to be doing is to be nice to her.

We're only about fifteen minutes from the shuttle now, even from our longwinded trek, and soon enough we start to leave the trees behind us. The woodland doesn't exactly end, but it does thin out so it's more like a park back home. I know the terrain of Ceres was supposedly naturally-formed, but I can't help but feel that some parts of it were put here purposefully. It's the animals I can't get. Before I came I delved into research and discovered there were literally hundreds of different large animals here; hundreds more than there seems to be room for. And yet we're not overrun by monsters so they must all have found somewhere to live. Nature finds a way, I guess, although I had thought I'd be doing a lot more shooting of things.

"It's beautiful isn't it?"

Harper may have been talking for a while, but I drifted off. She's staring at the sky, and I instantly tense, fearing there might be more winged beasts circling. But then I realise she's only looking at old Zeus himself. The sky of Ceres is a deep unnatural blue, the heat and light of an artificial sun pulsing through to blast us with its lovely radiation shower. But there's something else in the sky aside from clouds, something which I very much doubt you could ever get away from on Ceres.

The planet Jupiter is fifth out from the Sun and the largest planet in the Solar system. A massive gas giant, Jupiter is a roiling storm of power. The swirling orange, red and white gases churn brilliantly above us, the great red eye – a storm several times the size of Ceres – staring down at us piously. The colossal planet consumes almost half of the sky, lazing around and casually observing yet somehow not casting an immense shadow over half the world. Unlike the rock planets Jupiter is constantly changing and romantics have sat watching the churning gas much as others would lie back and stare at clouds. I have to agree with Harper in that Jupiter is indeed a beautiful sight. It's hardly something I haven't seen before though.

Colonising Jupiter is of course impossible, but the gas is collected through various mining operations, and used to power most of our amenities. Several of Jupiter's moons were terraformed years back and the Jupiter system was established, just like all the other planets have their own systems. We're like different countries in the old way of looking at things, when everyone used to live on Earth. (Of course, each world has its own countries, so that makes everyone even more distant.) Nowadays we police ourselves and don't have much to do with other moons in the Jupiter system, let alone other planets in the solar system.

Ceres was always an odd one though. It wasn't ever an actual world, but was drawn together from some of the larger asteroids in the belt between Jupiter and Mars. The rocks were shoved together to form a world Jupiter claimed, but which somehow Earth managed to grab. Just who owns Ceres has been hotly contested for more years than I've been alive, and I really couldn't care that much for the truth. The fact is Ceres is unstable, because whoever put it together did it wrong, and could break apart at any moment. Why anyone would fight over it is beyond me.

Why anyone would populate their brand new world with dinosaurs is an even more hotly debated question. I don't much care for the answer to that one either. All I know is that Jupiter and Earth have always agreed that Ceres is off-limits. Over the years there have been people landing here of course; usually criminals on the run, hippies seeking peace and love, or scientists like the plant lady here. Whenever we get such a report, sometimes someone's sent in to retrieve them. The quarantine of the world is so strong, however, that in most instances by the time all the legal hoops have been jumped through there's not going to be anything left of the people to save. I read a case once where some hippies tried to make peace and love with a pack of coelophysis and ... well, it didn't end well for the hippies.

Harper was lucky I managed to find her before something like that happened to her, but I don't expect any gratitude, just attitude.

I'm so funny today I kill myself.

Rambling on like this, I'd forgotten she'd mentioned Jupiter being beautiful and thinks I'm ignoring her so she's walked off again in a huff. Oh well, like I give a toss.

The ridge comes into sight now, beyond which I've parked my shuttle. We're at the top of the slight decline, but I left my ship down there purely because all the animal activity was centred up here. Peering down to the scrubland below I can see my little shuttle nestled in the vegetation and out of anyone's way. But there's something wrong. The door's open for one thing, and I know I didn't leave it that way. And there's no way a dinosaur ever developed the ability to open doors.

"Stay here," I tell the professor as I make my way rapidly to the decline. She opens her mouth to protest but I shoot her a stern glower and whatever it is she intended to say never emerges. I don't mind saving her life, but dragging her down into potential danger just to do that seems a little stupid.

A faint stream of gravel and dust accompanies me as I half run, half slide myself to the bottom of the incline. The rocky outcropping upon which the professor still stands shelters my shuttle from the elements and from the prying eyes of anything large enough to, even in curiosity, do any damage to my ship. I draw my pistol as I tentatively approach the poor thing, but I can already see it's in bad shape. The dorsal fin has been torn almost entirely off and the rudder has been damaged beyond repair. The door is half off its hinges, not even swinging mildly in the breeze: even the door doesn't think this is funny. There doesn't appear to be too much damage on the outside of the shuttle, and the rudder and dorsal fin I can do without since they're mainly involved with the steering. I'll know better once I've been able to give the ship a good once over, but right now I'm more concerned with the open door.

As I approach I wrinkle my nose at the strong stench of animal urine. Whatever's attacked my ship certainly wanted to leave its scent. Marking its territory perhaps; maybe I stupidly landed slap bang in the middle of something's hunting grounds.

There's little light within the shuttle, but as I reach the door I can see pretty much everything. It's only a small vehicle, little more than a single large room from which a lone occupant can operate everything. I can certainly see there aren't any animals inside, which is probably the only good thing about what I'm seeing. I step into the shuttle and lower my pistol with a sigh of frustration I should be beyond in my line of work. The chairs have been shredded by powerful claws, the console has been attacked similarly, and pieces of apparatus are scattered, mainly broken, about the floor. Something catches my eye and I retrieve something from the upholstery. Holding it up to the light I can see it's a claw of some kind, belonging to a small theropod most likely. I know for a fact there are coelophysis packs hunting over pretty much all of Ceres, so it's likely they forced their way in and just started breaking things. One probably knocked the console with its tail and a light came on or something, or something beeped at it, and the poor console was torn apart in fright.

There's also a sickly yellowing stain over pretty much everything and I really don't want to touch that: the smell is bad enough for me, thanks.

I try the radio, even though I can see it's broken, and I'm not surprised when I get no answer. So I detach the entire thing and place it in a durable bag, slinging it over my shoulder. There's hardly anything else worth taking, especially since I can see the theropods have even go into my food stores and have torn those apart. I spend a few moments trying to sift through some of them, determining whether anything's still edible, but what they haven't eaten they've urinated over so quite frankly I'd prefer to eat grass.

Heading back outside, I examine the door more closely. I still can't figure out how they managed to get inside. This door should be strong enough to repel a grenade: there's no way a dinosaur would risk injury by throwing itself against it. And no carnivore would ever bite something it didn't understand: that was a sure way of breaking its teeth and thereby starving itself to death through lack of being able to catch food. Except for sharks of course, which have rotating teeth, but somehow I doubt a shark attacked my shuttle.

That's the weird thing about the claw I found inside, the claw I'm still fingering while I think this through. A lot of the dromaeosaurids, such as the velociraptor or the unenlagia, had developed a large and extremely sharp claw. They would always keep this claw above the ground, never allowing it to make even brief contact with anything other than prey. It would have been a menacing sight (and still is actually, considering there are likely some around here), to see that huge claw forked in the air as though it was already involved in an attack upon you. To have an animal take so much care not to blunt their most effective weapon, only to lose it by tearing up my chair ... it's a bit odd to say the least.

But then I guess the dinosaur would have been spooked by the unnatural environment, and the lights and sounds, so maybe that explains it.

I can see an indentation in the doorframe now I hadn't noticed on my way in. It looks as though something heavy has indeed slammed against the frame, which would have created a sizable gap in the door. From there it would have been easier for a small theropod to widen it enough to gain entry. I still can't see a carnivore attacking the shuttle though, but suddenly my thoughts return to that minmi. If an ankylosaur with that great massive clubbed tail had taken this ship for a threat it might well have assaulted the shuttle. After a few whacks it might have determined with its simplistic brain that the shuttle wasn't a threat after all and gone about its business. The theropods could have moved in afterwards, curious, and gained entry that way.

Suddenly it makes more sense than it did a moment ago. A team effort of various dinosaurs, all out to make my mission a lot more difficult than it has to be.

I could blame the dinosaurs, but I blame Professor Harper more. Without her I'd be soaking in a nice lavender bath right about now.

Harper's eyebrows are raised by the time I scramble back up to her, which I do slowly since I'm in no hurry any more. "Shuttle's gone bye bye," I tell her, removing my pack from my shoulder and shoving it into her chest. "That's what I could salvage from the radio. I'll fix it, send a signal and get the lieutenant down here to pick us up."

"And why do I have to carry the pack?"

"Because I have the guns." Which sounds like I'm threatening to shoot her but really means if anything attacks us I'll need to have my hands free to shoot *it*. Does Harper realise that? Do I care?

I look into the sky, the great omniscient eye of the world king staring down laughing at me. I'm going to be here a while – we're going to be here a while. And that means I should probably try to get along with Miss Daddy's Girl. I feel a tightness in my chest at the very thought, but as Jupiter gazes down upon me I realise it's practically telling me I need to obey.

"You looking for your ship?" Harper asks.

Not such a stupid question as it sounds, although in the daylight there's not much chance of seeing the ship from down here. The lieutenant will still be in orbit, and hopefully should have realised by now my radio's ceased transmitting. With any luck she's already on her way down, but so far I can't see any sign of her.

"Just thinking we might like to bury the hatchet since we're going to be stuck together." I don't tell her just where I'd like to bury the hatchet, but I guess she still needs her head for something at the moment. I extend my hand and even try to smile. Harper looks warily at the gesture, at both gestures in fact, and I can see by her face she clearly thinks this is some kind of trap. Which is fair enough, since we both know neither of us is ever going to consider the other a friend.

"All right," she says slowly, taking the hand rather limply, still frowning. "No more jibes 'til we're off-world."

I'm sure I'll try to keep to that. "So," I say with a sigh, trying not to make it look as though it's a great effort just to be civil, "what should I call you? Marigold is a bit ... long." Stupid is what it is, but for the sake of our newfound love I don't say as much of course.

"You don't like my name do you?" she asks.

I shrug. "What's in a name? A rose by any ..." I stop myself. "To be fair, I didn't actually intend that one."

She smiles. Genuinely smiles, and it's actually kinda nice. There's no upper class imperiousness to the action, there's no condemnation, there's not even any sarcasm to it. It's just a smile, and I figure if this girl can smile at me like that the least I can do is try to stick to my promise and be a little nicer.

"Mary," she said. "My friends call me Mary."

I nod, knowing if I say anything it'll only screw with our freshly uncovered girl love. I'm feeling tingly already with what this heart-to-heart might lead to. "We should head for high ground," I tell her. "It'll give us cover so I can fix the radio, and it'll give us a good position to see if the lieutenant lands anywhere nearby."

Harper does not argue, which is almost as though she's agreeing. Perhaps she's accepting that of the two of us I know more about survival. "While you're doing that I might collect a few more samples. There are bound to be some in the mountains if that's where we're going to camp."

I don't care about her samples, but if it keeps her happy it'll keep her quiet, so I don't argue. Which is almost as though I'm agreeing.

I can tell this relationship is already going places.

Heading off together, skirting the tall grass entirely, we head for the mountains. From what I've read up on the terrains, there are dinosaurs that live there too, but I can't see any carnivores braving the area. It'll mean we'll be relatively safe while I work, which is one less thing to worry about.

I catch the great eye above me once more and really do believe it just winked at me. I hate it when planet god kings flirt with me. But then if ya got it ya got it.

I think the heat of this world's getting to me already.

CHAPTER THREE

We're eating an animal which looked like a rat or a vole or something. I have no idea what it was: there was only so much research I could do prior to coming here. Nor did I intend to be here long enough to need to shoot and cook my dinner. We made good time to the dusty valleys above which the mountains towered and I figured I could ignore my grumbling stomach no longer. Harper, for all her faults, had not complained even once during the trek, and so I figured it was time I at least fed her. So I went out to shoot something and left her to get the fire started. She had a good blaze going by the time I returned, remembering to surround the flames with a circle of stones so the fire can't spread, even though that's not very likely in this dry terrain. I also rather suspect Harper didn't bring this fire into being by rubbing together two pieces of wood, but then it doesn't really matter how she made it: I'm not a scout leader.

I cooked the meat thoroughly, not knowing what it was and therefore what diseases it might contain. I have an odd belief that so long as something is cooked well it can't possibly poison you; or at the very least if you're going to die you might as well die with a good meal inside you. While we eat I take the time to properly observe our surroundings. The mountains here on Ceres are huge, or at least they are in this part of the world. The valley in which we currently sit stretches on for miles by the looks of things, and while I was hunting small mammals I certainly couldn't see an end to it. The ground here is dry and sandy, scorched almost as though it gets really hot here during the day. Right now night's falling in quickly, and I remember reading at how suddenly darkness descends here. Something to do with the artificial sun and our close proximity to Jupiter or something. I don't need to understand it for it to happen, and being in the open when night falls is not a good idea. From what I read about Ceres there are a lot of these dinosaurs which hunt at night.

"Things here are a bit weird," Harper says, looking over some plants she's managed to gather along the way. "I mean, I'm not sure this is quite what I was after when I came here."

"What did you expect then?"

She shrugs, chewing on her meat. "I won't bore you with the details, but these are more re-creations than actual prehistory."

I consider that in silence a moment while I eat. "So what you're saying is that the life here isn't what it was like back on Earth millions of years ago?"

Harper puts her plants back into her satchel. "I guess whoever put these things here tampered with their DNA or something."

"Or maybe the creatures adapted to their surroundings. Remember this isn't Earth, this is Ceres. We're farther from the Sun, the world has a smaller surface area and there's a whacking great planet in the sky. And the world's cracking apart, from what I can gather." No one knows who constructed Ceres to begin with, hence the constant argument between the Earth and Jupiter governments, but whoever did it didn't do it too well. The various asteroids shoved together have been slowly shaking themselves apart for years. Quakes are apparently common on this world, and although we haven't suffered one as yet I can only assume they're not far off.

Harper shrugs again. "Maybe. Just so long as they contain the cure for cancer I guess that's all that matters."

There she goes again with the cancer thing. I'm not going to pretend I know anything about medicines beyond what basic training teaches me. Again, I don't need to know how something works for it to save my life. I know which plants can do what, but I don't know why. Harper is one of those people who knows why, and who makes the discoveries to begin with. I should respect her for that at least. After all, if she cures cancer who cares if people a hundred years from now don't realise what a pain she was?

"Why do you want to find the cure so much?" I ask.

"Fame? Money? Isn't that what you're expecting?" She answers whimsically, and I can detect almost a trace of raw anger and I wonder who it was she lost.

"I don't expect anything," I tell her. "Whatever I think about you, you're trying to do some good, and I can't resent that. How'd you get to Ceres then?" I ask, changing the subject. "We couldn't detect a ship down here at all."

"I was dropped off. You have enough money you can bribe anyone to take you anywhere."

"Then how are you getting off?"

"The government's getting me off."

"I don't follow."

"No one approaches Ceres without someone seeing it. I knew the government would send someone to fetch me, assumed it would be the army. I just wanted to get my research done before you got to me, and I didn't manage to do that."

"So you're using my unit as a shuttle service?"

"Pretty much."

The incredulity of the woman knows no bounds, but I keep my temper somehow. "Has anyone ever told you you have a lot of nerve?"

"Oh yeah, all the time."

Night is really settling now and I rise, tossing aside the bones and gristle of my meal. I kick the fire to death and wish I was stamping instead on someone's head. Harper rises also, dusting herself down and preparing her bags for departure. I haven't had a chance to properly look over the radio yet, but I can do that in the morning, when we've managed to gain a little height. Right now climbing would of course be ridiculous, so we'll have to find a place to make camp. There are various caves lining the ground of the valley, although I'm not too happy at the thought of wandering into somewhere any old animal could reach. All dinosaur carnivores were built of the same basic body; powerful rear legs, less powerful forearms, bulky body, neck, big head with wide jaws, counterbalancing tail. This structure does not enable the things to climb, so waiting on the ground for the night would be pretty stupid. Finding a cave someway up the mountain would be better; even if it contained a nesting herbivore, at least the thing wouldn't eat us if we had to fight it.

I scan around with my naked eyes and see precisely what I'm after. A small cave entrance a few metres from the ground. Far enough from any predators to keep me asleep all through the night I think.

Reaching the cave is going to be a little problematic since I didn't bring any rope, although we're both young and fit and there are more than enough juts of rock to help us reach it. I take the lead, shouldering the pack containing the radio since I'm built stronger than the professor. She does not argue about my preceding her: she knows full well the cave may be occupied and isn't stupid enough to want to face such creatures first. The foot- and handholds are proving more than adequate and soon enough I'm chucking the pack over the edge and hauling myself up. The ground here is as dusty as the valley floor, and I see no prints in the thin layer. Night is really falling fast now and yet I know this can't be hastened. I don't want to get either of us killed, and right now there's more chance of danger lurking in this cave than stalking the professor down in the valley.

Instructing Harper to wait a moment I draw a pistol and start into the cave. The darkness is almost absolute in here, but I dare not strike a light. I continue for only a few metres however before I come upon something I had not expected, and reaching out a tentative hand I confirm my suspicions. My hand touches the bare rock and I realise the cave is hardly deep enough to be even considered such. Still, if it's only a recess in the cliff it means there aren't going to be any native animals intending to use it as their nocturnal nest.

I return to the rocky edge and say down to Harper, "Come on up, there's nothing here."

"That wasn't a very long look, Corporal."

"It doesn't go very far, only a few paces. But there's a ceiling so it'll provide some shelter from the wind and cold. And rain if any comes in the night."

"Unless the wind blows it in our faces," Harper says quite correctly as she begins to climb. She makes good progress, not showing any fear at making the ascent, but then it's only a few metres. I've known people to look down and be afraid of falling, not seeming to take into consideration that their feet are over a metre and a half closer to the ground than their eyes so they don't have quite as far to fall as they believed. Harper would not know, since she doesn't look down even once. As she reaches the lip I offer my hand and she accepts it, although she doesn't really need it. I had expected her to rebuff my gesture, although perhaps she wants to carry on this unlikely friendship we appear to have struck up. Or maybe she likes for me to think she's more helpless than she is.

A nagging suspicion enters my mind suddenly that she's going to make a break for it during the night. I certainly don't want to have to go chasing her through the forest tomorrow.

We settle in the quasi-cave and don't talk of much. It's been a long day but neither of us is really that tired. Adrenalin tends to keep one awake, although I know it will fade soon enough and we'll both be able to get some decent sleep. I'm in two minds as to what I should do, however. To sleep and lose Harper would be infuriating, but to remain awake's going to dull my senses tomorrow. And having dulled senses on Ceres is a certain way to get oneself killed by the first roving carnivore one encounters.

With the fall of night so too does the temperature drop and we start another fire. A small one only, and one properly constructed so as not to spill over onto us when we're asleep. I watch the professor sit cross-legged before the fire, shivering and rubbing her hands before its warmth. I can see her breathing is laboured through the cold as her heart pumps furiously to keep her warm, but I know the temperature isn't going to drop low enough to kill us. It's just lower than we're used to, that's all.

"Where are you from?" I ask.

"Europa."

"That would explain the cold then."

Harper shrugs. Europa, or Jupiter II as it was once known, is very different to when Galileo discovered it a millennium ago, and a heck of a lot hotter. For a long time it was speculated Europa might contain extra-terrestrial life, and it was in fact the most likely of all the solar bodies to do so. Its oxygen atmosphere and liquid oceans beneath the incredibly thick crust of ice did not of course reveal anything of the sort, so when the terraformers moved in they got rid of everything that anyone had ever romanticised about the place. There have been attempts in the last fifty years or so to recapture some of that romantic dream, with retro-architects and historians making great effigies to the past. Whole areas of the planet have been quarantined to try to return it to its original landscape and atmosphere, but none of it's met with much success. It seems a shame really to have messed so much with nature only to now try to turn it back to the way it once was.

I'm from Ganymede. We don't have that problem on Ganymede: no one ever liked it in the first place so terraforming it was a godsend. Ganymede, or Jupiter III as it was once known, is larger than the planet Mercury, which I've always found funny. The Jupiter system is the largest, most profitable in the whole Solar system, and I feel sorry for the poor chaps who tried to colonise Mercury. They don't even have any moons to branch out into, while we have a moon attached to our planet larger than their whole system.

Laughing at the unfortunate is never a proud moment in anyone's life, although sometimes you have to remind yourself how well off you really are. And the best way to do that is through laughing at the little guy.

"I take it you've never been to Europa," Harper says tartly. "Yes, I'll admit I'm cold because Europa's a hot place, but it's meant to be that hot. Why do you think we get all the tourists all year round? Why do you think the ruling class of Jupiter lives on Europa?"

"Because they're taking advantage of the failing terraforming which left the place burning in some parts? You do realise it's illegal to go outside during the daylight if you live within ten miles either side of the equator?"

"And it's only not illegal to go to the actual equator because there's no point because you'd instantly fry." She rolls her eyes. "Yes, I've heard all these things before."

"And you do realise they're true?"

"They are so not true."

"Of course they're true."

"Why? Because everyone says so? Do you believe every factoid you hear, Corporal?"

I shrug, drawing my knees up to my chest where I'm sitting. "Only the ones I find interesting."

"But you've never been to Europa?" she presses.

I think about how to answer that. I've been to Europa several times actually. I completed my desert training there for one thing. Second time I went there I was tracking down a particularly nasty serial killer who decided to hide out near the equator. That ended well (!). I've been back a couple of times since then, mainly to hit the nightclubs during hen nights, but I don't like to go too far from home and leave my son with my folks too often. He doesn't see enough of me as it is, what with my job and all.

"No," I say, deciding this is a debate I really can't be bothered with, "I've never been to Europa."

Harper snorts, uncertain whether the argument is over and if it is just who won. Then she goes back to rubbing her hands in silence.

I don't say anything either, just stare into the flames and wonder when I'm going to get back to see my son. The funny thing about all this is that Davey loves dinosaurs. In fact he's always wanted to come to Ceres, which of course I've told him he can never do, what with it being off-limits and all. Assuming this mission doesn't get stamped classified he's going to be so jealous when he finds out mummy's been here. I wonder what I'll tell him. I saw a flying reptile, I'll say. The ones that eat insects and fish. I won't tell him it tried to tear me apart and I was forced to blow its brains across a field. I won't tell him how god-damned terrified I was when it looked like it was going to rend the flesh from my bones. I won't tell him how hard my heart was thumping when I was in my shuttle, looking at the damage and realising that only a short while earlier there were horrific predators standing on the very same spot, urinating all over my food.

I'll tell him the good things, the things he wants to hear. I can describe the minmi: I can do that much at least. I don't know whether I'm going to have to shoot any more lizards before getting out of this place, but I'd be very surprised if I didn't. Davey wouldn't like me to tell him I came all this way just to shoot the things he loves so much. Mummy verses the dinosaurs ... it's a contest I think I've been facing his whole life.

"Scraggs."

I blink, my gaze shifting upward from the blaze. "What?"

"My cat," Harper says a little dryly. "Look, I realise what you were trying to do. Talk to me about my home, just making general chitchat. And I was short about it and I'm sorry. So, if you want small-talk so we can bond or something, I have a cat named Scraggs."

I realise I must have looked really miserable staring into that fire. "Strange name for a cat," I say.

"Not if you knew him. You have any pets?"

"No. Davey's allergic to cats, and to be fair I'm never home long enough to look after one."

"Davey?"

"David. My son."

"You have a son?"

"Yep."

"I'm sorry."

I frown. "Why are you sorry?"

She looks away quickly, which is odd seeing as though it's telling me she doesn't want to meet my eyes. "I'm sorry for dragging you down here," she says quickly. "With all these dinosaurs you might not make it back."

"I've been in worse situations than this, you know."

"Yeah, but dinosaurs?"

"I've always found people are a lot worse than animals. People are vindictive, manipulative, bear grudges and can plan ahead. Animals are just animals. If one attacks you and you get away it doesn't trail you but goes after different prey."

"I guess."

She's an odd girl, and I can't quite figure out whether she's trying to be nice or just trying to freak me out. Either way, I've decided I'm getting too tired to stay up all night watching her. If she's stupid enough to go running off into the forest while I'm asleep then she fully deserves whatever happens to her. I'm not leaving Davey all alone just because I'm not getting enough sleep.

"Goodnight, Professor," I say, lying on the dusty ground and trying to get comfortable despite the cold.

"Goodnight, Corporal," I hear her mumble and watch through the small flames as she does the same. She's a strange girl all right, but come tomorrow I'll be able to get a signal out and I'll be rid of her for good. Even if I can't get the radio fixed the lieutenant will come get me tomorrow. Either way this is the only night we'll be spending here on Ceres.

A distant howl cuts through the night air and I lie to myself that it was just a wolf. Yes, leaving Ceres behind forever is going to be the best thing I've done in a long time.

CHAPTER FOUR

A screech, a scream, my eyes snapping open from darkness. Still darkness. Cold, wet, another scream. Movement, flashes, my head exploding, my knees scuffing, my shoulder bleeding on the floor.

And suddenly I'm properly awake. Everything comes back to me in moments. The mild form of cave I found for us to spend the night in, the crackling fire, the thought of leaving this Godforsaken world. I must have jumped up, cracked my head: it feels like it's on fire. My body's aching where I've fallen, but it's nothing serious. Just scrapes through the material. The armour's holding: it's what it was built for after all. I'm wet; the rain's not too hard but it's blowing into the recess and making the ground slippery.

A scream tears through the air once more and I'm back on my feet in an instant, more aware than ever of where I am. The scene before me freezes my heart and widens my eyes to such a degree I don't think I'll ever be able to close my lids again. Professor Harper is standing a few metres before me, frantically waving a floundering burning brand in both hands, the rain attacking it like a mass of piranhas intent on stripping the faggot of its every ounce of flame. Before her looms the huge and hideous head of the largest creature I've ever seen. A theropod far in excess of anything which might have torn through my shuttle. All I can see of it is its snout, and the head itself when it rears to bellow a roar into the storm. Its head is the length of a human being, and over half of that is jaw. Two cold piercing eyes stare out hatefully at the professor while it attempts to gnash at her with teeth well over half a foot in length.

I know what the creature is, for the records show this to be the primary large theropod upon Ceres. I had prayed not to run into one of these things, prayed to a God in which I don't believe and several more besides. It seems for my lack of true faith an entire pantheon of deities has seen fit to drag one of these things from Hell and send it straight to my door.

"Get back!" I shout at Harper. "You can't fend that thing off for long!"

Harper shouts something over her shoulder, but it's devoured by the storm. Even in that brief instant I could see the panic bleeding across her face and know I have to do something. The daspletosaurus was not the largest of carnivores by far, but it's nine metres of pure strength and muscle, with teeth longer than even its more famous descendent the tyrannosaurus rex. The tyrannosaurids were among the largest predators, and anything larger doesn't even bear thinking about. A tyrannosaurid is more than enough to kill a dozen human beings; there's no reason to be thankful it isn't one of the largest.

"Corporal!"

I shake my head, realising I've fallen into shock and have dropped back into what a soldier does best in such circumstances: assessing the situation. But no amount of research is going to get us out of this. From everything I learned during my studies of this creature, if the daspletosaurus has you in its sights you're already dead.

Backed into this foolish choice of cave, unable to flee farther than the creature's jaws can reach, I think I may have just succeeded in killing us both.

For the first time since landing on this world I actually feel sorry for Professor Harper. Without my interference she may well have avoided this encounter altogether.

Suddenly grateful I decided to sleep in my clothes, I snatch my pistols from their holsters and open fire indiscriminately. The sounds of the explosions are swallowed by the fury of the storm, although I see several of their impacts as blood ruptures from the dinosaur's face. It rears back, roaring hatefully at us both, its colossal breath knocking me back and spoiling my aim. In those few instants of recovery I can see the monster eye to eye, and I realise just how angry I've made it. The wounds my bullets have torn into its jaw are being washed clean by the torrential rain, and I understand with horror that not all of my shots even connected; and of those which did several had been turned by the sheer defensive power of its armour-like skin. Enough of my shots got through to hurt the thing, although nowhere near enough to cause it any real problems.

I estimate I let off six or seven shots from each gun.

Upwards of a dozen bullets did nothing but annoy the thing.

The great head comes for us once more and this time I know it's not going to be put off by Harper waving her little flaming faggot before its face. I dive, colliding with her, encircling her waist with my arms as the two of us tumble across the rocks. The daspletosaurus misses us by inches, and as I stumble to my feet in the rain, dragging Harper along with me, I duck as the massive head swings our way once more.

But the carnivore wasn't trying to kill us that time, and my heart leaps with no uncertain joy to see that we've been granted a momentary reprieve. In attempting to snag us the daspletosaurus has managed to bite down upon the pack containing what's left of the radio. On opening its maw has the strap of the pack caught between two of its teeth and it's swinging its great head about in an attempt to dislodge the heavy anchor, weighing down one side of its face.

It's a distraction which will only last a few moments longer, and it means losing the radio entirely, but the alternative is staying to fight that thing bare-handed. I grab hold of Harper once more and run, throwing her before me and forcing her to climb. Our only chance is to get high enough, out of the reach of the monster. At first she doesn't react, but I don't care for her shock: it's only going to get us both killed. I press my face close to hers and scream down her ear, fighting the raging storm, and finally she begins to move. Her progress is slow, one hand finding a hold, the other hand coming up, followed by one foot. I turn to see the dinosaur is swinging its head madly, and I know Harper's moving too slowly.

I watch as the pack slams into the cliff side, pieces of the useless radio showering down. The latch must have shattered, because the main bulk of the radio transmitter follows, tumbling away into dark nothingness. I don't know whether it's the sudden jarring of the movement, or whether the material's finally worn through, but the strap snaps in that instant and falls away.

With a last shake of its head, as though to regain its bearings, the daspletosaurus growls deep within its throat and trains cruel, tiny, narrowed eyes upon my position.

Even should I begin my ascent right now I no longer have time to make it off this ledge alive.

That's hardly going to stop me trying my damnedest.

I stand still, watching the great beast, fully aware that every moment we remain impassive is another Harper has to scrabble to freedom. I can hear her ascending: the frantic grunts, the scrape of rock, the laboured breathing. A flurry of dust falls upon my shoulder, but I do not turn my head from the daspletosaurus. We simply stand there staring at one another, each of us knowing I'm not getting out of this.

And then it lunges, and raising my pistols I charge. My guns blaze in the rain, pinpricks of light in the maddening storm. My aim is more accurate this time, although even as I watch the tiny explosions of blood upon the thing's snout I can see all I'm doing is making the thing mad. The dinosaur ignores every shot, concentrating on the attack, and as it reaches me does it snap its head horizontally, seeming to dislodge its mandible in the manner of a dog, that it shall gain more force when those awesome jaws lock upon me. I leap from the ledge, guns hammering into its face, dropping from my precarious position, all but passing through its open jaws, to tumble to the ground several metres below.

I land upon my feet, bending to fall into a roll that I might survive the impact with no bones broken. A massive foot slams down almost atop me, and my eyes widen at how thickly-muscled is the attached leg, how the claw of even one toe could easily tear straight through me with one mild slash.

The daspletosaurus rounds upon me, enraged now, Harper entirely forgotten: I can't even see her any more through the dark storm. The dinosaur shifts its feet, angling itself to a position whereby it might see me better, and I think about my chances of outrunning this monster. With legs thicker than my entire body, there's no chance I'd survive such folly.

Discarding my pistols, I don't even watch as they squelch in the mud as I whip the rifle from my shoulder. If I survive this I'm going to need my pistols to get off this world, but right now speed is the only thing that's going to keep me alive, and having the rifle in my grip affords me a slight sense of comfort. Or at least less of a sense of panic.

I fire as soon as I sight the creature, although with such a bulk it's something I could hardly miss. I watch as larger explosions of blood erupt across the beast's underside, and it rears its head to roar in anger at my temerity.

Snapping down with its jaws, it misses me only because I stumble in the rain-slick mud in my attempt to evade such monstrous death. My face slams into the mud and I actually feel the dinosaur's chin brush across my back. Spinning to face the thing, lying in the mud with my rifle raised, I can only watch in horror as the thing raises its head to the heavens once more, screaming in victory this time. We both know I can run no further.

And then the night erupts with light, the entire area being suddenly lit with a yellow-white beam brighter than the day's sun. Wincing, I raise a hand to shield my eyes as I stare in shock at the thing hovering ten metres above the ground, just slightly higher than the dinosaur itself although nowhere near out of its reach. The wind hits me at that moment, more intense than the storm, churning rain into my face like tiny stabbing knives. Through the bright glare I can see make out some of the details of the hovering thing. It's around four metres long and two tall, with a rotor blade projecting from its roof. There are no walls upon any of its four sides, merely a skeletal structure of metal holding the thing together and minimising weight. I can see the casing at the rear which marks the engine, and the basic landing gear on the underside resembling thick skis. There's a woman, I think, sitting at the pilot's controls, and a large man in the rear trying to keep his footing. Greater details are a little difficult to tell through the storm and the light being directed at me from the contraption.

The daspletosaurus turns towards the machine, bellowing in rage and snapping its mighty maw threateningly. It won't chance breaking its teeth on an unknown quantity, but having a three tonne dinosaur snapping its jaws at you would put the fear of God into anyone. The copter backs off a pace and the dinosaur presses forward, lowering that powerful tail that it might gain extra height with its neck. A giant foot crashes down close to me, but by this point, with the rain pounding down upon me, I'm all but oblivious. I never thought I would see the day when a giant theropod was fending off a helicopter, light blazing into its face.

The daspletosaurus shakes its head, slamming its skull into the side of the copter, which wavers uncertainly. I hear the pilot shouting, but the dinosaur strikes again, and this time there is a terrible shattering of glass and the light dies. The daspletosaurus roars in triumph and presses forward, its tail shuffling along the ground as it attempts to gain even greater height. I'm vaguely aware of the tail slapping the mud directly to my left and something in my brain shrieks at me to get up.

I try, slipping in the mud once more, my weapons entirely forgotten now: even my rifle's left my hand somewhere. My legs won't respond, won't allow me to stand, and nor can I tear my eyes from the fight. I can see the large man in the rear of the copter trying to keep steady as he holds something, although I can't for the life of me see what it is exactly.

And then something slips beneath my armpit and I'm dragged to my feet, my arm thrown over someone else's shoulder. I'm aware someone's shouting at me, but it's not just the storm which is drowning out the words. I can't hear anything, my mind seems to have frozen, and a small part of my brain, deeply buried but highly trained, is telling me this is shock. This is my mind telling me none of this can possibly be real so therefore it isn't.

And quickly, silently, I feel myself dragged from the scene, but my eyes never leave the dinosaur.

The copter has spun about by this point and, maintaining the same distance from the ground, it's moving off farther down the valley. The daspletosaurus gives chase, and my heart catches in my throat. There were apparently scientists years ago who theorised that the large carnivores were too heavy to run, that they must have all been scavengers. As my eyes track the rhythmic pounding of the immense legs of the daspletosaurus I find I can attest to their speed in equal measure as I can to their fearlessness. The copter suddenly increases in speed to compensate as its pilot realises she's also underestimated the hunter. The only difference is that a palaeontologist making a mistake with dinosaur habits never cost anyone their life.

I feel the reassuring arm leave me as I sag against a rock, watching the monster disappear into the darkness of the storm, still chasing the demon bird which dared to defile its realm.

The woman beside me is laughing, relishing the storm, raising her arms to allow the rain to soak her. I still can't hear what she's saying, but it doesn't matter. I can feel my brain shutting down, but I know I'm safe. The professor and I are rescued at last.

The lieutenant has come to save us both.

CHAPTER FIVE

I open my eyes to daylight; it's a welcome sight indeed. And the silence: the silence is almost worth having gone through that nightmare. After everything I've seen in my career I shouldn't have been spooked by what I experienced last night, but I challenge anyone to come face to face with a daspletosaurus and still have control of their urinary tract.

Presently I'm lying on a rock, and I sit up slowly. My body aches and I'm tired, and I know it's the come-down from the adrenalin high I was on last night. Professor Harper is huddled nearby, hugging a flask of steaming tea. I notice now the fire before us, over which is cooking some small animal. I decide I don't care what it is, don't want to know in fact; there's no room for fussy eaters in the survivalist's world.

There's another woman with us as well. Tall, well-built and menacing, Lieutenant Winter seldom smiles and when she does it twists her scarred features. Slashed across her face are three tears, indicative of an old encounter with a big cat. If ever I wonder about those scars, I only shudder to think of just how much pain the cat was in before she allowed it to die.

Winter wears a lot more armour than me, but then she's always been that way. Whereas I've always opted for the lightweight armour which offers more than reasonable protection, Winter prefers to look like she's going out into the cold laden down with a dozen layers. I guess the attitude fits her name though. The only annoying thing is that no matter how heavier her armour, she never seems to move any slower than the rest of us.

She catches my eye and offers a mild growl. No one could ever be accused of finding the lieutenant a beautiful woman. Even if she wasn't built like an ox, she shaves her head to a military black stubble, while her nose has been broken several times and never properly reset. She sports a trio of scars across one cheek and the corresponding ear is torn and withered. That she's actually married surprises me, although no one in the unit's ever met her long-suffering husband. We reckon he might be made up, but none of us is brave enough to ever raise the suggestion.

Right now Lieutenant Winter is doing what she does best: drinking whiskey out of a flask and not giving a damn about whether we think it's water. Winter's a hard woman to work with, a terror to her enemies; but she's always got your back. If you're on her unit you're in her family and she'll look after you properly no matter what it costs her.

"Morning, Corporal," she grunts. "Seen any more dinosaurs you want to run away from?"

I ignore the jibe, assuming it not to be an actual question. "Thanks for the save, ma'am. Professor, you all right?"

Harper nods, staring into the flames. She's either still in shock over everything that happened last night or else she's already got on the bad side of the lieutenant. To be honest I'm surprised the lieutenant hasn't hit her yet for dragging us all down here.

"Where are the others?" I ask. "Did they get away from the daspletosaurus?"

"Aye. Must have learned how to run from that running school you teach. I've got 'em checking out the terrain, setting up sensors and stuff. Don't want any more of those nasty beasties getting the drop on us."

I can feel the barbs to her words, although not having any sensors to set up was hardly my fault. "My shuttle was totalled, ma'am," is all I say.

"So the professor's been telling me. You should've made sure you locked the door properly, fall-girl."

It seems the professor's been spreading her nickname for me already. Looks like it's back to her being Goldie then. "If your shuttle's close, ma'am, we should get off Ceres before we can worry about anything tripping those sensors."

The lieutenant gives me a look half sympathy, half wondering why she ever let me on her team. "Sweet, Corporal. We didn't stay here just because we didn't want to disturb your beauty nap. We're parked a few hours to the east of here, but that storm was worse than we thought. It was brought about by a tectonic shift, which means we're cut off from the shuttle, at least on a direct route. We're going to have to skirt the mountains, which'll add a couple days to our stay here. Nothing major; it'll give you a few more opportunities to run away from the wildlife."

Again I ignore her. I tend to do that a lot by the way. "Do you know what's in the area? I got the impression the valleys were home to ankylosaurs."

Winter shrugs, but she doesn't fool me. She's done just as much research as I have; she'd never walk into a situation without having planned every single step she knows she'll be taking. "Herbivores don't concern me," she says. "What have you found out since you got here? I asked the professor, but she started going on about plants and I felt like strangling her with a vine."

Harper does not react to this, and I wonder how long the lieutenant's been subjecting her to these insults. I briefly fill in the lieutenant on what's happened so far, mentioning I couldn't identify the type of theropod which tore apart my shuttle but that it had to have been a lot smaller than that daspletosaurus. It's something to be on the lookout for anyway.

She listens in silence, and once I'm done takes the animal from the flames and tosses it at me even as she gets to her feet. "Eat en route. We have to meet up with the others."

"Can we not just fly to the shuttle?" I ask.

"Copter's gone."

She does not elaborate, but I don't have enough reason to enquire for details. I presume there was an accident last night. Perhaps the daspletosaurus was faster than they expected. Perhaps we're all underestimating the dinosaurs living in this place. It might be an idea for us to start remembering that this is their home and that we're just interlopers. If we march around with our guns cocked thinking everything will fall in line for us we're going to end up dead. It's not something the lieutenant will ever admit to, but a lesson she has no doubt already learned since landing here.

Harper rises once the lieutenant has walked off. She's been strangely silent, sullen-looking even. She seems to struggle to meet my eyes.

"You sure you're all right?" I ask.

"Yeah," she replies with a sheepish smile I can see is faked. "Thanks for saving my life back there."

"Not sure you should thank me. I think you've already found out the lieutenant's far worse than any dinosaur you could ever face." It was meant as a joke, although Harper doesn't even crack a smile. Something's wrong, that much is certain; and I'm not too sure it's just because the lieutenant's no doubt given her verbal hell over what she's put us all through. All I can think is that Winter's threatened her somehow. Whatever it is, we're going to have to be working together for the next couple of days so I'm hoping people can start acting as though they're getting on, even if they're not.

"I'll keep you safe, Goldie," I say, clapping her shoulder as I pass, taking a bite out of my rat-thing. God, it's awful. But it looks as though I have another couple of days of this to come.

The three of us don't talk much as we travel, but then the lieutenant always likes to concentrate when we're in the field. Moving through the valley is at the same time a great idea and a terrible one. With cliffs rising either side of us and almost level terrain before and behind, there's very little chance of any predators sneaking up on us. However, it also means that if something does appear there's equally very little chance of our getting away. I've retrieved both my pistols and rifle and found thankfully none were damaged, but my bullets were incredibly ineffective against that daspletosaurus yesterday so unless the lieutenant's packing a rocket launcher I don't see we're going to have much better results should the thing return for another round.

The lieutenant doesn't seem fazed at all by the possibility of attack; she just keeps taking swigs from her canteen and walks ahead moodily. But then that's the lieutenant for you. I find myself at the back once more with Professor Harper, although we don't have anything to say to each other so the journey is a long one.

Ahead of us, the lieutenant stops suddenly, holding up a balled fist to tell me she senses something. I grab Harper by the arm and lead her quickly to the side of the valley, searching for a cave or some other safe hiding hole. There's a slight trench formed likely by rainwater and I drop her into this without a word. She understands there's danger and thankfully doesn't voice any complaint as I leave her and jog back to the lieutenant.

I can see by her face the lieutenant is concentrating hard, although as I strain my eyes I can see nothing.

Then I hear a strange sound, like a braying, and I unshoulder my rifle. Winter doesn't have a gun in her hand yet, and I can see by her expression she's still trying to figure out the situation. In this valley echoes will play havoc with sound, and it's entirely possible the creature is heading for us down the sides of the cliff, or from behind.

Something appears before us then and we both tense. The beast which emerges from around a bend in the valley ahead is large, plodding along fairly slowly on four legs, the rear of which are much larger and better muscled. Its body is bulky without being bulbous, and a thick tail protrudes from the back. Its neck is thinner than that of the daspletosaurus and not much longer. Its head reminds me of a horse, with flaring nostrils and a long face ending in an almost beaked mouth. Its eyes stand upon the side of its head, although from their positioning in the skull I can only assume it can see ahead perfectly well.

Upon its back are two people: a large, barrel-chested man and a smaller, younger woman in the front, holding what appear to be leather reins. The younger woman is waving at us and beaming a genuine smile.

Winter grunts and starts towards them while I signal to Harper that it's all right to come out. Together we go to meet the rest of our unit.

We're reunited only a minute or two later, and the two people dismount their seven metre steed. These of course are Corporal Summer and Private Spring: a name we love so much I doubt she'll ever be promoted because then we'd lose our personal spa. She always reminds me of Major Major Major Major, but Spring doesn't read books so doesn't have a clue what I'm talking about.

Spring is our communications expert, which would have come in handy yesterday. She's young – I never learned her age but I'd guess she's about nineteen – and still has that positive outlook on life you tend to have when you haven't quite grown up yet. She's short, slim and always ready with a smile and a joke. She wears her blonde hair to just above her shoulders and hides most of it under a cap; that she's wearing a hat in such a hot environment just shows how clever young people can be sometimes.

Corporal Summer is the only man in the unit. At six and a half feet and built of pure muscle, Summer's our strongman of the group: I reckon he'd even have no problem wrestling the lieutenant to the ground and that's no mean feat, let me tell you. He has an obsession with guns, but that doesn't mean he enjoys wanton killing. He's also the team's medic, having trained extensively for the role and having achieved qualifications to actually be termed a nurse. In fact Summer could easily have gone into the medical business, but the man likes his guns too much and there isn't much cause for swinging guns around in a hospital ward.

"Transportation?" the lieutenant asks, eyeing the creature.

"It's some sort of ornithopod," Summer says. "We found it grazing, figured it was more than large enough to accommodate at least a couple of us. We could potentially get four on its back together, so long as none of them was me."

"I think it's a drinker," Spring says helpfully.

"It's a draconyx," Harper says. "Drinkers were a lot smaller than that."

I frown, not having heard of either name before. "Hold on, you're telling me there's a dinosaur called a drinker? That's a pet name, right?"

"Named after some dinosaur explorer called Drinker," Harper says. "You know, like the Marshosaurus?"

I'm surprised Harper did any research before coming to Ceres, but then I'm finding out a lot about her the more time passes. "OK," I say, "so how fast can this ... draconyx go?"

"What, you're intending to race them now?"

"We won't need to move fast," the lieutenant says, seemingly not caring at all about my rather useful line of enquiry. "We can use the draconyx for scouting while we head back for the shuttle."

"Let's just hope yours is still in one piece," I say.

"Why?" Spring asks. "What happened to yours?"

"Some dinos broke in," I say. "Totalled everything. The food, the radio, the chairs. I doubt it could even fly again."

"Dinosaurs are that clever?" Spring asks, some of the omnipresent joy bleeding out of her to be replaced with nervousness. "Didn't you lock the door?"

"Of course I locked the door," I snap. It's been a long couple of days, but at the girl's crestfallen face I instantly regret taking a pop at her.

"Well now we've all peed each other off," the lieutenant says, "let's see about reaching our own shuttle. Which incidentally does have the doors locked. Autumn, Summer, Spring; you take the draconyx and scout ahead. I'll bring up the rear with the professor."

It seems an odd arrangement, for the leader of our unit to be looking after the civilian, but I get to ride a dinosaur so I'm hardly going to be complaining about it. Summer vaults onto the back of the creature and grins as he helps me up before him, Spring taking the driver's seat and clutching the reins tightly. The dinosaur is warmer than I expected, the scutes softer and more responsive. Nor does the dinosaur itself seem to mind our being here, and even gives a little hoot of joy.

"Ride 'er out, Private!" Summer shouts, and Spring cracks the reins. The dinosaur jerks and I realise this isn't going to be quite the smooth ride I'd expected. But I'm on a forbidden planet riding a dinosaur and I can't help but grin from ear to ear. When I get home, Davey's going to be the most envious kid in the world.

CHAPTER SIX

First, let me tell you that riding a dinosaur bareback is the greatest experience anyone could ever have. I've skydived through the Magenta Heights, I've walked the bottom of the Blue Ocean in a naked-wetsuit, I've even driven a motorbike through the gas clouds of Jupiter (don't ask), but none of that has ever brought about a thrill the like of which is running through me now. That's not to say riding a dinosaur is more thrilling than anything else I've ever done, nor that it's more exciting. And certainly it's nowhere near as dangerous as a hundred other things I've done in my life. But there's a simple pleasure in sitting there, my naked fingers holding onto the sides of the dinosaur hide, the skin to skin contact affording us more intimacy than a lover's caress. Even the rhythmic bumping of the ride as the dinosaur moves is beginning to feel like some form of aphrodisiac. That I'm not alone in my supreme enjoyment only heightens my own pleasure, because I realise in the years to come I'll have someone to talk to, to remind myself that this actually even happened.

We ride through the valley, leaving the rockiness of the terrain behind as we come to some fields. I can see the trees in the distance indicative of another forest, which seems to make up most of the world in fact, although we're not heading in that direction so I figure the route to the shuttle must be across the clearer fields. I trust that Summer and Spring know where we're going, which leaves me to just sit here and enjoy the moment.

Since coming to Ceres this is the first thing which has made me actually glad to have come after Harper.

The sun's beating down upon me, there's no trouble in sight and I'm riding the back of a dinosaur. What more could a girl want from life?

"You know," Summer says behind me, his big frame offering more psychological protection than anything I've ever known before, "I've never really thought about Ceres before. Sure, every kid likes dinosaurs, but I never actually wanted to come here."

"Never?" Spring asks from before me. "God, I've always wanted to find an excuse to visit this place. Man, I'm glad that professor smuggled herself down here."

I laugh. "I'm sure she didn't come here just so you could have an excuse to pay Ceres a visit."

"You don't like her much do you?"

I try not to shudder; there's no way I'm allowing Professor Marigold Harper to ruin this glorious moment. "If she'd learn a little respect for other people I might."

"No you wouldn't."

"You think she's that bad?"

Spring laughs, and that in itself is a joyful sound. "No, silly. I know you, that's all. You don't like people pushing you around, telling you what to do. You only put up with the army because your direct superiors are in the army with you."

What the girl's saying is true. I know I have a problem with the upper classes, but then what self-respecting working class girl doesn't? The way I see it there are only two classes: upper and lower. If you work for a living you're working class: if you don't you're upper. Anyone who goes around calling themselves middle- or upper-middle class or whatever other nonsense they come up with is deluding herself. And such delusion feeds the upper class machine which just lies on its back all day watching the rest of us whore ourselves out to keep them from having to lift a finger.

That Harper's come here off her own back isn't evidence that she's working: it's just showing she hasn't anything better to do with her time. Yes, her theories could cure cancer, and that can only be a good thing; but she only has the time to think about these things because she doesn't have a proper job. If she worked for a company or taught in a university, those would be proper jobs. Instead I don't think she does anything. She just has a few degrees because once someone who doesn't need to work gains a degree, what's the next move? Go back and get another?

But there's no way I'm saying any of this out loud. Spring and Summer are more than aware of my particular pet hatreds and I'm not going to ... but I've already ruined the mood so anything I'm going to say from now on's bound to come out a bit grumpy.

"What's that?"

"What?" I ask, realising there was no humour to Summer's voice. No fear either, more curiosity than anything.

"Thought I saw something over the rise," he says. "Spring, stop this thing would you?"

The communications girl obeys and the draconyx grinds to a halt, almost reluctantly from what I can tell of dinosaur behaviour. Summer pulls out a set of binoculars and studies something in the distance. I strain to look but can't see anything: if he managed to see something without the aid of the binoculars while moving at speed on the back of a bumpy dinosaur I take my hat off to him.

"Yeah," he says, handing me the binoculars. "Take a look at that."

I do so, frowning as I peer through the glass. There's something reflecting light over by the far trees. Something which seems to have a fairly large mass in fact. It could just be a trick of the light of course, but if both Summer and I have come to the conclusion that it's a mite odd it means it's worth investigating.

"Well?" Spring asks, and I realise we haven't said anything aloud yet.

"Probably nothing," Summer says. "But regulations say we should check it out. We should head back for the lieutenant."

Spring adopts that cute annoyed look of hers and I understand why: Summer didn't explain anything at all to her. Deciding the cute annoyed look is kinda cute I opt not to tell her anything either as I hand the binoculars back to Summer.

Spring turns the draconyx around and whips the reins, sending the beast off at a gallop. I dig in my knees and feet, clasping my hands upon the dinosaur hide for dear life. Behind me Summer almost tumbles off, and only manages to stay on because he encircles my waist with one big, strong arm. Spring alone seems light enough not to be bothered by the sudden increase in speed and the smooth bumpiness of the ride. That she's getting her own back on us isn't lost to me, or my jarring teeth. To have Summer's arm holding me like this almost makes it worthwhile, but sometimes I wish Spring didn't have to be so petulant.

Still, she's ten times the woman that Professor Harper is.

Harper and the lieutenant have just reached the outskirts of the field by the time we come upon them. I can't help but feel that's strange. I know they're on foot, but I would have thought the lieutenant would have made Harper move at a fast trot at the very least. Nor does Harper look especially annoyed, so I can't see the delay has been down to the lieutenant shouting at her. Perhaps Harper feigned a sprained ankle or something and for some reason the lieutenant fell for it. I've never taken her for a soft touch, but maybe she's made friends with the professor or something. The very thought rankles me no end.

Summer briefly explains what he's seen, but the lieutenant's not too happy about the suggested detour and doesn't bother to hide it.

"If it's not on our route," she says, "we don't need to know what it is. Like you say, it's probably nothing. Just a reflection of this weird sun."

"What's with the sun anyway?" Spring asks. "It's a lot hotter on Ceres than anywhere else in the Jupiter system."

It seems no one's ever been able to figure out how the sun thing works here.

"Ma'am," Summer says to the lieutenant, "regulations say we have to check out any potential criminal activity."

"And what potential criminal activity could you have found?" the lieutenant asks.

"If it's a manmade construct it means whoever put it there came here illegally. We have to check it out, just to make sure it's nothing."

Summer's a brave one, I'll give him that. The lieutenant narrows her eyes at him, but we all know he's right. Quoting regulations at a superior officer is never a good idea at the best of times, and I can see in Winter's eyes that all she wants to do is get out of here. But regulations are regulations and we have to make the sidestep.

"All right," the lieutenant says begrudgingly. "Corporal Summer, take custody of the professor here. The three of you take that dinosaur and clear the way to the next rise, see what's over there. Autumn, you're with me. We're going for a quick look, and when we find nothing we're coming to rendezvous, Summer, so things better have got underway by then."

Summer nods, snaps off a salute, and motions with a genial smile for Harper to climb aboard the dinosaur express. Spring retakes her position behind the reins and they move off slowly.

I look to the lieutenant, who takes a swig of whiskey and grumbles something about this taking far too long as it is and not having the time to check on every damn fool thing shining in the trees. Or words to that effect. I can't say I disagree with her, to be honest. We're here legally, but only because we're a retrieval operation. The instant we found Harper we should have lifted off. With the damage to my shuttle and the quake preventing an easy route to Winter's it's made us stay far longer than we should have. There's every chance that our debriefing's going to turn into a stern telling off. If we're here too much longer we might even face disciplinary action, even court martial. Risking our jobs just because we've seen something which may be nothing more than light reflecting off water seems a little foolish. Even if it does turn out to be someone having built a home on Ceres, there's not a lot we can do about it. In theory we could drag them back with us and extract them along with the professor, but without knowing who they are we might well be treading on government toes. The Jupiter system of course does not have the single government, with each satellite having its own rulers, most of them having separate countries on just the one world, and therefore separate governments. But the law against trespass on Ceres is universal so in theory it shouldn't matter who these people are, we could still legally extract them. Depending on where they're from it might open a can of worms over what they were doing here, and why we side-tracked from our own mission long enough to even find out they were there.

Politics, as you can see, are not something I ever like to get involved in, and here I and the lieutenant are in total agreement. We've found Harper and should be leaving, but events are conspiring against us.

I catch the lieutenant staring at me as we move. "Tell me about it," she mutters, and clearly our minds are at last in sync. "Quick look, Corporal," she tells me. "And I mean quick."

I nod but say nothing. The less I speak the quicker I walk.

We make good time across the field and enter the trees cautiously. Thus far the daspletosaurus is the only carnivore we've seen, yet whatever tore my shuttle apart is likely around somewhere, and the trees are a perfect place for an enemy to hide. Ordinarily we would not even be passing through them, but there's no other way to find what Summers and I saw, so we move through regardless of common sense. The lieutenant and I both have our rifles to hand, the safeties off and held almost to our shoulders. Should anything leap out we don't want to have to think before cracking off a shot or two.

I take note of the trees as we move through them. They're not that different from those back home. Tall trees with thick trunks and large leaves. There are a lot of ferns in this area, which I believe was the principal food for dinosaur herbivores, so that at least makes sense.

And then I frown. There's been something nagging at me ever since coming here, before that in fact, and I've just realised what it was. Harper came here to study plants which could only be found on Ceres, plants which have been extinct on Earth for millions of years. I can see before me ferns and various other plants suitable for dinosaur consumption. But how could someone bring plants back to life? Even if DNA stretches to plants, which I have to admit I don't know for certain, how could scientists possibly have located enough complete DNA strands to successfully bring them back? Dinosaurs are a stretch enough of the imagination as it is, but plants?

I guess since no one knows who built Ceres to begin with, no one knows the methods they used for populating it with life. There are even people back home who think God put Ceres here and sparked life anew upon it. It's a common enough theory among the religious groups, since Ceres has started with early life, just as Earth did. And since no one has yet to put forward a decent theory of how life settled on Ceres it's as good as any I guess. In fact, Ceres being declared a sacred world is one of the major reasons it's forbidden to come here. Catholics see it as a second Garden of Eden, upon which it is sacrilege to tread. That would of course make me and the others serpents, which is an analogy with which I'm not entirely comfortable.

The lieutenant's trying to get my attention and I silently curse myself for drifting off during a combat exercise. She has her back to a tree and is holding up two fingers, moving them forward. She's either telling me to precede her or she's trying to call an aeroplane down to landing. I go for the former and raising my rifle I drop to a crouch and move swiftly to the edge of the treeline.

Beyond there is indeed something, although it's entirely surrounded by further trees, with moss and vines growing all about and across it. Whatever I had expected, however, this is certainly not it. The thing is made of metal, mostly, and measures about thirty metres in length. And that's only because it's not all here. Its basic shape is cylindrical, although there are pieces torn away, leaving gaping holes across its side. My foot brushes against a piece of metal grown over with plants, and I reckon there must be a thousand more pieces of debris scattered about the place.

Looks like my assessment of the lieutenant's finger signals might not have been that much in error after all.

"We're getting serial numbers," Winter tells me in her usual gruff tone, "checking for survivors, then getting back to the others."

I nod mutely. That it's a commercial plane is obvious: I can even still make out the company logotype flared across its side. By the growth of the forest all over it I suspect it's been here some time, maybe even going on a dozen years or more. I don't know enough about planes to be able to tell how old this particular model is, but the lieutenant's right. If we can find serial numbers, or better yet a black box, we'll have something to take back home with us to aid in the identification.

The lieutenant disappears inside the plane and I scan the outside one more time just to make sure there are no obvious signs of activity. While it's doubtful there would be any survivors in a wreck like this it's always possible. But there's nothing, no indication at all that anyone walked away from this. And even if they did, the forest closing in would have wiped away all traces a long time ago.

I join Winter in the plane. It's dark inside, shafts of sunlight spraying down through cracks or holes in the bodywork. There are rows of seats here; some still intact, although in the main they've been torn away from the ground. A few of the seatbelts are still fastened and there are traces of bones upon some of them. One contains what appears to be a complete skeleton, lying almost horizontally in an upturned chair as though waiting for the pilot to flag up the 'unfasten seatbelt' sign.

Playing the laser sight of my rifle about the plane I can see nothing moving, no signs of life at all. It seems when this plane came down there were indeed no survivors.

I find the lieutenant in the cockpit and mention such to her.

"You think," she asks as she rummages around in search of the black box, "any survivors would necessarily unstrap their fellow passengers and give them a proper burial?"

"It's what a decent human being would do, yes."

She pauses in her search, looking at me as though trying to determine whether I'm serious. I'm not naïve, and straighten my back in protest at her treating me like a child.

"Passenger plane crashes," she says slowly, "on the forbidden dinosaur world. You're lucky enough to survive, everyone else around you is bleeding and dying, most of them are already dead. First thing you do is stop to see if anyone else made it, and bury those who didn't? Did you even see that daspletosaurus we faced earlier?"

She's right, and that annoys me. Smaller carnivores would easily swarm over this wreck and strip it bare, and anyone in their right mind would want to put as much distance as possible between that situation and themselves. Without a complete passenger manifesto, however, there's no way we're going to be able to tell whether anyone made it out of the plane. And even if they had, they would have been swallowed by the jungle long ago, or else a theropod or two.

"Got it," Winter says, tugging free the black box. It isn't of course an actual black box; it's more like a chip the size of a woman's thumbnail. Winter removes a device from her bandolier and slots the chip inside. She shakes her head at the data she receives. "Commercial plane, like we thought. Went down fifty years ago. I'll check it against records when we get off-world," she adds, shoving the device back into her bandolier. "Right now there's nothing we can do. The plane's been sitting here half a century, nothing we can do about that."

"Then we just find Spring and Summer and pretend we didn't stumble upon this at all?"

"No, we find Spring and Summer, get off Ceres and file a full report. Then this incident can be looked into. But without anyone alive here to rescue there's no way another team's going to be sent here. It'll cross off one mystery though, and will give the families peace of mind at last."

That's true, as is the fact that we can't do any more here. The lieutenant heads back out the plane, keeping he gun handy in case any carnivores have taken the opportunity to set an ambush or something. I hang back for several moments, visually scouring through the detritus. I see a small device lying in the dirt and moss and tug it free. It's a music device, and I smile as I think about how someone must have been sitting there listening to his or her favourite songs, entirely unaware of the impending doom they were plummeting towards. It's amazing how little such devices have changed over the years. By the Twentieth Century human society was being pushed towards commercialism, so that technology was becoming obsolete a year, even six months after it was unveiled. There was a sudden stop in societal progress, such as space exploration or feeding the hungry, as the world made a profit-making move to owning the next big thing.

That all changed with the colonisation of other worlds, and while I'm sure a lot of places in the solar system are still commercially-minded, no one system can afford to be exclusively so, else they would fall out of communication with the rest of us. And that would be fatal.

This music device is testimony to the fact that technology doesn't always move forwards too quickly. A song is a song, after all; and if it can be stored on a small device there's not much room for improvement.

I pocket the device and head out after the lieutenant. I don't like leaving all this behind, and would very much like to bury the bones of the long-dead. But Winter's right. We can't stay on this world longer than we're supposed to, and we've already overstayed our welcome. There's no one alive here now, and we have to re-join the others.

With deep sadness I depart the plane also and head back into the forest, leaving the wreck once more to the moss and lichen which now rule what was at one time a noble conqueror of the sky.

CHAPTER SEVEN

The lieutenant briefly fills the team in on what we found, although doesn't dwell on it. Summer and the others report they've come to a lake and that we have two options to continue our journey to the shuttle. Go around the lake or cross it. Since we're already having to skirt around the quake area in the first place, adding extra time by skirting around a lake as well is not something Winter's going to go with. It comes as no surprise to me then when she declares we're going to build a raft and go across. It will mean leaving the draconyx behind of course, but the lieutenant wants to waste no time.

Summer directs us to the lakeside, and I stop, staring at the vast expanse of water. Strangely it never really occurred to me that there would be any great bodies of water on Ceres, when of course there would have to be for the life to survive. I had heard somewhere that there were no oceans on Ceres, but I don't now know how true that was. It's possible of course the information was right and that there are no actual oceans, but a number of extremely large lakes and lagoons. The body stretching before me would attest to this theory, and I all at once agree with Winter that we shouldn't try to work our way around it.

I would not like to estimate the length of the lake, although I can't see its end when I look to either side. Across from us I can see the jungle rising in the distance, but the mild fog upon the lake blurs the images to almost obscurity. It's as though the trees are beckoning like some dark will-o'-the-wisp, enticing us out to our doom. The water itself appears muddy, but not in a polluted way. Without human beings Ceres has to be the most unspoiled body of life in the entire solar system. I don't know much about lakes and can't say whether the water will become clearer the farther we move out into it; but it stands to reason that it would, with deeper water and less contact with the mud.

Of course, none of us has any idea what might be lurking within this lake, and I can't believe it would only contain herbivores. I must admit I didn't research any water-based prehistoric creatures prior to coming down to Ceres, and it's an oversight I'm beginning to regret already.

Under instruction, we set to forming the raft. It's an exercise all soldiers have to go through when you're part of a unit like ours. Basic raft-building is a matter of selecting the right wood, cutting it down, forming beams and binding them together. But we've never been a unit to do anything by the basics, and we have no idea what might be in that lake. None of us want our lives to be placed in the hands of a few pieces of wood, no matter how sturdy.

The vessel we're constructing then may take a little longer, but it'll stand a much better chance of getting us across. It will be larger than the basic raft, with barriers upon the edges and a defensible central pillar in which we can hide and be able to mount a gun or two in order to fight back. It's ambitious, and something none of us has likely attempted before, but it should only take a couple of extra hours. We will no doubt be exhausted come the end, but it will be worth it if it saves our lives.

The draconyx all the while looks on sleepily where it lies, entirely oblivious that we're on the verge of abandoning it to the forest once more.

An hour into the work and we've obtained most of the wood we need. Summer's immense strength has been useful in cutting down the necessary trees, while the physically weaker Spring and even Harper have been constructing the rope with which the wood shall have to be affixed. There's a knack to rope I never could quite get the hang of, where you have three pieces and somehow twist them into one, more powerful, strand. Of course we're not using rope, so whatever vines they're finding better be good ones.

While the lieutenant and Summer are dealing with the cutting of the wood I drop down beside Spring for a short rest. Harper has gone to fetch some water which will have to be boiled before we can drink it, which means I can stop working without having Harper annoy me at all.

Spring smiles at me as I pass her my canteen and a biscuit I was keeping in my belt for a special occasion. Poor thing looks exhausted, with sweat pouring off her brow and soaking through her cap. We sit there in silence for a few moments, savouring the food and more than that the shade we've managed to find behind what we've already managed to construct of the raft. I never realised how much of a blessing being out of the sun could be.

"I'm going to miss that ride of ours, you know," Spring says while we rest. "I've grown quite fond of him, and it sure beats walking."

"Yeah, but getting the hell out of here's going to make it worth it." This is one of those times when I sure wouldn't mind knowing the girl's real name, but then it's polite not to ask and put her in that position. Our unit's one of those you've never heard of. We deal with all the stuff no one else likes to, all the things our superiors later claim never took place. Like pulling people off hostile worlds it's illegal to even visit. The best way to explain away our presence here is to deny we ever came, and if it comes to light that we did we just tell the truth and say we came to pull Harper out. Harper's the only actual name that's ever going to be associated to this mission, so if the lawyers want to come after anyone it's going to have to be her.

Still, I've often wondered what Spring's real name is. Spring suits her well enough, but I've always pegged her for an Anna or a Louise.

But it's useless to think about such things. People like us don't exist so far as enquiries are concerned, and for that to be true we have to remain anonymous.

"So what did you really find in that crash?" she asks. "The lieutenant's keeping tight-lipped about it, but you must have found something, yeah?"

I smile at her naivety in thinking that there must be meanings behind every meaningless action. "There's nothing more I can tell you, Spring. We found a crashed commercial plane and Winter took the black box." I shrug. "That was all there was to it really." I try not to think back to the skeleton still sitting in its chair, waiting for the plane to properly land so he or she could unbuckle the seatbelt keeping them safe. My fingers absently play through my pocket and I realise I'm fumbling with the music device I took from the crash.

Pulling it out, I check the charge. Even after so long in the forest its battery life is still good. I'm not sure whether the humidity will have destroyed the thing yet though. I fumble with the buttons, a part of my conscience reminding me this belonged to someone long dead and that I'm nothing but a ghoul for having removed it. But there's also a part of my mind which tells me this is the only thing remaining of that person. Stored on this one device are the hopes and dreams of an individual. I'm holding something of her soul, something which made her who she was in life.

It's sacrilege to listen to it, but perhaps more a sacrilege not to.

I toss the thing to Spring. There's no way innocence could be corrupted by music, so it's best she relives the poor dead woman's life. Spring attaches the headphone to her ear and smiles slightly, which I assume means the device is still working.

I close my eyes and lean back against the wood, wondering what other bodies this world holds, how many further lives it's destroyed.

"You have good taste in music, Corporal," she says.

She thinks the device belongs to me, and I realise I hadn't told her otherwise when I tossed it her. I've been so drawn into my own thoughts and feelings lately I'm forgetting to communicate with those around me. I'm not sure why a girl as young as Spring thinks me having a taste in music fifty years old is good taste in music. When I was a teenager anything my parents listened to was strictly outdated, and this music's even older.

Spring hands me back the device. "Never took you to be a fan of *Sins of our Sister* though."

"Who?"

Spring laughs at my expression. "Come on, don't tell me it came with the machine." When she gets no joy from me she continues. "Arcto-found?"

Now that's something of which I'm vaguely aware. Music trends change so much, so quickly, that there are always these weird terms rising to describe a new and supposedly different type of sound. Rock, pop and classical will likely be around forever, but there are a shedload of others that come and go all the time. Arcto-found, however, was after my time. It's what the teenagers listen to now. In short, I'm simply too old for it.

"And that's on here?" I ask seriously, holding the music device in the air as though it's a stabbing finger of accusation.

"Uh, yeah?" she says, the lower half of her face still amused, but her eyes are a little concerned now. "You don't know what's on your own player?"

My mind explodes with what this means. A thousand possibilities circle through my brain, none of them good. Lieutenant Winter confirmed the wreck had been there for fifty years, she had insisted there was no sense in checking things, and had taken the black box regardless. Yet this device could not have been there more than a couple of years, five at the most. Could the lieutenant have been wrong? Could she have been so determined to get out of there quickly that she messed up in her search? Is it possible that she could have been out by fifty years though?

But what's the other alternative? That the lieutenant lied to me? That she could see full well the plane had only crashed recently but lied to me to get me out of there? Is she really that adamant about getting away from Ceres that she's willing to not properly investigate a crash which potentially could have had survivors?

A third, more rational, explanation comes to mind then. Perhaps the lieutenant had not been wrong and had not lied. What if someone else was on Ceres and had found the wreck? They could have dropped their music system and left without it. It would mean I could still trust the lieutenant's judgements, but also means there's someone else running around Ceres.

I don't like to think badly of anyone in my team, but that Winter could have made such a gross error is unthinkable. I know she drinks too much, but it's never impacted on her observation skills before. She's always managed to get the job done: she's the best soldier I've ever served with.

Spring's still looking at me strangely and I know I have to say something, have to placate her somehow. I can't go over and accuse the lieutenant of either negligence or lying, so that leaves only the option of sitting on the information until I have the opportunity to have a quiet word with her.

"It's new," I say, shoving the device back into a pocket. "Like you say, must have come with the machine."

Spring shrugs, and I can tell she doesn't believe me. Nor can she possibly know what's going through my mind, which means Winter clearly didn't tell them the plane had crashed years ago. But then why would she? Just because she didn't give them all a pointless fact doesn't mean she's keeping something from me. Winter never tells anyone anything unless they need to know it: it's the military officer in her.

"We should get back to the raft," I say, and Spring is only too glad to be returning to something other than the awkward conversation we appear to be having. I look over to see Summer and the lieutenant busily cutting the wood into the correct sizes. Even Harper's back at work fashioning rope. We're all working together to get out of this. We're a team. It doesn't matter what we're telling other members of that team, we're all working for the survival of this world. That's the one thing I have to remember, the one thing that's going to keep me sane here. We're all working to survive. We're all in this together.

I catch the lieutenant's eye and freeze, although there's nothing accusing in the stare, just a silent question of why I'm not working to that end.

Breaking away eye contact I set to arranging the wood. I can't afford to be stirring up trouble here, not when everyone else is working so well together.

But still the thoughts nag at my mind.

The yearning to know the truth.

CHAPTER EIGHT

Within two hours of our deciding upon a plan the raft was ready. A full twenty metres long and six wide, it was a monster construction, complete with a tower of strong wood in which we could seek refuge should it become necessary. Saying our farewells to the draconyx, we set off into the lake, the raft charging across the surface as though it had every right to be there. For only a few moments did the lake voice complaint as it attempted to force us back to the shore with a series of powerful waves, but we weathered such attacks and spat in its face. Eventually the lake simply gave a shrug and turned its back, deciding it did not care whether we were there or not. There are few feelings in life which can rival fighting nature, and it's always the greatest achievement when you realise you've conquered it.

I doubt any of the others are thinking of this leg of our journey in quite such romantic terms, but then that's their problem.

The sun is a menace on Ceres, and upon the open waters like this there isn't much protection. However, after but a few minutes the raft becomes one with the gentle sway of the lake and it's almost a pleasure to be making the trip across. Spring's been positioned at the top of the tower as lookout, while Summer and the lieutenant deal with the rowing: one powerful figure positioned upon each side of the raft. That leaves me to steer, which consists of repositioning our rudder and informing the two rowers when they're veering off course. Professor Harper has been told very politely to stay out of the way, although even she has a role on board this raft. By stretching a large, thick leaf across a hollow log we've been able to fashion a primitive drum which she is rhythmically beating so the two rowers can keep their movements in time.

One can only imagine the sight of us to anyone who might happen to be standing on the shore doing a bit of fishing. It would be like a group of reject Vikings were rowing past them.

I chuckle softly at the absurdity of it all and catch Summer's eyes as he works, seeing the reflection of my humour in him. He's the only one of us who's removed everything from the waist up, which is probably a good move for him considering how hot it is and how much physical work he's having to do. Working the rudder and having to keep an eye on those huge sweat-laden muscles is perhaps the worst job I've ever had to endure, but I guess one of us has to do it. The lieutenant and I have kept our uniforms, purely for the armour in my respect. It's hot, but I'd prefer to be hot than dead. In the crow's nest Spring's tunic hangs over the side, so presumably she's feeling the heat as well.

"You know what this reminds me of?" Summer asks as he rows.

I shake my head and he laughs.

"Yeah," he says, "having a hard time answering that one myself."

Summer may be a big imposing brute of a man, but he's always game for a laugh in the worst of situations.

Our good humour is suddenly broken by a shout from the tower. Spring isn't one to panic – nor is she now – but a shout is a shout nevertheless and the lieutenant calls up to her without missing a beat.

"I don't know what it was, ma'am," Spring says. "But something broke the water, ma'am."

I look in the direction indicated but can only see a wake. It might easily be the wake of our raft, since it's behind us, but if Private Spring says she saw something break the water then Private Spring saw something break the water.

"There's nothing much we can do about it," Winter says. "Just carry on as we are, and we'll deal with it if we need to. Private, set your rifle up there and shoot by your own judgement."

"Ma'am."

The lieutenant is trying to remain calm, which is all we can do really. I detect a sharp increase in speed as she and Summer row harder. Other than that there's nothing we can do. We're out upon the surface of a lake and are entirely at the mercy of anything which might be lurking beneath its depths. I can't help but stare out across the water in case I can see a repetition of the sighting, but it's as I look that I realise the drumbeats have become somewhat inconsistent.

"Harper," I call across to her. "Get back in the rhythm. And a little faster. I think our rowers have gained a little extra strength."

We speed along nicely and yet I know that if something wants us dead we're not going to survive much longer. I can no longer see the shore we've departed, and looking ahead I can't quite make out anything in that direction either. The fog's set in without me even being properly aware, as though the creature beneath us is vampiric or akin to the mermaids.

The raft suddenly jolts and I cling to the rudder as it settles. Spring releases a mild yelp and Harper screams, but Summer and the lieutenant don't even seem to have noticed, as though they think we've just passed over a speed bump. I nod to Spring, who's all ready with her rifle. She's mounted the gun on the side of the wooden tower and is swivelling to see anything surface. So far there's nothing and I'm hoping whatever it was that bumped us did it accidentally and is now half a mile away from us, stunned and trying to work out just what it hit.

I hear the water behind me churn just as Spring gives a shout of warning. I duck, hand still on the rudder, but as I turn it's to see nothing but a fine spray come for me. The lake water soaks me through, but nothing else happens. I look up to Spring, who seems a little shaken. That she's reliving the moment when she was peddling a helicopter backwards from an enraged daspletosaurus is evident. I had meant to ask her just what happened to that copter, since we sure could have used it to get back to the shuttle quicker, although I doubt I would much like the answer.

And then I see it. A dark form moving by the side of the raft, along the side upon which Summer is rowing. Water is a superb mask for anything and as such I can't be sure of its size or family, but that the creature is keeping time with the raft is unsettling since it means there's no way we're going to be able to outrun this thing. That only leaves staying to put up a fight, which is something I don't think any of us especially want to have to deal with.

I blink and the creature's gone, presumably having dived. I don't know if that means it's gone or if it's done that in preparation for attack. I wish I'd paid more attention to what creatures might be living in the waters of Ceres, or even of underwater threats in general. It's something to make amends upon when I get home, but getting home to do so is going to be the trick.

The raft rocks again and I see two of the logs rise momentarily. The creature is testing the strength of the raft. Never having seen one before it doesn't understand the thing, and is curious. Perhaps this means it wants to eat us but can't understand what we're riding, perhaps it just means the creature is wondering what we are. Either way could prove fatal for us, but if we're lucky its curiosity will be turned if we can just scare it enough.

Again the raft rocks and this time I briefly see something splash out upon the side. It was thick and pale, looking incredibly slick. It had to have been a tail, but it was larger than anything I've seen before. Whatever owns that thing is something I really don't want to have to tangle with.

"Private!" the lieutenant shouts. "Put a few bullets in the brine!"

It's not brine, it's freshwater, but I don't correct her. Spring snaps off three shots from her rifle, the bullets spearing through the water. She's not going to hit anything, and I have no idea what sounds bullets make once they hit the water: certainly the creature won't have heard anything of the gun's rapport. A machinegun would come in handy right about now, although with any luck those three shots are going to prove enough to curb that creature's curiosity and enable us to reach the far shore without any ...

The rudder suddenly turns of its own accord, almost throwing me to the floor. I keep firm hold, wrestling with whatever has the other end. I don't even know why I'm doing it, but perhaps if I can show this thing it shouldn't mess with us it might even go away.

I fall back suddenly as the thing must have released the rudder, and the waters go still once more. I cast a nervous glance ahead to see how far we have yet to go, but all I can see is the omnipresent fog and it's really starting to get on my nerves.

The raft shudders, water sloshing over the side and drenching Summer before the raft levels off again. He does his best to ignore the attack, his eyes set in a fiery determination as he concentrates on the steady rhythm of his rowing. Harper has stopped her drumming by now, although neither rowers need her at the moment, working under instinct to save all our lives. I keep hold of the rudder, knowing my own position aboard this raft is just as vital. At the moment the waters are calm again, with only the backwash of the monster's passing still gently rocking us.

Harper shrieks. I look up to see a great beak has broken the lake and my eyes widen in terror. The head is almost crocodilian, with two piercing eyes standing at the rear end of a long snout bearing a maw containing razor teeth. The powerful jaw muscles snap at the professor, although she's just out of reach, and swiftly does the head slide back into the water.

It all happened so fast I can barely understand that it happened at all. The image of the monster is burned into my mind: the crocodile head almost two metres in length attempting to tear into prey nowhere near so large. Suddenly our raft hardly seems big enough to combat the horrors of this lake.

"Focus, Corporal!" Winter shouts and I realise I've fallen into a daze. Tightening my grip upon the rudder, I correct our course and try to put from memory the terrible thing which almost took Harper in one bite.

My eyes fall upon the water and I can see a dark shape just below the surface. No longer is the beast hiding, and I can no longer believe it is just curiosity keeping its interest in us. I'm fully aware that water and fear are both agents of exacerbation, yet I estimate the shape circling the raft is somewhere in the region of eleven metres, with a large bulbous body, a seal-like tail and two powerful flippers pushing it through the water. That this thing is not a crocodile is obvious to me now, although what it could be I have no idea. The only water reptiles I know about are the plesiosaurs, and this doesn't seem to fit the description. I'm under the impression they all had long necks for one thing, like that Loch Ness monster hoax.

The shape disappears beneath the raft and we shudder once more as the thing strikes us. I'm entirely grateful for the military training we've all received in raft construction: I can't help feeling if we were a group of scouts the only badge we'd be earning today would be the badge of being eaten by an extinct reptile.

Gunfire tears through the air and I see Spring taking careful aim with her rifle. I can't see a target but it's not my job to take care of those sorts of things. A spray of water stings my face, but I ignore it, entirely focused on my job. I'm vaguely aware of a commotion towards Summers, can see something rising from the water, but there's nothing I can do so I close my eyes to the sounds of gunfire and just hope Spring's managed to kill the thing.

The gunfire ceases, the water begins to calm once more, and after half a minute I realise there's every chance Spring has indeed managed to kill it. I scan the water with my eyes, but can see no sign of any creature circling. Either Spring killed it or frightened it off to seek out easier prey. I look over to the rowers, but they don't seem injured and are continuing their work. Both look more than haggard and neither is entirely happy about the situation, but there's nothing they can do but continue to press on. My eyes track up to Spring, who seems tense but a little more comfortable than she was. Harper looks as though she's going to vomit, perhaps has already, but she's still in one piece and that's the main thing.

I think we may have beaten the beast.

And then the raft all but shoots in the air as something smashes it hard from the underside. I hear wood splinter, see water gush through several large cracks, can hear people shouting, but feel nothing. My fingers are numb with cold, stuck to the rudder which is my lifeline; my eyes are stinging with lake water, my body heavy through a soaking. Gunfire tears the air once more, and I can hear a woman screaming but can't identify who; in all honesty right now it could well even be Corporal Summer.

Harper is suddenly coming towards me, sliding across the wood and in no control at all of her actions. Wood explodes behind her as a crocodilian maw erupts through the raft, snapping at her and missing entirely. Harper is half running, half falling, but I can see she's headed for the rails. I can't leave the rudder to save her, but it would be a damn fool extraction mission if we let die the person we're extracting. Deciding in one moment that the rowers should be fine without me for a few moments, I release the rudder and leap at Harper, catching her about the waist and preventing her from tumbling over the edge.

Wood cracks beneath us, knots untangle, and suddenly the ground beneath us becomes unstable, water sloshing our legs, slapping our faces and obscuring our vision. I can hear someone shouting at me, I think it's Spring, and I snag the rail to keep the both of us aboard the raft. Harper's gone limp in my arm and I know to release her is to lose her. A terrible strain tears through my other arm, but I cannot relinquish my hold upon the rail.

Then the rail surrenders for me and I watch as the ropes snap, the wooden logs come apart and the part of the raft upon which I so precariously stand comes away. We strike the water a second later and I tighten my grip upon the professor. I don't know whether she's unconscious, but she certainly feels it, and I'm not going to just let her die; not even to better my own chances for survival.

Flailing with my free arm I manage to catch hold of a log and try to drag myself atop it. The log bobs upon the uneven surface of the lake, going under and gasping for air as though it's still alive. After a few seconds I'm still no closer to being upon that log and try to control my breathing. Training will kick in if I just allow it, although I've never had to fight a lake before. Forcing myself to concentrate, to work with the swaying of the lake instead of trying to fight against it, I wait until the most opportune moment before dragging the log once more. This time I'm able to throw myself across it, so that my belly's clutching the log, my back facing the sun. I pull Harper up after me and just hope the log is sturdy enough to carry us both.

The log dips into the water uneasily and I realise my plan's just not going to work. I check on Harper again, but she's still unconscious, so I have to work with what I have, not what I would like. There's some vine trailing from the log, and I quickly put it to use, dropping myself back into the water and positioning Harper upon the log so her belly and chest are pressed against it. Quickly I tie the vine about her wrists beneath the water, doing the same with her legs. It will keep her securely upon the log, and just so long as it doesn't overturn with her weight she won't drown. Making sure of that will of course be my job. Removing the girl's glasses, I shove them under the collar of my suit. Losing them wouldn't be too good for her, and I might well need her eyes if the two of us are trapped here together for a while.

Casting a speedy glance about me I can see the fog is lifting slightly, as though it was the creature causing such weather to begin with. I can barely see the raft continuing in the distance. It does not appear to have stopped for us, but then there's every chance they haven't realised they've lost us. Either that or they've still got problems with that animal. Which is the only thing which is going to keep the two of us alive. Now the immediate danger of drowning has passed I'm suddenly reminded of what put us here in the water to begin with. There's no sign of that beast, and if it had noticed its success in throwing us off the raft I think it would have killed us both by now.

The waves are slapping me in the face at every pass and I know I have to get us out of this place before I freeze to death. So far I'm treading water through instinct, but I can feel my body losing feeling and cast my eyes about for the nearest shoreline. I can just make out some trees to one side and head for there. Throwing the vines over my head I hold them in my armpits and fashion a very primitive rein. Pushing off, I put every ounce of strength behind my movements and slowly drag the log and Professor Harper along behind me. My body is screaming out that this isn't going to be possible, my heart is beating furiously in a vain attempt to compensate for what I'm putting it through. My thighs are both numb and stinging at the same time, the muscles rejecting these foolish demands I'm placing upon them.

I realise with a sinking feeling that this is going to take me a long time, but it's the only way to keep Harper alive. Alone I would stand a much better chance at survival, but as I glance behind me to see the closed eyelids of the professor I realise I could never do that to her. In sleep she looks at peace, no different to anyone else. It's the best time I've ever had with her, and I'm not going to ruin that by cutting the vine and letting her fall into the water. No matter how easy that would be.

Pushing myself on, I keep the trees in sight and just pray I can make it there before my heart gives out.

CHAPTER NINE

I think I'm getting fed up with forests, but Ceres is full of them. Even when we cut them down they bite us in the backside by allowing lake monsters to smash through, but maybe that's just the forest getting its own back on us. It took the best part of an hour to reach the shore, and of course it was to find it lined with trees. I tried not to collapse as soon as I hit the mud and soil and somehow managed to cut Harper free of the log to drag her up into the cover of some of the closer trees. My head was pounding, my body burning with the heat of exertion, but I knew I couldn't allow myself to surrender to my body's wishes until I'd made sure Harper was alive. Lying her on the ground I carefully placed my ear to her chest to check her heartbeat. It was still going, and I smiled at the realisation since it meant I wouldn't have to try to resuscitate her.

It was at that point I believe I closed my own eyes and gave in to the wishes of my body. I had already put it through seven torments of hell and there was only so much demand I could place upon it before I let it have what it wanted.

I awoke about an hour ago: enough time to put into cohesive order those events which occurred after I reached the shore. It's strange how your brain doesn't register everything it's doing but always seems to record it for later evaluation. The human brain is a wonderful thing: I wouldn't be much without it in fact.

I have a fire going by the time Harper wakens. When I awoke I stripped off entirely to dry my clothes, my underwear being the first priority so I could at least be decent when the professor came around. Armour would have been the primary concern for a rational mind, but there's no way I'm going to be parading in the nude before Harper, so the armour can wait. I keep my guns handy of course, knowing a well-placed shot would be enough to deter most predators even if the loud rapport didn't prove sufficient. And if that daspletosaurus or one of its similarly-sized kin comes for a look I don't think any amount of armour short of a tank-suit would do me much good.

Harper wakes slowly, stirring and holding her head. Fright, pain and water pressure all play their part in her headache, I'm guessing, but she's alive and should be grateful for that. Whether she will be I have no idea, but then I'm not a stuck-up Daddy's girl so I wouldn't know.

She blinks, narrowing her eyes due to the pain in her head, and slowly takes in her surroundings. I say nothing, allowing her to come to her own conclusions in her own time. I carry on sitting there stoking the fire and trying to dry our clothes. She sits up slowly, and I can tell just by looking at her that she's stiff, sore and in a whole lot of discomfort.

"Hey," she says weakly.

I offer her a small smile. "Hey yourself. You OK?"

She nods slowly, noticing the blanket I've wrapped her in as snug as a sleeping bag. It's formed of lightweight material and is very, very thin. They're handy things which are factory-packed to become no larger than a paperback novel. Handy to fit into a belt pouch and essential for every soldier considering how well they retain heat. I watch with a twinkle to my eye as she looks at the sleeping bag strangely, lifting the top to stare down at her own naked body.

Her eyes snap up to me but I'm not looking at her any longer, my concentration back upon the fire. Yes, I took your clothes off, I think without comment. No, I didn't dwell on what you looked like naked: it's a rule of survival not to lie there unconscious in wet clothes. She does not say anything however, but does seem to hold the sleeping bag closer to her, as though I've intruded on some form of hallowed ground.

I toss over her underwear, all dried and laundered. She doesn't catch them, but takes them slowly, and they disappear into the sleeping bag as though to hide them from my sight will make me forget I just spent the past hour drying them for her.

"We fell overboard," Harper says. She doesn't remember precisely what happened, perhaps didn't even know fully at the time what was going on. She was perhaps even unconscious when she struck the water so no doubt she's a little confused as to why she's no longer on the raft at all.

"We fell overboard," I confirm, looking at her now. I expected to see defiant anger flaring her face that I had dared to place my hands upon her royal person. Instead I see nothing but a confused and frightened girl and I scold myself. Whatever her faults, Marigold Harper is still a young woman, little more than a child, and being attacked by prehistoric reptiles is not something which is ever going to go down well with her psyche.

"I don't remember anything," she says, and I can see she's desperately trying to work through what happened.

Perhaps it's time I threw her a bone and see whether she decides to bury it. "We fell overboard, I brought you here." I shrug. "That's about all there is to it really."

"You saved my life."

"Yes."

A pause.

"Why?"

Of all the responses I'm not sure I was quite ready for that one. Gushing gratitude was a long shot, but a grudging thanks might not have gone astray. Being asked why I saved her is like returning to the lake just to get a wet fish to slap in my face.

"Why did I save you?" I ask, just for clarification that this really is what she's asking.

"You could have died."

"I'm a soldier. It might sound cliché, but I do have to protect people."

"But you hate me."

"I don't hate you." I realise as I say the words that they're true. "I don't like people like you, Mary. I don't like people who throw themselves into bad situations because they know other people are going to come along to help them out of them. But that doesn't mean I hate you. And you didn't mean to be thrown off that raft. What did you expect me to do, just stay at my rudder and watch you tumble over the side?"

Her eyes widen then as she realises something else. "You mean you fell overboard because of me?"

Uncomfortable isn't the best word to describe what I'm feeling right about now, but I'm not sure a better word's been invented.

She's about to gush after all, and I'm not quite ready for that from her.

"Can we not talk about it?" I ask, certain this will please her also.

Her eyes become hard, her jaw tenses and I'm oddly aware she's fighting back tears. Angry tears which really have no meaning here. "You shouldn't have bothered."

All right, maybe she's not going to gush. "What? Why?"

"Because *I* wouldn't have."

"Well you're not a soldier. You're a botanist."

"That's not the point."

I'm not sure how this conversation turned so weird, but I feel more exposed before this girl than I've ever felt before anyone. "Here," I say, tossing her glasses over. "Figured you might not want to lose these."

She holds them in her hand, staring at them as though I've just given her the secret to eternal youth. "You saved my glasses."

"They would have fallen off your face otherwise."

"You saved my life because it's your job." She meets my eyes and I can see she's confused, almost angry, and certainly still on the verge of tears. "No one back home would care about my glasses."

It's an odd statement. "No, but you do."

"That was ... kind of you." The words are simple, but the way she says it one would think I'd just saved her pet from drowning instead of her glasses.

"Like I said, I don't hate you." The whole non-gush is making me more uncomfortable than ever, and I focus my attention once more on drying out the clothes.

"Did you get that because of me?"

I look down to my chest. There are dirty red and black marks under my arms, which incidentally are so sore I'm finding it difficult to put my arms down by my sides. There's a corresponding thick slash across my chest which has even started to bleed, although I've applied some salve to it already.

"Rope burns," I say. "Don't worry about them."

"Did you get them because of me?"

I look at her again. Her eyes are tight, her demeanour more mature than I've seen from her before. It's almost frightening, this change in her, and I'm not sure I didn't prefer it when she was lying there unconscious. Maybe I'd even prefer it if she *was* gushing right about now.

"Don't worry about them," I reiterate and hope that'll mark the end of the discussion.

The silence descends once more and I busy myself through it by playing with the fire. I don't normally feel this uncomfortable talking to people, but Harper's mood towards me seems to change too much for me to understand her. That she hasn't thanked me yet is something of which I am fully aware, although I can't help but suspect there's something more to her reasons than whatever I'm assuming.

She's shivering in the sleeping bag, but it has nothing to do with the cold. It doesn't matter what I think of this young woman, or what she thinks of me. No one deserves to be chased around by monsters. Leaving the fire I move across to her, crouching on my haunches. She doesn't even seem to notice, and I can see at last just how terrified she is. I reach out and place a comforting hand to her face, allowing my own warmth to infuse through her body.

"You're alive," I tell her at last, my words gentler than even I had expected. "You're alive, and I'm alive. And so far as we know everyone else in my unit's still alive. Nothing else matters, Mary. So long as we all get off Ceres alive, none of this matters at all."

She looks at me, our eyes closer than they've ever been. She's still afraid, still hateful, although now I'm this close to her I can see it's self-loathing. Whatever she's going through she blames herself. Probably because it's all her fault we're even here in the first place, but I'm not tactless enough to tell her that to her face. Maybe once we're all out of this mess alive, but not here, not now. Not while we're both lost in the jungle on a world filled with monsters.

I hold her to me, pressing her against my chest, and her resolve breaks. She sobs uncontrollably and I set my own resolve, knowing I could very easily join her but that I have to be strong for the both of us, else we're going to die here at this lakeside.

After a while her sobs lessen and her body calms, the shivering decreasing the more she's able to relax. Her heartbeat, shuddering through my own body, gradually slows, and before long it's as though she's a babe fallen asleep in my arms. I'm trained for combat situations, for adapting and for dealing with issues as they arise.

Harper has none of this: she's not even a soldier. I can only imagine how bad all of this is for her, and to even attempt to understand what she's going through is never going to be possible for me any more. Not after everything I've been through in my career.

"You all right now?" I ask, raising her face to stare into her red-rimmed eyes.

"No," she says, wiping her nose and pulling away from me.

"At least you're honest. Come on, we need to get dressed so we can try to catch up to the others."

"They're too far ahead," Harper says a little too quickly for my liking. "Even if we could get to them they'd have left Ceres by then. We'd be better off finding someplace to hole up for a while, maybe try to get a message out to someone else."

"There is no one else. The world's quarantined remember? And the atmosphere messes with any communications."

"But we'd never reach them."

"We won't know if we don't try. Besides, if I have our position right I think we're closer to the shuttle than they are. I don't think that quake last night did quite as much damage as the lieutenant thinks it did. If we head inland through the forest we might be able to find the shuttle before they do."

She wants to argue, I can see she desperately wants to argue, but she doesn't. Perhaps she recognises that I'm actually the authority on survival here, but I can't help feeling that she's hiding something. I have no idea what it could be, but my mind is drawn back to when I left her alone with the lieutenant earlier. I can't shake the feeling the two of them were arguing about something. At the time I took it to be the lieutenant giving her a sound telling off, but now I'm suddenly not so sure.

"Professor," I say carefully then, "about this cure for cancer."

She sniffs. "Yeah?"

"How much would it be worth?"

She avoids my eyes. "You mean if you were the only person holding the cure?"

"Yes."

"What do you think?"

It's enough of an answer but not the one I wanted. I can't think badly of the lieutenant, can't think for one moment she would be the type of person to try to make some money out of this venture, but nor does any other possible explanation come to mind. But what would Harper say if I asked her whether the lieutenant was blackmailing her? Would it ease my mind if she said yes or no? Would I believe her?

Something sounds through the trees then and I cast all such thoughts from my mind. I hold up a finger for Harper to be silent, and she obeys, hugging her knees through the sleeping bag and looking like the most terrified caterpillar I've ever seen. I rise slowly, drawing my pistol from my holster and wishing I was wearing more than just my underwear and a belt. The only thing worse than wet armour is armour wet with my own blood, and it's a mistake a survivalist should not have made.

The sound recurs and I judge the direction of the creature, straightening my arm and holding the pistol level. I'm somewhat surprised my arm's not wavering in the slightest, but that won't matter much when something leaps from the underbrush to tear through my unprotected stomach.

A shape moves swiftly through the trees and I track it without being able to see very much. From the movement of the trees I would believe the creature to be big, which means it's not going to be a small theropod like the ones which tore up my shuttle. And if it's big there's every chance that daspletosaurus might have found us once more.

A roar fills the trees as something charges through. I spin my pistol to cover it but the thing slams into my arm, sending the gun tumbling. A terrible stench of breath blasts my face as something wet and sticky slaps down upon my breast, slicing straight up my throat, chin and across my face. My heart pounds at the thought of the horrific wound which must have opened up clear across my body, but there is no pain.

Harper laughs, which I find exceptionally cruel. Then I realise what the creature is and my heart almost explodes with relief.

The draconyx bounds joyously before me, its tongue lolling like a lost puppy.

Laughing, clutching my poor heart, I look back to Professor Harper. "Get dressed, Mary. I think we've just found our way of definitely getting to that shuttle before the lieutenant."

Harper looks as disappointed as she is pleased, and I stop trying to work out the mind of that woman. All I know for certain is that here we may have a chance of getting away, and I grin like a schoolgirl in a chocolate factory.

Things, at last, are looking up.

CHAPTER TEN

Riding through the alien forest on the back of Onyx is the most exhilarating thing I've ever done. Sitting at the front and holding the reins, we're able to make good speed. Harper sits behind me, clutching tightly about my waist. I won't say it doesn't hurt, what with the injuries I took getting her to the shore, although I voice no complaint. We need to get to the shuttle as quickly as possible and I can't have her holding into the sides of the animal. She's not an experienced rider and I can't afford for her to fall off the back.

The professor's been quiet during our travels, withdrawn would perhaps be a better word to describe her. Again it nags at my suspicions, although what those suspicions are even I can't say. I'm glad of Onyx's company, so much so that I've decided to name him at last, and can't believe he came looking for us. Where we came to shore was a fair distance from where we left him, but it seems his sense of smell must be incredible. Either that or he was heading home and just happened to see a couple of women cavorting in their underwear and went for a closer look.

By now I'm back in my armour, fully dry or not, with all my weapons in place. My rifle's taken a bit of cleaning to get it back to proper efficiency, but when all else fails I always have my combat knife. Harper's clothed as well, but still hasn't thanked me for the rescue.

Sometimes I wonder what her problem is.

An hour into our ride Onyx becomes a tad nervous. I snap the reins to keep him going, yet it's clear something's bothering him. At a guess I'd say we're entering the hunting territory of something he really doesn't like. A large carnivore perhaps, although I can't see how a large creature would be able to hunt well amongst all these trees. A smaller predator would not cause a seven metre herbivore such nervousness unless it hunted in packs. That puts a damper on my plans to charge straight through. In my reading of the smaller theropods I've found quite a lot I really don't like. They may not be as powerful as the tyrannosaurids and their ilk, but even a small theropod is likely to be as large as a human being.

I debate upon whether I should mention any of this to my companion, but Harper seems at peace at last, leaning against my back and possibly even asleep. Disturbing her by telling her we might be just about to die hardly seems fair; yet nor does not telling her when death's approaching.

Onyx slows to a trot and I allow him the change, pulling forth a pistol and spinning it so its butt is facing behind me. "You ever use one of these?" I ask.

I don't have to see Harper to know she's not only fully awake now, but looking at the gun with more than a little fear. "No."

"It's simple," I say, pressing the thing into her hand. "Just aim, squeeze. Don't pull back, don't raise the gun as you fire, and watch out for the recoil. If you're shooting at a moving target try to lead it; but then if you're shooting at a moving target you're likely not going to hit it anyway."

She accepts the gun nervously and I realise I've just scared her witless.

"It's just in case," I assure her. "There are going to be a lot of unsavoury beasts between us and the shuttle, and I wouldn't like you unprotected if we get separated."

"I've just ... I'm not a soldier, Autumn."

"You don't need to be a soldier to fire a gun. Just try not to use it at all if I'm still with you. I don't want you hitting me by mistake."

She nods, looks more worried than I thought she would, and tucks the gun into a belt clearly not designed for such things.

"And remember to remove the safety before you shoot anything," I say, hoping she will never have to draw the gun at all. But it's always best to be prepared.

My earlier thoughts about a group of scouts not being able to make it this far come back to haunt me. I'm not that sure we're even doing all that much better.

Onyx continues to trot, although I can tell he's wary now, skittish even. He keeps looking from side to side as though expecting attack. My own eyes scour the trees for signs of predators, although my senses aren't anywhere near as acute as his and I can't see any ...

Movement, possibly a shadow, to my side. An instant later, when I'm staring intently at that area, it's gone, as swift as a hawk. Behind me Harper's tensing, realising something's wrong, but I say nothing. My eyes continue to rove, hoping I'll be able to find something, hoping I'll see nothing at all.

And then something emerges from the trees ahead and to the left. It's small, about the size of an adult woman. Its body is long and thin, with two powerful hind legs for running, and two shorter arms which are longer in comparison to those of the daspletosaurus and therefore deadlier. Its tail is snake-like, thinning towards the end, while its neck is also longer than that of the daspletosaurus before it. The head is almost the shape of a rugby ball, with sharp and horrific teeth. Two yellow eyes stare out at me with menace as the creature tries to work out whether it's going to be able to take us down.

Another of the creatures emerges from the trees to the right and runs parallel to Onyx, although keeping a careful distance. They're gauging speed, reach of their prey and reaction. It's a clever move for them, and what I would expect from pack animals. They're taking their time in the stalking, knowing that with so many of them against just one of us they have all the time in the world to decide upon their attack.

The thing is, it's not just one of us. They don't realise this draconyx has two armed women on its back.

Loosening my rifle I take aim at the creature running parallel to us and crack off a shot. The bullet takes the thing through the eye and it collapses upon itself. The remaining creature barks at us angrily but flees into the trees.

Onyx pounds on, apparently free of pursuit.

"Good shot," Harper says from behind me, clinging tighter than ever, which thankfully didn't ruin my shot a moment ago. Somehow.

"Coelophysis," I tell her. "I was expecting to run into them sooner or later. They're apparently the most widespread predator of this world and they always hunt in packs. Their territory stretches through the forests, and since there are a lot of forests here I figured they'd be around here somewhere."

"Still, it was a good shot."

It was a great shot, but I don't let it go to my head. It's possible the brain of one of their fellows suddenly exploding might put them off. But then again it might not. So long as Onyx can put a fair bit of distance between us and them we might get away before they decide on what course of action to take against us.

After a while Onyx slows a bit and I can feel he's a lot less nervous than he was. It likely means the coelophysis are long behind us, but I'm not going to relax until we've reached that shuttle.

"I reckon," I say over my shoulder, "those must've been the things which tore apart my escape craft."

Harper says nothing and I wonder whether she's scared again. Not that she shouldn't be scared, but it's not something I expected from her. When we first met she was pretentious, arrogant, far too sure of herself. She was standing in that field taking samples as though entirely unaware that there were these dinosaurs even running around the world. Maybe that was even the case. Maybe she was just too absorbed in her worthy cause that she never even bothered to do any research at all about this place. It would fit with what I've always thought about her, so why am I so nervous at her silence?

We come to a break in the trees and dismount. The view is amazing. We're at the rise of some form of cliff, the forest continuing below us for the most part, although there are patches of plains upon which roam massive sauropods, their long necks raised like giraffes as they plod along in complete safety, even from the greatest predator. Even one sauropod is too large to be anything's prey, but walking in herds as they are there's nothing which could even come close to bringing one of those things down.

I scan the area with my binoculars, searching for the shuttle or signs of the lieutenant and the others. They could have returned for me and Harper after the incident at the lake, but I doubt they would have stayed long to search. They would have given us up for dead and continued with the evacuation, knowing that if we had survived we'd be heading for the shuttle as well. I can't see anything of the group, but there's something in the middle of one of the plains that quite takes my fancy. Closing upon it I smile to myself at the familiar sight.

"Shuttle's located," I say, handing the binoculars to Harper so she can take a look herself. I gaze over the terrain of our route. A lot of it's open plains, and if we could get amongst that sauropod herd we might even stand a better chance of making it. There's a little bit of forest left to cover, but not much. With any luck we should be at that shuttle by noon tomorrow, although it does mean spending another night in this place. We could continue moving, but the lieutenant will likely stop, and it seems pointless to risk our lives just to reach safety.

I watch Harper carefully as she concentrates on the shuttle. She isn't calm, far from it, but she seems to be thinking too much; and I can only wonder at what.

"What do you think about that plane that came down?" I ask, somehow knowing I'm going to regret this.

"Nothing," she says, handing back the binoculars. "Your lieutenant said it crashed here years ago. Planes go missing all the time. One mystery solved, I guess."

"Lieutenant lied," I say simply, my gaze across the forest but my attention focused upon Harper without her knowing it. "Plane only came down a couple years ago at most."

Harper tenses, but that could just be a natural reaction to being given this news. "How can you know that?"

"Just know." I'm guessing, yes. But I reckon if a teenager went to inspect that wreck recently she would not have lost her music there. That music device came from a passenger, I'm sure of it. Well, as sure as I can be with a guess.

"I don't know anything about plane wrecks," Harper says distantly.

I turn a frown upon her. "That's an odd way of phrasing things. What *do* you know about then?"

Her eyes narrow and I realise I've handled this wrong. "Nothing. I don't know anything about anything."

"Why did the lieutenant lie?"

"How should I know? I don't know her."

"You were arguing before."

"She was shouting at me before."

"So you've never met? Prior to coming to Ceres I mean."

"No."

"You sure about that?"

"Of course I'm sure."

"And there was no blackmailing going on? From either side?"

Her confusion is genuine. "What are you going on about?"

I shrug once more. "Maybe nothing. Maybe something important. I just feel there's more going on here than I'm being led to believe."

She looks away. "I wouldn't know anything about that."

"Who wrecked my shuttle?"

"Dinosaurs. You told me that."

"Dinosaurs that could open the door? Really?"

She says nothing.

I gaze back across to the shuttle, far, far away. "The lieutenant destroyed my shuttle. Why?"

"I don't know."

I look back to her with a raised eyebrow. "So she *did* destroy it then?"

Harper sighs, and I can see conflicting emotions battling their way across her face. "I don't know everything, why would I?"

"But the lieutenant destroyed my shuttle?"

"Yes! All right, if that's what you want me to say, then yes." She meets my eyes at last and I can see a purity of spirit there I've not seen before. She straightens her back and I get the impression she's decided to do the right thing at last, that she's been pushed into a corner long enough. "Yes, she did. I don't know everything, I really don't."

"But you know something?"

"I know ... I ... I was sent here."

I blink, waiting for more. "Sent here by whom?"

"By the government. Our government."

"To find a cure for cancer?"

"No. No, that's just me. That's what I wanted to come here for. I planned to come here, planned to somehow hire someone to drop me off. One day these guys grabbed me off the street, just kidnapped me but did it so sneakily you'd never know they'd done it. Turns out they worked for the government and they'd heard about my secret plans. Not so secret plans as it turned out. I thought I was done for, that I was going to disappear or something. But they told me they thought it was a swell idea to beat cancer and that they'd help me get to Ceres.

"I didn't believe them of course. I figured they were up to something, that they were setting me up for some big fall. But they kept their word. They got me here. And I had all the equipment I needed to get on with my work. My plan, like I told you, was for the government to realise I was here and wait for an extraction. They had the same idea, and sent in you guys. They said the leader, a Lieutenant Winter, would be the only one of the unit who knew I'd not come of my own accord.

"When I met Winter before she wasn't happy, started shouting at me as though I was some form of traitor. That was when she told me she'd destroyed your ship. Whatever she wants here, she needs to be here."

I shake my head at the bleeding obvious. "So you're a front. The government wanted to send Winter here for a reason but they couldn't violate the law, couldn't just send her in. Unless it was as a part of an extraction team."

"I figured that much. I'm nothing to these people, which is why I don't know anything."

"I take it that midnight quake was a lie as well then?"

Harper nods, not looking at me now. "I guess Winter needed a little extra time to do whatever it was she needed to do."

"And you have no idea what she's doing here?"

She shakes her head.

I wish I could say I had a better idea, but where the government's concerned none of us has a clue. That Harper's telling me the truth I don't doubt, but it calls into question everything my team's doing. I've worked with these people for three years now, Spring for only a year. Soppy as it sounds, they're like my family. We watch out for each other and never leave a woman behind. Now the lieutenant's been lying to me this whole time? I shouldn't believe Harper, shouldn't take the word of a woman I don't even like. But it sounds plausible, and more than that it answers a few questions.

The plane is the key. Then I remember the lieutenant took something from the wreck. "The black box."

"You think that's what she was sent here to retrieve?"

"It'd make sense. But why? It was just a commercial plane. It didn't have any military potential."

"I'm not the right person to ask."

She's not wrong there. Whatever the truth, no matter how infuriating, I won't find any answers without consulting with the lieutenant. The only thing we can really do then is continue our journey towards the shuttle and hope Winter doesn't leave without us.

"You fit to travel?" I ask.

"You're still taking me with you?"

I frown. "You thought I was just going to leave you here?"

"I've been playing you, Corporal."

"The lieutenant's been playing me, girl. Anyway, whatever you'd done I'm not going to just leave you for the dinosaurs to eat. Did you actually think I would?"

"I ... wasn't sure."

"You really don't think much of me do you?"

"I'm trying not to."

I can tell there's something else and debate whether to press my luck. But I don't want her clamming up, especially since she might well reveal a few more tidy facts along the way. Whatever it is she knows and hasn't yet said, it can keep a little while longer.

"I'm not the monster you think I am," I say, mounting Onyx and holding out my hand for the professor to take. "Now come on. We have a lot of ground to cover."

She hesitates only a moment before accepting the gesture and hauls herself onto the back of the beast behind me. Her arms encircle me once more and this time I find it almost pleasant to have another human being depending on me so much for her safety. It makes me feel necessary, makes me feel that I'm not going to be able to die on this stupid world because someone here needs me. Just as Davey needs me to come back home.

We start trotting without another word. There's been far enough spoken just now for me to have enough to think about. Far, far more than I ever wanted to learn.

CHAPTER ELEVEN

We reach the continuation of the forest just as night falls. It took a lot longer to descend the cliffs than I would have liked, especially with the draconyx. We've already had proven to us why we shouldn't travel the forest during the night so decide to make camp. I select a large tree and clamber into its branches. The formation of the leaves provides a natural bedding and the branches themselves are thankfully almost horizontal so I figure it would make a good place to sleep. Using Onyx as a stepping stool, Harper is able to reach the lowest branch as well and I help her to a more comfortable position. Onyx himself can make do on the forest floor: he's used to sleeping here so knows what he needs to do to make sure he survives. We could I suppose have remained with him, for if he started it would mean trouble was approaching; but I have a horrible feeling I'm going to need all the strength and wits I can muster tomorrow, so wouldn't mind an uninterrupted sleep beforehand.

Harper doesn't complain about the makeshift bedding, and I'm once again not so sure I like the change which has come over her. It's true I prefer not to have some antagonistic rich-girl continuously carping on at me, but this new persona is unsettling. I know there's something she hasn't told me, but the more she stays withdrawn the less I'm liking it.

"Do you want me to tie you down?" I ask.

"This is only our second night sleeping together, fall-girl. You could at least wait 'til we're engaged."

It's a half-hearted attempt at humour, and there's none of the previous insult lacing her words. She's trying at least, and I have to give her points for that.

"I meant to stop you falling out of the tree in your sleep. Or I could just hold you all night if you'd prefer?"

"Your unit must be a very happy place to work. I'll be fine. I haven't studied trees for all these years just to die by falling out of one."

So we settle down for the night on the same two branches where they meet the tree itself. Beneath us Onyx settles down himself and I just hope the lieutenant doesn't decide to march through the night. I get the impression a part of Harper is hoping for just such an occurrence.

I awaken immediately alert. That's not natural for me, but has taken a great deal of training. In fact it's one of the things I've put the most effort into, since it's just so difficult for me. But sometimes waking up instantly knowing where you are and what you were doing the night before can save your life, and as such it was the one thing the lieutenant always insisted I perfect. Thinking of how the lieutenant always looks after her unit makes it so difficult to accept everything Harper was telling me last night. That Winter could be lying to us all is ridiculous, and yet I believe it entirely. It makes me wonder what else she's been lying to us about over the years.

Harper isn't beside me, which is the first thing I notice when I open my eyes. Frantically I check the base of the tree, but she hasn't fallen to her doom, and for that I'm grateful. The next jump for my heart is that she may have taken Onyx and departed silently in the night, stranding me here in a tree. But Onyx is still there, dozing by the looks of him. I look about for signs of Harper, and see her on the ground a few trees away, standing at a position where I can barely see her arm but none of the rest of her.

She's probably gone over there to relieve herself, I decide. But she's standing up, and the more I stare, the less certain I am of anything. Since I can't think of anything else she might have gone over there to do, my suspicions begin to churn my insides with doubts. She also seems to be leaning her back against the tree, if the angle of the visible arm is anything to go by. So she's not relieving herself.

So what's she doing then?

Without a sound I drop from the tree and stalk through the forest floor. The closer I get to her the more I'm certain I can hear her talking, and it's as I reach the tree and pause upon the opposite side that I recognise the words she's hastily mumbling.

"... just asking you to wait. Please! I'm a couple of hours behind you at most. You won't have to wait long." She pauses as if listening. "I know all that," she says now. "But come on, it's not going to do you any harm. And what's it going to look like if you return without the person you were supposed to extract? Come on, all I'm asking is for you to fulfil your mission." Another pause. "All right, I'll try. But if I'm not there just remember how rich I can make you for just waiting an extra hour."

She swears angrily and storms straight past me, heading back to where we were nestled for the night.

"No joy?" I ask.

Harper freezes, her entire body going rigid. I reckon she probably doesn't need to relieve herself any more after that fright.

She turns to me slowly, her eyes afraid, an excuse already bubbling from her lips.

"Not interested," I tell her. "Strange the lieutenant gave you her frequency."

"It just suddenly occurred to me she might answer if we called her."

I never thought of that, stupidly enough. Still, after everything I'm learning I'm starting to think maybe it's for the best I haven't tried to contact anyone. "So you're arranging our trip back? What makes you think the lieutenant would leave us behind?"

"I swear I didn't mention your name."

"You didn't mention my name? What does that matter? Hold on, you're telling me you didn't even tell her I'm still alive?"

"I told her you got eaten by that brachauchenius."

"By a what?"

"That thing in the water."

So that was its name. "Why would you want her to think I was dead? Are you planning on leaving me here, is that it? You trying to get me back for calling you Goldie all this time? You think it's funny to tell my friends I'm dead so they'll leave me behind on some dinosaur world? Eh?"

She's backing away, but that's likely because I'm stalking towards her. Anger boils within me and I'm desperately trying to control it, but I don't think I even want to. Ever since coming to this place I've been running for my life, saving Harper or finding out a whole heap of things I really don't want to know. Anger is not a word which even adequately describes what I'm feeling.

"You don't understand," Harper says. "I was trying to help."

"Help?" I'm close enough to push her so that's precisely what I do. She stumbles but doesn't fall, so I shove her again and this time she goes down. I watch her scrabbling back uselessly and I feel a fire burning within me at last. "Help? You think we're pals, don't you? You think you've wheedled your way sufficiently into my good books that I'm about ready to turn on my friends. Is that it? You want to make me think the lieutenant's ready to abandon me to get me riled up?" I kick dirt in her face. "You think I'm going to believe Winter's going to abandon me?"

"You don't know everything," Harper says, more fearful now than I've ever seen her before. Whatever she has to say is something I don't want to hear, and I grab her by the shirt, tossing her through the air without letting go, slamming her back into a tree. Her breath explodes from her body as she attempts to gasp words, but they don't come.

"I know everything I need to know," I say through gritted teeth, trying my level best not to punch her head in. "I know that everything was going fine before I met you. Now suddenly I don't trust what the lieutenant says, and I don't know who to turn to. And the only person I have is you. Do you understand that, Goldie? The only person I have is you, and you're nothing."

"Her orders ..."

"I don't care what you think of her orders," I snap, pulling her back and slamming her against the tree once more. "Tell me what's happening, Goldie. Tell me what the lieutenant told you, what you're not telling me."

"We have to get to the shuttle first. They don't know we have Onyx. If we ..."

"I'm through with your manipulating!" I strike her then, my fist backhanding her across the face. Blood spills from her split lip, spattering the fallen leaves. Her glasses fly from her face. It shuts her up instantly, and as she turns terrified eyes upon me something within me bursts. The frustration of this mission, the stupidity of being here at all, being chased by beasts which died out millions of years ago ... None of this makes any sense. Adrenalin rushes might be my life's blood, but this entire situation isn't even real.

I draw my fist back to punch her full in the face, not even realising what I'm doing, and Harper bursts into tears before I can even land the blow. Suddenly I feel rotten that I've snapped, that I'm taking things out on this girl, the one person who's still stood by me through everything.

I lower my fist, loosen my hold upon her shirt. "I'm sorry, Mary. I ... I don't know anything any more."

"You're going to die."

For a moment I don't think I've heard her right. My eyes narrow just as hers begin to tear once more, and in a trembling voice she repeats those words, damning to someone though I'm not sure who.

"What?" I ask.

"Orders. Winter didn't like them: she was giving me a rough time over them when we met. That's what she was having a go at me about: as though it was somehow my fault."

I blink, none of this making any sense at all. "What?" I repeat.

"They need a patsy. Someone to take the blame. The lieutenant retrieves whatever it was she needed to retrieve and goes home a success. The blame's laid on me because you had to come retrieve me. But they needed someone else, someone within the team. Someone to be lost, killed by the dinosaurs so there would be a sad story to the tale if it ever got out to the media. And because ... because the government knows my father would protect me, so a cover story had to be made."

"That's absurd."

"They're going to pin the blame on you. Someone who won't be able to refute whatever crimes they heap on you."

"No. No, that's ... this is ridiculous. I ... you're telling me I'm nothing but a fall girl?" And then the nickname suddenly makes sense. I figured Harper called me that because of my codename – Autumn. But maybe she's been trying in her own way to warn me of this the whole time.

"I'm sorry," she says, trying not to cry but not entirely succeeding. "I told the lieutenant I was an hour or two behind her, but I figured with Onyx we could make it there before her. I thought

... I thought if you could stow away on the shuttle, they'd never know."

"Winter wants to kill me?"

"No. No, Winter doesn't want to kill you. But they're her orders."

I shake my head, releasing her at last. The orders stink, and I can't believe the lieutenant would go through with them. Actually scratch that, yes she would. Over the years the lieutenant's done a whole lot of bad things just because she's been ordered to do them. Losing me would be something she could live with compared with some of the others. It's no wonder she's always drinking.

"Do Summer and Spring know about these orders?" I ask.

"I don't know."

They can't. There's no way either of them would have gone for it. Which means all I have to do is turn up to the shuttle alive, surprise them all, and unless Winter's prepared to shoot me dead in front of everyone they're going to have to take me back. But would she do that? Alienate her entire team just to see the mission through?

Possibly. You never can tell with the lieutenant.

"I'm sorry," Harper sobs from where she's fallen.

I crouch beside her and hold her tight, clutching her to me like a lost sister. "I'm the one who's sorry," I say in a gentle voice. "You're a screwed up kid, aren't you? You don't deserve to have all this responsibility shoved down your throat."

She sniffs. "Thanks."

I help her to her feet, whether she wants the assistance or not, and place her glasses back on her face. "We should get back to Onyx and start moving if we're going to stand any chance at all of making that shuttle before Winter gets there."

"I don't want you to die, Autumn. I ..."

"Claire." It's almost comical the size her eyes become as I say that single word. "My name's Claire," I say. "If we're two women alone against this crazy world we might as well know each other's names."

She doesn't understand just how important this is, me telling her my real name, but she seems to grasp that it's something big. It could be accused that I've only decided to be open with her because I want her support. That would be true, I don't refute it. But Harper and I have spent a lot of time together and I think I'm actually starting to like her. Against all my better judgements certainly, but as stubborn and antagonistic as she is, she's just a kid. And she's tried to do the right thing. I can respect that.

"Your son," Harper says. "I ... I didn't want him to grow up without his mother."

"You're a better girl than you were a couple of days ago, Mary. Just remember there are people in this life worth trusting. Now let's get a move on. We have a shuttle to catch."

She tries to smile, tries to maintain a sense of optimism, but the truth of the matter is that neither of us knows what to expect when we finally meet up with the lieutenant. We don't know whether she'll carry through her orders or whether she'll have the balls to throw her orders out the window and carry on protecting her soldiers.

If she turns on me, I honestly don't know what I'll do. Or what I'd prefer to do. It's something I'll have to decide when I reach it. Be prepared, those annoying scouts would have said, but I've never met a scout who's had his scoutmaster planning to kill him.

With any luck Harper and I may yet be killed by a dinosaur before we ever make it back to that damn shuttle.

CHAPTER TWELVE

With Harper having lied to the lieutenant about her speed of travel I have it figured there's an even chance we will be able to make it to the shuttle first. I still have no idea what I'm going to do once we arrive, and riding on the back of Onyx at his fastest gallop, the wind kicking my hair and blasting cold sense into my face, I realise that on this primitive world the only survivors are those willing to do whatever it takes to stay alive. That does not for one moment mean I am in any way willing to kill the lieutenant, but at the very least I have to disarm and try to reason with her. I won't even attempt to talk to her, however, without first making sure she's powerless to kill me.

These thoughts continue to bombard my brain: over and over they churn. I don't know what to do, I don't even want to know what to do, but I know I have to do something. If only for Harper I have to be willing to do something.

We left the forest some time ago and entered the rolling plains. There are no more trees between us and the shuttle now, of which I'm glad since it means there won't be any more dinosaurs hiding in ambush. It means all I have to worry about henceforth is human problems. Unnatural enemies.

Onyx is beginning to slow and I know he's tiring. He's not designed for such a hard run, and I feel bad for running him down so. I espy a small stream ahead and rein him in so he can catch a few minutes' rest. Harper and I dismount and leave him to it, moving quickly to the top of the nearest hill so I can reconnoitre. There's no sign of the lieutenant through my binoculars, but that doesn't mean she's not out there.

"I could call her again," Harper suggests. "She might lie about her position, but with any luck she may reveal something."

"I'm more inclined to contact Spring or Summer. God knows what the lieutenant's told them about me. She might have turned them against me already for all I know. Convincing them of the truth is going to be tricky."

"Or impossible."

That's a point I readily concede. Then I notice something and put the binoculars back to my eyes. I feel my heart beat a little faster at the sight; something I really could have done without. There are several forms moving through the grassy plains about two miles away, heading in a direction away from us thankfully. They're keeping low, but the grass masks them well. I had thought coelophysis were confined to the forests, although it seems our records of Ceres are somewhat lacking. Which would make sense since no one's allowed down here to catalogue the dinosaurs or anything. All we really know is what dinosaurs were like on Earth millions of years ago, not what they're like here on Ceres now.

I tell Harper about the coelophysis. There's no point in hiding anything like this any more, and we've both agreed on total disclosure from now on. Secrets kill, and when there are only the two of us there doesn't seem much point in taking such foolish chances.

"Well there's nothing we can do about them now," Harper says somewhat more maturely than I had expected her to. She's beginning to grow up and doing so very fast in fact. It seems this excursion to Ceres was good for some of us at least. "How much more distance do we have to cover?"

"I'd say an hour, maybe slightly more. It all depends on how quickly Onyx there's going to be able to make it."

"He'll come through. Onyx hasn't let us down yet, Claire."

It sounds very strange someone using my name like this. In my life outside of the military of course people call me Claire, except for Davey for obvious reasons. But to be at work and have someone even knowing my name is not something that's ever happened before. It's strange, yet at the same time makes this situation more real to me. It's hammering into my brain just what I'm going through here, making me realise that this is indeed life-changing. Whatever outcome this has, it's not going to be good for everyone, and amidst it all it's just nice someone knows who I really am.

We head back to the stream and take a little water ourselves. There are likely colonies of bacteria in that water, but we don't have the time to properly process the stuff. But then again we swallowed a lot more when we were almost drowned by that lake creature so if we're going to be infected with something it's already inside us.

Onyx seems ready to complain when we mount him again so soon, but we can't afford to let him rest much longer. If I'm right and we are indeed only an hour from the shuttle he can have all the rest he wants when we get there.

The final leg of the journey speeds by. It's difficult to tell the time of day here on Ceres since the artificial sun never moves and the great head of Jupiter is there whether it's night or day. Charging across the plains, a dark shape finally comes into sight and I realise with glee it's the shuttle. It's still a full ten minutes before we reach it, although as I draw the draconyx to a halt it's to note the stark emptiness of the area. The shuttle itself is larger than the one I lost, a full twenty metres in length and ten wide. It stands silently a metre from the ground via three metal landing legs, no thrum of the engine or, more importantly, of the cannon warming up to fire.

"I think we beat them here," I say, dismounting and reaching up to help Harper. She leaps into my arms and I set her down gently, patting Onyx on the side of the head. "Take a nap, pal: you earned it."

"Thanks, Onyx," Harper says, stroking the side of his face and laughing when he tries to lick her. It's one of those moments when I'm reminded as to how young this girl is, and how wrong it was of the government to use her in this fashion. For all my earlier anger and insults towards her, Marigold Harper is still very much a child. This is a heck of a way to have the meaning of adulthood kicked into her head.

"If we can get inside," I say, "we'll have the advantage."

"What about Onyx? If they see him they'll know we're here."

"I'm not hiding, Mary. I want to have it out with the lieutenant, and the best way of doing that is to train those guns on her. The really big guns on the shuttle. That way she'll have to at least listen to me."

"You think she'll admit what's going on to the others?"

"Lieutenant Winter, for all her faults, is a good woman. She's just following orders. Once I give her the opportunity to come clean she'll do so. I think she'll be glad to be disarmed. It'll take the responsibility from her so she can return to her superiors a failure as opposed to a traitor."

"I hope you're right about her."

"Yeah. No more than I do."

I approach the shuttle and key in the unlocking sequence for the door. I'm not surprised to find the lieutenant's changed the code, and this is the final moment upon which I could have had any doubts about her. I believed Harper, she was too sincere in everything she was saying, but there was always a nagging hope in the back of my mind that she had fabricated the entire thing and that the lieutenant wasn't really under orders to kill me so they could blame everything on me if it became necessary.

Now it seems I have to at last own up to the fact that the lieutenant's turned on me.

"Claire!"

I look back to Harper, startled to see she has a gun to her head. Corporal Summer is a large man, but it would appear he can sneak up on people like a snake when he has to. Standing off to the right is Private Spring, her own gun raised but not pointing anywhere in particular as she nervously looks from one person to another, trying to work out what's going on. The lieutenant stands on the left, her own rifle levelled directly upon me, a sad look of tired resignation clouding her eyes.

"Sure wish you hadn't come, Corporal."

"Yeah," I say. "But then that'd be letting you off nice and easy, ma'am. And being in the army's never been about taking the easy option has it?"

It's a taunt she ignores, and I don't blame her. Facetiousness never becomes a junior officer.

"Spring, Summer," the lieutenant orders without taking her eyes off me, "get the professor into the shuttle."

Summer's looking a little awkward, but his gun's still to Harper's head so there's not much I can do about anything. "Ma'am, what's going ..."

"Now, Summer: this isn't a debate."

"Ma'am."

I'm now certain Summer and Spring don't know anything about the lieutenant's orders regarding me. Allowing them into the shuttle would be very foolish, for I don't want to be left alone with the lieutenant. If I can get the others on my side then it'll be all of us against the lieutenant, and there's no way she'd kill her entire team, especially without orders to do so.

"I know everything, ma'am," I say quickly, before Summers can move anywhere. "I know you've been instructed to kill me in case the government needs plausible deniability later."

Summer had forced Harper one step forward, but stops at these words, casting a questioning look at the lieutenant. Spring, bless her, still looks like her gun's too heavy in her hand.

The lieutenant doesn't meet any of their eyes: I'm surprised she's even meeting mine, but then she knows if she looks away I might just shoot her. "You have your orders, Corporal."

I wonder whether she's talking to Summer or me.

"If you want to kill me, ma'am," I say, "then I'd rather you just got on with it. I mean, your mission's completed isn't it? You have the black box you came here for. You do remember your actual mission, don't you? The one you were sent in to do after the government sent the professor in ahead of us just so we could extract her?"

"Hold on a minute," Summer says, his confusion turning to anger; at me for spreading these lies, at the lieutenant for their being true; at the government for turning us against each other. "Lieutenant, what's she talking about?"

Winter finally breaks eye contact with me and lowers her weapon. "Two years ago the Jupiter government put into operation a plan to collect data on Ceres. Data they needed to obtain from the ground. They attached a probe to a commercial flight, to its black box. Then they hijacked the plane and purposefully crashed it onto this world. The probe's spent the past two years gathering intelligence and now the government wants it retrieved."

"And you knew about this?" Summer accuses.

"No," she snaps back. "Of course I didn't know about it. I found out before we left. By that time the plane was crashed and everyone on board had been dead two years. There was nothing I could do to save them, and I had orders to retrieve those data. And that's just what I did."

"What sort of information did the probe gather?" I ask.

Winter shrugs. "Didn't ask. Not my place to know." She scratches her cheek absently, at the three scars which run across her face. I realise something very obvious has been staring me in the face for some time now.

"You've been to Ceres before," I say. Not an accusation, not a question, just a statement.

She meets my eyes once more and nods very slowly. "Years ago. I was much younger then. And teetotal. Once you've fought these monsters hand-to-hand it drives you to the bottle, trust me."

"So you're doing me a favour by killing me?" I guess.

Winter ignores me. "The government's been here a whole lot more frequently than anyone likes to believe. More than I reckon they have as well. I'm not their only agent to come here, and I'm likely not their only agent to come here twice."

"So what do they want with Ceres?" I ask.

"No idea, didn't ask. But I reckon it has to be something to do with military potential. Covert missions are always about military potential."

"You really don't care do you?"

"Autumn, when you've seen what I have you'll learn not to care any more either."

I don't know what she means and I don't want to. "So," I say in a small voice, "what happens now then? You kill me and return home as planned?"

"Screw that," Summer says defiantly.

"You shouldn't have said anything," the lieutenant tells me sadly. "By rights I should kill you all now and go home alone. Just me and the black box."

"And that's what you're going to do?" I ask.

She stares at me for some moments and I see something of the old protector in her at last. "No," she sighs. "No, I'm not. I don't know what I'm going to do."

"I'll tell you what we're going to do," Summer says heatedly. "We're going to take that black box to the media and expose the government for the murder of everyone on that plane."

"No one would believe us," Winter says. "They would for a week or so, but there would be a cover-up and then we'd be arrested and disappeared."

"So what's the alternative?" I ask.

"The only thing we can do," Winter says, "is follow the plan. We leave you here, Autumn, tell our superiors you died. They're happy, you're alive."

"For how long?" Summer asks. "No one can live on this world."

"It's better than a bullet in the head," Winter snaps. "And it's all I can offer."

"Then I'm staying too," Harper surprises us all by saying. I look at her questioningly and she straightens her back even where she's being held. Her eyes are still trembling, but there's more determination there than I've seen in her before and something in my heart breaks for her. I've never been prouder to have called her a friend than in this very moment. "You can say we both died," Harper continues. "They'll believe that."

"Your father will not be happy," the lieutenant says. "He'll sue the government for inadequacy."

"Good," Harper replies and I love her for that. "If he pushes hard enough maybe things will start to unravel."

The lieutenant thinks about all we have said and I can see we're getting through to her. "All right, we'll give it a shot. We ..."

The plain erupts with the crack of a single explosion and I stare with wide horrified eyes as Summer topples, a crimson spray cascading from the side of his head. Harper stands petrified, while Winter jumps back a pace in shock.

Spring, her arm entirely steady now, trains her rifle upon me and the lieutenant with a scowl. "This was a simple operation, Winter. You really should have put a bullet in this woman by now."

"What the hell ...?"

"Back-up," Spring says with a tight smile. "Our government always has a back-up plan. Plans within plans as it were. Just as you didn't inform the group as to your real mission, I didn't tell you about mine."

"I trained you," the lieutenant rages.

"And a good six months it was, thanks. But all things come to an end. If it makes any difference I've put this off until the last possible moment, but I don't have any choice now. If you hand me that black box right now I'll disarm you both and leave you here to fend for yourselves. I'm not a total jerk."

Winter doesn't even so much as look at Summer's corpse as she replies, although we all know she's thinking about him. "The black box is going to the media, Private. We'll take our chances."

Spring makes a sound of complete disrespect. "Don't be stupid."

A loud rapport cracks the air once more and I dive, knocking the lieutenant to the floor where we both roll to behind cover of the shuttle. Spring screams angrily and I see her swing around with her gun. Harper, entirely forgotten and considered useless by Spring, has matured considerably over the past two days. Where once before having a man's brains blown over her might have sent her into bowel-moving despair, today she's a different woman. And she seems to have remembered I gave her a pistol.

She's never fired one before though, so her shot, even if it was meant to hit Spring, didn't come close. The attack was enough to jar Spring, however, enabling me and the lieutenant to get out of there. I lay down rapid cover-fire and shout for Harper to get to cover herself, watching as Spring dives beneath the shuttle to find cover of her own.

We can't all hide behind the same cover, though.

"Sorry about all this, Autumn," the lieutenant says beside me.

"Like to say you're forgiven, but you're not. Mary! Can you hear me?"

"Claire!"

The shout comes from behind a rock, which is good since it's unlikely Spring will bother going all that way just to put a bullet in her. If she can retrieve the black box and get off-world she'll be happy enough. Which means she's going to be coming our way instead.

"This isn't clever," Spring calls. "You know I don't want to hurt anyone else."

"Like I care what you think, you little ho."

The lieutenant holds out a hand for my silence and I realise I shouldn't be replying to the woman's baiting. All it's doing is giving away our position. She can see as much by looking under the shuttle of course, but the landing struts are very thick and there's every chance we could be moving from one to another.

"I don't want any more deaths," Spring shouts. "Seriously, I'm behind schedule enough as it ... what's wrong with your dinosaur?"

It's a trick, and an obvious one, so I don't look. Then I hear Harper's shout, for she clearly didn't know it was an obvious trick and took a look anyway. "Claire!" she shouts. "Onyx: he's nervous!"

Now I do look and see that indeed Onyx is on his feet, shaking his head from side to side. It's fear from the gun discharges, I tell myself. It has to be, since the alternative is ...

"Autumn!" the lieutenant says and I follow her eyes to the crouched form of a familiar theropod, its red eyes glaring at us from the end of its long snout. Behind it there's another one, and another, and my heart sinks when I realise we're surrounded.

"Spring!" I shout without taking my eyes off the things. "We have to get into the shuttle. We have to all get into the shuttle right now."

"What are you harping on about?"

Harper screams and begins loosing shots wildly. I break from cover, charging over to her rock, bringing my own rifle to bear and releasing a sharp discharge which all but shreds the coelophysis which had launched itself at her. Harper shrieks as the body collapses beside her, its blood spraying across her and mingling with Summer's. The girl's blouse is soaked through and she stares at the blood and starts shaking. I can't afford for her to fall into shock and grab her by the arm, yanking her to her feet.

"Into the shuttle," I tell her. "Winter! Open the door!"

The lieutenant nods and keys in the correct number sequence. A creature leaps at her while she's working and I take it down with a barrage of fire. I would have thought the sounds would have kept the animals at bay, but it seems to be attracting them.

Spring appears from nowhere, a rifle in either hand, firing precision shots: short bursts which take down an enemy at every squeeze. She looks very annoyed, but if she's occupied with the coelophysis she can't be shooting at us.

The door of the shuttle opens and the ramp descends. The lieutenant stands at the base of the ramp, shooting anything that comes close as I run towards her, dragging Harper along behind me. There's a veritable carpet of coelophysis appearing around the shuttle now, and to stay and fight them all would be suicide. Protected by the lieutenant's cover fire, I reach the base of the ramp and shove Harper forwards.

"Go," Winter tells me, cracking off shots without pause.

"I've got this," I tell her.

"And I'm still in charge, so go!"

We can't stand here all day arguing, so I run up the ramp. Harper's terrified, but has learned to work through her fear and has strapped herself in securely. I rush to the main controls – the shuttle has only the one room aside from the storage area at the back – and fire up the engines.

Suddenly the lieutenant's beside me. She has a nasty cut to her forehead which drips blood into her eyes, but she grins at me wolfishly: she's suffered far worse in the past. I look back to see the doors are closed.

"Strap in," Winter tells me and as I head to a chair I glance out the window to see Spring continuing to fire, doing her best to keep the beasts back. I turn from her and take the seat beside Harper, strapping myself in and pressing my hand upon hers.

"We're clear," I tell her. "We're all right now."

"What about Spring?"

"I think we left her."

"Good."

It's a turning point for Harper, the first of many these past couple of days. As arrogant as I always took her, I never thought she would have been glad to have seen another human being left to die. I'm not sure I like it all that much.

The shuttle lurches as the landing struts are raised and the craft begins to lift. I look back out the window and see Spring cursing us, although I can't hear her words. My eyes widen as she tosses one rifle so she can reach into her belt and withdraw something. My years in the military have trained me to recognise the firing pin of a remote detonator when I see one.

"Winter!"

"I see it!" she shouts and slams a button. The shuttle grinds and the lieutenant turns to look directly at me. There's sorrow to her eyes, pity and more remorse than I could ever mention. "Good luck, Claire."

And suddenly the floor drops out and Harper and I are falling, our chairs being released from the shuttle. I watch as the shuttle careens above us in the air, looking like it's shooting away simply because of the speed at which we're falling from it. And then the entire thing explodes in a tremendous fireball as Spring's incendiary ignites: her final hateful revenge against those who would leave her to die.

I jar uncomfortably as my seat strikes the ground. The seat is designed to have absorbed the impact, although I'm sure they never work properly. We have no time to dwell on anything that's just happened, however, for the coelophysis will be nearby: we can't have gained too much distance from where Spring's fighting. Pressing the unstrap switch, I clamber out of my chair to help Harper with her own harness. I can see Spring some distance away, perhaps fifty metres, fleeing, her rifle flaming at anything that moves. Tearing Harper from the seat I draw my own pistol and loose a shot at a creature ten metres away. The bullet doesn't connect, but it gives the thing second thoughts about attacking us.

"Winter," Harper gasps, and again I'm afraid she's falling into shock.

"Forget her," I say, grabbing her face with both my hands and almost shaking her. I force her eyes to find mine and try to instil a little calm into her, even through my own panic. "Mary, focus. I need you, all right? I need you."

Slowly she nods and I take up my pistol once more. Our gun situation's not too good, and our ammunition is worse, but so long as the coelophysis don't flock our way we might be able to make it across the plain without being killed.

Something explodes to the north and I watch as what remains of the shuttle crashes to the ground, sending flames careening across the field, igniting the grass for a quarter mile. The coelophysis look towards it in confusion; it's just the distraction we need.

"Come on," I say to Harper, taking her by the hand and leaving the chairs behind. "We need to go."

I catch sight of Onyx and wave to get his attention. The fire's spooking him, but he comes at my signal, knowing I'll be able to lead him from the flames and to safety. A single coelophysis means nothing to him, but a frenzied pack is more than even he can cope with. I clamber onto his back when he reaches us, drawing Harper up alongside me, holding her tightly in front of me for fear of her sliding off if she sat behind. And I'm through leaving people behind.

"Autumn!"

I glance across to where Spring is still firing. She's using up an enormous amount of bullets, even though she's scoring a hit every time she fires. She can't have too many left if her body-count's anything to go by. And she has no cover, and no shuttle now she's destroyed it. Nor does she have a dinosaur steed.

"Autumn!"

There's something else she doesn't have either. A friend. Which is a shame, because it's only friends I'm not willing to leave behind.

I crack the reins on Onyx and he breaks into a gallop. Harper feels incredibly small and young curled up before me, but I'll look after her. I have to. She's all I have now. She's my entire world, my hopes. My life.

EPILOGUE

We returned to the wreck a few days ago. There was nothing there, no sign of anything useful. Certainly nothing left of the lieutenant I might be able to bury. Coelophysis corpses littered the field, but they had mainly been picked clean by scavengers. I even caught sight of a circling quetzalcoatlus and bade it a good day. Of Spring, or whatever her real name is, there was no sign either. No shred of cloth, no bloody head. It's possible she was entirely devoured, possible she survived. But I did find two familiar ski-like marks in the grass. It seems I may have discovered at last what happened to the copter when Spring piloted it away from the daspletosaurus. As with the bomb on our shuttle, it seems Spring had planned a great deal for her future. The marks in the grass aren't conclusive evidence, but I have to assume she survived simply because I have to prepare for her being a problem come the future.

Still, Ceres is a large place. The chances of her being able to find us are incredibly remote.

"You're back."

Mary's smile is infectious, and how she keeps her chin up under these conditions I'll never know. We've made something of a home for ourselves in the mountains. In a part of the world with fewer trees. There are caves here, and there's a quick route down to a tarn where we've found plenty of fish. We haven't starved or wanted for water and it seems we might be able to live here indefinitely. We've also taken care this time to make our home far, far above the reach of any roving daspletosauri.

"I'm back," I confirm, "and I brought goodies."

I unload a bag filled with fruit and Mary sorts through it methodically. Her botany training's come in very useful. I may know everything there is to know about survival, but I couldn't tell you which extinct plants are safe to eat. Thankfully Mary's story about being here to study the plants wasn't a part of the lie, and she's been a godsend lately. I wonder how Spring's managing to work out what to eat, but maybe if we're lucky her poor choices might well kill her.

Mary has a fire going and is cooking something, another vole it looks like. She's turned out to be a pretty good cook as well, which is handy since I'm not. She's also developed a mastery of small-talk, which helps to pass the time. Today however neither of us is feeling too talkative and we eat in silence.

The black box is gone, destroyed by Spring in her anger in blowing up the shuttle. The black box, the one thing Spring wanted; the one thing we need. Without that box we have no proof of anything. Without that box even if we were rescued we wouldn't be able to show the world what we've been through. And the box is gone.

"If Spring's dead," Mary says to break the silence, "and they do send a rescue ship, we could just deny all knowledge of the plans within plans. You'd be debriefed and go back to work. Daddy would do his best for me and hopefully I'd see the outside of a cell one day."

She's a sweet girl, but I know what she's doing. She knows I'm thinking about Davey. She knows he's all I think about. She knows full well he's never going to see me again and she's trying to make me feel better. She's a sweet kid, but it doesn't change anything.

"You forget something, Mary. There's no rescue ship coming. Ceres is forbidden territory. No one ever comes here."

"Aside from all the people the lieutenant claimed the government sent here. Sometimes twice. We just need to keep an eye out, and make sure we find these people before Spring does."

She's trying to cheer me up again. She does this a lot, and I respect her for it. But it's not helping. We're not going to be rescued. And I'm never going to see my son again.

But I can't feel badly for her attempts. At least one of us is managing to say positive.

"Yeah," I say, forcing a smile as I eat. "Maybe one day they'll send someone and we can get a lift home. Maybe."

We continue to eat in silence.

Above us the great face of Jupiter gazes down with satisfaction. There is a reason, it says, why Ceres is forbidden. Religious ground, it agrees. Perhaps Jupiter itself just doesn't like people walking on its sacred soils. I don't know any more. I just know I'm never going to see my boy again.

I wish I'd never come to Ceres in the first place.

DINOSAUR PRISON WORLD

CHAPTER ONE

Sparks flew in her face, searing her skin and almost blinding her in the process. She tasted blood in the back of her throat and there was a stabbing pain in her side. It was possible she had broken a couple of ribs, but it was more likely she was just bruised and a little shaken up. The fingers of her left hand darted across a small panel affixed beside her head, while her right reached up to grip a horizontal lever wrapped fastidiously in strips of leather. It was the one lever which would mean the difference between her life and death and she wasn't about to let her hand slip from it. She did not tug the lever however, ignored the flashing red light blazing about her face and the written indicator of danger burning into her corneas. Her eyes focused through the visor on the thing slowly approaching, and her right hand tensed.

The beast came to within five metres of her, its great nostrils flaring – either to test the air or merely in indignation she could not say – before it shifted its weight to crane for a better view. The creature was enormous, nine metres long and about half that in height; she didn't even want to consider how much the thing weighed in at. Its torso was huge and bulky, kept in the air by two thick hind legs whose thigh muscles were easily more powerful than anything mankind had ever been able to build. Its forearms were in contrast relatively weak, although she knew they were still able to deal a lethal slashing blow if she allowed them to come into contact with her. From the rear of its torso there was produced a thick, well-muscled tail which presently swished behind it as though it was debating which way to turn. She knew from experience the creature used the tail for counterbalance and it was often possible to predetermine which way the animal would strike if she kept a close eye upon this weapon – like watching an alpha male wolf and ignoring the rest of the pack.

It was the head of the beast which had caused many to quail, however, and very few who had such a thing so close to them had survived. The head was a powerful skull of serrated teeth, its eyes protected by two bony flat protuberances which many years ago had been termed horns, as though this was the Devil's own pet. She imagined this thing being Cerberus and did not stop to fear what this beast would have been like with three heads.

The creature leaned in closer, the thick neck, stocky torso and muscular tail all forming one straight horizontal line to keep the body of the creature in an upright position. The terrible head was close to her now, within a metre, and she could see its massive reptilian eye gazing down upon her, the breath steaming from its nostrils fogging up her visor.

Inhaling sharply and wishing her heart would cease pounding so loudly in her ears, Ashley Honeywood yanked down hard on the lever with her right hand, and the monster roared in pain and rage as a spray of light erupted from her.

Honeywood's fingers darted across panels once more and she shot out a fist, catching the beast on the side of the head. She knew she would have only moments before the thing recovered, and that once it did she would have no chance of surviving, let alone winning. But the creature thrashed too madly in its pain of sudden blindness and the great muscular tail came hurtling around as it spun, and smashed directly into Honeywood's chest.

She went tumbling, alerts flashing before her eyes, klaxons wailing at her, and she felt the dented metal pressing into her side. She did not know whether it had punctured the skin, but didn't want to think about such a thing. If she stopped to consider how much damage the creature had done her she would fall into shock, and then she would die.

Her fingers danced again as she attempted to regain control, but the world was literally spinning as she rolled across the dusty ground and she could see nothing of her tormentor. She was leaking fuel somewhere and instantly cut off the feed into any damaged sectors of her suit. Then she did the one thing she entirely dreaded. She took her hands from the controls and tried to assess her situation now that she had stopped tumbling.

Her suit was compromised in several places; a quick diagnostic showed several old wounds had reopened in addition to the rupture in her side. She attempted to raise the limbs of the suit, but they were unresponsive and she knew she was too damaged to deal with the thing outside.

Gorgosaurus. Let's give things their proper names, she thought to herself. That it had not attacked in the two or three seconds she had been lying helpless on the floor was a good thing, but there was nothing she could do with her systems from here. She had two options, so far as she could see. Her suit was useless to her, so she could abandon it and take her chances with the gorgosaurus without it. Honeywood was five foot eight, the gorgosaurus was over thirty in length; that just wasn't going to happen.

Taking a deep breath she did the only other thing she could, and hit the kill switch.

Everything went dark. The suit's power failed entirely, and Honeywood was robbed of both external sight and sound. The only things she could hear were her own laboured breathing and her incessant heart pounding. She couldn't even see that much.

Metal ground around her and Honeywood felt herself being raised bodily into the air. Shock waves hurtled through her body as she was dropped once more, blind and afraid, and suddenly she could hear something even through the blackness of the suit: she could hear the roar of the beast outside as it struggled in its own blind rage to get to her. Honeywood controlled her breathing, kept her hands to the sides where they wouldn't slam into anything at its next attack, and would have prayed if she thought it might have done her any good.

She was knocked onto her side and gasped as something pressed into her stomach. Metal from the freshly-dented suit, she reasoned, but as the beast retracted she stared in wide-eyed panic as light filtered through. It was light streaming through knife-like gashes made in the suit, and as she glanced down at her body in view of that light she could see where the teeth of the gorgosaurus had torn through her armour and pressed bloodily into her belly.

Then suddenly a red message flashed before her eyes and any prayers she may have inadvertently muttered were answered. The message read: SYSTEMS ONLINE.

Lights came back on in her cockpit and Honeywood wasted no time, her fingers once more flying to life. Her suit's right fist smashed out once more, catching the monster under the chin in a surprising manoeuvre, its left fist taking it in the side of the face. She struggled to her feet and called up a schematic for a visual, but the feed was down. She could see the gorgosaurus staggering before her, but then the image was gone.

Honeywood was not about to waste the advantage while she had it.

Disengaging the main visual screen, she slammed a naked palm into the faceplate retraction and the entire visor slid inwards. Real air washed into the cockpit of the suit, along with it the roar of the animals outside. She could see her surroundings, could taste everything with her own senses now, and she smiled. It was good to be alive.

The dusty ground was a roughly circular space fifty metres in diameter, about which were concrete walls high enough to contain her suit and the beast she fought. Above the concrete there was enclosed a massive clear area where upwards of five hundred people could gather. They were jeering, primitive brutes, calling for blood and demanding satisfaction. Today there was a turnout of probably somewhere in the region of four hundred, and Honeywood knew this was a main attraction. After all, it was one of the greatest, most ferocious predators of this world in the pit.

And then of course there was also the dinosaur.

Honeywood launched herself at the beast, entirely unmindful that she was exposed to the elements, that if the gorgosaurus could get its head snapping at the right angle its teeth could tear her from her cockpit before she could blink. Ashley Honeywood had never wasted time on worrying about possibilities, especially with an audience.

The crowd exploded with primal, vocalised praise as she landed blows upon the beast. The gorgosaurus backed away, but her attack was too vicious for it to counter. The beast snapped out its head to clamp its teeth about her arm, and the massive teeth shore through her armour. Sparks exploded into the creature's face and it automatically released its hold, allowing Honeywood to use her free fist to punch it to the floor.

She backed off herself, slowly, gaining distance between herself and the animal. She ran a quick check of her systems. The left arm was offline, most of the primaries were shot; but it was an old suit not in the best of states when she had donned it. All things considered it was holding up well. In contrast the gorgosaurus was lying upon the ground, its great chest rising and falling, its beady eyes locked onto her in hatred. There remained intent to kill her, but no ability.

Honeywood drew a blade from where it was sheathed at her thigh. She blocked out the tinny droll of the crowd's enthusiasm as she closed upon the animal. This was always the most dangerous part, where she could easily grow overconfident. She had seen more than one combatant torn apart at this point simply through growing too confident in the victory. These creatures were to be respected, and anyone who didn't understand that didn't last long in the arena.

She raised her blade, a full two metres of tempered steel, hardened through a complex construction of chevrons; simple beaten metal could snap after all. If the creature understood what the blade represented it gave no sign. However it did understand that her approach meant another attack, yet it did not fight to regain its footing. It was not giving the crowd what they wanted, but through no thought of stoic disdain. The gorgosaurus had given its all and was spent, and could only lie upon the ground awaiting its end.

Honeywood paused as she reached the creature, blade poised over its almost still form. A beast so magnificent … it was almost a shame to end its life.

Almost.

The blade came down and splintered the skull of the gorgosaurus, sliding through its brain. The beast thrashed once and was still, and Honeywood released the blade to take a step back from the carnage. Blood was pooling about the head of the animal, her sword standing firm as though it was a tombstone. Conan Doyle had claimed these beasts took minutes to realise they were dead, even once their brains had been destroyed, but she had slain enough of them to know Conan Doyle hadn't a clue what he was talking about. But then Conan Doyle had never met a real live dinosaur.

Honeywood gazed about the crowds above her, all chanting her name as though she was some Second Coming. She smiled, shouted something back she couldn't afterward remember, although she reckoned it must have been abusive. She raised the still functional arm of the metal suit to meet the cheers and drank it all in. This was her life, and she was damn good at it.

She did not enjoy even one moment.

CHAPTER TWO

"You know, for a while there even I thought you'd had it, Ashley. That would have been bad for business."

Ashley Honeywood had cleaned up as best she could after the fight. They didn't have showers as such, but then nor would they have been particularly effective in this humidity. Instead she had thrown water over her face and had stripped off her shirt so she could tend to her injuries. The gorgosaurus teeth had barely pierced the skin of her belly thanks to the suit, but her ribs ached and she was applying a salve to them to aid in the healing. Presently she was sitting on a bench in what could passably be termed the changing area. Her top lay on the bench beside her as she slowly tied a bandage about her bruised knuckles – it was surprising how she seemed to absorb the punches the suit made on her behalf. If she had one time felt uncomfortable sitting in front of men dressed only in her shorts and underwear (she, not the men), this place had long since blasted such folly from her. Honeywood had heard hundreds of arguments about heat verses humidity, but all she cared about was that it was so hot you never stopped sweating.

The man before her was named Dexter Valentine. For some reason he always dressed smartly in a carefully-pressed business suit, as though he was someone important, but then that was how he saw himself. He was tall, fairly thin by the average of people around here, with short blond hair and a clipboard. He always carried a clipboard. In contrast Honeywood was at least two heads shorter, with a stocky, muscular figure which bore no fat but would never have been considered attractive in the magazine sense. Her hair was dark and just longer than shoulder length, and always matted to her forehead in sweat. Her eyes were two dull pits of mud, her lips twisting her face into a permanent scowl. People like Valentine did not make that scowl ever want to go away.

He ticked two names off the paperwork he currently held on his clipboard, but Honeywood didn't much care about them. She didn't do what she did to keep Valentine happy, despite what he would have her think.

"If you died out there, Ashley," he continued, seemingly oblivious of her scowl, "things would go very badly for me, you know."

"I'm sorry," Honeywood all but rasped. "I'll try harder not to die next time."

Valentine removed his glasses so he could rub at his tired eyes. Tired, as though he ever did any work. She would very much like to see Valentine enter the lists sometime. "We have enough volunteers for the security details, why don't you finish cleaning up and get some rest."

"I don't tell you about my work, Valentine, I'd appreciate it if you kept yours to your clipboard."

She finished tying her bandage and walked away before she could thump the man. She supposed she couldn't blame him for what the way he was. Valentine kept the place running, that much was true. After the riot a couple of years back the whole place had been liberated. It had been a great victory, but no one gave any thought to how they would run things. Simply getting rid of the people in charge didn't create new laws, so Valentine had come up with a system. They had no money, no reason to want any money and no access to it even if they did, so Valentine had proposed the fights. Everyone was hot on the idea of watching people fight dinosaurs, especially since they had a few mechanical suits and other weapons to hand. There were herbivores of course, both small and large, and there were small theropods which could be fought by teams even without suits. No one would take on a tyrannosaurid like gorgosaurus without sufficient protection, however. Valentine had tapped into the people's primal need for violence, and took bets on the outcome. Instead of money, the losers would take on the various work details until the next fight. The winners would be guaranteed a break from the details if they were already on one, and if they weren't they would get whatever perks there were available. That could range anywhere from extra food to a night with one of the losers.

It was a decent system and one to which they all obeyed. There had not been another riot since it was implemented, so it must have been doing something right.

If Honeywood agreed with anything Valentine had said to her it was that she should get some rest. First though she was hungry, and that was fortunate because her lover owned the best café in the bayou. That it was the only café in the bayou didn't make the blindest bit of difference; Garret Seward was the finest chef the entire world over and Honeywood was thankful he had purposefully poisoned an entire delegation of Spain purely because they had insulted his mastery. Honeywood remembered the papers the following day, for Seward denied nothing, and had stood over the bodies with his arms folded, declaring to the police that they could arrest him, but that those he had killed had committed a far greater crime.

Seward was passionate about his work, and went on many trips into the swampland about his café that he might forage for the freshest fruits and obtain the choicest cuts of meat. That he was a perfectionist annoyed many people about the institution, but no one complained when they were sitting in his café. For one thing there was nothing to complain about when the finest food was sitting on a plate in front of you; for another, they all knew why he had been arrested all those years ago.

Being a perfectionist also meant he was the best lover Honeywood had ever experienced. It did not mean she was actually in love with him, but out here people took whatever pleasures they could find, and there was little which could meet the adrenalin rush of fighting monsters for her life.

Honeywood left the institution via the front door. It was a huge affair, bearing multiple locks, and there were of course people on guard duty who had made losing bets on the fight. That they had wagered for her to die was not something she was going to hold against them. Life was cheap out here and Honeywood was not one to hold a grudge. As she watched the guards open the great doors for her she marvelled at how much of this place they had kept the same after the riots, and was thankful the riots themselves had not destroyed too much. Taking charge would have been useless if it meant they were all killed.

Moving out into the afternoon air of the swamp was not pleasant, but Honeywood was used to it. The air was oppressive and damp, and her thin sleeveless shirt became instantly stuck to her skin. The chirruping sound of a thousand insects hungry for her blood came to her ears, but long living in this swamp had all but cured her of their bites. If she hadn't been killed by them yet she figured she probably never would be.

Keeping her foot-long knife in its sheath at her thigh, Honeywood entered the swamp proper. There were firearms back at the institution, but they were kept under strict lock and key. Fights were frequent after all and they could do without people shooting one another. Plus they had only a limited supply of ammunition. They had a great deal of it, but there was no more coming to replace it so once it was gone it was gone.

Through long experience Honeywood had learned how to keep to the firmer ground, for the swamp was a deceptive beast and a person could be dragged down to her waist, or even drowned, before she even realised she had placed a step wrong. She kept close to the trees, creeping vines that they were, and followed the well-travelled route which people took to the bayou café. She had more reason to travel this path than most, but today she was hungry and all she intended to sate herself upon once she arrived was a kentrosaurus steak.

It would of course be nice to see Seward again though. It had been a week since she had found the time to leave the institution and she had become hardened because of it. Seward's simple ways of viewing the world always grounded her to reality, for everyone back at the institution was a sadistic thug whose only thoughts concerned violence, sex and getting one over everyone else. Seward was a dreamer, a thinker. They would often sit together on top of his shack in the swamp gazing at the stars and of course the great godly eye staring down upon them all. Seward believed one day they would be rescued, that someone would come to take them from this hell. He did not seem to understand that if anyone should come, they would be far from rescued; if they were lucky they would be arrested and tried for the riot. Either way they would be executed. But Seward's childlike fantasies inspired Honeywood. They made her see another side to life, made her accept that perhaps there was more to living than killing.

She intended to contemplate such things over her burger.

Breaking from the trees, Honeywood began the final thirty metre walk across flat, usually solid ground (it all depended upon whether it had been raining the night before). Seward had chosen to build his shack at the end of this stretch because it enabled him to draw carts right up to his café should he require their usage. After all, if he was serving something large and heavy like a ceratopsid he would need several people to help him bring the carcass back to his shack. Seward was a skilled surgeon of course, and would often cut just the choicest meats from his kills – and he never scavenged – but the bones could often be made into a delicious soup, and there was so much bone in the skull of a ceratopsid that Seward was able to work wonders with them.

Honeywood had taken two steps onto this flat plain before she realised something was wrong. The shack was before her, in the distance still, but it was not as she had always remembered it. It was a single-storey affair with a thick chimney breaking through the centre, allowing the heat and smoke from the internal fires to escape. The chimney seemed crooked from her distance, and this made her eyes rove the rest of the structure.

Then she realised the stakes Steward had set outside to mark his territory and the seats he had placed in the shade were all destroyed. Something large and something heavy had torn through this place.

Honeywood ran, not even considering the danger inherent in the swamp, not even checking first whether whatever had done this was still around. She covered the distance in moments and burst through what remained of the front door. The shack was formed of wood and twined vines, so the walls somewhat resembled a hanging basket. The front door came off in her hand but she hardly even noticed as she cast her gaze about the common room. The tables and chairs were overturned or shredded, there was a great gouge taken out of the counter as though by some claw.

Moving slowly now, forcing herself to think clearly, Honeywood surveyed the damage with a clinical eye. There was no blood spattered about the walls, which was a good sign. It was possible Seward was alone when the attack had come, for indeed there were no bodies strewn about. If Seward was attacked, however, he would have not gone down alone, for he kept a small array of firearms behind the bar. That Seward had not been here at the time of the attack was also a possibility: he could easily have been out hunting or gathering berries. He might also be lying dead out the back amidst a heap of ornitholestes corpses, although that was a possibility she would deal with once she had finished down here.

She examined the claw marks upon the broken furniture and bar. She could not identify them all, but certainly they seemed of the correct size and height to have been made by a dromaeosaurid. There were known utahraptor packs operating towards the far edges of the swamp, although they had never come so far towards the installation before. They had local problems with small carnivores, but dromaeosaurids were not common aggressors. The nature of the claw marks, however, suggested otherwise. Honeywood ran her finger absently through the deep impression left upon the counter and knew of no creature which would be able to survive such an attack. The dromaeosaurids were small carnivores in comparison to the gorgosaurus she had just pounded to death, but she had been encased in a suit of technological armour, while Seward had only a shotgun and kitchen knife to wield.

It was time, she decided with a deep breath, to go out the back.

Stepping over broken girders, Honeywood made her way carefully to the far door. She was a prize fighter and knew the advantages of stealth; in fact she could move silently if she had to. However, there was so much debris scattered about the floor here it was difficult not to tread on at least something. Her booted feet managed to miss crunching the broken glass and wood, but a girder had fallen across the door and there was no way she would be able to pass through without first moving it.

Assessing the situation with a keen eye, Honeywood bent her legs, taking the weight of the beam in her arms. When she was certain she had the weight evenly distributed she heaved, and a flurry of dust and wood fell into her eyes. Dropping the girder, she blinked rapidly, further dust flying into the air from where the beam struck the ground. She stood tensely for several moments, but if anything had noticed the noise she had made it gave no indication.

She wasn't certain whether to take that as a good or bad sign.

Pressing on into the back rooms, Honeywood made her way to the kitchen, which was where she knew Seward would make his final stand. He would never let a potential meal chase him out of the kitchen after all. She found the sacrosanct room not even touched, and decided the fallen beam over the door may have prevented anything reaching this far. If that was the case, it meant Seward could well be hiding here somewhere. But no, he wouldn't hide in his domain. It would be like an artist cowering behind his prize canvas. Seward was just too damn proud of this kitchen to live while it was it destroyed.

Perhaps he had got his wish.

Moving back to the main room, Honeywood checked the place over once more, thoroughly this time. Again she could find no indication of a struggle, although there was ample evidence of attack. It cemented her theory (hope?) that Seward had not been here at the time of the attack, perhaps that he was not even aware his precious café had been destroyed. She wished she could just phone him, but communication on this world was never very reliable, and while there was supposedly a satellite in orbit for this very purpose it didn't seem to work.

She left the shack to return to the swamp and extended her search. It did not take her long to find the animal tracks heading from the swamp towards the shack. It seemed she had been right about the dromaeosaurids. She found many prints of the right size and shape, and indications of the raised claw on each foot which would accidentally touch ground on occasion. Every species of dromaeosaurid had such claws; curved knives which would tear into its prey as it attacked. They kept the claws from the ground so as not to blunt them and they were the single deadliest weapon nature had ever evolved.

Perhaps excluding the human race.

Standing straight once more, Honeywood gazed into the darkness of the foetid swamp and slowly shook her head. "Garret, just what have you got yourself into this time?"

CHAPTER THREE

"Leaving? But Ashley, think about the bouts."

"You can still have bouts without me, Valentine."

Honeywood had returned to the institution to gather some equipment. A hunting rifle was the least she would insist upon, although a backpack of provisions and survival necessities was something she could not follow Seward without. Valentine had been buzzing about her since her return, and seemed more frantic about the running of his operation than he did Seward's life. But then life was cheap here in the swamp, and Honeywood could hardly blame him. What she had just said was accurate though; she wasn't the only combatant and work details could still be planned around other people's fights. She was simply the only person crazy enough to take a large theropod head-on.

"We don't even know if he's still alive," Valentine persisted. "If he was dragged back to a nest or something he'll be long dead by now."

"If he was dragged away there would have been blood," Honeywood told him. She did not understand it herself, although the logical assumption was still that Seward had not been in the café at the time of the attack. Her gut was telling her otherwise, but there was no other explanation she could think of. "Besides," she said, "once news gets out that Seward's not going to be serving up his famous dino-burgers your people are gonna be impossible to keep in line."

It was true, and she could see in Valentine's eyes that he understood this. He was a man afraid though, and Honeywood knew why. This whole place was kept together so precariously that something like the disappearance of the café was liable to tip people over the edge. If Valentine wasn't careful in how he handled things there would be another riot, and this time it would end with Valentine lying face down in the swamp.

"All right," he said, moistening his nervous lips. "But I need to make an announcement."

Honeywood shrugged as she continued to shove things into her bag. "Do whatever you want, Valentine. But I'm heading for the door right now."

Valentine knew better than to argue with her and hastened away. Honeywood wondered what he was up to, but put it from her mind. She supposed she would find out sooner or later. Performing a final check of her equipment, Honeywood finished strapping armaments to her body before hefting the pack onto her back and heading for the swamp once more. She passed through several empty corridors before coming to the door which led to the main atrium. It was this room which was the easiest route to the outside, especially with all the fences up, and it was also the room which was fed by several doors and staircases. As she entered she could sense a lot of activity and saw a dozen people standing to her left doing very little. There were more to the right and for a moment she thought Valentine had got them to stop her from leaving. She tensed her muscles for a fight, but kept her head low and walked through them. They made no move to stop her.

"The hero of the hour!"

Honeywood stopped. The voice had come from behind her, and above, and had belonged to Valentine. She turned very slowly to see him standing on the landing a level above her, surrounded by a score or more people. Others were gathered on the stairs, or by the doors on the ground level, and Honeywood counted at least sixty bodies in the large area. Valentine was beaming, and she decided whatever he was trying to pull this was going to be it.

She kept her mouth shut and let him speak.

"The staple of our lives," Valentine was continuing, "is the fights. Human against dinosaur, brain against brawn. It upholds our laws and creates order. Ashley Honeywood is the greatest scrapper we have ever known; but she is a hero for more than that this day."

Honeywood had never been called a hero before and wasn't so sure she liked it. She shifted uncomfortably as her skin crawled, but continued to hold her peace.

"There is one other pleasure which makes our lives bearable," Valentine said, "and this is the establishment in the bayou. Seward's eatery. You may have been hearing rumours of Seward, and I am sorry to inform you these are true. The café has been destroyed, and Seward is gone." He paused to allow the requisite gasp to flow through the crowd. It didn't actually happen, so far as Honeywood could determine, but Valentine continued regardless. "Honeywood has volunteered to venture forth to locate Seward and bring him back alive. The café shall reopen, we shall have order."

Honeywood already knew all of this, had told Valentine herself in fact, and wondered whether he had a point to make.

"But the swamp is a large place," Valentine said, "and who knows whether there is anything which exists beyond? Honeywood, hero that she is, cannot do this alone. Who shall answer the call to accompany her on this arduous mission?"

So that was it. Honeywood rolled her eyes, wishing Valentine would just leave her the hell alone. She preferred her own company, moved at her own speed, and the last thing she wanted was a couple of guys hanging around telling her how to track someone. She opened her mouth to speak, but someone beat her to it.

"I volunteer."

She looked at the man who had spoken. His name was Stiggs, and if he had another name Honeywood did not know it. Nor did she know whether Stiggs was his forename or surname. Stiggs was a wretched thin man with shifty eyes. He was always grinning, in an unnerving leering way, and bobbed his head when he spoke as though he was a duck diving for fish. He tended to agree a lot with people, trying to curry their favour, wanting to get them to fight his own battles for him. She could not imagine Stiggs had ever been in a fight in his whole life, and as someone who valued strength over everything else, Honeywood despised the man. He was also a known lackey of Dexter Valentine, always eager to please his master. Honeywood had no doubt at all that Valentine had put Stiggs up to this, so his could be the voice to gather others to her side.

"I really don't need anyone," she said before Valentine could respond to Stiggs's volunteering. "I can move faster alone."

"And such modesty is worthy of fine praise," Valentine said theatrically. "But come, is there no one here as brave as Stiggs?"

Honeywood groaned inwardly. That was his plan then. To shame people into stepping forward by claiming anyone who didn't was weaker or more cowardly than Stiggs.

"I'm going too."

Honeywood appraised her next volunteered companion. Abe Garza stood three heads taller than Honeywood and was built like an ankylosaur. Broad-shouldered did not cover it with him, for his chest was an oozing powerhouse of muscle. His arms were thicker than an average man's skull and his thighs were like tree trunks. Honeywood had no doubt he would be able to outrun even a dromaeosaurid, which would make him useful to her. It would be interesting to see him wrestle one as well. Garza had yet to compete in the bouts, although he was eager to prove himself, and was scheduled for a match sometime next month if her memory served. He was likely taking this to be a preliminary test then, and to garner support to his name.

In a couple of years he could be stealing her crowd, but at least here she could keep an eye on him, get to know him perhaps. And if he could indeed wrestle a dromaeosaurid perhaps she would even consider retiring.

"I'll take Garza," Honeywood said. "Stiggs you can keep."

"Your party shall be made of four," Valentine said, and Honeywood knew he had already selected the fourth member. Garza was someone he could not refuse, now the offer had been made, but Honeywood doubted Garza was someone Valentine had selected for her. She had no idea why he wanted to keep such a close eye upon her, but she wasn't liking it.

"I'm in."

Valentine's face fell at the sound of the voice, and Honeywood realised whoever had just volunteered it had not been who he had expected. Indeed there was someone already calling his own response, but it was too late, for someone had beaten him to it.

Honeywood regarded the young woman stepping forward, the one who had spoken before Valentine's man could manage to. She was young, probably no more than twenty, which was too damn young to be in this place. She seemed physically capable, but far from brawny. Athletic might have been a good term for her, and Honeywood reflected that perhaps athleticism was the one sure way of dealing with a dinosaur anyway. Only an idiot charged them head-on, and this young woman had the air of someone who was clearly not an idiot. She met Honeywood's gaze and projected a calm stoicism beneath which Honeywood could see fear and trepidation.

Honeywood shrugged. She had no idea who the girl was, but she was certainly better than Valentine's choice.

"What's your name, girl?"

"Cassie, ma'am."

"Well, Cassie Ma'am," Honeywood said, extending a hand, "you're on the team."

Relief flowed through the girl as she accepted the hand.

"My party's formed," Honeywood said. "Stiggs, Garza, gather some stuff and be ready to move in ten. Cassie, I'll help you pack. Come on, people, we have a way of life to save here!"

Everyone departed in high spirits. Honeywood had no intention of helping Cassie to pack, but nor did she want Valentine to get to her. If he could convince the girl to back out he could still get his man inside. Sticking close to Cassie meant Valentine would have to try his luck with Garza, and there was no way Valentine was a brave enough man for that.

Cassie tried to make small talk while she packed, but Honeywood grunted it all away. The girl even at last understood, and stopped asking stupid questions after about the dozenth. Once the girl was ready Honeywood noticed Valentine heading their way. Cassie went to leave them alone, but Honeywood stopped with her with a simple hand gesture.

"Well, Ashley," Valentine said, "this is good luck then."

"And to you, Dex. God knows how you're going to cope without me."

"Oh I'll manage, I'm sure."

"Any particular reason you want me surrounded by your people?"

"To the point as ever, Ashley."

"Evasive as ever, Dexter."

Valentine lost some of his smile. "I'm looking out for you, Honeywood. Seward ... There may be more to this than meets the eye and I don't want you getting hurt."

"I'm touched."

"I need you back here, Ashley. I can't have people like Seward ruining that for us."

"You make him sound like a gooseberry."

Valentine shrugged.

"You know anything about what happened to his café, Dex?"

"Know anything? No, of course not. I ... You think I did it?"

Honeywood shrugged in mockery of his own action.

"This is a tight ship I run, Ashley," Valentine said, and she could see the fear to his eyes now. "But I would never dare do anything to that man. God, I'd be lynched."

And Honeywood knew then precisely what his fears were. They had already lost Seward; Valentine didn't want to lose her as well. If he lost them both in one day he would lose control over everything. The only difference then was that Honeywood hadn't yet given up.

"Keeps the coffee hot, Dex," she said, "and prepare a feast fit for a hero's welcome." She signalled Cassie to trot after her and the girl obeyed. She might prove a useful pack animal after all.

"You really think you're going to find him don't you?" Valentine called after her.

"The most impossible thing I've ever done, Dex, is walk into a pit with a gorgosaurus and still be here talking to you. Finding a guy in a swamp pales beside that." Valentine did not reply and Honeywood wished she felt as confident as she sounded. But she could not accept Seward was already dead. She did not know what she would do then. Lose herself to the fights probably. It would be all she would have left; she would have nothing to remind her she was even still human.

She had to find Seward for herself. Otherwise she was lost.

Valentine and his precious institution be damned.

CHAPTER FOUR

It turned out that Cassie, whose surname was actually Aubin, proved to be a very handy woman to have around. As the group entered the swampland just beyond Seward's shack it was to bathe themselves in the oppressive humidity which stuck their clothes uncomfortably to their bodies and generally slowed their progress. Honeywood and Garza had been out in the swamps many times before and knew to wear as little as possible; consequently they were dressed in thin trousers and boots, but wore very little above the waist; Honeywood wore a durable lightweight brassiere while Garza himself wore only his scars. The trousers were necessary in order to affix knives, pouches and a firearm or two, while the boots were needed in order to trudge through the marsh. If neither had been necessary, modesty be damned they would likely both have opted to slosh through the swamp naked.

For Stiggs and Cassie Aubin, however, this was not an obvious thing. Stiggs had come wearing light armour, as though the stab vest would actually prove able to deter a dinosaur's teeth. The girl had come dressed in a hardy travelling top and trousers which offered her no protection at all. She was even wearing shoes, which had no doubt let the water in by now and were only adding to her discomfort. Stiggs was someone Honeywood cared nothing about, but the girl was carrying Honeywood's backpack so she had to feel a little sorry for her.

"We'll stop here a while," Honeywood declared after only a few minutes into the swamp. She needed to get her bearings and check the tracks, and she also needed to have a talk with Cassie Aubin about what the hell she thought she was wearing and how she intended to act whilst on this expedition.

Garza grunted his agreement and set down his pack while he went to check the perimeter of their camp. Stiggs collapsed, overheated and already exhausted. Honeywood watched Aubin set down one pack before struggling out of her own, and approached the girl.

"Your first time out of the institution?"

"It's not an institution, ma'am, why does everyone keep calling it that?"

Honeywood could tell the girl was hot and bothered, and likely regretting her choice of attire. It wouldn't cost them much time to head back for her to change, but it would cost them face. "Your first time in the swamp then?" Honeywood rephrased.

Aubin nodded as she sank to the ground. The damp immediately soaked through her trousers to her backside, but it was so humid she likely didn't even realise. Her short blonde fringe was already plastered to her forehead and her long pristine hair was matted with sweat and dirt. She certainly looked a little more lived-in now, Honeywood reflected, if lived-in was a term which could actually be applied to people.

Aubin produced her canteen and Honeywood reached out as it touched the girl's lips.

"We're in this for the long haul," Honeywood reminded her. "And no one's going to be sharing their water with you when you run out."

She could see the girl considering her words, then she stoppered the flask of tepid water and refastened it to her belt. It was the first smart thing Honeywood had seen her do.

"So," Honeywood said, "tell me something about yourself. I've never seen you around the institution."

"I don't watch the fights, why would you have noticed me?"

"There's more to me than dinosaur wrestling, Cassie."

"Really?" she asked dryly. "What do you do with your spare time?"

"Push-ups."

Aubin raised her eyebrows and pulled a face.

Honeywood smiled. For a woman who valued strength over everything else, Honeywood was actually starting to like this girl. "So what do you do that's so different then?"

"I like to read."

"You seem the type."

"Which means?"

"Nothing."

"No, you clearly meant something, ma'am."

Honeywood cast a look about their position, but could see no trouble. "Just never saw the point in books, Cassie."

"Escapism mainly. God, we could do with some of that here."

"Why are you here, Cassie?"

"Because I volunteered."

"I meant why are you on this world. But if you want to talk about why you volunteered, I'm good with that."

"I volunteered because I was curious about life outside the prison. Sorry: institution. Sort of regretting my curiosity now."

"And why are you in the prison?"

Aubin met her eyes and asked casually, "Why are you? How many people did you kill to be resigned to this place?"

It was a subject Honeywood did not like to speak of and she looked away again. "What makes you think I killed anyone?" she asked casually.

"Because you're a killer?"

"Maybe this place made me a killer."

"You enjoy it too much. I've seen your eyes after a kill, ma'am. No one without the killer instinct enjoys death that much."

"Thought you'd never been to any of my bouts?"

It was Aubin's turn to look away. "Maybe I'm here for lying then."

It was as good as Honeywood was going to get, and if she wasn't prepared to have the girl pry into her own affairs it was somewhat hypocritical of her to press her further. "I'd advise you to lose your top as soon as you wise up," Honeywood told her, stretching her legs to head over to where Garza was pretending to rest but had never stopped being alert to their surroundings. She entirely ignored Stiggs, who was greedily gulping his water as though he expected a monsoon in the morning.

"How's the kid?" Garza asked flatly. He didn't care about her welfare, only that she would slow them down.

"Eager to get this over with. Anything out there?"

"Of course there's nothing out there. But the tracks lead further in."

Yes, Honeywood thought. The tracks. When she had first set out upon this search she was certain she would find nothing beyond the edges of the marsh. The swamp tended to look after its own, and if something had indeed dragged Seward away it would not be leaving any visible tracks for them to follow. If she had found nothing by the time she reached the edge she knew it would never reveal its secrets. Instead they had found a spoor; an indication that someone had passed through here recently. Not that something had been dragged, but that someone had most likely walked of their own volition.

It gave her further hope that Seward had just gone out hunting. If that was the case then all this was for nothing. Except that whatever had attacked his café would likely now have Seward's scent, and could well be tracking him just as they were.

"Any chance we could drown Stiggs and get away with it?" Honeywood asked.

Garza grunted. "Don't give me ideas." He turned away from his observations in order to get his pack ready, leaving Honeywood staring through the bog. It was dark in the swamp, with overhanging weeping willows blocking out almost all light as they reached down with snaky tendrils at the travellers. The ground underfoot was deceptively moist, and Honeywood was debating whether to construct a canoe to get them across the worst of it. A million insects buzzed just above the water's surface, feeding or performing whatever mating dances were native to their individual species. From somewhere nearby Honeywood heard the tinny chirp of a frog, but she could see no sign of it in the vastness that was the swamp.

The swamp was far more dangerous than people seemed to consider. Pot holes were of course able to suck a person down in an instant, and at the points where a river or other body of water flowed through there were created rapids. The monsters out in the swamp could take a person's head off – and had done in the past – while they bent to tie their shoelaces. The biggest killer in the swamp by far, however, was the insects. Malaria was not a nice way to go, but out here it was a new world, which brought with it new diseases.

Honeywood was just contemplating death by mosquito when she saw something move in the water ahead of her. It may have just been moss floating downstream, but there was a wake behind it which suggested there was more to it beneath the surface. Her hand moved slowly to her thigh and found her knife, her eyes never leaving the clump of floating moss. It was not moving towards her, however, and came to a piece of solid ground ten metres from her position. She watched as the lithe form slipped out of the marsh and marvelled at its simplicity.

The creature was over a metre in length and was possessed of a long, lizard-like body. As with the gorgosaurus, the tail was long and tapering, although unlike the previous monster this creature walked upon four thin legs which did not seem anywhere near as powerful. The rear ones were longer, meaning the creature's head was kept lower to the ground, and all its limbs ended in a splay of what appeared to be webbed claws. Its body shone with hard scales, while its head was bony and likely extremely thick.

Slowly Honeywood drew her knife.

"Simosuchus," Aubin said, suddenly behind her. Honeywood had not heard the girl's approach, and sensed she was shouldering her pack, trying to get it into a comfortable position.

"What?" Honeywood whispered without taking her eyes from the beast.

"Simosuchus," Aubin replied, finding she had tangled her hair in the pack's straps. "Prehistoric crocodile."

"That's not a crocodile. The legs are too long."

"Lives on land too."

"So what was it doing in the water? Going for a swim?"

"Probably."

Honeywood realised the girl was being serious and shot her a quick look to see she was not worried in the slightest. "The one thing I know about crocodiles," Honeywood said, "is that they're fast critters. Can outrun a jungle cat, and can certainly outrun four humans wandering through a swamp."

"Sure," Aubin said. "But Simosuchus was a vegetarian."

Honeywood blinked, finally taking her eyes from the creature. "You're trying to tell me that crocodile walks on four long legs, lives on land and doesn't eat meat?"

"Yeah. Amazing what you can learn in a book these days."

Honeywood blinked. She stared at the girl for some moments and then a broad smile broke her face. She had assumed Aubin to be weak and soft; she certainly looked and acted the type. She had also assumed that Aubin's interest in books was a useless endeavour. But if Aubin was reading books which enabled her to survive on this stupid world perhaps it was Honeywood who was the weak one. The first victory in every war was won through intelligence, and on this world they were at war with nature itself.

"I think I'm gonna enjoy having you around after all, Cassie," Honeywood told her and picked up her own pack before shoving it onto the girl. "Now get moving. We got a lot of ground to cover."

CHAPTER FIVE

It was a screwed up world, but then it never should have existed anyway. Abe Garza looked heavenward and felt unnerved by all the tree coverage. He was used to seeing the great red eye glaring down at him from its orange and white cloud, and to be cut off from such a thing made him edgy. He should have taken it as a welcome respite, would have believed he would have in fact if asked yesterday; but the truth was he had grown used to seeing that great eye in the sky. It was the same with the whole world. When they had initially left Earth none of them had thought they would get used to these surroundings, but it was amazing how humans adapted to any given situation. It had not taken them long to master their confinement, be it within the prison or upon the world as a whole. Perhaps one day they would even leave, but Garza knew such dreams were foolish. Seward may have sat on the roof of his shack gazing at the stars longingly, but it was a pipe dream. And pipe dreams did nothing to further their lives.

Garza had taken the lead for the moment, and hardly minded. Honeywood did not throw her weight around as he had expected her to, being a big-shot pit fighter as she was. He had volunteered in order to get to know her, and she was surprising him. He had never intended to get to know her personally of course; he just needed to grow to understand her moves, the way she acted and why. He did not care for her as a person, but if he intended to become a better pit fighter than she he would have to learn her tactics. She was after all indisputably the best they had, and if he wanted to be better he would have to take everything that she was and put his own spin on it. He did not like to admit that he was growing to like her, but that was only because Garza did not believe the best way to succeed in life was to make friends. Allies, yes, but allies denoted an ability to help one another for mutual benefit. Friends were people who helped one another for the sake of it, and Garza did nothing simply for the sake of it.

"Damn it's hot."

He glanced at the girl then, Cassie something or other. She was sweating like a pig and seemed to want everyone to know it. She had dressed oddly for the swamp, and her long hair was plastered across her face already. Her top was hardy but not suited for the swamp, and her sweat had all but stuck the thing to her body, revealing curves she likely wanted to keep hidden, otherwise she would have done the clever thing and discarded the top ages ago. Modesty was a stupid thing to have on this world, and Garza presently didn't even wear a top at all. But then he was a man, she would have argued. When the girl fell down dead from dehydration and exhaustion he would be willing to bet she'd wish she hadn't been so vain.

Not that dead people could wish for anything, but that was all beside the point.

The trail was easy to follow and Garza was beginning to wonder whether Seward intended for people to follow him, and if so who? Perhaps he did this every time he went hunting though. After all, he was their only decent chef and he knew if he went missing at least someone would come searching for him. He would therefore need to leave as blazing a trail as possible, and he had done so indeed. From scorched wood, flattened moss and carved arrows his trail was simple to follow.

Perhaps too simple, Garza's paranoid mind warned him without good reason.

Garza thought then about the dinosaurs. It was a stupid notion, and no one back home even knew for certain whose dumb idea it was. There were theories, a dozen people had taken credit through history, but the truth was no one had a clue. Putting this world together from a collection of asteroids between the fourth and fifth planets of the star system was bad enough, but seeding it with prehistoric sense made absolutely no sense. That he was wandering through a swamp filled with long dead monsters was the most ludicrous thing he had ever contemplated. Of course, every schoolboy knew of this world and wanted to visit. But it was illegal to even come here, probably because A) the world was put together wrong and too unstable, B) was filled with monsters and C) had a penal colony taking up half the swamp. This was a world the government used to shove its undesirables, and Garza wondered not for the first time whether there were any other penal colonies across the face of the world.

"What's that?"

The girl again, and this time she sounded positively exhausted. Garza had long since given up caring what she had to say, and pointedly ignored her. She said something else, sounded like she was about to pass out, and he realised too late her voice was frantic for a reason.

Garza saw the thing explode from the swamp before he could do anything to react. It was a huge black form, scissoring wide and coming straight for him. He tried to drop, to dodge, to raise his arm, but his feet slipped from under him and he went tumbling. Which was probably the only thing which saved his life. The huge bullet-shaped form slammed down upon his legs, and while the intense weight of the creature sent a surge of pain through his body at least the maw had failed to rip into him.

The monster crocodile slid back into the water, and he had barely caught even a glimpse of it before it was entirely vanished once more.

Honeywood was dragging him away from the water's edge before he even registered what was going on, and he fought furiously not to descend into shock. Stiggs had vanished, probably clambered up a tree or something, while the girl Cassie was dancing up and down screaming. She was afraid, he knew – terrified – and was doing his head in with her noise. Then he saw the dark shape make a snatch for her from the brackish water and he realised what she was actually doing was drawing the beast's attention so Honeywood could get him out of its reach.

He was touched by her kindness, and his estimation of her went up a notch. He would never have done that for her of course, for it was the act of a friend and not an ally. Still, he appreciated the save nonetheless.

It took him a few moments to realise Honeywood was talking, and talking rapidly. She was asking whether he was all right, if he could move his legs, if he fancied getting up any time soon, and he felt a wash of shame as he realised he was letting two women do all the work. The least he could do was assist in his own rescue.

"I'm fine," he said, throwing off any further assistance. He tested his legs by standing and found no bones were broken. They felt a bit sore, but then he had just had a prehistoric crocodile land on him.

Honeywood released him at that moment and drew a pistol from her belt. The girl had stopped prancing around by this point – Aubin! That was her name – and the crocodile had disappeared. Garza quickly fought through what he knew of crocodiles, which was surprisingly little. He had never needed to know anything about them before coming to this world and since he had got here had seldom ventured out into the swamp. He supposed if he intended to become a better pit fighter than Honeywood he should have been learning all that sort of thing.

"I can't see it," Honeywood said slowly, her concentration on the water. Garza was searching frantically where he stood also, and suddenly the air was cracked by an explosion. Honeywood had fired into the water in hopes of either hitting the thing or stirring it up to action; likely the latter considering how calm she was in these sorts of situations. It did nothing to bring the crocodile to them however.

Aubin was by their side an instant later. "It's a baurusuchus," she said breathlessly, fear having just as much do to with her state as exhaustion. "Or at least I think it was. Anyway, the nostrils are at the front of its snout."

"I'm suitably amazed," Honeywood said. "If you don't have anything useful to say, just ..."

"The nostrils aren't on top," Aubin continued frantically.

Honeywood and Garza were still staring into the water, awaiting the thing's reappearance at any moment. Garza knew crocodiles were one of the fastest predators, knew from experience of only a few minutes ago in fact.

"So they don't drown when it rains," Honeywood drawled. "Now go away. Maybe I should fire again."

"Maybe it's gone," Garza suggested.

"Will you two listen to me!"

Garza broke his eyes from the swamp then to see the veritable pleading in the young woman's eyes. He realised whatever she was trying to say, it was important, and his mind worked quickly through what little she had provided. Its nostrils were on the front of the snout, so what? Maybe Honeywood was right and it was so it didn't drown in the rain … Or maybe it didn't need to have its nostrils on top of its head because it didn't spend any huge amount of time in the water.

Garza shoved Honeywood just as he caught something charging him out the corner of his eye. The baurusuchus, if that was what it was, had a scaly leather skin almost jet black, and ran at them on the long legs of a dog or cat. Its body was bulky, dense, and from the tip of its thick tail to the nostrils on the front of its razor-filled snout it was at least three metres, probably more. Its head resembled so much the ordinary crocodile of Earth it was uncanny, but it had been placed onto the body almost of a lizard.

As with the simosuchus before it, this beast lived and hunted on land. It was perhaps simply that here in the swamp even a land-dwelling creature had to enter the water at some point. Perhaps the things were even adapting, just as well as the humans here.

The beast careered through the space between Garza and Honeywood, would have taken a chunk out of a leg had Garza not reacted in time to shove her out the way. Aubin had backed off, a terrible blank fear to her eyes, her heart all but stopped in her chest. Garza was thankful she had not taken to screaming, so at least he could think, and put the girl from his mind.

The baurusuchus spun to face them once more, its tail slashing about and catching Honeywood a glancing blow across the side, sending her reeling. The thing opened its maw and hissed like a snake or a jungle cat, and Garza found himself completely ignorant of how a crocodile should act; still, he was certain they didn't tend to hiss.

He could run, knew he probably should, but Honeywood was momentarily down and this was his opportunity. This was his chance to prove himself to her, to prove himself to himself. He wanted to wrestle these things in the pit, he would have to practise. And what better time to practise than when in the company of a master of the art.

"Keep back," he told Aubin, for it would not hurt for her to think he was being chivalrous in his defence of her. Perhaps it would win him some favours later on, allies over friends and all that. If she considered him a friend and he considered her an ally perhaps that was even better. She obeyed, not wanting to face the creature at all, and he crouched as he began to stalk the thing. The crocodile seemed to sense he was a formidable opponent because it began to ape his moves, circling him even as he was it. He locked eyes with the beast and bided his time, for if there was one thing he had a great deal of it was patience.

The thing struck, launching all three plus metres at him, and Garza met the attack, dropping at the final moment to encircle the beast with his thick meaty arms. He had long ago heard someone quote someone else about having a lever to move the world, and knew in his training that leverage was indeed his best weapon. His weight and strength didn't hurt either, especially in situations like this. Thus did he put all his weight behind his efforts, and pivoted, throwing the beast onto its back, where it crashed down amidst the marshy ground, and instantly began thrashing as it fought to right itself. Garza knew he would have several seconds before it managed to do so, and drew his hunting knife that he might make a show of ...

Pain shot through his leg as the mighty jaws clamped onto his shin and he fell, dropping the knife, throwing his arms about the snout of the beast. The speed of its recovery astounded him, and his mind screamed that he could not allow the thing to turn its head. He knew enough about crocodiles that their method of attack was similar to a shark. It would grab its prey and twist its head to tear out a huge chunk, or to sever a limb entirely. It would then retreat and wait for the animal to die of either shock of blood loss before moving in to claim the meal.

Garza could feel the crocodile trying to turn its head for just such an attack and clung on for his life, turning his own body with the beast's so that it could not have the chance to tear him apart.

The swamp exploded once more with sound sudden enough to send a flock of what may have been birds flying from the trees. Another explosion followed, and another; then screaming. Garza felt the pressure on his leg ease and he was flung to one side. He landed heavily and could see Honeywood facing off against the brute, firing shot after shot into the face of the animal. One bullet tore through its maw, shattering teeth, and that was the one thing no predator would ever risk. The baurusuchus backed off swiftly, limping slightly and trailing blood. It charged straight past Garza without giving him a second glance and he watched the thing disappear into the rushes.

His chance at greatness was gone.

Suddenly there was a hand being held out to him. He looked up to see mild concern upon Honeywood's features, although now the crisis was over she was returning to her usual stoic self.

"Your leg should be fine, what with the armour you have in your boots," she said.

Garza batted the helping hand aside, wondering how the hell she knew about his reinforced boots, and scrambled to his feet. "I had him."

"Sure looked that way."

He narrowed his eyes at Honeywood, wondering what she had to prove. Did she really feel so threatened by him that she would interfere to this degree? Did she really feel the need to all but empty her gun to prove that he couldn't handle the situation? And how many people did she plan on telling once they returned to the institution?

"Here," she said, handing him one of his guns. It had dropped from his side during the fight and he hadn't even noticed. "You might need this, although I was using it along with mine and it didn't seem to do much."

"It's filled with blanks," he said, snatching it back from her. "Thought it might come in useful in scaring the animals away without hurting them."

"Wow," she smiled sarcastically, "you care for the animals now. How sweet."

"An animal's at its worst when it's wounded," he snapped, "and the best way to avoid a wounded animal is not to wound it."

"Or to kill it."

"Get out of my face, Honeywood."

She raised her hands in placation, although there was still a sneer to her face. "Just trying to help, Garza."

"I don't need your help," he barked and turned his back on her. Aubin was there, more than a little stunned at his outburst, and he growled as he passed her. He could have done without her witnessing all of that as well.

He would not become the greatest pit fighter if he was never allowed to fight. It did not matter to him that he had summed up his foe so badly, that it had almost killed him. That he had needed the rescue was bad enough, but that it had come at the hand of the woman he was trying to outdo was intolerable. It did not occur to him for several hours that perhaps he was mostly angry about his own failure, and the fact that Honeywood had indeed proven herself his superior. It was something to reflect upon perhaps, but at that moment he was simply angry, and would not have listened were anyone to even suggest such a thing. And when Garza was angry he needed to be by himself to cool off. Hang the women, they could do whatever they wanted for a while, but right now he needed to be alone.

There was still no sign at all of Stiggs.

CHAPTER SIX

Ashley Honeywood seemed a very kind woman, but that didn't count for much so far as Aubin saw things. She had learned the hard way that people only ever wanted what was best for themselves and that they feigned caring and understanding for the sake of convenience. Garza was a man like that; she had only known him for less than a day but she could already see what he was. He would use people for his own ends and discard them when something more profitable came his way. Stiggs … well at least Stiggs was upfront about what he was. There was nothing likable about the veritable rat of a man and Aubin kept out of his way as much as possible.

Honeywood however was different. She did genuinely seem to care at least on some level. Which meant she was the worst of them all. The woman was a pit fighter and long used to enticing her prey to the optimum position whereby she could take it down. Plus Honeywood was making her carry her pack through the swamp, in addition to her own, and through this Aubin could see the woman's true character.

The event with the crocodile had been largely forgotten and no one had even bothered to thank Aubin for her knowledge of the creature which had initially saved their lives. Stiggs had come down from his tree shortly after he was certain the danger had passed and no one even bothered to berate him. They just continued trudging onwards through the endless marsh.

Just why Seward would have come this far was not something Aubin could understand. Honeywood had said Seward was likely looking for something to take back to his café, but that just didn't make any sense to Aubin. If he was gathering berries he could just as easily have taken some which weren't so many hours into the swamp; and if he was after meat there was no way he would be able to drag the carcass all the way back to his shack. She was beginning to think that Honeywood was wrong about all this, or at least that she was lying. But then what was the alternative? What else would Seward be doing out here so far into the swamp?

Perhaps he had been taken. It was all she could think of, but it made no sense. No one back at the prison would attack the man who made all their best meals, and so far as they knew there was no one else on the entire world. So far as they knew. She had never really stopped to think about it before, but what if that had not been true? Just because there was a penal colony on this world, it didn't mean there wasn't anything else. There could have been a city five miles away and they would never have known about it. Of course if there had been a city, likely there would have been some communication during the riot and help would have been sent. Valentine had been in charge of the prison for around five years now and they had seen no sign of anyone else around the area. Nor had they seen any craft come down from the sky, but then they had no sensors to detect such. Aubin had no idea how large this world was, but it had been formed of asteroids clumped together so she couldn't see that it could have been too big. Certainly not as big as the planet ever in the sky above them.

Night was setting in by the time Honeywood called for a rest, and Aubin was glad. Her legs were aching from trudging through the swamp and her arms and shoulders were pounding from having to carry two packs. She collapsed as soon as Honeywood gave them permission to stop, and sat trying to catch her breath while she watched as Honeywood and Garza produced materials by which to make a form of tent. Aubin knew enough about the local insect life to realise what a bad idea it was to stay exposed during the night, and figured she probably should start setting up her own tent soon. She noticed Stiggs wasn't doing much of anything, just eating some form of energy bar he had brought along with him. He even tossed the wrapper into the mire, which Aubin found kind of rude.

She felt something on her face then and for an instant thought it might be a splash of blood. Dabbing at her cheek with a finger she couldn't see anything wrong, and then felt something else strike her. Thunder rolled in the distance and the drops intensified. Aubin raised her face to the heavens and closed her eyes. Rain was the best part about this world, for it was always hot in the swamp and it was nice to be able to drench oneself; and the showers back at the prison weren't exactly in the best of shape.

"Cassie," Honeywood said, and she opened her eyes. "You're not keeping an eye out for monsters if you have your eyes closed."

"I'm supposed to be keeping an eye out?"

"Well Garza and I can't do everything, and Stiggs there can't do anything."

It was true. Aubin would not have trusted her life to Stiggs no matter what the situation. "Sure," she called back, and focused her attention on the undergrowth. It was dark by this point, and she fished a light from her backpack, or it might have been Honeywood's backpack. They would have to set up some kind of sonic field to keep the creatures away while they slept, but that was easily done so long as they had brought a generator with them. Alternatively they could just set a fire burning, but the swamp would douse it in moments.

The rain intensified within the next minute and she was beginning to grow uncomfortable sitting where she was. Shifting her weight, she found her foot sinking into the mire, and pulled it out before she could lose her shoe or something. She was not too proud to admit, at least to herself, that she had made some bad wardrobe choices in coming out here, but she wasn't about to lose any of it.

Then she realised one of the packs was sinking into the mire, so she took two careful steps over to it and drew it out with a dull sucking of swamp water. She looked about for drier land, but there didn't seem to be any which wasn't quickly turning into sludge. Even her clothes, long stuck to her body through the heat, were now drenched through and far more uncomfortable upon her than they had been previously. The rain was intensifying very swiftly and she realised she could hardly hear anything above the harsh wail of the wind as it came screaming through the willows.

She looked about for the others of her party and saw Honeywood was shouting at her, her words lost to the sudden storm. It took Aubin too many split seconds to understand just what was going on, but as she turned in the direction she could see Honeywood was urgently looking in horror she suddenly remembered the precise recipe for a flash flood.

The wave of sludgy water struck her square against her hips, the water level automatically having risen to such a level. She staggered under the impact, but no matter how hard she fought there was nothing she could do to fight nature. Aubin felt herself yanked from her feet and released her hold on the backpack as she careened through the suddenly water-logged swamp. She tried to scream out, but her mouth instantly filled with marsh and she choked as it entered her lungs. She tumbled end over end, her mind frantic, for she knew she was going to die. She fought to gain footing, to stay upright, but her flailing limbs could find nothing to suggest she was not in a deep and thick ocean.

Light exploded in her world and she took a single gasping breath as her head broke the surface, but it was only a momentary respite, and once more she was tumbling. Her back struck something hard, she felt rock scrape down her arm and a thousand stings assailed her body as she was dragged across something sharp.

Suddenly she could breathe again and gulped air in a panic, then expelled it involuntarily as her body was slammed into the mud. She could feel the water sluicing across her back, although she had stuck fast in a patch of mud beside what had become a fast-flowing river, and she frantically clawed at the soft surface in an attempt to drag herself to drier land. Rocks cascaded against her legs as they were taken up by the flood and carried downriver, but Aubin ignored the pain. She tasted blood in her mouth and blinked away a dark haze she knew would be fatal if she allowed it to consume her. She knew she was bleeding from a score of cuts across her entire body, but if she could just sink into the mud as she moved she would be anchored.

And then something grabbed her and she was torn forcibly from the mire. Aubin tried to say something, but her mind was fighting unconsciousness and all she could manage was a strangled groan. She felt herself fall to the ground and knew it was solid beneath her. She tried to keep her eyes open, but a red haze was clouding her vision and she knew she had probably taken a head wound. She tried to speak again, but blood and bog bubbled in her throat and her efforts came out a hacking wheeze.

She rolled onto her side and her body convulsed as she vomited half the swamp from her lungs, leaving a sickly aftertaste of mud and sludge. Her heart was hammering, her breathing almost insane, and her eyes were hardly registering her surroundings at all. She knew it would have to have been Garza who had dragged her from the marsh, for no one else of the party had that sort of strength, and as her eyes focused for but a moment upon her saviour it was to see something which did not even make sense.

The creature was not human. It stood in a crouch as though it was examining her, gazing at her with curious but blank eyes. Its skin was a mottled green and ochre, and it was clearly one of the indigenous beasts. But in that single second of sight she had Aubin could see something utterly frightening about the thing. Crouched though it was, the thing stood upon two legs, like a theropod, although its arms were long and muscular, and she could tell by its body structure it wasn't just bipedal; it was humanoid.

"Over here!"

Aubin felt herself being shaken, which was perhaps not the best of medical practises, but it cleared her head and she gradually forced her eyes open. The red haze had diminished somewhat, and she could see vague forms before her. The rain had stopped, and she could no longer hear the rushing torrent created by the flash flood. She felt a flask placed to her lips and she drank in the sips she was allowed before the flask was taken from her, then returned so she could resume sipping.

Fighting to focus her eyes and mind, Aubin could make out the forms of her three companions now. Honeywood was the one who was cradling her in her arms, feeding her from the flask.

Aubin coughed once more, vomited further sludge, and felt her entire body shaking from within.

"She'll be all right," she heard Honeywood say and wished she could agree.

"We're lucky to have found her at all," Garza said. "The current could have taken her for miles."

"Thanks," Aubin managed, her first actual word. Garza had pulled her from the swamp, she knew that much. Only he had the strength to do so, although an odd image formed in her mind of some form of theropod. Perhaps something had stalked her and the noise of the flood or her searching comrades had frightened it away.

"How do you feel?" Garza asked her. "She's pretty cut up, Honeywood. We need to get those injuries tended to."

"I'm fine," Aubin wheezed. "Thanks to you."

Garza managed a reassuring smile. "And here I was thinking you were the one who knew the terrain and all its pitfalls."

"Only so much books can teach you," Aubin said, her breathing slowing at last. Pain was beginning to set in now and she knew she was hurt in many places. She could feel the warm dampness over her legs to indicate she had been torn quite badly, but she couldn't feel that anything was actually broken. Which meant she was a very lucky young woman indeed.

"Hey!"

Aubin realised it was Stiggs who was shouting. Garza went over to see what he had found, while Honeywood helped Aubin to her feet. She seemed to ask silently whether Aubin was all right to move by herself, which of course she wasn't, so Honeywood helped her hobble over to see what they had discovered.

And then she saw it. The odd set of footprints in the mud. She could see it had been left by some kind of theropod, but the impression of the heel indicated something peculiar indeed.

"What makes that kind of print?" Honeywood asked flatly.

"Nothing," Garza said. "Whatever left these tracks, it was walking upright, and by the length of its stride I'd say it was human."

"Those aren't human tracks," Honeywood said, more than a little fear lacing her voice.

"I know," Garza said, and Aubin could see such fear reflected in his eyes. An image flashed into her mind of the thing which had pulled her from the mud, for she knew now it had not been Garza. The curious thing which had watched her and then vanished while she was unconscious. She had thought, hoped, she had simply imagined it, but she knew now she had not. It was real, and it was out there. And whatever it was, it was no more natural than the prehistoric extinct animals roaming the swamp in the first place.

Fear crept into Aubin's soul then as she realised at last that there was more to this world than they had yet discovered in their five years of being free. And perhaps they did not want to explore further lest they find out just what else this world might be holding in secret from them.

CHAPTER SEVEN

The bird was about three quarters of a metre in length, but then it had a long brightly coloured feather tail which made it sound larger than it was. Its beak was sharp, its eyes full and alert, and it looked very much like any other bird which might still be found on the Earth. Its neck was relatively long, its talons sharp, and there was a slight crest, a tuft of fur almost, upon its head.

Stiggs watched as the bird took flight from the branch upon which it was perched, its wings exploding outward in a beautiful spray of brilliance. It caught a mosquito mid-air and landed upon another branch. It had been as though the bird had leapt instead of flown. Stiggs had seen birds catch insects like that before – swallows were a perfect example – but that was back on Earth. The birds on this world were far more intriguing.

"Thanks," he said to the bird. The mosquito may well have been headed for him and his friend the bird may have just saved him a nasty bite.

The bird was known as the changchengornis, or the 'Great Wall of China bird'. When it had lived it had done so in China, obviously, but out here the name seemed somewhat redundant. With so many large extinct creatures roaming the lands, Stiggs was surprised such a thing was even here. Whoever the architects of this place were, Stiggs was grateful for their choices.

Of the creatures roaming the swamps, from the crocodiles to the dinosaurs, Stiggs cared very little. His passion back on Earth had been birds, and when he had first come to this world he had been as depressed as everyone else. But then he discovered his first bird out in the swamp and he had become fascinated. Immediately he had taken up his books to identify the creature, but of course it was in none of them. A thorough search of prehistoric records (which was something of an oxymoron), revealed the bird to have been confuciusornis. It was, so the records told him, the first bird to have developed a beak. He realised then what wonderful blessing he had been given; to be able to see the origins of birds on this prehistoric backwater world.

Since that time he had devoured the archives and sighted several more species. The changchengornis he was observing currently was a bird he had seen many times in the swamp, but it always fascinated him.

There were theories of course that dinosaurs evolved into birds, and that the dromaeosaurids had sported feathers. There were also theories that the dromaeosaurids had evolved directly from lizard birds such as the archaeopteryx. Either theory was intriguing, but both together made for a thought-provoking notion indeed. What if birds had evolved into dinosaurs, which then evolved back into birds? It gave the whole 'chicken and the egg' scenario a whole new twist.

The changchenornis took flight once more and disappeared into the upper branches. Like the confuciusornis, the changchenornis possessed a feathered tail which gave it absolutely no help during flight, and Stiggs could actually see as much as he watched it disappear. He wondered what had spooked it, and heard the dull clomp of booted feet moving through the swamp. He had heard carnosaurs make less noise than that.

"There you are," Garza grunted when he found him. "What are you doing back here anyway?"

"Nothing you'd understand."

Garza shrugged. "Well get a move on, we're leaving."

Night had come and gone and Stiggs had woken early in order to catch some birds feeding. No doubt the others thought he was off for some nefarious means, but he found he didn't much care what they thought of him. He knew he should not snap at people so much, not entice them to hate him, but since he didn't care what they thought of him it didn't matter much how he treated them. Stiggs preferred birds to people, and made no secret of it.

He made his way slowly back to camp. The girl, Aubin, had been washed away by the flash flood, but had been recovered and her injuries tended to. She had managed to lose two packs in her stupidity, however, which meant the others were insisting Stiggs share his supplies. It was an annoyance for him, but had been something he had entirely expected. Had he been the one to lose his pack however he doubted they would have been as forthcoming with sharing their own provisions and equipment.

The camp was breaking up by the time he arrived. Aubin was moving very slowly, placing each step carefully, and was moving with a pronounced limp. Honeywood was securing the tents so they could be carried once more, while Garza was packing away some meat he had cured the night before. They would need food for the journey, of course, but it was water they would be more likely to run out of. Even despite the flood of the previous night. One could not drink from the swamp after all, not unless you wanted a slow death from disease.

There was very little for Stiggs to do so he did nothing. Shouldering his own pack he stayed out of everyone's way until they were ready to go. No doubt they would glower at him, probably make a jibe at his not helping, but their comments would not bother him. He was only here as Valentine's representative anyway, and Valentine didn't want much.

As they set off once more Stiggs noted Aubin was somewhat withdrawn. Having been swept away like she had and almost killed it was understandable. He did not care for her of course, but it seemed a shame for her to be so afraid. Then there was the nonsense of the supposed man-dinosaur which had saved her, the tracks of which Stiggs himself had found and foolishly revealed to the others. Stiggs knew nothing about animal tracks and had simply been worried there was another crocodile lurking around. That Garza should then decide the tracks supported Aubin's near-death experience about a man-dinosaur was ludicrous and to Stiggs's mind Garza should have just said they were ordinary animal tracks. That way Aubin would not now be as fearful as she was and everything would be hunky-dory.

As such it was partly his fault Aubin was so afraid, and while he did not care for her well-being, if it was his fault he needed to do something to make amends.

Stiggs found himself falling into pace alongside her. He did not ask how she was, for she would likely take that as unusual and he would only freak her out further. Instead he decided to engage her in something she knew about, to put her somewhat at ease.

"It's a good thing you read up on the crocodiles," he therefore said. "Otherwise we might all be dead."

"Except for those of us who ran up a tree."

Stiggs shrugged. There was that. "So what other crocodiles should we be looking out for? There are vegetarian ones, ones with long legs which live on land. Anything else?"

For a moment she seemed as though she was about to quicken her pace to get away from him, but then she said, "There's Crocodylia and then there's Crocodylomorpha: crocodile-shaped. Some Triassic crocodiles were tiny, so that's the distinction. Erpetosuchus and gracilisuchus were only about a foot long for instance. They were swifter, would have been like hyenas of our day probably."

"So they were scavengers then?"

"No." She frowned. "Why?"

"Because hyenas are scavengers." She continued to stare at him blankly so he pressed on. "So what distinguishes a dinosaur from a crocodile then?"

"How should I know?" she finally snapped. "I'm not a palaeontologist, I just read up on some of the local wildlife 'cause I didn't want to get eaten."

She stormed off then and Stiggs wondered whether he had done more harm than good. If she was angry, however, it meant she wasn't so frightened any more, which could only have been a good thing. Pleased that he had done his part in her recuperation just as he had done his part in her needing recuperation, Stiggs walked now with his head raised just that little bit higher.

Honeywood slapped him across the back of the head as she passed him, shot him a stern glare, and said nothing at all.

And people wondered why Stiggs didn't like anyone.

They continued walking for another hour or so before Honeywood and Garza stopped to get their bearings. The heat of the swamp was stifling and Stiggs was continually finding it difficult to breathe, although he knew his complaints would be ignored so did not bother to voice them. He could not understand how Seward's tracks could still be visible after the flash flood and knew the two expedition leaders were just taking them onward without any knowledge of where they were actually going. Aubin didn't seem to have realised this as yet so Stiggs thought better of telling her. She was freaked enough about the dinosaur-man footprints they had found and didn't need to be told they had lost Seward.

He stopped to consider that a moment. Perhaps the reason they were continuing at all was because they themselves were lost. Maybe Garza and Honeywood just didn't want to admit it, or didn't want to worry Aubin (Stiggs was under no false belief that they cared one whit how *he* felt). Since the riot they had done very little exploring of the local swamp, and had never ventured this far, so far as Stiggs was aware anyway. He had always assumed the entire world was swampland so there was no need to explore any of it. Now it seemed they would be exploring it whether any of them wanted to or not.

"Why do you like birds?"

Unused to anyone talking to him as he was, the question threw Stiggs somewhat. It took him several moments to realise Aubin was even speaking to him. Her eyes were firmly fixed upon Honeywood and Garza some way off, as though the girl knew they were discussing the possibility they were lost. Perhaps Aubin wanted to speak to him just to anchor herself in what she knew of as reality.

Still, it was true that Stiggs liked birds.

"I don't know really," he admitted. "Every Christmas we'd have this little robin pop up in our back garden, looking for worms I suppose. It was amazing to think that something so small could be so complicated, so engrossing. Up until then all I'd seen in the wild were pigeons, and I'd never seen anything special about them. But this robin would just appear on our window sill and chirp away to his little heart's content. I guess from there I started noticing other birds, then actively went looking for them whenever I was in a different country."

"So you're a proper bird watcher?"

"No," Stiggs reflected. "It just gives me a reason to travel."

"Oh. You must miss home then."

Stiggs shrugged. He had never really thought about it before; there had always been too much for him to be doing for Valentine. Out here there were prehistoric birds, true, but there was no chance of him ever seeing a real terrestrial bird again. "I think I miss that robin every Christmas," he said at last.

Aubin offered him a small smile, which was a disconcerting sight which brought him back to reality. No one smiled at him, especially not attractive young women – and there was no denying that Cassie Aubin was attractive. He realised he had already said far too much about himself.

"We're lost," he told her bluntly, wondering why he had done so. A knee-jerk reaction to getting too close to someone, perhaps. "We're lost and we're likely walking farther and farther from the prison every moment."

"I know."

"You know?"

"It doesn't take a genius, Stiggs."

"Doesn't it bother you that we're lost?"

"No. Why should it? What's back at the prison that's so hot anyway? Maybe out here we'll find someone else. Maybe we'll just find something which isn't swamp. Whatever we find, it has to be better than drawing out our lives in that place anyway."

Stiggs had never thought about it like that before. The prison, or institution as they liked to call it, was their home. It was everything to them, yet Aubin was right; it was also nothing. But then perhaps Aubin thought that way because she was herself nothing. Honeywood was their prize pit-fighter, and Garza was a potential rival. Even Stiggs had his role, and it was a very important one to their leader, Dexter Valentine. Aubin was just a nobody, dreaming of a better life. Well there was no better life, Stiggs decided, and she was deluding herself to think there was anything better for her out here.

He could see she knew what he was thinking, for he knew what they all thought about him. He was yes man to Dexter Valentine, and they all hated him for it. Some were jealous, others simply could not understand why he ran errands for the man. Valentine ruled the institution and Stiggs worked directly for him. That made Stiggs more important than any Honeywood there ever was.

"There's always something better beyond the horizon, Stiggs," she told him. "By the way, do you even have a first name?"

"Maybe Stiggs *is* my first name," he shot back. "Maybe I don't need two. Now, if you'll excuse me." He stepped away from her and saw her face distort as she reached for him. He could not understand the reaction, but suddenly he was falling as his foot passed through what he had taken to be solid ground, but was actually a pot hole. It sucked him down with a sickening slap of wet juices and he threw his arms above him for a reason which eluded even him. His fingers clawed frantically at the lip of the hole, but it was wet and loose and all he succeeded was to tumble dirt upon his head.

Something yanked his arm then and he realised Aubin had managed to grab hold of his hand before he could disappear entirely. He could feel soil and swamp draining away beneath him, sliding down his body and being sucked away below. If she released him he would go down with it, into the world's natural sewer system, forever entombed beneath the swamp. His eyes met hers and he could see hers were frantic so wondered what his own must have been like.

She grabbed his arm with both hands and attempted to drag him out, although her feet were finding no purchase and he could see her sliding all the way towards him. If she wasn't careful she would be sucked down with him, but he wasn't about to snap his hand away to save her. Instead he managed to get his other hand clasped about one of her wrists and he attempted to haul himself up, all to no avail.

Out the corner of his eye he espied a thick root sticking out the side of the hole, and he grabbed onto this, tugging it to test its strength. It held, and with a deep breath hauled against it. With Aubin still pulling, he felt himself slipping out of the hole, managing to rescue his waist at least. He did not stop for a rest, knowing at any moment he could still be sucked straight down, and nor did Aubin's adrenalin rush seem to be abating. Seeing he was coming free, she tugged harder, and with a resounding plop he was pulled free, collapsing on top of her to roll in an untidy heap.

They lay upon their backs for some moments, breathing heavily, their adrenalin burning off slowly. He knew he should thank her, knew she had saved his life at great risk to her own. But she was not his friend, and he did not understand why she had done what she had done. Reflex, probably. Probably she already regretted her actions.

Once he was certain he would be able to speak a full sentence he said, "Where's a handy dinosaur-man when you need him?"

Aubin scowled at him as she rolled to her feet and, brushing herself down, walked over to join the others. Stiggs did not much care what she did. He was alive, and that was all that mattered. People like Cassie Aubin could go to Hell for all he cared.

Still, he was beginning to wish Valentine hadn't sent him on this expedition after all.

CHAPTER EIGHT

When Honeywood was a child she had never imagined she would be spending the rest of her life in a swamp. But then she had never really given that much thought to what she would actually be doing with that life. She had a terrible temper, but that didn't mean she was violent. Most people assumed she was; after, all she was the greatest pit fighter they had ever had. But the pits were somewhere she found she could work out her aggressions, and that left very little room in her life for anger. Once it was drained from her it was gone, at least for a while. Her temper had been what landed her on this world in the first place, and so many times would she sit on top of Seward's café, the two of them watching the stars and wishing they could just go home.

That Seward was dead was not a possibility Honeywood wanted to consider, although it was the most likely scenario. Whether he had gone willingly or been coerced, Honeywood knew they would have been able to find some trace of him were he still alive. That they had become a little disorientated was not lost on her, and Seward could even now be returning to his café, wondering what all the fuss was about.

It was a jolly scenario, and one Honeywood did not believe for a moment.

With Aubin having lost two of their backpacks, however, Honeywood knew they would have to locate a supply of fresh water. It was easy to become dehydrated in a swamp, which was ironic considering how much water there was about them. Honeywood did not want to die lost out in the marsh, face down and breathing in quagmire.

"That's odd."

Honeywood was only paying half a mind to where she was walking and almost didn't catch Garza's statement. She turned casual eyes upon him to find him frowning over something. Instantly her mood changed, her mind became more alert, and she asked, "What?"

"There's a trail here."

Honeywood stared at the hard ground indicated, but she could see nothing. "Animal tracks?" she suggested. "Maybe there's freshwater somewhere nearby and they use this trail to get to it."

"Maybe."

Honeywood had never been much of a forester, or rambler, or whatever the term was for a place like this; she had never cared enough about exploring the swamp. She hated the swamp so much the last thing she wanted to do was trudge through it. That Garza could see a trail where clearly she could see nothing was only indicative that Garza had a greater survival instinct. But then if this world was all they had to look forward to for the rest of their lives Honeywood didn't care all that much about survival.

Garza moved almost more quickly than Honeywood could react, but she saw him lunging for her and parried his arm with her own while delivering a horizontal swing with her other fist. Garza's momentum kept him going and he collided with her, the two of them tumbling to the sodden ground. It was a feeble tackle, and yet as Garza's body pressed into hers she felt a stifling wave of disgust and shoved him off. Garza rolled onto his side, stunned at her swift reactions, and Honeywood rose slowly to her feet, her chest heaving through the sudden adrenalin rush, her confused eyes fixated upon him in lethal fury.

"The hell?" she asked.

Garza stumbled angrily to his feet and snarled at her, before turning away and striding off. "Screw you, Honeywood."

Honeywood's anger was beginning to abate somewhat, and she was aware both Stiggs and Aubin were staring at her. "What?" she barked.

Neither replied, but both were staring at her, their eyes darting to something a little way to her right. Honeywood forced herself to look and saw the foot-long rusting steel bear trap she had almost stepped inside. She knew she should have felt relief, should rush over to Garza and apologise, but all she felt was a wave of anger that she had reacted so quickly, and with such detriment to Garza. He was here to learn from her, she knew that much without even the need to be told, but that didn't mean for one moment he was here to replace her. There had been no indication he meant to kill her to assume her role, and she hated that she could even have thought such a thing of him.

This whole world was messing with her head, turning her into a monster. Seward had been right all along; they really did need to get off this rock as soon as humanly possible.

"Someone set that trap," Stiggs said, which was both true and useful. It was also so blindingly obvious that Honeywood should have realised such already, and likely would have if she hadn't been feeling so sorry for herself.

"Of course someone set it, you idiot," she snapped.

"It's old and rusted," Aubin said. "It could have been put here years ago."

"Could Seward have set it?" Stiggs asked. "We *are* on his trail still aren't we?"

"You have something to say, Stiggs," Honeywood accused, "just come out and say it."

"I don't have nothin' to say, Honeywood."

"You think we're lost, don't you? You think I don't know how to follow a spoor."

"I never said nothin', Honeywood." He raised his arms and backed off a step.

Honeywood took that same step forward, not allowing him to put any distance between them. "You want to lead this party, Stiggs? That why Valentine put you here? Eh?"

"Honestly, Honeywood, I ..."

"Hey," Garza said, coming back to them then. He eyed both Stiggs and Honeywood with the disgusted look of a father coming home to find his two boys scrapping. "If you two are finished, I found something."

Honeywood immediately forgot Stiggs even existed and moved after Garza, who was heading back the way he had come. He made no mention of the incident with the trap, and nor did he make a fuss of the bruise forming on his cheek. However, he did not seem especially happy either, and Honeywood decided against apologising. Garza was a big boy; he could take a few lumps.

"What do we have?" she asked, joining him at the edge of some trees.

"Take a look."

She did so, and could not believe what she was seeing. The swamp continued all about them still, yet nestled upon some dry ground there was a small building formed of wood and what appeared to be woven reeds. It had one storey, a series of wooden steps leading to a seemingly secure door, keeping the interior off the ground of the swamp, and several windows dotted about which were covered with some form of transparent plastic. There was even a chimney poking out the roof, and looked similar to the shack Seward used for his café.

"Seward have a second home out here?" Garza asked.

"Not that I know of."

Garza nodded in silence.

The house, if such it could be called, likely contained two or three rooms, judging by its size, and Honeywood had a strong suspicion that this was where they were going to find their missing comrade. Why he would have built a house out here in the swamp she could not say, and the only thing she could think was that he used it as a stopover whenever he went hunting. Perhaps the entire shack was some form of larder.

Still, there was only one way to find out.

"Aubin, Stiggs," she said, "keep an eye out for trouble. Just in case." She and Garza headed across to the shack and approached it warily. The truth was they did not know anything about this place and could not simply assume that Seward was inside. And even if he was, it was possible he was being held by someone. There were a lot of bad people back at the prison, after all, and after the riot several of them had simply wandered off into the swamp, not intending to stay in the building which had served as their incarceration. None of those people had ever been seen again and it was generally accepted that the swamp had claimed them. Perhaps some of them had survived, however. Perhaps they had had the right idea to leave the prison after all.

Honeywood placed one foot on the first step to test it. The wood held and did not creak, proving the shack was built of sturdy materials, and by an expert hand. She glanced to Garza for affirmation, who nodded back his assent, so she pressed on. She was at the door within seconds and with Garza keeping watch she set to examining the lock. It was a simple catch, there was no actual key needed; but then she supposed it just needed to be complicated enough to keep the animals out.

Glancing back to Garza to indicate she was ready to go in, Honeywood lifted the catch and pushed the door inward.

The door opened to a cramped yet homey room. The lighting was poor, and while Honeywood noted a bulb in the ceiling she did not dare throw the switch. She assumed there must be a generator out the back, although could not hear the hum. She wondered whether the shack had been abandoned long ago, and that the generator no longer worked. Taking a cautious step into the shack, her eyes began to adjust and the details were brought out to her.

There was a table at the far side of the room, two rough constructions which passed for chairs. The room was decorated with two paintings, both chipped and faded, which might well have come from the institution. The swamp was never kind to such things, and seemed to despise art in any of its forms. Honeywood could see a kitchen area, with a section of cupboards. The door was open on one and she saw several items of cutlery and a saucepan, all but destroyed in this coarse atmosphere. Everything in the room was built from scraps of recycled material or torn down trees; she could recognise leather torn from seats and hinges ripped out of other doors to name but two. There was one other door, leading to another room, and since there was no indication that this room was used as a sleeping area she assumed the door led to the bedroom. The bathroom, it seemed, was simply the swamp outside.

"I don't see any food scraps," she said as Garza joined her in the shack.

"No," he said in a tone which indicated it was obvious why there shouldn't be. "There are a lot of animals out there, Ashley. Any of them got wind of there being food in here they'd work their way in somehow, catch or no catch."

Honeywood did not like the way Garza kept making her feel stupid all the time, but supposed she had slugged him for saving her life so let him off this one. She made her way slowly across to the other door and placed her hand upon the handle. She turned it slowly, silently, and pushed her way inside.

There was a crude cot within, formed of a base of wood covered with some form of vines and moss. There was an actual sheet which must have come from somewhere, and several storage cupboards. Honeywood supposed everything had to be stored away so the swamp air took longer to deteriorate it. Glancing around slowly, Honeywood found nothing of interest, and took the lid off a box to find a small stack of well-worn hardback books. Damp had found its way into them and Honeywood did not linger on them. It seemed whoever owned this shack spent at least some time here, however.

"I don't think this place belongs to Seward," Garza said.

Honeywood turned a raised eyebrow his way and he tossed something at her he had pulled out of a drawer. She caught the item and realised it was a woman's underwear. It was clean too, if a little damp, which meant whoever lived here was coming back. No one liked to do the washing, after all, and it was an age-old practice to never throw away a clean item of clothes.

There came a shout from outside, and the report of a shotgun. Honeywood and Garza stared in frozen horror at one another, and then bolted for the front door. They were pretty certain neither Aubin nor Stiggs had brought such a weapon with them, and knew whatever was happening out there it could only be trouble.

Honeywood exploded through the door and was down the steps without touching any of them, her booted feet slamming into the thin mire and bringing her into a crouch from which she was ready to leap into her attacker. She could hear Garza clumping clumsily down the stairs after her, but put the man from her mind as she focused on the scene before her. Stiggs and Aubin knelt on the sodden ground, hands clasped at the back of their heads. They looked a little shaken, but Honeywood could not see that they had been harmed in any way. Before them there stood a woman holding a shotgun whose barrel was pointed skyward. Honeywood assessed her quickly. She was aged somewhere in her forties, maybe fifties, and was dressed in sturdy trousers tucked into her boots. Her hands were gloved, even in the heat, and the material of her clothes seemed lightweight, allowing the air to circulate. She wore a flat-cap which kept her eyes in the shade, and clearly knew well how to survive the swamp.

The woman fixed Honeywood with cold eyes which sparkled with passion. It was an odd contrast and Honeywood decided this woman, whoever she was, really wasn't pleased at the company.

"Thought that shot might get yah attention," the stranger said, lowering the gun so it was kept handy but not focused upon anyone in particular. "Now what are ya doin' in mah house?"

Honeywood could not place the accent and was curious about how she had got here, because she certainly didn't recognise her from the prison. Not that Honeywood was familiar with every prisoner who had left the institution, however.

"We're looking for someone," Honeywood said slowly, truthfully. "Put the gun down."

"Yah don' get ta tell me what ta do in mah own home, sweetheart." The woman was not angry, was almost amused in fact. Honeywood desperately wanted to tear the gun from her hands and beat her around the head with it. "Who are ya'll?"

"My name's Ashley. Abe, Cassie, Stiggs."

"Stiggs? What kinda dang fool name is Stiggs?"

"Who are you?"

The woman seemed about to refuse the question, but decided it couldn't hurt any. "Hargreaves. Sally Hargreaves. This here's mah home and I'll thank yah kindly not to go messin' with it."

"We don't want anything to do with your home," Garza said, annoying Honeywood that he wasn't letting her handle this. "We're just looking for a man named Seward."

"Seward?" Hargreaves asked, a small smile playing at her lips. "And what yah be wanting Garret for now?"

Honeywood's heart skipped. "You know Garret Seward?"

A twinkle came to the woman's eye. "Ah guess ah do, sweetheart."

Honeywood's eyes narrowed and she felt a sudden and intense loathing for this woman.

"We think he might be in trouble," Garza pressed. "We've tracked him this far and thought he might be inside your home."

"Ah take it he's not?"

"No."

Hargreaves shrugged, shouldered the shotgun and strode past them. "Well ah suppose ya'll'd best come in then. I'll put a brew on."

She disappeared up the steps and Honeywood was aware Garza was waiting for some form of response. All Honeywood felt however was loathing and anger; with perhaps a little confusion. She did not know what this woman had to say for herself, but it was clear Seward was not here, and that meant they should continue their search through the swamp. There was no sense in wasting time when they could be searching.

"You coming?" Garza asked as he headed after Hargreaves.

Grumbling, Honeywood followed. She definitely did not want to set foot in that shack once more, yet a part of her had to know the truth. Because if her suspicions were right she wanted more than ever to find Seward now; so she could take up a big rock and beat him with it.

CHAPTER NINE

"Oh, make yourselves comfor'ble."

The shack was not built to house a family, and the air was somewhat oppressive with so many bodies inside. Stiggs sat in the corner, staying out of everyone's way, and Aubin held her tea in shaking hands; it wasn't every day she had a shotgun pointed in her face. Garza and Honeywood were more leery of their situation and kept their wits about them, although in truth Honeywood was wound so tight it was a miracle she didn't snap back and strike the woman across the face. Hargreaves had supplied them all with tea and pottered about, tidying up to make space for them all. Honeywood could tell Garza wanted to press her with questions, and literally bit through her lower lip in order to stop herself from trying to take a chunk out of their hostess.

"So," Garza said conversationally, "when was the last time you saw Seward?"

"Oh, Garret came by 'bout two weeks back," Hargreaves answered with a smile, her eyes distant at a memory. "Thought it might ah bin him now, but it turned out to be you fellas."

"Sorry to disappoint," Garza said diplomatically. "Are you expecting him by soon?"

"He don' keep to a schedule, sweetheart. Jus' comes an' goes when he pleases. Comes through on his hunts and foragin'. Always drops by to say hi."

"That all he says?" Honeywood said with surprising calmness. She ignored the shot cast her way by Garza.

"Well," Hargreaves said with a slight sigh, "Garret does have a way with words, but we don' do a lot a talkin', sweetheart."

Honeywood growled deep within her throat. Since they had entered the shack Hargreaves had removed her hat and her tunic to reveal long curly scarlet locks and a trim well-muscled figure. She was far from what Honeywood would have considered female perfection, but she was ten times what Honeywood was in appearance. Honeywood had always known her own shortcomings in the looks department, but Seward had never seemed to have even a wandering eye. Honeywood had felt herself blessed by being involved with such a man, and now it seemed she had been played for a fool.

"Why ya want him any road?" Hargreaves asked.

"His café was destroyed," Garza said. "Some form of theropod tore through it, possibly a pack. We saw a spoor going into the swamp and we came in after him."

"Mighty kind a ya'll."

"No one tosses a burger like Seward." Garza's attempt at levity did not go down too well and the resultant silence was oppressive. He decided not to do that again any time soon.

"You're not from the prison," Honeywood said, almost an accusation. "Who are you?"

"Prison?" Hargreaves asked with a frown.

"Prison," Honeywood confirmed acidly. "Seward did tell you he was an escaped convict, right?"

Hargreaves looked even more confused.

Honeywood pushed her advantage to the limit. "There's a prison a day or so from here at a march. We're lifers, sentenced to this mudhole for eternity, whether we're guilty of petty crimes or grand larcenies. No one checks on us, no one comes at all. This world's off-limits, illegal to even come here. So we're shoved here and abandoned, with just the minimal staff in guards."

"And they let ya'll out on day trips?"

"The guards are dead," Honeywood said flatly, enjoying this. "Most of them died slowly. There are a lot of killers a day's march away, a lot of fellas with anger issues. Anyway," she said with a smile, "that's us. Where are *you* from?"

"Ashley, this isn't helping," Garza hissed. She met his gaze coldly and she could see he understood the origins of her anger. He wanted to complete the mission however, and she honestly couldn't say she was all that bothered any more. She looked around her group and wondered why they were even all here. Honeywood was tracking her lover, Garza wanted to become a hero, Stiggs had been ordered and Aubin just wanted to get out of the prison by all accounts. But they were all here because they needed their chef back, and Honeywood found she no longer cared much for it. There were other people who could cook, even if she wasn't among them. It seemed a stupid reason for carrying on with this trudge.

"You know what?" Honeywood said, rising, "I'm done."

"Where are you going?" Garza asked.

"Back to the institution. I have fights to train for, I don't have time to be chasing off after idiots like Seward. He's probably back there already, laughing at us right now."

"Well he sure as hell won't be laughing when you find him," Garza said, "so why don't we carry on 'til we do, yeah?"

Hargreaves followed some of this, and addressed Honeywood with a frown. "You sweet on mah Garret?"

"Sweet on him?" Honywood rounded on the other woman and took slow aggressive steps towards her. Hargreaves edged away slowly until her back touched the wall and Honeywood stared daggers down upon her. "You're lucky I don't break your face – *sweetheart*. And you're welcome to him. If you do happen to see him tell him from me ..." Her mind blanked and she found no words coming into her head. It was the stupidest time in her entire life for her to be speechless, and she was fully aware everyone was staring at her. But she could not stop the thoughts flying through her mind, the image of Seward together with this woman, rutting in the bed of vines in the very next room while Honeywood was back at the institution or the café patiently waiting for her man to return. Honeywood wasn't in love with him, she would never have made the mistake of falling in love again; but if that was the case why couldn't she find the words?

She spun on her heel and pushed her way out the stupid stifling shack. Her throat was tight and she felt tears stinging her eyes, but she would sure as hell not let the others see her like this. She was a pit fighter, she had personally beat the living hell out of dinosaurs twice her size; she wasn't some stupid schoolgirl with a crush on the cool kid in the playground. She wasn't in love, she hated the very idea, and had made it perfectly clear to Seward that what they had was just physical.

She stopped at the edge of the swamp and gazed up at the sky poking through the thick veil of trees. She would look at the stars with Seward and they would pray for a release. Now all she could see was the huge orange ball of gas, the blazing red eye staring back at her in silent mocking laughter.

"Screw you!" she shouted, hurling a rock high into the sky. She did not see it land but heard it do so with a dull plop. The great eye continued to laugh at her foolishness.

Honeywood took several deep breaths, her throat still tight and painful. Seward just wasn't worth this, no man was. He wasn't worth even half of what she was.

And she refused to admit that, even in passing thought, she had ever loved him.

"You OK?"

Honeywood had not heard anyone approach, and wiped at her eyes even though she had no intention of turning around. She ignored the question and it was not repeated, and she wished Aubin would just leave her alone. She knew the girl hadn't moved anywhere, however, knew she was waiting as though she was her new best friend or something. At last Honeywood spun to face her, her emotions afire, her every intention to shout out all her aggressions upon the girl. When she saw Aubin, however – standing there nervously, eyes downcast, her entire body language indicating she was herself about to burst into tears – Honeywood's resolve melted and any anger towards the young woman, to anyone, was lost to the wind.

"No," Honeywood said at last. "No, I'm not OK."

"I don't think you should be, ma'am," Aubin said in a small voice. "I think you have a right to be angry and I think you have a right to be upset. But the swamp's a dangerous place, ma'am, so you go and shout all you need and I'll just stay here and watch your back."

Honeywood stared at her in silent incomprehension. She had never given this girl any indication that she wanted to be friends, had shouldered her with her own pack, had treated her as badly as she could; and still was Aubin treating her like a human being. She wasn't laughing at her misery, wasn't grateful Honeywood had at last got her comeuppance. Instead she was being genuinely sincere. Honeywood had no idea what she had done to garner such loyalty but knew she didn't deserve it.

"I think," Honeywood said slowly, "the most dangerous thing in the swamp right now is me, Cassie." She tried a small smile, although it came out more of a scowl. Shaking her head, she sat upon the ground and tossed a stone into the black waters. "God, what a mess."

"Yes, ma'am."

"And stop calling me ma'am." She realised she probably shouldn't have snapped, and Aubin didn't quite seem to know what to do next. "Sit down," Honeywood said, patting the ground beside her. After a moment's hesitation Aubin complied, and looked the most uncomfortable she had ever seen her. In fact she looked a lot younger than Honeywood had always imagined, and for the first time since meeting her she genuinely wondered about her. "Cassie, how old are you?"

"Nineteen, ma'am."

"My friends call me Ash. Or at least they would if I had any. Most everyone calls me Ashley though."

"Yes, ma'am."

The corners of Honeywood's lips quirked uncontrollably and Aubin returned the smile shyly. Perhaps the girl was good for lifting her spirits after all. "Hold on," she said, frowning, "if you're only nineteen and we've been here five years, that means you were shipped out here when you were a minor."

Aubin shrugged.

"What did a fourteen year old do that was so bad they dumped her on this rock to be forgotten about?"

Aubin gazed out across the swamp and Honeywood knew she had hit a nerve. She didn't look as though she was going to cry, didn't even look annoyed, which were two ways she had bettered Honeywood already. She just looked as though she didn't want to talk about it.

"Sorry, I should know not to pry," Honeywood said.

"No, it's fine. To be blunt, Ashley, my father abused me for three years and one day I clobbered him over the head with a table lamp." She spoke so flatly and embellished nothing of the telling that Honeywood knew the girl just wanted to get it out of her lungs as fast as possible. "Did I mean to kill him? No idea. Do I regret it? No."

"Whoa, back up a ... They don't ship minors off to backwater penal colonies for that."

"They do when her father's brother owns one."

Neither woman spoke for several minutes, the only sounds those of the insects chirruping, the frogs croaking and the distant crocodiles sliding into the brackish waters. Everyone on this world was a convicted criminal, with varying degrees of horror to such crimes. Honeywood did not know everyone's reasons for being in this swamp, but whenever she met someone new she fully accepted they were likely a murderer, rapist or just a generally violent thug. It took a lot for a court to sentence someone to this place, or at least that was the theory. Honeywood had learned never to ask too many questions of a person's reason for being here, since she knew it would taint her view of them. Garza for instance was a big, aggressive man. He had likely killed someone, perhaps was even here on rape charges. As closely as she was being forced to work alongside him Honeywood really didn't want to know. It was why she deigned not to make friends at the prison. She simply didn't want to associate herself with criminals, and since there was no one else on this entire world her only alternative was to keep to herself as much as possible. In the pits she fought monsters, but in reality she knew the creatures were at least just doing what came naturally to them.

But what happened to Cassie Aubin was a travesty. The girl needed help, counselling, a doctor at the very least. She didn't deserve to be stuck in a swamp where she couldn't tell at a glance which of her neighbours had molested other girls just as her father had her. She must be living a life of constant fear, Honeywood reasoned, and it was a wonder the girl was still sane, and no wonder at all that she had volunteered to get away from the prison for a while.

"I'm sorry," Honeywood said, the words sounding lame even to her own ears. She couldn't even bring herself to look the girl in the eyes, she was so ashamed of her species. "If there was any way off this rock I'd take you with me, Cassie."

"My friends call me Cass, Ash."

Honeywood hesitated once more. Perhaps the girl was right. Perhaps it was time to start making friends with the right people.

"Sure, Cass. Look, I've been thinking. Maybe we shouldn't return to the prison. Maybe we should just keep walking, see where we get to."

"No one does that," Aubin said cautiously. "Those who tried it disappeared; you and I both know they're all dead. The safest place is the prison."

"And you feel safe there?"

Aubin looked away.

"This woman Hargreaves," Honeywood said with a nod of her head. "She didn't come from the prison. Maybe there are others like her. Sure, this world is off-limits, but since when has a 'Keep Out' sign ever actually kept anyone out? Hargreaves doesn't have a space craft, but maybe someone else does. Maybe there's a whole city of people living on the other side of the world."

"There's no one on the other side of the world, Ash."

"We won't know 'til we look."

Aubin was silent a moment, and finally looked up at her once more. There was a fiery determination set into her eyes now and Honeywood found the sudden change in the girl both frightening and stimulating. "We'll likely be dead within the month," Aubin cautioned.

"A month of living verses a lifetime of prison?"

A slow smile spread itself across the girl's face. "All right, you've convinced me. What about Stiggs and Garza?"

Honeywood had forgotten about them. "They can do whatever they like. Maybe we should just sneak off without them, I don't know."

"They could come in handy."

"Well Garza could."

"I think you underestimate Stiggs."

Honeywood almost laughed, but saw the girl was serious. "We don't even know what they're in prison for, Cass."

"I don't know what you're in prison for, Ash."

"What do you think I'm in for?"

"Well you obviously killed someone. Drunken anger? I don't know."

"What makes you think I killed someone?"

"You're a pit fighter, all you do is kill things."

"Yeah, well that's pit fighting. I never killed anyone, Cass." Honeywood was hurt the girl could have thought such about her, and wondered whether everyone back at the prison thought the same thing. It would explain why people showed her respect, but she had always assumed that was because of her status as greatest pit fighter they had ever had. "I've never killed anyone in my life and I don't intend to."

"So what are you here for?"

"Aggravated assault. Turned out my fiancé was seeing someone else. So I … well … punched her. A lot."

"Ouch."

"Tell me about it. My only regret is that I chose the wrong punching bag. He's likely still laughing at me."

"Wow, you really do know how to pick the wrong guys, Ash."

Honeywood glowered at her, until she realised Aubin had meant it as a joke. She thought about it, realised it was actually quite funny as well as entirely true. Honeywood had never had any luck with men, ever since she was fourteen and her mother had to lock her in her room to keep her away from some biker whose name she couldn't even now remember. She found herself laughing at the memory, laughing at the absurdity of life that every man she had ever been with had cheated on her. Within moments the two women were in hysterics together and Honeywood wiped the tears from her eyes once more, although this time they were tears of almost painful joy.

"God, I needed that," she said, shaking her head as she re-examined Aubin in an entirely new light. "Come on, we should get back inside. Find out whatever this Hargreaves woman knows of the area before we move off. Who knows, maybe she has a space craft hidden beneath the swamp or something."

The two women headed back together, in higher spirits than when they had come out. Honeywood had never intended to make a friend on this trip, and it seemed she had possibly even found something more; it was entirely likely she had found someone with whom she would be spending the rest of her life. It was just a good job she actually liked her then.

CHAPTER TEN

Storming out into the swamp was never a good idea, but if Honeywood wanted to get herself killed Garza wasn't going to go running out after her. He didn't want her to die of course, he just didn't care enough to save her. When Aubin had gone chasing after her he wasn't at all surprised: as unsurprised perhaps as the fact Stiggs had remained behind.

Hargreaves in contrast didn't seem at all annoyed to discover her lover had someone else on the go, but then perhaps she was just a realist. Also Hargreaves may have been at least twenty years older than Honeywood but she was certainly better looking. And if Seward had this little love nest out here in the swamp no wonder he was out here so much.

He did not say any of this aloud of course. What he actually said was, "Any more tea?"

Hargreaves continued to prove the congenial host, but could not provide much information as to where Seward might have been. She did however produce a crude map sketched over several A4 sheets of paper. Apparently Seward had specific routes he liked to travel, had located certain areas where he could find the best herbs. The maps didn't mean much to Garza, but then all the swamp looked the same to him, so he allowed Stiggs to take a look. His reasoning was that Stiggs was so used to doing other people's work for them he would have to have built up a multitude of skills.

Stiggs devoured the maps avidly and muttered to himself while he leafed through them. Indeed he seemed to be putting them to memory, which was a good thing since Garza very much doubted Hargreaves would allow them to take the maps with them when they left.

"No idea where he might have gone to then?" Garza asked.

"He didn' come this way, sugah. If he stopped by the house ah could tell ya which way he headed, but he didn' pass here so ah couldn' tell ya."

"And there's no way to know what he was running out of," Garza said more to himself. "Assuming he even came of his own volition."

"If the dinosaurs wanted him, sweetheart, they woulda jus' killed him at his café."

"I wasn't really thinking the dinosaurs might have nabbed him."

"Yah think there be people out in the swamp? Ah lived here a long while, Mr Garza, and I never seed another soul. Aside from Garret a course."

"I wasn't necessarily thinking of people either," Garza admitted distantly.

Stiggs looked up from the maps. The two men exchanged a worried glance before he went back to memorising the sketches.

The door opened then and Aubin re-entered, followed by an Ashley Honeywood slightly more subdued than when she had gone crashing out. She was distant, aloof, colder than Garza had ever seen her; but at least she didn't appear as though she wanted to tear Hargreaves's head off any more.

Garza could not resist baiting her. "Better?"

Honeywood ignored him and noticed Stiggs poring over the maps. "Do these help any?"

Stiggs offered a mild shrug. "We'll see once we're out there, I guess. Seward's a halfway decent cartographer though; he knows how to record landmarks which won't shift with the changing swamp."

"Hold on ah moment," Hargreaves said. "Goin' back ta what yah was sayin' before. If yah think someone took Garret but don' think they were people … who do yah think they were?"

Garza would have preferred not to have to divulge their knowledge of a potentially non-existent race of dinosaur-men, mostly because he didn't want people to think they had all been breathing in too much swamp gas. Thankfully neither Honeywood nor Aubin seemed about to say anything, so he replied for the group. "I think the main thing is finding him. We can worry about everything else later."

Hargreaves looked at him with a frown and he could see she was attempting to work out the meaning behind his words. "OK," she said slowly. "Jus' don' go huntin' the Swamp Men. Las' thin' I need is for you to make them angry with me."

"Swamp Men?" Honeywood asked.

"'Smy name for 'em. They don' speak, so I can' 'xactly ask them what they call themselves, sweetheart."

"You mean the dinosaur-men?" Aubin asked, more than a little afraid.

Hargreaves nodded in satisfaction that she had gained the truth from these travellers. "That I do, miss."

"So you've seen them?" Aubin asked. "What are they?"

"Whatever they are, they keep ta themselves, chil'. They don' bother me and I don' bother them. I can tell you they carnivores, or omnivores at least. They never taken any int'rest in eating me though, so ah'll thank y'all for keeping it that way."

"Dinosaur-men don't exist," Garza said stupidly, and it even sounded stupid to his own ears. "This world was seeded with prehistoric life. Life that already existed. It wasn't built to house freaks."

"And how did they get the DNA for the prehistoric life to begin with?" Aubin asked.

"Bones, I don't know."

"You can't get a complete DNA sequence from the bones of an animal that's been dead for a hundred million years, Abe."

"I don't know where they got the DNA," Garza snapped, "but I refuse to believe there are dinosaur people walking around out there."

"There was a theory once," Aubin said. "A theory that the troodon would have evolved into the dominant species of the Earth if the dinosaurs weren't wiped out."

"There are theories about everything; you don't need any proof for a theory. That's why they call them theories."

"Maybe it's more than a theory."

Garza could see Aubin wasn't about to let this one go. "Fine," he said, getting his argument into order and raising a finger. "One; why would the pinnacle of evolution have to involve being humanoid? Are we that arrogant as a species to think every superior animal has to look like us? Look at sharks, or crocodiles. They haven't evolved since the time of the dinosaurs and they do all right. Two;" he held up a second finger, "evolution is itself a theory and there's very little direct evidence that it's even a valid one. Three; this world was built by mankind about a hundred years ago. Even if we put troodons here, how could they have possibly evolved into a humanoid state in less than a century?"

Aubin was silent and Garza could see he had her. He also realised she wasn't arguing for the sake of it, but because she was trying to justify what she had seen out there in the swamp and was trying to stay sane and as fearless as possible. He felt a stab of guilt to have thrust it all back in her face like that, but her argument *had* been rather stupid.

"So what do you think they are?" Aubin challenged.

"Swamp gas?" Garza suggested. "We're all thinking it, just none of us wants to say it. Maybe they're people in suits trying to scare us. Maybe there are people out there who found out there's a great big prison nearby and they're trying to scare us into staying there because they're quite rightly afraid of us. Primitive tribes always wear animal skins, right? Shamans wear the skins of bears and whatever, thinking they can become possessed by the animal's spirit."

"So where did primitive people come from?"

"I didn't say they were primitive, I just said they'd adopted primitive behaviours. And it looks like it's working too."

"Whatever these things are," Honeywood cut in, "Hargreaves says they're harmless, and they didn't kill Cassie so I'm inclined to agree with her. I reckon we should just press on and find Seward. If we don't run into any of these dinosaur-men, or Swamp Men, I'll be more the happier."

"You're in charge," Garza told her. "Stiggs, you done with those maps yet?"

"Hmm? Oh, yes."

"Good. Then I think we should be going."

"If Garret comes by," Hargreaves asked, "yah want for me to give him a message?"

"Yes," Honeywood replied before Garza could. "Tell him we'll meet him back at his café."

It was a far more civilised response than Garza had expected from her. Hargreaves also seemed somewhat surprised by it, for she hesitated several moments before nodding. "Will do, sweetheart."

Honeywood and Aubin left the shack together and Garza felt relieved Honeywood hadn't struck their host for continually calling her that.

"Thanks for the tea," Garza said.

"Any time, sugah." Hargreaves smiled. "An' I do mean any time."

Garza managed a quick smile and hastened out. He had a feeling that woman would be more trouble than he could handle.

Back in the swamp, they headed out under the guidance of Stiggs. He had indeed memorised the maps Seward had drawn up, and pointed out several landmarks as they walked. They had not gone far however before Garza frowned in thought of something. If Seward had made those maps, why then was he presently walking around the swamp without them?

CHAPTER ELEVEN

After their encounters with the crocodiles Cassie Aubin was growing a strong dislike of the swamp. Thus far she had been the only one of the party to have seen the dinosaur-men, but now that Hargreaves had verified their existence they somehow became more real to the girl. While in the shack speaking with the older woman Aubin had felt no fear at all; but now they were back in the stifling humidity of the swamp she was once more on edge. It wasn't that the meagre shack would have offered much protection against a determined predator, but clearly Hargreaves had lived in it for a long time so it was obvious the local wildlife avoided it.

Wildlife. Aubin was finding it very difficult thinking of the local creatures as ordinary animals, yet that was precisely what they were. Certainly they did not exist naturally any longer, but they were still natural creatures, in their own era. Which was what made the dinosaur-men so creepy. Whatever they were, there was no way they should ever have existed at all.

It was still daytime, although the overhanging trees cut off most of the light. Night was odd on this world, because it came upon them very suddenly and vanished just as quickly. Aubin didn't know much about astral physics but suspected it might have had something to do with their close proximity to the gas giant their world orbited. Day or night, it was always scorching, and at last Aubin had discarded the heavy top she had been wearing when she had set out. Beneath she was wearing only a thick brassiere, although modesty mattered little when one was trudging through such a damnable place, and none of her companions seemed even to have noticed her veritable strip-tease. All except Honeywood, who had nodded in something akin to pride that Aubin had taken the plunge and done the sensible thing. Garza had started off topless and Stiggs had his head in a book most of the trudge, and she felt angry with herself that she had not taken her top off sooner. It had been embarrassment because of the men which had stopped her, and neither of them even seemed to have realised, let alone cared.

She pondered whether she should ditch her trousers as well and see if that got a reaction.

"What is that anyway?" she barked at Stiggs, not even knowing why she was so annoyed with him. "I thought Hargreaves wouldn't give us any of Seward's maps."

"Oh this isn't a map," Stiggs said as he turned another page.

Aubin glanced at the book then. It was small enough to carry on long treks, to fit neatly into a breast-pocket, and looked very much like a diary. "You're keeping a diary?" she asked conversationally.

"No. But Seward has. Sort of anyway."

Aubin stopped walking, blinking rapidly in shock. "You stole Seward's diary?"

She must have spoken louder than she had intended, because suddenly Honeywood had come back to where the two of them were lagging behind and snatched the tiny book from Stiggs's hands.

Stiggs did not hide his annoyance at the older woman, although knew better than to try to wrest it from her. "It's not a diary per se," Stiggs said. "More a catalogue. Which is why I took it, because it's useful."

Honeywood had flicked through the pages and tossed it back when she realised it was use*less* to her. With a disgusted grunt directed towards Stiggs, as though it was his fault the book didn't provide her with an insight into her (former) lover's mind, she resumed her scouting with Garza.

Aubin raised her eyebrows at Stiggs expectantly and he said with some annoyance, "It's a record of all the animals around here. It seems Seward set out to make a list of all the edible plants and animals, what herbs he could use for seasoning, that sort of thing. Then he seems to have realised he was being attacked far too often for his liking, so he started making notes on the local predators. Like those crocodiles you knew something about earlier."

"What does he have to say about them?"

"Not much. He names them, puts their measurements if he knows them. Their colours, habits, that sort of thing. Even a bit of scientific knowledge. I reckon he must have noted down whatever he could about them, then looked them up when he got back to the institution."

"So he could prepare himself for when next he met them."

"So he could avoid them, presumably."

"I think I can see why Seward's stayed alive as long as he has."

"Hmm."

"Uh, Stiggs?"

"Mmn?"

"If you're the one who memorised the maps, why are we at the back of the group?"

"Because," he said without looking up from the book, "Garza and Honeywood don't trust me. Nor do they like me. They think Dexter Valentine put me here as his eyes and ears."

"And why are you here?"

"Because Dexter Valentine put me here as his eyes and ears." He cast her a queer expression.

"Oh."

"Stiggs!"

The shout came from Garza and Stiggs and Aubin hurried to see what he had found. The two scouts had stopped and Aubin slowed even before reaching them. The oppressive heat of the swamp was well-known for allowing meagre circulation of air, and the thick abrasive stench of blood was prevalent about them. She could hear an incessant buzzing of insects and knew Honeywood and Garza had come upon a body. If they had found Seward their trek would be over, as well as being a tad disappointing. As she reached their side however she could see immediately it was not the body of Seward they had found.

The creature was half in the mire, half on the moist land, as though even in death the carcass had attempted to crawl to safety. It was about a metre in length and had pale green skin, thick and rubbery. The armoured scutes washing across its back had done little to protect it, for there was a great hole torn out of the creature's side where some big carnivore had been feasting. The four flat limbs, all legs, of the dead animal were all intact, as did seem its tail, although that was lost to the swamp now. There was little neck to speak of, although the head was covered with blood which had poured through a series of uniform holes in its throat and side of the head. Whatever had killed the animal had likely launched itself upon its back and torn out the throat, or else pressed upon the windpipe until the thing had suffocated.

"Any idea what it was?" Garza asked.

Aubin shook her head, holding her nose. A wave of flies erupted from the carcass as the group approached, although they knew better than to get too close. "Stiggs is the one with the book."

"Nothing in here," Stiggs reported, not sounding bothered in the slightest. "But then it's not going to pose a threat to us so who cares?"

"I don't much care," Garza said levelly. "What I do care about though is what this creature's natural predator might be. A beast this big and heavy must have been taken down by something huge."

Aubin realised what he meant and nodded eagerly. "This wasn't a crocodile attack. Crocodiles seize their prey and twist to snap the neck. And the way this creature's been devoured isn't consistent with crocodiles either."

She realised Garza was looking at her with a neutral expression. "Think I just indicated that," he said.

No he hadn't, she fumed, although said nothing.

"If we have a dinosaur in the area," Garza told Stiggs, "I'd like to know about it. Especially if it's the dromaeosaurids we think attacked the café."

"Uh," Stiggs said, "I've found something which might fit."

"Hit me."

"Five metre long heavy predator. Marshosaurus."

"How appropriate," Garza grunted. "Is it a pack hunter?"

Stiggs shrugged his lack of knowledge either way and looked up from the book. "No."

Garza frowned. "I thought you just shrugged as though you didn't know."

"Yes," Stiggs said fearfully. "That was before I looked up."

They all slowly turned to see what he was staring at, and Aubin felt her heart freeze. About twenty metres from them through the open swamp there stood a true monster. It was perhaps two, two and a half metres tall, and was unlike any crocodile Aubin had ever seen before. The dinosaur stood upon two powerful hind legs, incredibly well-muscled and rising almost to the top of the beast. Its back was held horizontal so it could maintain its balance, its thick tail held out straight behind it to aid in this purpose. The forearms were small and pathetic, while the head projected forth from an amazingly-muscled neck, swaying slowly from side to side as it peered at the group with its tiny beady eyes.

"Don't move," Honeywood whispered urgently. "Back away slowly and don't run."

"Don't move and back away slowly?" Aubin asked, her terrified mind making her stammer.

Then the creature, returning to its kill, raised its head to the sky and bellowed a mighty, angry roar; and charged.

"Run!"

Aubin did not know who had shouted the command, felt it might well have been herself, and the four of them exploded into action. She did not see where the other three went, did not know whether they had each taken a different path; all she knew was that she was running through the swamp, her feet slamming wetly against the marsh, her heart hammering within her breast, while behind her she could hear the double drumbeat of a stampeding demon.

She turned her head as she ran, could see the thing bearing down upon her, and her body lost its balance. Aubin fell, her elbow striking the swamp, her arm disappearing. She struggled to rise, felt the swamp fill her mouth once more, and was on her feet and staggering an instant later.

It was an instant longer than she had.

The marshosaurus bore down upon her and roared. Aubin could see the physical vibrations in the water caused by the bellow as though the tide was going out, as though even the brackish swamp was afraid of this powerful god of the marshes.

Her feet slipped out from beneath her and Aubin managed to twist her body as she fell, landing awkwardly on her back. She scrabbled backwards on her elbows, her eyes staring out in sheer panic at the thing closing in upon her. The marshosaurus stood barely five metres from her, but did not approach. It took her several moments to realise it was still standing upon the solid ground, while she was in a marshier area. At any moment she might fall farther into the water, where the crocodiles lurked, but the marshosaurus was too large, too heavy, to risk falling in. Keeping to the dry areas, it hissed at her, moving around to follow her progress without actually approaching her. It tracked her with its reptilian eyes, daring her to come to the shore, and Aubin stopped moving, forcing herself to think straight. Her brain was screaming at her that she was going to die, but she was still alive and she had to think quickly if she was going to stay that way.

"Help!" she shouted, but no one responded. Perhaps they could see her, perhaps they had all fled. Either way no one was coming back for her, and she didn't blame them. Of them all it had been Honeywood she thought might have cared something for her, but Aubin knew better than to count on anyone for support.

The marshosaurus took a tentative step into the swamp, testing the waters with one toe. The entire foot sank soundlessly into the mire, as though the swamp was afraid of making any noise which might upset the beast, and the creature seemed content with the feeling that the swamp would withstand its mass. Aubin watched in mounting horror as the beast raised its other leg, like some thirty stone man stepping gingerly into the bath, ignoring the fact that she was already in there.

She looked about herself frantically, but there was nowhere to go. The swamp lurked ominously behind her and she knew she would have to give herself up to it. She would not be able to touch bottom, would have to swim through the thick mire, and knew her muscles would give out within the space of a single minute and she would be sucked down and asphyxiated. Perhaps it was a better death than being torn apart by a dinosaur, but it wasn't a decision a nineteen year old girl should have been forced to make.

And then suddenly the marshosaurus shook its head as something struck its snout. It was a bag of some kind, a small brown water flask to be precise. Its strap caught on the snout of the beast and while it shook its head vigorously to dislodge the thing it only succeeded in entwining it further about it. The marshosaurus roared in annoyance, attempted to scratch the bag from it with its small forearm, before leaning back to lower its head so it could use its powerful hind legs for the same effect.

Aubin watched the entire thing with a mute fascination, not understanding anything of what was happening, when hands grabbed under her arms and hauled her to her feet. "Up! Move!"

And Aubin was running, and did not stop running until she was out of the marsh and standing with twenty metres between herself and the dinosaur; twenty metres of swamp water the dinosaur would have to skirt around.

She collapsed against a tree, sweat and swamp water pouring off her body, her sodden hair falling over her face. She clasped her shaking knees with her hands and felt bile rise in her throat. Her heart was beating with anxiety and a surge of adrenalin now, for her body and mind had yet to fully realise she was even still alive.

She looked up into the face of Stiggs, who seemed equally as afraid as she was, if not half as wet.

She tried to say something, but words would not form and she could only manage a near-incomprehensible, "Wha ...?"

"Seward made some notes," he explained mechanically, and she could see in that moment just how afraid he actually was. "The marshosaurus is allergic to certain herbs, and I happen to have some of them on me. So I put them in my water flask and tossed it."

"That was some toss."

Stiggs shrugged. "Never expected the strap to get caught like that, but at least I can prove to Garza and Honeywood I'm not a useless tosser."

"You saved my life." Of all of them, it had been Stiggs who had come back for her.

"I couldn't let you die."

"You saved my life."

"You said that already."

Aubin threw herself from the tree, her arms encircling this man whom no one liked. Her weakened, trembling body pressed against him, finding stability in his ability to stand. Her lips pressed to his, and she could taste his own sweat and fear. He was too shocked to push her away, and in a moment of indecision they stumbled, falling to the relatively dry ground. Aubin continued to kiss him, her lips clinging to him like a swamp leech, her mind still not having caught up with her senses. Stiggs attempted to push her away from him, to get his own mind in order, but she did not give him the chance. Her fingers worked at his clothes, tearing his shirt from his body, fumbling with his belt buckle, and finally he surrendered and acquiesced.

Across the swamp from them the god of the marsh bellowed in rage, but Aubin could no longer hear the creature over the blinding of her own animal yearnings. The roar was merely a backdrop in the confusing miasma of near-death, survival and ecstasy. Aubin cared nothing for this deity; she was alive and she was living. Beyond that she cared nothing for the moment at all. Soon enough she added her own wail of primal lust to the echoing roar of the marsh god.

CHAPTER TWELVE

She wasn't Aubin's mother, but Honeywood felt a strong revulsion forming within the pit of her stomach once she was reunited with the girl. When they had split severally in their flight from the marshosaurus Honeywood had panicked that her entire party was going to be torn apart. She had struggled to make her way back to the others, although the more she moved the more lost she became. It was an incredible stroke of luck that Garza had been purposefully trailing her, and together the two of them attempted to find the others, and to discover what had happened to the dinosaur. Honeywood felt no small degree of apprehension that Aubin might have been ripped to shreds, and while that anxiety had transformed to palpable relief upon seeing Aubin alive and well, it had settled badly within her stomach when she realised there was a change that had come over Aubin. She seemed a lot more at ease around Stiggs than she had been, they were almost friends. Stiggs said something Honeywood didn't catch and Aubin smiled, even giggled slightly. It was certainly the most disconcerting thing Honeywood had ever seen.

"Just leave them be," Garza told her afterwards. They had continued along the trail Stiggs was leading them along, and stopped presently to get their bearings. Stiggs and Aubin had taken the lead so they could determine just where they were, and Honeywood did not like it one bit.

"Leave them be?" Honeywood asked, not realising she had been so transparent.

Garza wasn't paying much attention to her. He had found a rock to sit on and was busy cleaning his gun. Honeywood had never been one for guns, otherwise she would have known she should probably have cleaned hers also. Why they had not used their weapons against the marshosaurus she could not say, but when faced with such an immense predator the natural instinct was always to run as fast as one could.

"They're not harming anyone," Garza said without looking up. "They're just a couple a scared kids finding comfort where they can get it."

The statement threw Honeywood. She was herself in her thirties, as was Garza. Aubin was nineteen, and she would have placed Stiggs at somewhere in his early twenties. She knew she was older than them, but had never thought to call them kids. Honeywood had never been especially vain, yet Garza's somewhat blasé attitude was forcing home some unseemly truths.

"I still don't like it," she said somewhat petulantly.

"No one said you had to. But you're not her mother. Big sister," he corrected when he could likely sense her glower. Then he smiled. "Grandmother?"

Honeywood threw a clump of mud at him and wished her hand had managed to find a rock.

The underbrush parted noisily then and Honeywood drew her knife in instant fear that something was upon them once more. She saw the excitement upon Aubin's face however and knew whatever had happened it was far from bad.

"You have to see this," Aubin said. "Come on!"

And she was off again.

Honeywood raised her eyebrows at Garza. "She suddenly seem a lot younger to you, Abe?"

Garza shrugged, carefully putting his gun away before starting off after the young woman. "Kids are allowed to be young, Ashley."

They followed Aubin's spoor of excitement and after a couple of minutes saw Stiggs waiting for them up ahead. There was no sign of Aubin, although Honeywood did not take this to be necessarily a bad thing. She pointedly ignored the toady and marched straight past him, and stopped in shock as she entered a clearing.

The area had been cleared of shrubs and brush, anything which might provide cover for a sneaky predator. A small fire had been burning in the centre of the glade, rocks positioned about it as though whoever had set the fire had been afraid of the swamp catching fire. The swamp was not a forest of course, and Honeywood decided whoever had set it had their surroundings confused. There were rocks scattered about for seats and evidence of a half-eaten meal. Aubin crouched in the clearing, studying a plastic plate which had at one time contained some form of stew, although which now housed only a congealed mess.

"Seward must have stopped here," Aubin said excitedly.

Honeywood absently pushed her toe against an abandoned plastic bottle of water. It was half-empty, and Honeywood could think of no good reason for leaving a bottle of water in a place like this.

"This camp was attacked," she said. "Whoever was here had to leave in a hurry."

"The marshosaurus?" Stiggs asked.

"Possibly."

"How far behind do you think we are?"

Honeywood looked once more at the plate of former food. "No idea, but I'd say a while." The swamp had a tendency to rot food at a swifter rate than they were used to, but even without taking that into account Honeywood had no idea how quickly food turned to sludge. She had left a bowl of porridge in her bedroom once for an indeterminable amount of time and it had looked something like the plate Aubin was currently holding.

"Of course," Stiggs said, "this might not have been Seward at all."

"Who else is going to be out this way?" Honeywood asked.

"The dinosaur-men?"

She suddenly wished she hadn't asked, and saw Aubin's face fall. She wondered whether Stiggs was purposefully trying to scare the girl just to get her to run back into his arms.

"Sure," Honeywood said. "And where did they get the plate?"

Garza joined them then. He had vanished about the edges of the camp in order to perform an examination of the area, and did not appear too happy with things. "This wasn't Seward."

"You're sure?" Honeywood asked.

"And it wasn't no dinosaur-man either," he snapped at Stiggs before he could say anything. Garza tossed something at Honeywood. "We either have a problem, Ashley, or a solution."

Honeywood caught what he had thrown her way and unfolded it. It was a newspaper, a Jupiter newspaper, and it was dated only two months ago. No one lived on Jupiter of course, although each planet and its worlds tended to keep to themselves, had developed their own social systems. The Jupiter system had newspapers which were distributed across their little universe, and if someone had picked up a copy which had been printed so recently, it meant whoever had made this camp had not come from the prison.

"They may be investigating why they lost contact with the penal colony," Garza said seriously.

"The penal colony belongs to Earth," Honeywood reminded him, although it did not mean an Earther could not have picked up a local paper along the way.

"Whatever their motive," Garza continued, "someone's come here from the outside world. They came here for a reason, and we have to determine whether we are that reason."

"What if," Stiggs asked tenuously, "they took Seward from his café and made it look like a dinosaur attack?"

It was a decent enough question, and Honeywood didn't even berate him for voicing the fear.

"We should get out of here," Aubin said in a quiet voice.

"Not without Seward," Honeywood said. "At the very least he could lead these people back to the prison. He could give them enough information to finish us."

"I agree," Garza said. "We have to press on. At least now we know we have an enemy."

"Maybe we don't," Aubin said. "Maybe they're friendly."

"Better to assume they're not," Garza said, "and be pleasantly surprised."

What had begun as a simple tracking manoeuvre had spiralled into a miasmic confusion. First Honeywood came to realise her lover was unfaithful, and now they had discovered he may have been taken by off-world visitors. On top of all the creature attacks she was beginning to regard this as a very bad trip after all.

They set off once more, leaving the camp just as they had found it. If whoever had made it had been scared off by dinosaurs and returned to the camp they would find no evidence of Honeywood and her party having tramped through. Stiggs once more pointed the way, and this time Honeywood made him walk ahead of them. She kept Aubin by her side, allowing Garza to keep an eye on their untrustworthy cartographer. Garza understood Honeywood's reasoning, even if he did not agree with it, and obeyed her instruction. Aubin, for her part, did not seem to realise just why Honeywood was keeping her as far from Stiggs as possible.

"If we can find this person," Honeywood told her, "we're likely going to discover it's a scout and that there are a whole lot more people waiting in orbit."

Aubin shrugged.

"I'm going to try to convince them," Honeywood said, "to take you with them."

Now Aubin looked at her, and there was more than a hint of curiosity to her eyes. "Why?"

"Because you've done nothing wrong, and you don't deserve to grow up in a penal colony. You were convicted as a child for having had a crime committed upon you, and you shouldn't be here."

"No, I meant why do you care what happens to me?"

It was a good question, and Honeywood wasn't about to get soppy with the girl. "We're all here because we've done bad things, Cassie. Maybe we deserve to be here, maybe we don't; but the crux is we've all broken the law. You haven't."

"I know that," she said rather innocently. "And that's not what I asked. Ash, why do you care what happens to me?"

"What, because I'm a pit fighter I don't get to care about people once in a while? I've hardened myself, Cassie. Surrounded by criminals it's all I can do. But if I can get you off this world I'll do it. Whatever I have to do, I'll do it. The rest of us they won't take with them, but maybe I can talk your way out of this."

"Oh. Well, thanks, I guess. But they're not gonna much care, Ash. I was put here, same as you. If anyone cared about us a patrol would have been by by now. There are no records of our even existing, otherwise someone would have come looking. And if there are no records, no one's going to believe you, whatever you have to say. Whether I like it or not I *have* grown up here. And I'm gonna die here too, you know. I'm resolved to that, or at least I've accepted it. Maybe you should too."

She did not speak with hostility, remorse or any negative inflection at all. Hers was the most mature viewpoint Honeywood had ever seen in this place, and the older woman found she could learn a lot from her. Perhaps they all could.

"I wish I had your resolve, Cassie."

Aubin grinned, punched her lightly on the shoulder as they walked. "Maybe I can teach you. Tell you what, we'll make a game of this. Whoever can find out what Garza was sent down for has to do the other's laundry when we get back to the institution."

Honeywood could not deny she had long wondered what Garza had done. "What about Stiggs?"

"Oh he's easy. He killed someone."

"How do you figure that?"

"He told me when we were alone, looking for you guys. He's insecure, the way I see it. Likes for people to think something of him, but lacks the self-esteem to think anything of himself. He likes to do things for people because it makes him feel as though they'll like him more. He just fell in with the wrong people and ended up killing someone to try to fit in. Turns out he was fitted up for the murder and sent here. He just didn't learn his lesson and fell in with Valentine, went right back to his old habits. I guess it was easier for him than coming out of his shell, especially when surrounded by violent criminals."

Honeywood blinked. "He told you all that?"

"No. I figured out all the psychological stuff from what he did tell me though. Wasn't hard. He just needs someone to like him for who he is and he'll be fine."

"He's also willing to murder people in order to be liked, Cassie. You have to be careful with someone like that."

"I'm careful, Ash."

"Really?"

"Yeah." She seemed uncomfortable to talk further so Honeywood dropped the subject. The girl may have a more mature attitude than most people Honeywood presently knew, but in some things it seemed she was still every bit the adolescent she appeared. It was sad to think Aubin had to choose prospective lovers from the detritus that existed on this world; sadder still to consider that maybe she had even managed to pick someone who wasn't as bad as some of the others.

It was a sobering thought, and one which drove Honeywood with even greater determination to make sure Aubin left with whoever had come down to the surface of this Godforsaken world. Cassie

Aubin would not die here, that much Honeywood promised herself. No matter what it took, she would have a proper life somewhere else.

CHAPTER THIRTEEN

The heat was beginning to get truly oppressive now, although there was little more in the way of clothes that Garza could remove. His naked torso was grimy with swamp, sweat and dust; and his legs were itching from a thousand insect bites. He was trying not to say much to his companions because he knew how grumpy he got when he was too hot. He didn't much care what any of them thought of him, but Honeywood was liable to snap right back at him and he could do without a slanging match. It was bad enough the woman had turned all maternal on Aubin, but Garza certainly had no desire to watch. He was just glad Honeywood still hated Stiggs, although he was certain that given a few more days she would come around to liking even him. At which point Garza would likely shove his own head into the swamp and end all his misery.

He kept Stiggs in sight ahead but made no attempt to catch up to him. That Stiggs was reading Seward's maps and notes was good enough for him; for while he did not trust the little weasel of a man at all, so long as he was reading the map for them he was proving himself of some use.

He could sense the two women falling further and further behind, or maybe Stiggs was moving further and further in front, and debated on whether he should go back to hurry them up a bit. The last thing he wanted to get in between however was their girlie chat, so just kept at his own pace as he trudged through the swamp. He had long aspired to be Honeywood, to have everything she had. The more time he spent with her however the more he realised what a milksop she was. In the pits she was fierce, determined, merciless; while in reality she was every bit the woman. He had always been attracted by her power, and it was with a certain desirability that she would dispatch each and every monster thrown against her. It was far from sexy of course, but her movements, her grace, her strength … it all added up to something incredibly attractive. The reality of her though was that she was just an ordinary person who coped well in times of high stress combat. There was very little he could learn from her aside from mental control.

With a grunt of annoyance he realised he had allowed his mind to wander, and now he could see no sign of Stiggs. Nor could he hear any indication that the two women were even behind him any longer. That he had wandered off in the wrong direction was probable, and he began to trace his trail that he might rejoin theirs. It wasn't anything to panic about, since any idiot could read a trail, but it was somewhat annoying to have allowed his mind to walk away with him, quite literally.

Following his footsteps back, however, he froze. He could see his boot prints in the soft mud, left only a minute earlier, yet there was something overlapping them: a trail of prints which had been left in his wake. They were familiar tracks, for he had seen the strange prints before, and he knew them to belong to the creature, whatever it was, that had dragged Aubin from the flash flood. More disconcerting was the fact the two paths did not actually cross; instead the tracks overlapped. The creature had not just moved across his trail therefore. The thing was following him.

Instantly Garza became more alert to his situation, lost and alone as he was, although aside from a slight tensing he allowed no indication to show that he had noticed he was being followed. The creature was likely watching him even now, and if he reacted adversely here it would likely leap out and attack immediately. He needed to play this carefully, and use his one advantage: his superior intelligence.

Garza continued to retrace his steps, his every sense alert and ready to react to an instant's attack. He had not gone a further ten metres however when he stopped and stared in abject horror. His tracks were no longer there: they had been purposefully wiped clean.

His gun came to his hand in that instant, his other hand producing his hunting knife. Garza had never been especially good with a firearm, yet the noise of its firing would alert the others and with any luck bring them running. He held off firing that shot, however, not knowing in which direction the enemy actually lay.

Suddenly it was before him. There was no rustling of bushes, no sucking of mud, no scent even to indicate its approach. It was simply standing there on the path behind him. Garza stared at the creature and any doubt of young Aubin's wild tales died instantly within his wide eyes.

The creature stood at around seven feet. It was thin and lean and walked directly upon two legs, with a vertical straight spine. Its legs were long and thin, its arms shorter than a human being's, ending in hand-like claws bearing opposable thumbs. The thing wore neither clothes nor armour, although its slick dark green body appeared to glisten with what may have been a tough leathery hide, may have been a plating of scutes. The chest was broad and powerful, and appeared very much human to Garza's eyes. Its head was the shape of a man's, for it bore no snout, although its lipless mouth revealed a row of razor predator's teeth. Its nose was formed of two simple nostril slits, while its eyes were large and almost luminous, and clearly it was well adept at nocturnal hunting.

None of that, however, even began to explain the most shocking aspect of this beast. For held comfortably in its two hands, and pointing towards the floor, there was a rifle.

Garza blinked in astonishment. There were theories put forward in the twentieth century that if the dinosaurs had not become extinct they would have evolved. No one knew of course just why the dinosaurs died, and there were a thousand theories abound throughout the solar system. It was an age-old question and even after the generally-accepted theory of the meteorite was at last debunked, still was there nothing concrete to fall in its place. Whatever had killed them was irrelevant, however, for the theory Garza was presently more interested in was the one concerning the troodon. He didn't believe it, had said as much earlier, yet with a human-like dinosaur standing armed before him he could theorise nothing which even came close. But the troodon wasn't even all that clever to begin with. It may have possessed problem-solving capabilities, but that was a far cry from computing algebra equations in your head.

Still, what stood before him was clearly some form of evolved dinosaur in the shape of a man.

This world was constructed by humans, though. As he had argued before, there had not been the necessary time for this thing to have evolved. That meant it had either been placed here at the world's creation, or it had been put here since. Either way mankind had placed this creature here, which meant mankind had created it to begin with. The beast was an experiment, then; something created in a laboratory. It was the only explanation which made any kind of sense.

But why would someone want to create a humanoid dinosaur? To prove centuries' old stupid theories correct? It didn't seem likely.

The creature stared at him stupidly and slowly its claws clacked down upon the rifle as though it was tapping out a rhythm.

Garza decided he had nothing at this point to lose by attempting communication.

"So, come here often?"

The creature did not so much as crack a smile. It had been worth a try.

"My name's Abe Garza," he tried again, trying not to speak loudly and slowly like a typical Englishman on holiday in a foreign country. "Do you have a name?"

The creature continued to stare.

"You saved the life of my companion," he thought to remind the thing; he could not even tell the sex of the creature. "Thank you for that."

Silence.

"Do you live around here? I met a woman who says you don't harm anyone, just go about your daily business without bothering her."

More silence.

"I don't mean you any harm, my friend."

The creature slowly raised the rifle and Garza tensed. The weapon was pointed directly at him now and Garza could see whatever this creature was it had been trained in the art of warfare. What its creators had had in mind Garza could not say, but he was getting a fairly good idea the more time passed.

"I'm not your enemy," Garza promised, backing away slowly.

The rifle was brought up to its shoulder.

Garza flicked his hunting knife through the air, the blade somehow making contact and taking the creature through the shoulder. It screamed, snapping about and dropping its weapon. An arc of crimson blood shot through the air, and Garza stared dumbly as though having expected the blood to be green or something. His petrification lasted bare seconds however and he realised if he wanted to live he would have to run.

Turning, he charged through the undergrowth in what he believed was the general direction in which he had come. Thrusting his arms up before him he simply ran, heedless of the branches tearing into his naked flesh. The terrible angry wails of the wounded creature carried him onwards, and echoed throughout the swamp as though it was communicating with the trees, telling them to slow him and cut him deep.

Garza all but fell into a glade and saw movement ahead of him. He fell into Honeywood, who cast a frown to the underbrush behind him. Stiggs and Aubin were rushing up to see what all the commotion was about, although as Garza collapsed in a breathless heap it was to see he was not being pursued at all.

"What was it?" Honeywood asked, drawing her own knife as though it would do her any good. "Marshosaurus?"

Garza fought to get his breathing under control and didn't speak until he knew he would be able to string a few words together. His heart was racing, but now he was relatively safe his adrenalin was levelling off and he was having trouble concentrating. "Aubin was right."

Aubin's face turned ashen.

"Thing's not natural," Garza said, taking a deep breath. "Had a weapon."

"You mean like a club?" Honeywood asked fearfully.

Garza shook his head soundly. "Rifle. Human rifle."

"It took it then," Honeywood decided. "Saw it and stole it."

"Was trained how to use it." Garza was at last finding he could speak properly. "It was trained, Ashley. Whatever's going on here, we don't want to get messed up in it."

Honeywood's eyes had never once left the path Garza had taken, although now she slowly nodded. "We need to press on," she determined. "We need to find Seward and get back to the prison. Valentine can put some people on this to investigate. Whatever's happening Valentine will be at the bottom of it by the end of the month."

"Have a feeling," Garza said, "we might all be dead by the end of the month."

It was not something they could do anything about, however, so Honeywood chose to simply get on with the mission. Garza had to respect that about her, but then she hadn't yet come face-to-face with that creature. It was all right to be blasé about the thing, but the fact was none of them knew what they were up against here. It was as though the world was against them, punishing them for venturing too far into the swamp.

Casting one final look into the underbrush Garza wished he had never volunteered for this assignment in the first place. Perhaps he didn't want to be the next Ashley Honeywood after all. Not if it was going to cost him his sanity, or his life.

At a quickened pace they moved off, farther into the unknown; into the territory of the dinosaur-man.

CHAPTER FOURTEEN

Dinosaur-men were simply something Honeywood didn't want to think about. To a layman they sounded an entirely ludicrous idea, a sentiment with which any decent palaeontologist would have agreed. Most of the population of their world however were neither; they were people who had to live with monstrous creatures lurking outside their home every day of their lives. Most people at the institution never left the grounds, never had to even consider what kind of animals were roaming the world. Many people didn't even venture out to Seward's café. For people like Honeywood, who either did venture out on occasion or simply wanted to know how to survive should they wish to, dinosaurs were a reality. Accepting there were ten tonne lizards living in the swamp was far different however to believing in the existence of man-like dinosaurs. Man-like dinosaurs trained in the art of wielding firearms took her straight back to the ludicrous.

Yet that was the situation in which they found themselves, and Honeywood hated this stupid world more and more. As they broke into a clearing she cast her eyes skyward to the great orange orb spattered with swirling red gases and its single massive all-encompassing eye. They often joked the thing was their god, and yet this was the first time Honeywood was actually starting to seriously consider such a thing. After all, it could not have been more foolish than accepting the existence of gun-toting dinosaur-men.

Evening was setting in by this time, and Honeywood knew from long experience just how quickly night could fall. They should probably start looking for somewhere to make camp, although she wanted to be on the trail of Seward again by first light. The sooner they could get out of the swamp the better. Stiggs was ahead of their party, examining Seward's diary, his map firmly locked within his head. Garza had proved of especial use in tracking Seward's spoor, and Honeywood found herself pleasantly surprised by her feelings towards him. At first she had expected to resent him, but he was calm, professional and knew not to let his mouth run away with him. That he was learning from her was obvious, although Honeywood didn't mind the competition. People never fought one another in the pits, just animals, and Honeywood didn't care to be the number one pit fighter. That she was didn't mean that much to her, and if Garza could steal some of the limelight he was welcome to it.

Watching him scout the area, his muscled naked torso glistening with sweat in the fading light, she wondered whether he was seeing anyone. After all, if she was finished with Seward it meant she was single again.

But was she finished with Seward? They may have been lovers, but neither had ever really declared their love for the other. They didn't whisper sweet nothings in the other's ear, didn't give the other expensive gifts, didn't embrace at all unless it was during the act of love-making. They were more sexual partners than lovers, and just because Seward had strayed during their relationship it was no reason to fault him for it. Maybe he just assumed she had been doing the same. It wasn't as though they were married or anything.

It was something she could take up with Seward once she found him. A part of her wondered whether not finding him at all would actually make things a lot easier in her mind.

"Something's been through here recently," Garza said, coming to join her then.

"Hostile?"

"No. And not a dinosaur-man either, thank God. Some form of ceratops I figure, but I'm no expert. Ran through about half an hour age and headed off in that direction."

Honeywood glanced to where he was waving, but it wasn't the direction in which they had come or the direction they were going so she didn't think much about it. Herbivores were only dangerous if they had young to protect or if they were themselves attacked first, so if one had wandered through recently it didn't mean much to her.

"Anything else?" she asked.

Garza shook his head.

"Then we should set the tents and see about getting some sleep." They had a few provisions remaining, although with two of their packs lost they had been forced into strict rationing. Honeywood had little appetite in this oppressive heat anyway, and her mind was too anxious about dinosaur-men to consider much about eating. She glanced to where Aubin was hanging back, looking at the trees nervously as though she feared pursuit. "Do me a favour, Abe," Honeywood said softly. "Stay close to her. All this has spooked her."

"Ashley Honeywood taking an interest in another human being? What would Valentine say?"

"He'd probably throw her in the pit and take bets on how long I could protect her from a megalosaurus."

Garza smiled tightly. "Wish you were joking. Don't worry, I'll keep an eye on her."

Honeywood reflected once more just how wrong she had been about Garza. While she doubted he was a nice guy – no one on this world was nice – he certainly had a softer side to him. She watched as he carefully approached Aubin, although Honeywood could not hear the words. Whatever he was saying, it calmed the girl somewhat, and within the space of a minute she had smiled and even chuckled at something. Honeywood was pleased something was going right at least, although she had a sudden sobering thought that the only reason Garza was being so nice to the girl was because he was trying to get in Aubin's pants. Aubin was certainly the youngest person in the entire colony, the only teenager in fact, and instantly did Honeywood become protective of her all over again.

Still, it was something to be dealt with later. There was no way Garza would try anything while they were all out here together in the swamp.

She moved over to where Stiggs was still studying the book he had taken from that Hargreaves woman. Stiggs was a good thirty metres from the others, and as she approached Honeywood had time to reflect upon him also. She still didn't like him, and wouldn't pretend she did, but whatever Valentine had put him among them for, he hadn't hampered their progress in any way. Likely Valentine just wanted someone to keep an eye on things; maybe he intended to make a documentary out of their adventure and present it before Honeywood's next pit fight.

"We're bedding down," she told Stiggs as she reached him.

"Oh. Thanks."

She shrugged and went to turn away, although asked instead, "Anything useful in that book? You don't ever seem to keep your nose out of it."

"Useful? Not sure. Interesting though. Did you know there's a diceratops? It's like a triceratops, but with only two horns."

"That could be what wandered through here."

"Hmm?"

"Garza found tracks."

"Oh. What did the tracks tell him?"

"That a certatops came through."

"Well, obviously. I meant what else did they tell him?"

"What else *could* they tell him? He said an animal ran through here about half an hour ago, what more do you need?"

"Excuse me, did you say run?"

"Yeah. Why?"

"Have you ever seen a ceratops?"

Honeywood thought back. She had never seen one in the flesh, but everyone knew what a triceratops looked like, with its bony crest, three horns, sharp beak and big lumbering body. "So what?"

"So what? Honeywood, ceratops are large herbivores. They're like rhinos or elephants. When was the last time you saw an elephant run?"

"When it was charging something?"

"Or?"

Honeywood's face fell. "When it was running away."

"How sure is Garza that the creature came through half an hour ago? And more importantly did he find any tracks following it?"

There had been no second set of tracks. Which meant if the creature was indeed running away from something, its pursuer had yet to appear.

"Uh, Honeywood?"

"What?"

"That depression you're standing in?"

Honeywood looked to the ground, and slowly brought her eyes up. The ceratops tracks continued behind her, and ahead she could see their origins, where they had sprung from the trees before her. And standing silent just beyond those trees she could see a large form several metres tall, five metres in length, staring straight back at her.

"Hell," she muttered.

Stiggs snapped around and emitted a shrill shriek at the sight. The marshosaurus stepped from the trees, keeping its head low, its powerful tail raised as it centred upon its prey. It stood barely ten metres from their current position, and Honeywood doubted her meagre weaponry would have any effect on such a beast. She did not take her eyes from it, did not dare blink, and did not move in the slightest.

"Ashley!" Garza shouted. "Don't move!"

She doubted Garza had any greater plan than that, but then that was just as far as her own stretched. "Abe, run," she said without shouting, although knew he would be able to hear. "Get Cassie out of here, now."

"There might be something we can do."

"Like what?" She tried not to shriek, did not want to alarm the dinosaur in the slightest, although her heart was pounding so hard she could feel it attempting to explode out of her breast and Garza saying stupid things to her wasn't helping matters any. "Just get Cassie out of here."

"I'm coming back."

She wouldn't be here when he came back, but it was the thought that counted.

The marshosaurus took a single step towards her and Stiggs, its unblinking, coldly calculating eyes focused upon them both. It was trying to provoke a reaction, she knew. It wanted to know what they would do. There were two of them and perhaps it was hungry enough that it wanted to make sure it got both of them. It went against everything she knew about predators, who would focus on one single target and make every effort to bring that one down; but perhaps dinosaurs had a completely different way of thinking. Maybe it was what helped them to extinction in the first place.

She could hear Stiggs shaking beside her and hissed at him not to run. Of course if he did, the beast would go after him and she would be free to make her own mistake, but it didn't matter how much she didn't like the man; she wasn't about to leave him to be torn apart by this creature.

In an instant Stiggs was running and Honeywood barely managed to force herself from giving chase. The marshosaurus seized the opportunity and snapped at him with its massive jaws and Honeywood knew there was nothing more she could do for the annoying little yes man.

The dinosaur, however, was not giving pursuit: it had simply taken an experimental snap at him in passing. Slowly did the creature turn its cold, reptilian eyes back upon Honeywood and she realised it had indeed been waiting for one of them to run. Not to chase that one, however, but to determine which was actually petrified.

Honeywood felt her heart all but stop within her chest.

With a roar the monster came for her and something in Honeywood's mind snapped. The seasoned pit fighter took over, reminded her that she had faced such creatures as this many times before. This time she wasn't encased in a metal suit, but it would not stop her brain from deciding it wanted to fight rather than simply stand there and meekly die.

With a primal roar of her own Honeywood charged the behemoth, and in two strides it was upon her. Dropping, throwing herself into a roll, Honeywood somehow managed to evade its lethal claws and came out behind the thing in one piece. She knew the clever thing to do would be to keep running, but her mind had all but turned to soup in her terrified haze, and instead she turned to face the monster once more, screaming at the top of her lungs, adrenalin burning, passion flaring. She was queen of the pits; she could take on the world.

The dinosaur turned to face her, its thick tail slapping audibly across her face: the sound of a thunderclap echoing eerily through the swamp. Honeywood flew through the air, twisting several times before slamming into the ground. Lying on her face, fire coursing through her body, Honeywood's adrenalin rush had been purged, leaving her only wondering what the hell she thought she was doing.

The swamp was filled with the victorious howl of the marshosaurus and Honeywood fought to raise her bleeding face from the sodden mire. The creature was facing her, but gone was all of its posturing as it closed in upon her, dropping its mandible to tear her apart.

And then it stopped as another sound engulfed the swamp. The steady repeat of miniature explosions. Honeywood's tired mind fought to make sense of what was happening, but the dinosaur was paying only half attention to her now. It wanted to devour her, but every few moments something seemed to be biting into its flesh; perhaps a handy swarm of mosquitoes had moved in.

She saw him then; Stiggs had returned for her, was standing twenty paces away and holding two pistols. His aim was terrible, but it wasn't difficult to hit the side of such a monster, and he was systematically firing shots from each of the guns in alternation. It was an odd sight which her mind was refusing to register, and it took her a few more moments for her to realise he was shouting at her.

'Get up' probably.

Honeywood tested her limbs, found them all in working order, and struggled to her feet. The dinosaur had forgotten her entirely now, concentrating instead upon the annoyance that was Stiggs. He backed off a couple of steps – who wouldn't? – and Honeywood fought for some way to help him. She pulled her own pistol, but it had been bent out of shape by the striking tail, and she tossed it aside. All she had left was her hunting knife, and she couldn't see it doing much against such a monstrosity.

Then she saw Stiggs had dropped one of his pistols and had pulled free a grenade. That Stiggs had come so armed didn't surprise her at all, and she watched with a calm detachment as he hurled the thing. It sailed through the air and Honeywood could not help but wonder whether it would even do any good.

Then she realised she should have been running.

The grenade exploded in the air, having bounced off the snout of the marshosaurus. Honeywood was already several paces away by this point, and the blast did nothing to her save psychologically propel her onwards. She turned in her run to see the dinosaur had been barely dazed by the blast, and could not help but wonder how much damage it would have done were Stiggs able to have timed it so it went off when it struck the beast.

Stiggs himself was floundering, attempting to run, but the marshosaurus was upon him, scraping down his back with one gigantic foot and pinning him to the ground. Honeywood saw the streaks of blood the claws had made and her eyes met his and saw the pleading in them.

She knew any decent human being would go back for him.

Honeywood turned her back and ran. She did not see the great maw come down upon its prey, although she heard the sudden cut-off of the fearful wail. She hadn't asked Stiggs to come back for her, and didn't much care what kind of person it made her to leave him now. It made her a living one, and as her flight carried her into the protection of the weeping willows that was all that was going through her mind. She was alive, and on this world that was all anyone ever cared about at all.

CHAPTER FIFTEEN

"I hate you! I hate you!"

Honeywood was bruised, battered, bleeding and hardly in the mood to take another assault. As the young Aubin hammered her weak fists upon her, however, Honeywood did precious little to stop the attack. Finally she managed to grab hold of the girl's wrists and held her at arm's length.

"There was nothing I could do to save him," Honeywood said dryly, her voice sounding as haggard as her body looked. "I didn't do so well against the dinosaur without a suit."

Aubin's face was a mess of tears and grime, and she collapsed, weeping, to her knees. Honeywood attempted to console her, but it was half-hearted, and from where he watched the women Garza knew Honeywood hadn't done anything to help Stiggs. Neither Garza nor Aubin had seen what had happened, of course, although it didn't take a genius to know Honeywood hated the little guy. Garza didn't doubt for a moment what had happened; Stiggs had fled, the dinosaur had chased him and Honeywood had quietly slipped away. They had heard a lot of pistol shots, and, since Honeywood had let slip that hers had been bent and discarded, Garza had to assume Stiggs had at least made a stand against the brute. Well good for him, at last he had done something worthwhile in his life. Garza could not help but believe that if Honeywood and Stiggs had been willing to work together they may well have both come through.

Ah well, he thought; at least it had been Honeywood to come out alive. If they got into any more difficulty he would much rather trust her to have his back than a coward like Stiggs.

"You always hated him," Aubin was still wailing. "You left him to die."

Garza was surprised Aubin had actually figured that out already.

"There was nothing I could have done to save him," Honeywood repeated and Garza wondered why. Life was cheap on this world, and all of them were hardened criminals. They weren't nice people, none of them had ever claimed to be, and no one expected anyone to come to anyone else's rescue.

"Whoever's to blame," Garza said, stepping in, "we really should get a move on before that thing comes back."

Aubin fixed him with hateful eyes now as well, yet he did not regret his words. Harsh and insensitive they may have been, but this was not a forgiving world. If they didn't get going they were *all* going to die.

"Abe's right," Honeywood said. "We need to press on, find Garret and get out of here."

"I hate to mention this so insensitively," Garza said, "but Stiggs was the one who memorised the map."

"Damn."

Aubin glowered at them both but thankfully kept silent.

"Then we follow his spoor," Honeywood decided.

"We're a little off the beaten path, Ashley," Garza reminded her.

"So what do you suggest we do?" she snapped.

"Go home?"

"You mean that? After we've come all this way, just to give up now?"

"Hey, I like Seward's burgers as much as the next guy, but dying for him isn't gonna get my belly filled. The guy cheated on you, Ashley, what do you care what happens to him anyway?"

She scowled at him, and Garza realised both women were doing it now. This was turning into such a great evening for him.

"Tell you what," Garza said, more than a little anxious to leave and growing fed up with their over-emotional attitudes, "I'll get out of here and if either of you two fancy staying alive you can follow me if you like." He stormed off, hardly caring in fact whether they even followed. This entire venture was turning out to be the worst mess imaginable. When Honeywood and Valentine had pitched the idea Garza had taken it to be a great opportunity to prove himself. Now Stiggs was dead, Aubin was an emotional mess, and they still hadn't found Seward. Garza doubted the man was even still alive, otherwise they would have found some actual trace of him by now. And then of course there was that weird dinosaur-man out there and

…

He stopped walking, frowning to himself. They had found a campsite and believed it to have been made by someone who had landed on this world. They were chasing Seward but he always seemed to be able to stay one step ahead of them; he knew the swamp better than they did after all. And they had this dinosaur-man lurking around various corners.

What if all three were the same being? What if for some reason Seward was purposefully eluding them, had feigned the visitor from space and somehow turned into a dinosaur? Maybe he had skinned something and wore its hide. Garza was certain whatever he had seen had not been a man in a suit, but he had been afraid, tired and confused. Perhaps that had been precisely what he had seen; or maybe Seward was some weird kind of Jekyll and Hyde; it would explain why he went out into the marshes all the time anyway.

Garza shook his head. The oppressive swamp air was starting to get to him if he thought even half of that was true.

"Abe."

He turned to find the two women approaching him slowly. They stood apart, and he could tell by the red-eyed haughty expression from Aubin that she still wasn't talking to Honeywood. Honeywood however seemed to have shaped up a tad and Garza was glad. She was still the most capable of them, and therefore the most likely to survive. If Garza intended to get out of this place in one piece he could do far worse than sticking as close to Honeywood as possible.

"Glad you changed your mind," he told them. "Do we have any particular direction to go or are we just guessing at the moment?"

"We'll head in roughly the same direction we were before. Maybe we'll get lucky. What we really need is somewhere to spend the night."

That much was true. Darkness was coming quickly upon them, and upon this world you could blink and it would suddenly be pitch-black. They resumed their march therefore, each step taking them further and further into blackness.

Before long they came to an odd feature to the landscape, for the darkness before them was absolute, while behind and to the sky there was still some semblance of light. Garza desperately wanted to shine a torch on things, but that was a terrible idea when so many of the predators of this world were nocturnal. Instead he moved forward, his hand held before him as he slowly examined the area. His fingers brushed against something and his initial instinct was to recoil. Reaching out once more he found his fingers contacting something which was solid, hard and cold.

"It's rock," he said, perplexed. "It's a rock wall of some kind."

Honeywood was by his side in an instant, her own hands feeling around. "Well it's not manmade. I'd say it was a mountain."

Garza felt very foolish for not having made that connection himself. "Yes," he said. "I didn't know there were any mountains on this world."

"Sure beats swamp. Come on, let's take a look."

It was an exciting discovery, since no one had ever found anything outside the swamp. It was possible they had actually reached the edge of the swamp and Garza marvelled at all the things they may well find beyond it. They had no flight within the prison: no gliders or probes or anything. They had no idea what could be out this far, and the very thought that the terrain might be different on the other side of the mountain was exhilarating. Even the mountain itself represented something they had never considered before.

The three of them eagerly followed the mountain around, keeping a hand to the rock when the undergrowth allowed them to. Garza was moving so quickly he almost fell and barely caught himself as he realised there was an opening in the ground before him. He peered into the gloom, although could see nothing.

"This is silly," Honeywood said, and suddenly there was a flare of light and Garza realised she had struck a match. She dropped it immediately into the hole and Garza could see the rocks illuminated as it fell. In the brief moment before it flickered out he could see it was a gap in the mountain, rather than a hole in the ground, and led down to the valley floor.

"We need to be careful here," he said. "Perhaps we should camp out here for the night and descend in the morning."

"Or we could lose the trail of that marshosaurus," Honeywood suggested, "by passing through a hole it won't fit through."

It was a good enough argument, although since they really didn't know what lay awaiting them on the valley floor Garza wasn't all that certain it was an especially valid one.

They took their time moving down the rocks. Honeywood went first, and Garza helped Aubin as much as he could. The light was poor, and a single misstep could send them all careening down to their deaths. The girl accepted his hand one or twice when she slipped, although otherwise gave no indication that she intended to lean on him for support. The formerly bright and cheery girl had devolved into a morose, pallid mess, and not for the first time Garza wondered whether she was correct and Honeywood had indeed left Stiggs to die just so she could herself escape. Speculation aside, however, the truth was Aubin would never trust Honeywood again, and if Garza put a foot wrong he would be on her hate-list also.

They reached the bottom of the descent within only fifteen or twenty minutes and Garza found the ground here sandy, which led him to believe this was a real mountain valley. The sheer rock faces standing on all sides blocked out what little light there was, and Garza wondered what manner of creatures might call this place home. He desperately wanted to explore, for this was an environment otherwise unknown upon this world. Everyone back at the prison assumed the world was all swamp, and yet if there were mountains and dry valleys there might well be deserts and forests, even oceans. Worlds needed oceans to support life, of course, although he knew full well this was an artificial world, and for all he knew there could be some form of weather machine at the centre of the globe, churning out rainclouds and absorbing precipitation.

He breathed in deeply of the cool, swamp-free air. The scent was unusual, dry and fresh. This was certainly no swamp, he thought with a smile.

"We'll camp down for the night," Garza decided before Honeywood could decide to press on into the darkness. "We can pick up the trail again in the morning."

"What trail?" Honeywood scoffed. "We're not following a trail; we're just walking around now. Any sign of Garret is long gone. You got any food left?"

Garza had not thought of that, although he was the last remaining member of their party with a backpack: they had not gone back to retrieve anything Stiggs may have had upon his person.

They did not erect their last remaining tent, for it was a one-person affair and would never have fit them all. Instead they simply bedded down with what they had. They lit no torch and ate dry, cold rations in silence. Garza set his back to one of the rock walls and arranged his backpack behind his head to use as a pillow. He noted Aubin had curled up into a ball some way from both of them, and nowhere at all near Honeywood. Honeywood herself had made no attempt to aid either of them and lay on her back, staring at the stars.

Garza reasoned this was going to be a fun journey after all.

CHAPTER SIXTEEN

In her dreams Stiggs was running around with a gun, being chased by dinosaur-men and a marshosaurus wielding a machinegun. In her dreams Honeywood had spent a great deal of time trying to explain why she had done what she had done, as though justifying to herself her terrible actions. In her dreams she was drowning in the swamp while Stiggs was trying to save her by tying up Honeywood's mouth with his bag strap.

As Aubin awoke she was brought back to reality, her dreams cascading away into gradual forgetfulness as they were wont to do. Would this be the same with everything that had happened so far? she asked herself. Would she eventually forget the events leading up to Honeywood abandoning Stiggs? Would she forget the marshosaurus and the dinosaur-man? Would she forget Stiggs?

Aubin had no answers to any of these questions, although she knew one thing for certain. She was not returning to the prison. The prison was a place where Honeywood excelled, where life roared with success and spat in the face of the law. Aubin was not like them, not really. She was a killer, and she didn't for one moment regret what she had done to be put here, but she was not like them. Personal gain for her meant something different to what everyone else in that place had done, and she was clearly not going to reoffend. Not unless circumstances put her in a situation where she actually had to.

Where she would go she could not say, but they had discovered this valley and that meant there was more to this world than any of them realised. When they had first taken over the prison during the riot several prisoners had set off and never returned. It had always been assumed they had perished, but there was no evidence of that. If they had made it through the swamp, as Aubin and her party had in only a few days, what reason would they have for returning? Why would they go back just to tell everyone they had left behind that there was a better life out here? They were murderers and thieves; they didn't care about their fellow man.

And that was what Aubin would do now. She would wander, explore, and survive.

To hell with everyone else.

Stretching her aching body and instantly regretting her choice of sleeping posture, Aubin glanced around for her first look at the valley. It was indeed dusty, and drove between the tall, majestic mountains without any swampland in sight. It was rocky terrain, yet passable, and Aubin had thoughts of simply leaving now, before the others awakened. She could see Honeywood sprawled across the floor in sleep and wondered of her dreams. Did she feel anything for what she had done? Did this woman even understand regret and the pain of others?

Perhaps, but if she did she didn't care. She was no different to the others, and if her crime had not earned her perpetual stay in this place surely her actions following had. She was the greatest pit fighter the world over: she had excelled in her exile.

Disgustedly, Aubin turned her head from Honeywood and saw Garza still asleep, leaning against the rock as he had been all night. It was a large rock unattached to the mountain, with odd protuberances poking out from it, circling its base. There were two especially large ones at the front which looked very much like horns, and in a moment of true fear Aubin realised the terrible truth.

"Abe," she whispered, a sibilant hiss all but lost in the silence. She tried again, finding her voice at last. "Abe!" Again he did not respond and she crawled over to him, inching slowly. She placed one hand upon his bare arm, her eyes ever upon the thing behind him. "Abe!"

It might have been the physical contact, but whatever the reason Garza's eyes shot open and he flailed with his arms, releasing a series of inconclusive sounds. Aubin winced, backing away and trying to indicate with her open hands that he should shut the hell up. Garza finally ceased his mindless flailing and frowned.

"What?"

"Abe!" she hissed again quietly, pointing behind him. "Slowly."

Garza, still frowning, paid no attention to her, and rose quickly, drawing a knife Honeywood had loaned him and expecting some monster behind him. When all he saw was a rock he laughed. "It's a rock, kid." And then he struck it.

Aubin wondered whether he had been born an idiot.

The rock moved, rising on four massively-powerful legs. Garza backed off slowly and Aubin felt like hitting him. The rocky form rose to two metres and shook itself into wakefulness. Its rear-legs were longer and thicker than those at its fore, and its underbelly veritably heaved with weight. It sported a short, thick neck with a flat, almost beaten face and small black eyes. There was a beak sitting at the front of its head, and no teeth that Aubin could determine, although its mouth was currently closed.

The entirety of the thing's body aside from all of this was armour-plated. Powerful scutes ran down its entire body, with bony protrusions seemingly built into its spine. There was a row of sharp horns running horizontally across its body, halfway up; at the base of what seemed to be its shell and the top of its legs. The two massive horns Aubin had noticed earlier were situated just above the creature's neck, almost a metre long. Its tail was broad and grandly sweeping, making the creature somewhere in the region of six metres in length. The tail was similarly spiked and armoured, ending in a flat, hard club which could likely shatter rock and would treat a human skull as human teeth would treat a grape.

The creature shook its head groggily, annoyed at having been awakened and trying to figure out what had just struck it. Garza quickly lowered his knife, but Aubin knew if there was any damage done it was already too late to start hiding things.

"We should back away slowly," she whispered without taking her eyes off the thing.

"What about Ashley?"

"What about her?"

"Cassie!"

It was nice that Garza still cared something for their leader, although in truth Aubin was more concerned with her own survival. "It hasn't attacked yet," she whispered back. "Maybe if we just leave it won't."

And then the creature raised its small head to the sky and emitted a nasal bellow which sounded somewhere between a horn and a wail. It repeated the sound, waving its head around as it did so, and

Aubin watched in horror as dozens of rocky mounds strewn throughout the valley began to rise, sporting thick legs and wondering what all the commotion was about.

"We need to get out of here," Aubin said urgently. "Now!"

Honeywood had woken to all the noise but Aubin didn't even notice as she and Garza fled down the valley. The raging beast raised itself on its hind legs and slammed itself down, almost sending shock waves through the ground. Aubin could see an area ahead of her which fell farther away from the valley: another path leading out of the valley through which the ankylosaurid could not follow. Her legs burned with pain as she ran, but she gave them no thought and simply ran.

Something struck her legs from behind and she fell, tumbling end over end and sliding across the gravel until her back struck harshly into the wall. At first she had feared the creature had hit her with its flat tail, although as she saw it strike again she realised what had happened. It slammed the tail into another rock, and the rock exploded, sending shards flying through the air. Aubin raised her arm before her face to protect her eyes, and felt the shards tear through her skin.

Garza dropped by her side, his own body slick with blood, panic in his eyes. "Come on, move!"

He grabbed her, but her legs refused to submit, and she stumbled once more. She was aware of Garza shouting at her but couldn't hear the words. He hauled her savagely to her feet once more and Aubin could feel tears streaming down her face in her fear. Her legs simply would not respond and she knew at any moment she would die.

A fresh shower of rock shards assailed them and Garza released her as one struck his elbow and he pulled back his arm in pain. Aubin immediately fell in a heap upon the floor, her mind frantic, her thoughts dying as her brain seemed to shut down with the inevitability of death. She heard gunfire and was vaguely aware of Honeywood attempting to hold the beast back. The shots would do nothing to penetrate the animal's hide, and the report of the gun was entirely drowned by the smash of the ankylosaurid's tail.

Dragging Aubin to her feet, Garza struggled to reach the exit she had spotted, and stopped. Aubin could see it now: the path she believed would lead them to salvation. It was indeed a way out of the valley, but there was no simple way down. It was a break in the valley wall allowing them to see beyond to the swampland outside. The sides of the mountain were sheer, with a drop of perhaps fifty metres before they would hit the brackish swamp, swallowed up by the trees and digested. It made no sense for the swamp to be that far down, but it seemed the mountain range marked a point of descent on this world. Behind them was the swamp from which they had come; ahead was a new swamp, one that existed at the base of the mountains.

Perhaps the world was swamp all over after all.

"We can't get out that way," Garza said lamely. "We'd never survive the drop."

"We can't stay here."

They both glanced back to see Honeywood hurrying their way, an angry dinosaur in her wake.

Garza gripped his knife so tightly he was trembling. He nodded to Aubin. "Get back. Hide yourself best you can. Ashley and I'll hold it back, maybe draw it off or something."

Aubin wasn't certain she had heard him correctly. "You fight that thing and you'll die, Abe."

"Sure," he said with a smile. "But at least I get to die saving a pretty girl's life."

Aubin's mind was a miasma of confusion. Since coming to this world her life had been an insanity bordering on delusion. Now she was faced with someone willing to die for her, and thought back to Stiggs. Perhaps it was her. Perhaps she brought out the protective instinct in people. Perhaps in another life she may have been able to draw people from their bad ways.

"What are you here for, Abe?" she asked in a small voice, not certain she even wanted to know but knowing she had to before the end.

"In prison you mean?" He grinned. "Tax evasion. Just don't tell anyone; would ruin the image."

"Tax evasion?"

"Hey, if it was good enough for Capone …"

"Move!" Honeywood shouted as she reached them. The dinosaur was coming directly for them, building up what speed it could muster. Aubin noted its femur was far longer than the rest of its leg and knew the beast would not be able to run properly, but even a half-hearted charge by the thing would be enough to kill them all.

Garza gave her a good-natured shove and Aubin fell behind a rock while he and Honeywood went back out, trying to circle the beast to draw its attention from them. Aubin peered over the rock and watched in horrified fascination as they baited and danced about the creature.

And then she saw something else; something the others could not see.

Crouching low upon the ground behind the ankylosaurid was a tall, slender reptilian form with a rifle slung over its shoulder. The ankylosaurid snapped at the two humans with its beak, as they darted towards it and back, but there was no room for it to bring its powerful tail to bear. And all the while the dinosaur-man closed the gap.

Aubin had no idea its purpose there but could not take the chance it was here to kill them and not the large beast. "Look out!" she shouted, and all eyes turned immediately to her.

Fear was etched into the faces of Honeywood and Garza, anger upon that of the dinosaur-man, while the ankylosaurid bellowed with unrestrained rage as it turned towards her and attacked.

Aubin ducked, feeling the wind of the tail as its flat club slammed into the rock which had been her hiding place. Stone exploded in all directions and she fell backwards, slivers having pierced her flesh. She landed upon her back, her body a quivering mass of pain and fear, and she looked down to see rock fragments standing as if to attention across her body, bathing in pools of sickly crimson ichor. She reached for one with a trembling hand and pulled it free. Pain seared her entire body. She cried out, clamping her eyes shut against the pain, and knew she was unable to move.

She opened her eyes to see the great dinosaur looming over her, rising itself on its hind legs once more to trample her as it brought its entire weight down upon her. The great black shadow engulfed her and something inside her cracked in terror as she wished she could just die of fright before the thing crushed all her bones in one great strike.

And then the dinosaur-man was in her vision, lithely and swiftly by her side. It scooped her up in its arms and shot forward even as the ankylosaurid stamped down, sending shock waves coursing through the ground once more. Aubin threw her arms about the throat of the dinosaur-man, not knowing whether she was saved, not knowing much of anything; and then saw the dinosaur-man had miscalculated its step and had plunged them through the gap in the mountain pass. Aubin saw the sky suddenly fill her vision, the swamp below, the tree cover like clouds beneath her. She clung tighter to the neck of her odd saviour as her body screamed in terror at such a suicidal plunge. Fifty metres straight down was far more than anyone could survive.

Mercifully she blacked out and did not experience the final, sudden halt. The last Cassie Aubin knew was that she was flying through the fresh air of the mountain path. She was flying, and she was free. Finally she was a prisoner no longer.

CHAPTER SEVENTEEN

There was no way down to the swamp, and even if there had been Honeywood knew all they would find would be the broken, battered body of the girl. Taking advantage of the ankylosaurid's distraction, Garza had dragged Honeywood away from the raging behemoth and together they scrabbled along the sides of the valley, keeping as far from the beasts as possible. Trudging wearily on, they could see the others of the species didn't much care for them and they were able to walk between them without any problem; even their initial antagonist seemed to have calmed somewhat by this point and had offered no pursuit.

They walked in silence – a sullen, damning silence – until they were clear of the creatures, and approached the end of the valley. All throughout the journey Honeywood's thoughts had never once left Aubin. She was the best of them, the one thing which had kept them all going, and now they had lost her and they couldn't even bury her or say goodbye. The swamp took back its own, and laughed in the face of the just.

What the dinosaur-man was Honeywood still could not say, and knew now she would never be able to. Perhaps it had been an experiment gone wrong, perhaps it had indeed somehow evolved, it no longer mattered. It wasn't coming back from such a plunge either, and its secrets had died with it. Why it had done what it had was the real mystery for her, since this was twice it had tried to save Aubin. Yet when it had confronted Garza it was to draw a gun on him. Perhaps it had a moral sense to protect women, perhaps Aubin reminded it of someone who was once kind to it, perhaps it just didn't like Garza. Whatever the truth, Honeywood knew she would never find out, and nor did she any longer much care. Aubin was dead, and nothing else about the situation mattered. That was the only truth that counted for anything.

"What do we do?" Garza asked while they walked, the first thing either of them had said to one another aside from cursing since Aubin had died. He sounded sullen, but if he had been in shock he had worked through it. It seemed everyone had liked Aubin.

"Do?" Honeywood asked. "We find Garret and get back to the institution."

"Prison, Ashley. Call a spade a spade."

"You don't want to go back?"

"You do?"

"I thought you wanted to become a prize pit fighter, like me."

He shook his head angrily. "I don't much care for anything any more."

She knew how he was feeling and yet could not bring herself to be nice about any of it. "We find Garret, then we can work out what to do from there."

He nodded; it was a good enough plan anyway.

Two minutes later they stumbled upon a grave. It was a loose mound of stones, the barest attempt at a hole had been dug. The headstone was a stick stuck in the rocks with a handkerchief tied about it.

Honeywood and Garza looked at one another, although neither had any idea what this meant. Whatever it was, it was liable to be something bad.

"Maybe someone passed through here," Garza suggested, "and the dinosaurs flattened one of them."

"Which means someone must have survived to lay the grave. Someone from the prison?"

"Or Seward."

"Seward was alone."

"Or so we think. Maybe there's a fancy woman neither you nor Hargreaves know about."

He had meant it as a joke, but Honeywood was hardly in the mood for such. Thankfully she was too tired to rise to the bait and simply ignored him. She silently pressed on, knowing that the answer to the mystery could not be far away. She could not shake the feeling, however, that their dinosaur-man might have been the one to make the grave. Maybe this was where it lived and this was where it had lost its friend.

As the valley came to an end they broke out into solid ground. There were trees dotted about, with rocks rising in the distance, but no sign of swampland anywhere. It was in fact more a dusky desert area than anything, although there was the barest hint of forestation farther along the road. Presently they had stepped into a large clearing and here they stopped, staring aghast at what lay before them.

It was large, probably around twenty metres in length, and six or seven in height. Its body was tough and plated, but not heavily armoured, while it rested upon the ground upon four stocky legs, each of the same length. It bore no neck to speak of, although its head was almost flat and compact, with a dull nose and a bright shine to the eyes. The tail tapered off thickly, raised from the ground to keep it horizontal with its body.

"What the hell ...?" Garza gaped.

"This isn't possible."

Yet it was there, so it was clearly very possible.

"Nice, isn't it?" a new voice said, and Honeywood spun with glee to see a ruggedly handsome, muscular individual stepping out of nowhere. He wore a week's worth of beard growth and could have done with a hairbrush, but there was a tender light to his eyes which made Honeywood want to leap into his arms and forgive him everything.

"Garret!"

"Seward!" Garza said at the same time. "You're alive!"

Seward gave a little shrug. "So, what do you think of my acquisition?"

Honeywood glanced back to the massive thing standing in the centre of the field. "It's an exploration shuttle isn't it? Where did it come from? I mean, who's even exploring this place? The whole world's off-limits." Her mind was buzzing with questions and as happy as she was to find Seward alive, she was far more excited by the notion that there was a very real chance they could now get off this world alive.

"It belonged to a surveyor," Seward explained. "At first I was wary, thinking she'd come to see why there'd been no contact from the prison. But she was only a surveyor."

"How did you know it was here?" Garza asked with a frown.

Seward smiled at Honeywood. "Ash and I always sit on my shack gazing at the stars, looking for ships passing in the night. I was up there alone one time and saw one come down. I knew then I would have to track it and find it."

"You were going to leave without me?" Honeywood asked, a tremor to her voice.

"I knew if my café was attacked by dromaeosaurids a party would be sent out to find me. And I knew you'd be at the head of it, Ash."

"Why not just tell us before leaving?" Garza asked, ever questioning. "You didn't have to wreck your own café."

"Why not? It's not like I'm going back there. I'm sorry, do I know you?"

"Abe Garza."

"Garret Seward. Nice to meet you."

"We've met before. I used to use your café. Before you destroyed it."

Honeywood could not understand Garza's hostility. They had finally found Seward, which had been the entire point of them heading out here to begin with, and Garza was just finding fault with it. "What does any of this matter, Abe?" she asked.

"I get seeing the shuttle land," Garza said, "and I get why he rushed out here before it could leave again. Just wondering why he went to so much trouble to make sure no one in the prison knew about it. If you're not intending to go back, what does it matter?"

"Because," Seward said amiably, waving away Honeywood's protestations that he should owe the man an explanation, "there are some very psychotic people back there. They may not like the idea of my leaving and they may want to stop me."

"You're paranoid."

"So they told me in court." He smiled once more.

"None of this matters," Honeywood said. "We have a shuttle, we can get out of here. We should go. We should go right now, before something happens to screw things up for us."

"What about Hargreaves?" Garza asked flatly.

Honeywood's face fell at the sudden remembrance of that woman, but she shook such thoughts aside. "She doesn't matter if she's staying."

Garza laughed without humour. "Good lord, no wonder he cheats on you if you make it that easy."

Honeywood fixed him with narrowed eyes. "You know, we don't have to take you with us, Abe."

"That right?" Garza asked, and there was something to his tone which gave Honeywood pause. There was trepidation to his eyes, and she could see he understood more to this situation than she had considered. She thought about it then, trying to work out what it was she was missing, and then realised they were indeed missing something.

"What happened to the pilot?" she asked Seward.

"Didn't make it," Seward said.

"Didn't make what?" Honeywood laughed. "There's not a dent on this thing, it didn't crash."

"Didn't make the cut," Seward said.

Honeywood blinked. "Say what? Is she the one buried under the stones we passed?"

"Thought it was the least I could have done for her. I do have some sense of morality after all." He spoke, as ever, in a dry tone. His voice was always flat, which was why he smiled so much, to convey emotion. But his eyes seldom shone, and Honeywood had realised a long time ago his smiles were faked. She supposed in his days as a chef he had had to force a great many smiles in his time, before poisoning his patrons for questioning his cooking methods. There were those who considered Seward psychotic all right, and yet for Honeywood that was part of the draw.

"I take it," Honeywood said, "she was crushed by one of those ankylosaurids back there?"

"The aletopelta? Harmless beasts, no, no. Takes a lot to rile up one of those things."

Honeywood felt nervous about where this conversation was going. "So she went to relieve herself in the bushes and didn't realise there were dinosaurs around here, right? Some carnivore got her?"

Seward stared at her blankly.

"Oh," Honeywood said. "Why? Who was she?"

"No idea," Seward said. "Oh, I got her name and everything. She was practically screaming information at me by the end, but none of it was relevant. Quite frankly I just didn't care; and then I tired of her company."

"Ashley," Garza said without taking his eyes from Seward, "how did you get so good at pit fighting?"

The question threw her. With so much information being flung her way she almost thought she had misheard the question. "What?"

"Pit fighting. Those machines you sit in when you fight the dinosaurs."

"Oh. I'm a mechanic."

"So you're good with machines?"

"Yeah."

"So you can fly anything?"

Honeywood knew what he was inferring. Seward was a chef, not a pilot, and if he had waited for them to get here it was because he couldn't get out alone. Honeywood could not know the reason the craft's original pilot had refused to cooperate, but she was no longer able to help at all. Honeywood knew full well how Seward could get carried away in his work, and could only imagine how much he cursed when he realised he had gone too far with her.

"He's quite bright really," Seward said. "Shoot him and we'll be going."

"Shoot him?" Honeywood asked. "Why?"

"Didn't we cover this?" Seward asked in mild annoyance. "We don't want anyone back at the institution to realise we're still alive, otherwise they might find a way to come after me."

"No one can come after you," Honeywood told him. "No one here has a space craft, otherwise they'd have left."

"Valentine has a craft."

"What?"

"He has it hidden," Seward said. "If he ever needs to leave the world at a moment's notice he can do so. Until then he's content to run things here. A whole world living under his thumb; why would he ever want to leave?"

"But he'd leave to get his chef back?" Garza asked.

"Naturally. The way to a man's heart is through his stomach, Abe."

Garza shot Honeywood a look which told him he thought Seward was beyond paranoia and had delved into insanity. Honeywood wasn't sure she disagreed.

"Now kill him," Seward said, raising a pistol and holding it upon Honeywood's head, his hand not shaking in the slightest, "or I kill you."

"What?" Honeywood yelped, her heart racing. "Why would you want to shoot me?"

"Because I'm paranoid?" He laughed. "No, the only way I can be certain you're still with me is if you kill Abe here. Then the two of us can leave and go … well, anywhere we choose."

"But you can't fly the craft alone," Garza said quickly.

"True," Seward said. "It'll mean having to go back to the institution and bringing back someone who can, and it'll be a lot of effort. But better a lot of effort now than leaving with someone who's going to stab me in the back the instant we're safe on another world. Now shoot him, Ashley. Please. For me."

Honeywood did not know what to do. She produced the pistol with which she had been shooting the aletopelta – one she had ironically swapped with Garza for her knife, since her own gun had become bent at the death of Stiggs. She held the weapon on Garza between trembling fingers, her eyes wide and unblinking, her mind frantically screaming at her to do something: anything. She didn't want to shoot Garza, but Seward was right. All she had to do was squeeze the trigger just once and she could get off this world and back to civilisation. She didn't even have to stay with Seward if she didn't want to. She could start a new life, they could part ways, she could be happy again.

And all she had to do to attain that life was kill a man she'd never been sure she even liked that much.

Her hand grew less unsteady and she controlled her breathing. Perhaps this wasn't such a difficult choice after all.

Garza shifted his nervous gaze from her eyes to the gun and back again. "You're not a killer, Ashley. You've never killed anyone in your life. You don't want to turn into Seward do you?"

"Standing right here?" Seward said.

Honeywood ignored both men and narrowed her eyes. All that mattered was getting off this world. Stiggs, Aubin … did either of them ever mean anything to her? And if Aubin was dead, why should Garza be allowed to live? How was that fair?

"Ashley," Garza said, taking a small step in her direction. "Ashley, put down the gun, we can ..."

And she fired, the explosion shredding her last trace of morality. Garza spun in the air, a look of complete bewilderment frozen upon his face. She fired again and again and finally lowered her arm, the gun stuck fast in her trembling grip. Her eyes were riveted upon where Garza lay upon his belly, his naked torso a mass of grime and muck and the blood collected from so many wounds across their journey.

A hand was placed upon her shoulder and she jumped, only to find Seward gazing at her, no longer smiling. His was a look of respect and, at last, of trust. "Good girl. Now get on board."

"They're all dead," Honeywood said breathlessly. "My entire team was wiped out to save you."

"Tragic. I'm sure Valentine will mourn you more than he will all of them put together."

"I'm not going with you."

"What? Why ever not?"

"Don't you see, Garret? We've killed people! We've killed people just to escape this place."

"That's what we do, Ashley. We're killers. It's why we're here."

"Then maybe we deserve to be here after all." She raised her gun before he could stop her and pressed the muzzle to the side of her own head. It should have been the most difficult, most controversial decision she had ever made, yet the action came so easily that Honeywood did not even flinch as the hot metal pressed against the side of her temple. Her life was a mess of her own making. She had tried so hard to make the best of a bad situation and all it had created was a sea of bodies upon which somehow she had managed to float. She could still see the young, smiling face of Cassie Aubin whenever she closed her eyes, could still hear her uncertain laughter tickling her upon the breeze.

But it was more than just Aubin, more than just the people who had died. This world was sickening, their society was a disease. It chewed on criminals and spat them out monsters. There wasn't anything on this world that wasn't a monster and Ashley

Honeywood knew whatever else happened she could not allow Seward to return to society. She didn't matter any more: she never had and no longer even wanted to. Her fingers tensed along with her resolve. If she could stop Seward getting off this world it would be a good thing: the only good thing any of them had ever accomplished.

Seward gazed at her in uncertainty and she could see in his cold calculating eyes he was more worried about losing his pilot than his lover.

"Don't be stupid, woman," he told her. "Put the gun down."

"Or what?" she asked, the question coming out half laugh, half wail of despair. "You'll shoot me?"

"Ashley, just put the …"

She pulled the trigger and the gun exploded with violence.

Seward started forward, then stopped, confusion to his face. Smoke lingered upon the gun, the acrid stench of burning metal wafted in the air, but Honeywood still stood before him, the gun held tightly to the side of her head.

"I borrowed the gun from Garza," Honeywood explained in a small voice. "He filled it with blanks to scare away the animals. Best way to avoid a wounded animal is not to wound it to begin with."

"Or to kill it," Garza said and shot Seward through the back of the knee.

Seward collapsed in agony, wailing at the top of his lungs. His eyes found Honeywood and he shot a stream of curses upon her. She looked upon him with cold indifference, her shock fighting a losing battle against her survival instinct as she looked upon this man and wondered how she could ever have allowed him to touch her. Trapped on this small world they all took whatever momentary pleasures they could find, but she could do so much better than this psychopath. She was so much better than him it hurt.

Honeywood dropped her gun and raced to the side of the shuttle, tearing open the hatch and launching herself inside. Garza came behind her, sealing the hatch. The shuttle was cramped inside, but to them it was blissful. Honeywood dropped into the pilot's seat and flicked the relevant switches while Garza fell into the seat beside her and asked what he could do to help. She pointed out a particular button for him to press and he did so.

"Most important button on the craft," she told him.

"Passenger eject?" he asked nervously.

"Air con."

Honeywood at last had time to recover and as the blissfully cool air blasted at her she tentatively pressed two fingers to the side of her temple. "I think I burned myself."

"Yeah," Garza said, "you just shot yourself in the head. Blank or no blank, you're still gonna burn."

Honeywood had never understood much about guns but was fairly hopeful she would not have to fire another ever again.

They both looked out the window then as Seward continued to scream. He had crawled towards them, leaving a bloody trail behind him. "Are we just gonna leave him there then?" Garza asked. "The way he's bleeding out it might take him a while to die. Unless the blood draws some predators around."

"The problem," Honeywood told him straight, "is the two of us aren't killers, Abe. I heard what you said to Cassie. Tax evasion? I mean, really?"

"I know, right? Seriously, you're just going to let him bleed out until he dies?"

Honeywood thought a moment, pouted, then shrugged. She flipped a switch and the engine came on. "Yup."

"Wow," Garza said, strapping himself in. "Remind me never to get on your bad side, Ashley."

"You're not my ex-lover, Abe."

"Well it's a long journey."

She cast him a curious glance and found his laughter infectious. "Call me Ash. Now, you still want to be like me?"

"If it means getting off this place, Ash, more than ever."

Amidst the roar of the ascending craft a desperate man's wails were drowned out entirely, and the two people within were able to forever put aside any thought of psychopaths, murderers, dinosaurs or swamps. They had no idea where they were going, but wherever it was, Ashley Honeywood had had by far enough of any of those things to last her a lifetime.

THE DINOSAUR THAT WASN'T

CHAPTER ONE

The creature raised itself to its full height and bellowed, its flabby mass rolling as though a particularly heavy wind had just struck against it. The thing was five metres in length, with a huge bulbous body supported by four thick legs which did little to keep its fat belly off the ground. A short useless tail sprouted from its back, while what passed for its upper torso flooded into something which could vaguely be termed a throat before its long snout of a head appeared from its end. Its skull allowed for a large mouth filled with an array of lethal teeth, beady eyes staring out from above.

Aubrey Whitsmith wrinkled her nose as she regarded the animal, deciding once she got it to the arena she would have to think of a much more impressive way of describing the thing. She watched as it brought its forelegs from the ground, slamming them back down with a great deal of noise as it shook its head in a circular motion, probably believing such was intimidating. Perhaps it even worked, Whitsmith reasoned, but then she was far from close enough to be worried about whatever it was doing.

Whitsmith was a short woman with shoulder-length red hair she often tied into a knot just to keep it out the way. Her clothes were always utilitarian and presently she was garbed in hard-wearing trousers the same shade of brown as the local trees. At her side there were strapped two pistols, although through all her time doing this sort of work she had never had to fire a shot. She did not like to describe her appearance, although had been told more than once that she had very plain features. That was a good thing around the institution, and that she even seldom injected any emotion into her face stood her in even better stead. Her life could be a dangerous one, and hardly any threat came from the creatures that roamed the outside world.

There were four men presently surrounding the bulbous animal, clutching nets and poles and a variety of further equipment

Whitsmith had never really understood. One of the men had managed to snag the creature about the fat throat with a metal hoop attached to his pole, and if the other three could follow suit they would be able to prevent the creature from moving very far. If they could hold it steady enough to get the tranquilisers in they could ship it back to the institution and away from anything that might want to eat them.

The animal was called a moschops and the entire species had died out some two hundred and seventy million years ago. It had been from moschops and other therapsids that mammals had evolved, so Whitsmith figured she should have held the creature in at least a modicum of respect. In reality all she saw was a blubbery seal-like beast that would certainly hold its own against an opponent or two. Its skull was around four inches thick and she had seen them in the wild smash heads with rival males. It was something male animals did a lot, whether they were stags or giraffes, so accepting that something as old as a moschops would do such a thing as well was not difficult to accept.

There was something else males did, no matter what their species, and that was find females of their own species attractive. Whitsmith had developed a rather odd system for getting these creatures into position for the ambushes her people would set. For the commonest animals she sought to trap, Whitsmith had identified the specific scents females of their species emitted while in heat. It was a useful tool which never failed to work, although she mused it had been applied slightly differently this time around. She had been hurrying down the corridor with a batch of the scent when her boss had turned a corner without seeing her. Needless to say the bottle had overturned and Whitsmith had half its contents spilled down her chest. Valentine had been profusely apologetic and had immediately begun dabbing at her chest with a handkerchief, but the last thing Whitsmith wanted was her boss pawing her in the corridor. It had taken some effort to convince the man that she could sort it herself, but his face had been a perfect picture of shame. Valentine was one of the only people back there who actually apologised over anything: he was sweet like that. Of course, there had been no time to shower or change, so Whitsmith had gone out covered in female moschops scent. This particular hunt could have proved quite interesting had her people not been able to get a handle on the creature, but just to be certain Whitsmith herself had decided to stand as far from the animal as she possibly could this time around.

A steady bleep emitted from her belt and Whitsmith unhooked the radio. She had been so caught up in watching the animal straining against its captors that the radio may well have been sounding for minutes without her realising.

"Go," she said as she answered it.

"For a while there I thought you'd been inconvenient enough to get yourself eaten."

"Moschops is herbivorous, boss."

She could almost feel Valentine's eyes boring down the radio at her. On first glance Dexter Valentine was not a man who commanded much respect, but he knew what he was doing and no one questioned him. Whitsmith had only survived with him as long as she had because she was too good at her job for him to let go. Her own feelings for Valentine were a little more complicated. He was a man of facts and figures, with his entire life ordered by spreadsheet and clipboard. He had no time for silly emotions and Whitsmith had never seen him with a woman. At first she had laughed at him behind his back, but the more she got to know him the more she realised she liked him being around. That he was generally abrupt with her did not put her off, since he was like that with everybody. It was as though he felt that having to talk to people put too many variables in his way.

"How many animals are you bringing me?" he asked tersely.

"Just the moschops. We had trouble tracking it or we would've been back sooner."

"Well don't dawdle. It'll be getting dark soon and you need to be home before then."

Valentine cut off the link and Whitsmith replaced the radio upon her belt. Valentine was a strange man who used a peculiar choice of words. This place was not home, not in any of the decent senses of the word. But it was where they lived now, and it was where they were going to die. Even if somehow they all managed another forty years in this place, none of them were ever leaving it. Whitsmith looked to the sky and shielded her eyes from the glare of what could not have been the sun this far out. The sky was as bright a blue as could be found on Earth, but instead of the gentle, delicate cloud structure and the promise of the stars beyond there was a massive swirling gaseous form. The churning orange and red mass had been a part of their lives for several years and Whitsmith knew she should have been used to it by now. The planet Jupiter acted as some form of jolly warden, keeping a constant watch over them all. Even during the night it was still possible to see the world king loitering in the sky, and Whitsmith hated it.

But Valentine had been right about night setting in. Around here things like that happened quickly, as though this world upon which they were trapped did not care at all for polite convention. She could see her people had at last got the moschops under control and sedated. It would take a few minutes for the tranquilisers to take effect, but once they had the thing unconscious they could get it loaded on the cart to take back to the institution.

It afforded Whitsmith a few more minutes to take in her surroundings. Stretching all about her was a vast spread of wild fields, while ferns, conifers and monkey puzzle trees rose wherever they could take root. Insects the size of her head buzzed around the plants, building nests or whatever it was insects did. Whitsmith had never been an authority on insects, for instead she had learned all there was to know about the larger animal life. Valentine needed animals and Whitsmith had made herself indispensable to him in such a regard.

Whitsmith could see something in the far distance and strained for a better view. Vague shapes moved upon the horizon: tiny figures striding boldly across the lands confident there were no mightier predators the entire world over. Whitsmith did not know whether she could agree with such a thought, for human beings had a tendency to ignore the way nature set things up. Not that there was anything natural about this place, of course. Between the extinct animals, the artificial sunlight and the great eye of Jupiter keeping them all in their place, Aubrey Whitsmith could only wonder how any of them were even still sane.

She could see her people finally had the moschops down and were struggling to load it onto a cart. The cart was little more than a thick flat slab upon which they would chain the unconscious animal. There was a two-seater cab at the front so the thing could be driven back, although the going was always slow over the bad terrain. Out here in the fields things would run smoothly, but within ten minutes they would hit the swamp and from there it was another hour until they reached the institution.

This was not what Whitsmith would have considered a good life, but it was the one she had so there was little sense in complaining about it. They were all stuck here on this strange world and the more useful a person was the better her life was. Sometimes Whitsmith came out here to gaze across the plains and wonder whether there was anyone else across this entire world. Legally there should not have been, for the entire world was quarantined. There were many rumours as to why. Some believed the world was beset by plague, others that religious fanatics had taken the resurgence of extinct species to be an act of God. There were more theories about the fabled dinosaur world than there were natural satellites of Jupiter, and that was certainly saying something, but Whitsmith did not care for the truth. The facts were simple: they were not allowed to be here, but they were here. It meant no one was ever likely coming after them, and also meant they could never leave.

But did she want to leave? Whitsmith could have named a hundred people who wanted nothing more than to put this world behind them, but she could not think of anywhere she would want to go. Here she had a purpose, a decent enough life even. That she had become Valentine's secretary was a grating notion, yet she was so much more besides. Having learned everything she could about the habitats and manners of the animals here, Whitsmith had crafted a better life for herself here than she ever had back home.

One of her men was calling her by this point and she indicated that they should start moving. Casting one final glance behind her, Aubrey Whitsmith heaved a heavy sigh and set out after them. For all its faults, this world was her home; and it could have been a lot worse.

Reluctantly leaving the plains behind, Whitsmith accompanied her unit back through the swamps. It was never a good idea to wander alone, for there were always predators lurking and preparing to remove stragglers from any group. By staying close to the noise-making trundling vehicle, however, it provided the hunters with far more security than other travellers would have been afforded. That was not to say their vehicle was supposed to make all the clunking, chugging noises that it did. They simply lacked any professional mechanics or replacement equipment. And the natural humidity of the swamp did nothing to help what ancient equipment they did have.

It was the humidity that struck her as soon as she re-entered the swamp. She did not know what it was about swamps, had never thought to look it up prior to coming out here. She reasoned it might have something to do with rising swamp gases, or the all-enclosing cover of the trees. It might of course have been for some other reason entirely, but Whitsmith did not much care. The fact was the swamp was a hot, muggy place to live and knowing the reason why would not make her feel any better.

Her trousers and boots may have been almost military issue, but the top she wore was extremely thin and covered as much of her arms as it possibly could. She had known for people to have been bitten by mosquitoes in the swamp; and there were not necessarily cures for every insect out there. Within moments of course the humidity had plastered her clothes to her body and she could feel sweat stinging her eyes. But she was used to such hardships and just looked forward to the nice cold shower she could have once she got back home.

Home. It was an odd concept, but one she had accepted.

While she trudged through increasingly boggy terrain, the light dwindling through both the coming of night and the leaf coverage of the swamp, Whitsmith looked to the moschops lying on the slab. Its chest rose and fell rhythmically but its life was essentially over now. Once they got it back to the institution they would put it to work. It would last one, perhaps two rounds before it died. It was a terrible way to go, and Whitsmith often reflected upon how cruel they were to the beasts that called this world their home. That the things should never have existed to begin with did not justify what Valentine had them do with them, but it was not something Whitsmith liked to dwell on. In a harsh environment like this it was survival of the fittest. She could do what she was told or be put out into the world alone, and that was only if she was very lucky.

The moschops was, after all, just an animal.

No one spoke on the way back to the institution, but then that was hardly surprising. There was so much danger in the swamp even without the local wildlife that a wrong step could sink someone into the mire so quickly those walking beside would not even see their fellow vanish. Between the mosquitoes, the swamp and the creatures it was a wonder there were any people left alive.

Finally the institution came into sight. From the outside appearance it did not look like much, but then even from the inside there was hardly anything to find aesthetically pleasing. It was a large stone and brick edifice already overgrown with moss and vines. Whitsmith did not know how long the place had been in the swamp, but this world did not like intruders and she would not have been surprised to learn it had only been here as long as she and most of the other prisoners. Time was something especially difficult to keep track of out here but she believed she had been here for about five years now. Five years which felt far longer than the twenty-five she had spent as a free woman.

Passing through the initial gate was easy since the swamp had reclaimed most of the outer fencing years ago. Whitsmith could still see portions of the fence sticking out at awkward angles like markers for the graves for what should have been their protection. Their approach to the building was of course noted and the large entryway was opened for them, the steel shutters rolling up as people inside operated the necessary machinery. The vehicle trundled through the shutters and Whitsmith gave the signal to lower it behind them. As she watched those shutters fall she could not help but breathe a small sigh of relief. No matter how many times she ventured into the wider world she always felt as though it would be the last. She would never of course admit her fears to anyone, but this world was harsh and she had seen far too many people claimed by its horrors.

Whitsmith left the workmen to take the animal to the pens. It would need to be washed and brought back to consciousness, then fed and made to understand it was not in any immediate danger. But that was someone else's job. Whitsmith had far worse matters to attend to. She had to make her report to her boss.

Unsurprisingly, Valentine was waiting for her in what passed for his office. Whitsmith had always found it strangely amusing how they had settled into this place. Initially it had been their prison; but when they had turned on their guards and taken over it had become something the prisoners owned. There was of course no means off the world and they were every bit the prisoners they had been before the takeover, but at least they were now masters of their own fates. That no one had ever come looking for the guards, that no one had even bothered to wonder how things were going down here, told Whitsmith that no one cared. The world was off-limits, so it had never made sense to her that there was a prison here to begin with. Close proximity to Jupiter also screwed around with radio signals, and long-distance messages were certainly out of the question. At the institution – which was their nice word for prison – they used industrial, military-issue walkie-talkies, which were good for a range of several miles. The world badly despised allowing transmissions of any sort, and if not for the impressive military hardware, even the radios would not work. Any communication device which relied on satellites was pointless and had been discarded or recycled into something useful.

Nothing was ever wasted on this world.

Valentine's office was that of the former warden. The actual cells themselves were still used as bunks for some of the people here, simply due to the lack of space, but whenever Whitsmith walked those corridors lined with the thick vertical bars she never looked into the cells. She had spent too long in a cell to ever be able to sleep in one again and was only grateful she was one of the lucky ones to have been assigned a proper bedchamber.

Valentine leaned back in his chair as she stopped at his desk. He was a smartly-dressed man in a business suit which he always seemed to be able to keep presentable and pressed. Whitsmith had seldom seen him without a tie, and today was no exception. He was a tall man with short blond hair, thinner than most people of importance Whitsmith had ever known. Why he cared so much for his appearance she could not say. Perhaps he thought he was impressing someone, but even then she couldn't say who that might have been since he certainly didn't impress her. If he wasn't so meticulous in everything he did, perhaps he would have impressed her by being normal. But, if he was like everyone else, he would not have been Dexter Valentine.

He had been writing when she entered, scribbling away at his work as though it meant anything. Valentine kept meticulous records, and Whitsmith's excellent memory was certainly the thing which had made him initially notice her. He pushed his thin glasses further up the bridge of his nose and leaned his elbows on the desk as he awaited her report. Just why he wanted a report she could not say. There was certainly nothing to report save that she had brought in the moschops like he had wanted.

"It went off without a hitch," she said. "We didn't lose anyone."

"You seldom do, Aubrey. What level shall we put the moschops down for?"

She saw he was eager to reach for his pen and wondered cruelly how he would react when he finally ran out of ink. "Put it down for a level four. Five if you want a tag-team."

Valentine pulled a face as he made the necessary marks on his paperwork. "I was hoping for something a little more powerful than a level four, Aubrey."

"I take what I can get, Dex. Maybe next time you could give me a shopping list."

He ignored her sarcasm and continued to write something. Or maybe he wasn't ignoring her sarcasm but was instead recording it. She craned her neck to read it, but his handwriting was terrible.

"We need a fiercer dinosaur to draw the crowds, Aubrey," he told her seriously. "Something better than a herbivorous moschops. People have been getting a bit bored with the tournaments lately."

Whitsmith could understand why. Throwing volunteers into a pit with an angry animal was perhaps one of the worst blood sports Whitsmith could conceive. If the volunteers survived they gained a variety of rewards; if they failed they almost always died. Wagers were made on the results of the combat, and some of the prisoners had even become legendary due to their incredible success rate and ability to please the audience. Whitsmith found the entire thing sickening.

"There are predators out there, Dex," she told him, "but they're a little harder to bag. And the moschops wasn't a dinosaur, by the way. It was from the Permian era and wasn't even a reptile."

Valentine ignored her, just as he always did when she corrected him about such things. He did not care that not all prehistoric animals were dinosaurs. He did not care that only certain reptiles from the Triassic, Jurassic and Cretaceous periods were dinosaurs, and that did not include anything that flew or lived in the water. All Valentine cared about was keeping the institution running. Whitsmith was not even convinced he had seen any of the wildlife up close.

"If you don't want me for anything else," Whitsmith said tiredly, "I'm going to hit the shower then go to bed."

"Actually there was something."

He wasn't supposed to say that and he knew it. He knew her routine following a successful hunt and had no reason to stop her like this. Whatever it was, it had better be important.

"We're getting reports of something strange out in the swamp."

"What kind of strange?"

"We don't know yet. Something reasonably small and extraordinarily powerful. Some of the water purifier equipment was destroyed yesterday and just this morning one of my patrols reported seeing something hanging around outside the perimeter we set up."

Whitsmith rubbed at tired eyes and fought to stifle a yawn. "Probably a dromaeosaurid. There are enough of them out there." Dromaeosaurids were a problem which should have been dealt with via shotgun, so far as Whitsmith was concerned. From the harmless-sounding bambiraptor to dromaeosaurus to velociraptor, the dromaeosaurid family consisted of all the vicious, feathered hunters with a scimitar claw on each foot perpetually raised from the ground. This claw was never blunted through contact with anything other than its prey, and the dromaeosaurids were easily the most fearsome creatures on this world. And that was even including the bigger tyrannosaurids.

Still, there was nothing Whitsmith was willing to do about it right now. Dromaeosaurids were often known to hunt at night and in almost all instances they were pack hunters. She knew Valentine would have his eye on her capturing one for his blood sports, and perhaps Whitsmith could even look into it. But she would have to take with her a lot more support and certainly more weapons than she could carry on her person.

"I'm not so sure," Valentine said and Whitsmith thought back to figure out what he wasn't sure about. "There were no tracks at all out there."

"So they're finally using their feathers to fly," Whitsmith all but snapped. The implication sank in immediately, however, and Valentine's face was a blanket of concern. "I'm going to bed," Whitsmith muttered as she left. As she continuously liked to remind Valentine, dinosaurs could not fly. The thought of something as powerful as a velociraptor having learned how to fly ... it did not even bear thinking about. The former prisoners were barely holding their own as it was some days; even with the ridiculous flying theory disregarded, if the dinosaurs were becoming smarter there was simply no chance for any of them to last much longer.

CHAPTER TWO

The pit fights were not going well, and Dexter Valentine was beginning to panic. During the planning stages it had seemed a wonderful idea to overrun the prison. Valentine had put a lot of thought and energy into the plans, had found the work both exciting and stimulating. He was of course not one of the people who had initially decided to attempt the breakout, but he was certainly the man they had come to in order to thrash out a plan of attack. That all the ringleaders had died during the takeover had left a gap in the command post, and Valentine had slipped into it nicely. He had restored order to the confusion he had seen seeping in. Anarchy had its good points, but the simple fact was someone had to be in charge. Given entire freedom, the escaped prisoners would have killed one another before the year was out, and any who remained would have made quick meals for the dinosaurs outside. That they had killed every single one of the prison guards was terrible, since they had no one who actually knew how everything ran. Also, they had no information on how to contact anyone outside of their stupid little world, and what call-signs and codes they would need in order to avoid having a squad of armed soldiers coming in to clean them out.

Restoring order was Valentine's first order of business and he had done this by appealing to the prisoners' baser instincts. No one wanted to perform the menial jobs such as guard duty or cleaning. In fact most of the prisoners didn't want to do much at all. So Valentine had created the fighting pits. Volunteers would be thrust against various wild animals and bets would be taken on who would win, if not survive. Those who lost the bets had to perform the menial chores no one wanted to do. Those who won gained perks and sometimes even money, although there did not seem any point in anyone having money any more. It was ironic that a lot of the prisoners were there in the first place because of crimes they had committed for money; and that now they were free they had no longer any need for the stuff.

Valentine had maintained order for several years now, although recently he had noticed people were beginning to tire of the games. They were always such a good crowd-pleaser before, yet there were only so many animals out there to be found. Initially he had pitted people against the various species of crocodiles lurking in the swamp. There were some large, mean crocodiles out there, in fact, and an array he had never before considered. There were crocodiles with long legs, those which existed primarily on land; and oddly vegetarian crocodiles, which even Valentine found fairly interesting.

Aside from the crocodiles there were various other species living about the swamp. Many vicious dromaeosaurids were found locally, although when Whitsmith had told him about the things he had had no idea what she was talking about. These dinosaur names were all Greek to him, he had told her one time. She had thought he was making a joke and had laughed. To this day he still didn't understand what was funny about that. Whenever Whitsmith spoke to him of the creatures out there he always made her use terms he would understand. Dromaeosaurids, it turned out, were like little tyrannosaurus rexes. They were nothing like them, Whitsmith assured him, but in Valentine's mind they were close enough. They looked vaguely the same and they would eat you if they could.

On the hunt for fresh animals to bring to the pits, Valentine had pushed Whitsmith farther into the outside world. So far as most of the prisoners knew things, the institution was located deep within a swamp and there was nothing else the entire world over. That the entire world could be a swamp would have been ridiculous, but no one seemed to question such a thing. Whenever Whitsmith travelled to the plains and valleys beyond the swamp, therefore, she had to select a group of workers from those few who knew some of the secrets of their world. Secrets, Valentine scoffed. There were secrets to their world all right, but Valentine didn't know any of them. He liked to pretend to believe that he did, but the truth was he was as much in the dark as everyone else around the place.

Discovery of the outside world was not his primary concern, however. He had kept its existence a secret all this time, and the monsters out there had kept the prisoners from venturing too far. When they had first overrun the prison, several people had set off to explore. None had returned. Perhaps they had died, perhaps they had discovered Paradise. Either way they were out of Valentine's hair and if he was going to maintain control of this situation he needed everyone where he could handle them. It was perhaps selfish of him, but none of them were there because they were decent folk. There were a few petty thieves in the prison, but for the most part they were murderers and rapists and Valentine had no pity for any of them.

The crime which had placed Valentine on this rock was something he never revealed to anyone.

"We need something different," he mused aloud. He was no longer in his office, but had taken himself to the roof of the prison. The building may have been infested with swamp vines, moss and damp, but nothing that could hurt him could get to the roof. The building had been a prison, which meant it was designed to keep the inmates in and unwanted visitors out. From the roof, Valentine commanded a poor view of things, for the trees rose about him and the green/brown murkiness of the swamp gave him little in the way of a pleasant sight. But being up on the roof got him away from everyone and allowed him to think. And when Dexter Valentine was given the opportunity to think, bad things happened.

"There's not much left, sir."

Valentine had almost forgotten he had brought Anthony Stone with him. Stone was a large, heavy-set man who had been put away for rearranging the body-parts of the man his girlfriend had cheated on him with. Stone had no remorse for anything he did, and very little patience for anyone. Valentine had offered him the position as his personal bodyguard, knowing Stone would protect him with a passion. Stone was afforded his own chambers and pretty much any perks he wanted. As soon as Valentine died he would lose all of that, and would never have been able to run things without him. Stone would be willing to risk his life to safeguard Valentine, and they both knew it.

Stone was no fool, but nor was he a strategic genius, which meant while Valentine might sometimes bounce ideas off him, he would never seriously discuss his future plans with him.

But Valentine had more pressing things to consider than his bodyguard. The moschops would buy him some time, but it wasn't the herbivores the prisoners liked to watch. It was all very good pitting a human against a herbivore, for there were some truly fascinating defences those beasts had developed, but if the animal won it would then just wander around the pit, growling a bit and sometimes striking the walls. A carnivore's kill invariably ended in the loser being torn apart and most of the time devoured. Valentine had himself never been a fan of blood sports and seldom watched the matches, but he understood this was what the prisoners wanted. And if he did not give them what they wanted they may well take out their frustrations upon him.

An expedition could be in order. An exploratory expedition to bring back creatures more exotic than those living about the swamp and the plains beyond. It seemed ludicrous to no longer consider any prehistoric animals exotic, but over the years they had simply become commonplace. An expedition could breathe new life into their meagre existences, but would also likely reveal to too many people that there was more to this world than the swamp. It was a dilemma he had faced before, and one to which he only wished there was an easy answer.

Behind him he heard Stone grunt something and figured the man had just decided to have an opinion on something. Ignoring him, Valentine leaned against the wall overlooking the swamp, wondering what else might be out there. Whitsmith should have left by now to look into that animal sighting: perhaps she would come up with something worth throwing into the pits. Or perhaps he should develop some new form of entertainment. Someone one time had suggested a theatre, but no one had really been all that interested. Valentine was not a man to have developed a stereotypical viewpoint on criminals, but certainly those within his prison were a mean-spirited violent bunch.

Stone grunted again and Valentine wondered whether the man was developing a cough. He looked over to him and froze, his eyes widening. Stone stood precisely where he had been standing before, but he was no longer alone.

The two women wore green/brown armour to camouflage them into the surrounding swamp. It was bulky and cumbersome and made them look like mobile tanks, but he did not doubt either would be able to move faster than anything Valentine could manage. They wore no helmets, and he marvelled at how their heads seemed to float upon the rim of the suit's thick neck-guard, giving them the impression of deep-sea divers or the earliest lunar astronauts. Their expressions were stern, calculated, and Valentine was surprised to see how young they were. The closest to him wore her blonde hair short and messy, although it was likely a current fashion somewhere. She could not have been older than twenty and he would have bet good money she was still in her teens. The other woman had darker hair, what there was of it, and colder eyes. Each woman held a rifle, one pointed at either man, and Valentine found the entire process fascinating. He was very glad the dark-haired woman had her gun pointed at Stone.

"Good morning, ladies," Valentine enthused, not being foolish enough to make any movement with his hands. He searched his memory for what their uniforms might have told him. They looked vaguely Jovian, but Jupiter had so many moons it was difficult to keep track of who was where. The planet itself, obviously, could not support any life and terraforming a gas giant would have been a fiscal nightmare.

"Name," the blonde barked, and while she was young Valentine got an instant impression that she had done this sort of thing before.

"Valentine," he replied amiably, flashing her a smile he hoped did not come across as too roguish. "Dexter Valentine, ma'am. This is my associate, Mr Stone. How do you do?"

"You're in charge here?" It was almost not asked as a question. Valentine knew for her to even ask that meant they had been watching the prison for some time.

"I am," he replied, deciding it would have been stupid and perhaps even fatal to lie to her. "I must say, your stealth is highly impressive. Admirable, in fact."

She did not seem nearly as impressed by his praise. "What happened to the guards?"

"Guards?"

"This is a prison."

"This is a prison?" He quickly thought better than to deny the clear fact. "Of course this is a prison, yes."

"So where are the guards?"

"I don't know. It was empty when we found it. Abandoned. As you can see, the swamp has tried to reclaim this building over the years. Possibly the dinosaurs got all the guards. And the prisoners, I don't know." He continued to speak slowly, making all his words clear so she would not have to question his motives.

"How long have you been here?"

"A few years," Valentine replied casually. "We're here to study the dinosaurs."

"Study the dinosaurs?"

"Yes. It's a research programme."

"This world is off-limits."

"Yes. We sneaked in." He paused for effect. "And you? If it's off-limits, what are you doing here?"

The two women exchanged a momentary glance, but it was enough to tell Valentine that quite possibly he was right and they should not have been here either. "Our unit's camped nearby," the blonde continued. "We need someplace to stay for a while."

Valentine spread his arms wide. "Feel free to accept our humble hospitality. Whatever we have is yours. I'm afraid we can't offer you much, but we'll do our best for such distinguished visitors. You're from Ganymede, no?"

"Io," she replied. "Twelfth Regiment."

"Ah." Io was a big place. Without a country he had no idea which Twelfth Regiment they could have been from. She spoke English with the tiniest hint of a Birmingham accent so it had to be somewhere in Io's northern hemisphere considering the south of Io was mainly of French descent. It didn't much matter where they were from, of course; a bullet from a gun would kill him just as easily from a French woman as it would an English.

He suddenly realised his mind was rambling into tangents. It tended to do that when he was under a lot of stress, and Valentine was not used to having guns pointed at him.

"Is there anything specifically I can do for you perhaps?" Valentine asked, having terrible visions of these two women bringing in their entire unit and all of them wandering about the prison. The instant the other prisoners caught the whiff of soldiers they would react badly and soon enough some would become aggressive. At that moment in time Valentine could only guess at the reason for their presence, but he had to assume the worst. It had been around five years since the prisoners had revolted and in all that time they had received no word from the outside worlds. It was entirely possible these soldiers were here to find out just what happened at the prison five years earlier.

Valentine needed to find out as much information as possible before making a decision. He was not averse to murdering their entire unit if it would keep him and his people alive, but that was a recourse he wanted to leave until the last possible moment. If it came down to that, he would make sure they were nice, clean kills. He could only imagine the horrors some of the prisoners could put two such women through and he would risk the wrath of his people to help the women avoid that fate.

With any luck, however, they were here on an entirely unrelated matter. They would stay a few days, as the blonde had said, and leave to continue with whatever their mission happened to be.

"We don't need anything," the blonde soldier replied. "Just a place to stay for a while."

"We could do with some information," the dark-haired woman said. She was a few years older and Valentine had been surprised she was letting the younger woman do all the talking. "If these guys have been here for a while studying the wildlife they should know something of their habits."

The blonde seemed annoyed to have her decisions countermanded before other people, although did not say as much. Instead she simply agreed. "Sure. And if they don't know enough about the dinosaurs at least we'll know they've been lying about being here to study them."

"They're not all dinosaurs, you know," Valentine said, trying to remember all the useless things Whitsmith had ever said to him: all the things he had never cared about. "Only land-based reptiles were dinosaurs, you know. Nothing that flew or lived in the water."

The two women exchanged glances which told him they found his response amusing.

"And only certain creatures from the Triassic, Jurassic or Cretaceous were dinosaurs," he continued, unperturbed. "Why, just yesterday my chief researcher brought me a report about a moschops in the area. Moschops predated the dinosaurs, you know, because it used to live in the Permian era."

"Yeah," the blonde said with a tight, wry smile, "but the Permian era sort of ended a few years ago, Valentine. Everything exists on this rock all at the same time. No one cares about eras any more."

That much was true, but Valentine felt his knowledge stash becoming somewhat depleted already. He needed to get them to speak directly with Whitsmith, although she would have already gone off to look into that animal sighting. Knowing his luck she would get herself killed by it. He knew she thought he had been joking when he had said as much to her yesterday when she was bringing in the moschops, but Valentine never joked about such things. He had trusted people before, had considered people extremely valuable, and they always let him down by getting themselves killed. He was surprised Stone had lasted as long as he had.

But all this talk about the eras merging could wait until he could get them to speak with someone who actually knew what they were talking about. "I think these philosophical debates can wait until we get your unit here safely," he said diplomatically. "Why don't you signal them now and bring them in?"

The blonde's eyes sparkled with a humour he did not like at all. She saw straight through him, there was no mistaking that. But she did not contradict him, and for that he could only be grateful. It bought him a little extra time in which to sort things to his own advantage.

Lowering their guns at last, the two soldiers shared brief words before the dark-haired woman walked to the edge of the roof and jumped off. Valentine assumed she was abseiling down the side and not committing suicide, although the latter would have been a big help to him. The blonde regarded him with an amused expression and said, "How about a tour of the facility?"

Since there was very little scientific equipment throughout the entire prison, it was the worst possible request she could have made.

Valentine smiled politely. "What a wonderful idea." He almost went to place his arm about her shoulder as they walked back to the roof hatch, but stopped himself just in time. It was at that moment he realised he did not even know her name.

CHAPTER THREE

There were always creature sightings around the institution and Whitsmith knew if she investigated every one of them she would never get any work done. Most of those creatures were any of the variety of crocodiles living in and around the marsh. She had catalogued the various species of crocodile so that future sightings which reached her desk could be categorised without the need for her to actually venture out into the humid, oppressive atmosphere of the swamp. Whitsmith had come to know a great deal about crocodiles over her years in the prison, far more than she had ever wanted to, and had even caught many herself for participation in the pit fights. Having watched her fair share of these fights, she knew just how mean and ruthless a crocodile could be. She had seen first-hand that a single swipe from their massively-muscled tails could shatter a person's spine; she had seen how they locked their jaws upon their prey and twisted, with the motion of a shark, to tear a chunk of flesh from its victim. While the prey died from either shock or loss of blood, the crocodile could sit back and simply wait for its meal to prepare itself for consumption; as though the crocodile was preparing a TV dinner, staring all the while in anticipatory hunger.

Whitsmith did not much like crocodiles, but she certainly respected them.

When Valentine had told her about the creature sighting and that it was potentially dromaeosaurid activity, Whitsmith had half hoped she would have been able to put it down to crocodiles. As she had read over the information they had received about it, however, she could distinguish the tell-tale signs which indicated whatever was out there was not a crocodile.

Oddly enough, the evidence did not point to a dromaeosaurid either.

That there were two creatures out there, separate from one another in their hunting, was the most likely explanation.

Unfortunately the only way for Whitsmith to make certain would be if she physically went out there and looked.

Without any alternatives, that was precisely what she found herself doing.

The swamp that morning was terribly close and Whitsmith found difficulty in even breathing. The oxygen content of their world was generally richer than that of her native Earth, perhaps because it lacked major unnatural pollution, perhaps because its environment had been designed to reflect a period from millions of years earlier, when the world had naturally contained a greater degree of oxygen. She neither knew nor really cared that much, for it did not help her in her life. Nor did it help her breathe any better in the enclosing swamp. Why Valentine would not let them move to a more hospitable part of the wold she would never know.

"You all right? You want me to carry you or anything?"

Whitsmith ignored the snide comment made by her companion. Whitsmith had a certain authority within the prison so could command whatever resources she pleased, within reason. As such, whenever she ventured into the swamps she never went without a full contingent. She took more people with her into the swamp than she did any other part of their world, in fact. Therefore she presently had a team of fifteen people, some of them nearby, others spread out to form a perimeter. The woman Whitsmith had kept close to her side was a vicious, violent individual named Katie Hudson. Hudson had been imprisoned for multiple counts of GBH. Whitsmith did not know the details, whether they were all against the same person or Hudson just like beating people up. All she knew was that the large heavy-set woman with the permanent scowl and broken nose was not a person who ever gave anyone any leeway. Weakness was a bad thing to show before Hudson, for there was very little keeping her in line even within the prison. But Whitsmith had one time seen her wrestle a crocodile. It had only been a two metre long brachychampsa, but the woman had broken its back by slamming it upon the ground with all her weight behind the plunge. It was at that point that Whitsmith had decided that while Hudson may not have been the greatest human being, she was certainly a good person to have at her back.

"This is the area the creature was last sighted," Whitsmith said. "Keep a watch out while I take a look around."

Hudson grunted and moved off to whatever position she thought best. Hudson had little respect for anyone, but she did seem to like it when people sucked up their inhibitions and just got on with the job. Whitsmith had once developed a theory that Hudson only beat on people who were too afraid to fight back. She had visions of someone standing up to her and the two becoming inseparable friends. Whitsmith did not intend to become that person: she liked to see as little of Hudson as humanly possible.

Momentarily putting the violent woman from her mind, Whitsmith crouched to examine some crushed foliage. The swamp about her was formed of tall, sad trees; weeping willows and other pathetic specimens sadly patrolled the area. The ground was half bog, half solid, but even the solid ground could turn into marsh at any given moment. They had constructed canoes to take them across the entirely liquid parts of the swamp, although there was still a surprising amount of solid, reed-strewn land around, scraggly and depressing as those reeds were. Whitsmith had known nothing about swamps prior to coming to this world and, as with the crocodiles, had only learnt through necessity.

The crushed reeds and pathetic grass showed an animal had been this way recently. She searched for more prints, for if she could determine how many feet the creature walked upon she could decide whether it was a crocodile of a dromaeosaurid. Her initial sweep leant her more towards the latter, which would have been a shame considering the dromaeosaurids were such a vicious bunch. Wrestling a crocodile and winning was one thing, but taking on an actual dinosaur in its natural environment was something she doubted even Katie Hudson could manage.

Brushing the dirt from her hands, Whitsmith rose and looked about her at the swamp, listening to the usual sounds of chirping insects and rushing wind. Whatever was out there, the swamp did not care and just carried on with things the way they had always been.

"There are rumours of utahraptors further north," Hudson said. Whitsmith had not even noticed the other woman was standing so close and tried to hide the fact she had been startled. The most common dromaeosaurids in the local area were all fairly small, and having to face something larger than a human being was not an idea which sat well with Whitsmith. Unlike the capture of the moschops earlier, Whitsmith was in the thick of things here. She may have had a contingent of people to protect her, but here she was far from in control. She did not even know the identity of the beast out here, and therefore could not tell its habits. It could easily have been watching them even now and she would have no idea.

"If it is a dromaeosaurid," Whitsmith said, "which seems likely, there won't just be one of them. They tend to live in packs."

Hudson did not need to be told that, although Whitsmith was nervous and whenever she was nervous she tended to tell people facts about their situation; as though knowing the danger they were in would somehow lessen its intensity.

A shout sounded from someway behind them and the heads of both women snapped about. The cry had been short and cut-off, and Whitsmith felt a terrible sinking feeling in her stomach that she knew what that meant. Without a word the two women hastened off in the direction of the cry. Whitsmith drew her pistols nervously, her sweating palms causing them to almost immediately slip from her grasp, but she clutched them for dear life. Hudson withdrew from its mooring upon her back a large gun whose barrel made it resemble some bizarre cross between a blunderbuss and a rocket launcher. Whitsmith could not imagine the gun being able to hold more than one shot at a time, but nor could she see any creature surviving a direct hit with the thing.

They slowed as they reached the edge of the marsh, where the ground slipped into the bog in an untidy slide. Several other people had gathered by this point, most of the perimeter guards in fact. That made Whitsmith feel a little better: with so many bodies around the chances of the beast selecting her as the next target were marginally small. With a clearer mind than a moment earlier, Whitsmith examined the scene without getting too close to the water's edge. There was indication that something had been dragged through the reeds and into the brackish water, but no signs of other disturbance. With the ground as slick as it was, there was every possibility the guard had simply slipped and slid into the marsh, disappearing beneath the foetid surface.

She would, however, suspect creature involvement until she had direct evidence to the contrary.

Giving quick commands to the remaining guards to focus their attentions on specific directions, Whitsmith searched for any animal tracks which might be able to tell her just what they were dealing with. Her instincts still said this had been a crocodile attack, yet the prints earlier had suggested a two-legged dinosaur. An utahraptor, or any of its ilk, would not have dragged the body into the mire, though, and again she wondered whether there was more than just the one animal to be dealing with here.

"Whitsmith!"

Whitsmith heard Hudson shout and leapt back without even looking to see the cause. She fell onto her backside in sheer shock at the thing sliding out of the water bare metres from her. The thing was called a deionosuchus and she knew it well. Ten metres of moss-green scales, an armoured hide which could shatter knife blades and a temperament of the fiercest Rottweiler. Four short, fat legs protruded from a bulky, massive body, the thick, muscular tail trailing in its wake. The head was a vicious snout of teeth almost as large as a human hand-span, while the head itself was easily as long as Whitsmith was tall. The gigantic prehistoric crocodile gazed upon Whitsmith with cold and baleful eyes as it shuffled towards her. Crocodiles were among the fastest creatures that ever existed, and its trepidation at approaching her could only have been put down to the close proximity of so many other figures. And those figures were panicking; shouting and running and wailing for all they were worth. The cacophony confused the crocodile, which was perhaps the only thing which had yet saved Whitsmith's life.

Scrabbling backwards, Whitsmith realised she had been granted a reprieve and intended to put it to full effect. She had not studied the crocodiles for fun but through necessity, and now that she knew just what they were capable of she did not fancy being torn apart by one. Sometimes dying in ignorance was a far more merciful end than the alternative.

Her movement alerted the deionosuchus, its head snapping back towards her. Her people's flight had taken them out of the thing's range anyway, and the only viable prey remaining was Whitsmith herself. Her mind screamed at her to get out of there as quickly as possible, but her body froze as the crocodile bore down upon her. She could watch its approach but was powerless to do anything about it.

And then the world exploded and the crocodile screamed in rage. Whitsmith had never before heard a crocodile scream and at first did not equate the noise with the animal; but the explosion helped clear her mind and suddenly she knew she had to move if she wanted to survive. Stumbling as she rose, she could see Hudson discarding the rocket launcher, proving it could indeed only be fired once before needing a reload, and was thankful she had kept the woman so close to her.

But Hudson was not looking at Whitsmith, and looked more shocked than she had ever seen her before.

Whitsmith spun about to see the crocodile coming for her still. Perhaps the shot had missed, perhaps the armoured hide really was more impressive than any of them had figured upon. Either way the crocodile was charging for her as fast as its four fat legs could carry it, its maw wide open and yawning for the kill.

To her credit, Whitsmith did not scream. Her mind panicked, but this time her body reacted. She had re-holstered her pistols when she had bent to examine the bank, but her fingers clutched around a large fallen branch and she held it out before her as though the pale and dying leaves upon its end would be enough to fend off the attack of an angry prehistoric horror.

The crocodile snapped at her, its head as large as Whitsmith's entire body, her branch not even noticed by the attacking monster. Whitsmith felt the jaws stroke her leg and she pulled it back just as the crocodile twisted its head and would have taken the leg from her body. Releasing her hold upon the useless branch, Whitsmith drew both her pistols and fired repeatedly into the monster's head. It was the first time she had ever had to fire a weapon during an outing, and as her bullets pinged uselessly off the creature's armoured hide she knew with absolute certainty it would be her last.

A terrible roar tore the air and Whitsmith jumped, more surprised to see the crocodile had started also. Then she caught the coppery stench of freshly-spilled blood and saw the side of the creature awash with blood. She could see Hudson now, to one side, lying on her belly and lining up for another blast of her shotgun. The shotgun was not a weapon designed to be fired from such a position, and Whitsmith could imagine the recoil alone was tearing into the other woman's shoulders. But Hudson had realised the only way to effect any sort of damage upon the deionosuchus was to attack its underbelly, and that the underbelly of a crocodile, even a ten metre one, was almost impossible to reach.

The deionosuchus twisted its body as it snapped at her in anger, and Whitsmith watched as the monster scuttled towards her on its four squat legs at the speed of a gazelle with a cheetah at its back. But Hudson did not panic, did not flee; she simply lined up another shot and pulled the trigger. The shotgun sprayed its lethal charge into the monster's face, slicing through the inside of its mouth and shredding one eye. The deionosuchus thrashed in pain and anger, slipping noisily into the bog. One moment it had been bearing down upon Whitsmith, the next it was gone.

Whitsmith stared at the water, her mind telling her to move, her every conscious thought telling her that to move was to die. The waters settled and the crocodile did not return, and soon enough it was as though the beast had never been there at all.

"You can get up now," Hudson said sardonically. She was reloading her shotgun and collecting the rocket launcher she had discarded earlier. Hudson made no attempt at all to hide the disdain she felt for Whitsmith, and her voice had triggered something within Whitsmith which told her she was still alive. Until that moment it was as though her body had been held in some static limbo, but now her brain was free to move once more she began to realise she was still alive. Her body shook uncontrollably and she clenched tight her eyes to force herself to calm. It would be stupid to survive the encounter only to have Hudson despise her for it. Within just a few short months Hudson would have found a way to use her weakness against her and Whitsmith might as well have died this day after all.

"So much for your raptor theory," Hudson said.

"Just because that crocodile attacked," Whitsmith said, trying to beat down her anxiety over the entire mess, "it doesn't mean there aren't dromaeosaurids out here."

Hudson raised her eyebrows as she finished loading her shotgun, but said nothing.

Whitsmith knew this was the moment. She would have to impress the other woman at least a tiny bit, else she might as well dunk her head in the bog now and get it over with. "The tracks," Whitsmith said, "still indicate a creature which walks on two legs. The crocodile, I think you might have seen, walked on four."

Hudson seemed faintly amused. "Go on."

"There's nothing else to say. The evidence points to a two-legged dinosaur out here. And since most two-legged dinosaurs were carnivores, and since we do have a lot of dromaeosaurid sightings around here, it stands to reason there is a dromaeosaurid out here and that was what our people saw yesterday."

"Are you trying to convince me or yourself?"

Whitsmith knew what she meant, but was surprised Hudson had picked up on it. "Are you asking me whether I believe the thing we're after is a dromaeosaurid?"

"You've told me it's the most likely thing: not what you think it is."

"All right. I don't think it's a dromaeosaurid, no."

"Because raptors always hunt in packs."

Whitsmith was indeed impressed, but, if she let Hudson know that, it removed any authority she had over her. If Hudson was as good as Whitsmith in the only thing Whitsmith had been better at her in, it negated the need for Whitsmith at all.

"The tracks were not left by a large carnivore," Whitsmith said. "They were too small. But no, I don't think they were left by a dromaeosaurid either."

"So what were they left by?"

Whitsmith smiled coyly. "I have a pretty good idea, don't worry about that."

Hudson's faint smile played about her lips once more and Whitsmith could detect even a grudging respect for her at last. "OK, I'll go with that. Lead the way, Whitsmith. I got your back."

Whitsmith walked ahead of her. She wished she had the first idea of what it could be they were hunting.

CHAPTER FOUR

The blonde soldier was named Aura Torrance, and she was a private in whatever army she served. Dexter Valentine had taken her back to his office and made her some tea from leaves his people had been cultivating in the swamp. It was far from what he had been used to at home, but over the years Valentine had grown somewhat accustomed to the taste. Now that they were sitting more comfortably, Valentine could see her forename printed onto her armour. It was a rather odd thing to do, but he supposed it must have been a current fashion. Torrance sipped at her cup and made an appreciable face. She had also taken two biscuits, which was annoying since Valentine had only offered her the one.

Torrance had revealed little since accepting Valentine's offer of hospitality. While he was growing keener to get to know her as a person, what he really wanted to know was whether she had anything to do with the prison. That it had taken five years for someone to realise the prison guards had not reported in was unlikely, and even factoring in how long it would take to organise some soldiers and get them from Earth to Jupiter, it still seemed ludicrous that five years would have passed before they arrived. He had to assume therefore they were here for entirely different reasons, and had indeed just stumbled upon their prison. Valentine could tell, however, that it did not matter how young Torrance was, she was far from stupid. She had worked out back on the roof that Valentine was not here studying the dinosaurs and likely knew precisely what had happened to the prison guards. Unless he came outright and told her, he doubted she would do anything about it. That she was awaiting the arrival of her entire unit may have meant she was simply distracting him until they could come in force and arrest him.

Since there was nothing Valentine could do about that anyway, he decided he would entertain his guest as the most gracious host he could be.

"I must say," he mentioned as he poured her more tea, "all the soldiers I've ever met were ugly brutes." In fact, there were more than a couple in the prison. "Io must have a great lack of ugly brutes, I take it?"

"We have mandatory conscription at eighteen," Torrance explained. She had removed some of her bulkier armour, but retained her uniform and light metals. Her form was slim and athletic, as Valentine would have expected of a soldier. She also carried the requisite knives and guns, although for a man who relished the danger of a true challenge, it only made the young woman more appealing. "We get one year of hard training," Torrance continued, "and then we're shipped off-world somewhere for proper graft."

"So this is your first assignment?"

"Are you asking me my age?" she asked with a winning smile.

"Well I wouldn't have said you were a day older than eighteen, but this is no training ground so I must be your first assignment."

She seemed pleased by his words, although it was only her eyes which said as much to him. She seemed to have no intention of saying anything she was actually thinking.

"So what exactly," Valentine continued in as casual an air as he could manage, "is your assignment here. You didn't exactly say."

"I'm not sure I'm allowed to, Mr Valentine."

"Please, call me Dex."

Torrance did not even try to hide her smile, and he could see now her companion had departed she had allowed her proverbial hair down.

"We're not here to cause any trouble with your research," she promised him. "When Hunter comes back with our sergeant perhaps you'll find out, but until then I can't really tell you much. You wouldn't want to get me in trouble would you, Dex?"

Valentine was taking a sip of his tea at the time and almost choked at the coy twinkling to her eyes. He coughed, settling the cup back into its saucer. "Farthest thing from my mind," he said. He assumed Hunter was the other woman who had confronted him on the roof but knew it would be a stupid question to ask. "How long do you think until they get here?"

Torrance shrugged. "Are you asking whether we have time for a little personal tour of your facilities, Dex?"

"You want to see the building?"

"Wasn't thinking of leaving this room actually."

Valentine shifted uncomfortably. Torrance was certainly younger and more attractive than any of the prisoners on this rock, but she was also an unknown quantity and he tended to keep those at as great a distance as he could. Nor was he used to having attractive women practically throwing themselves at him, and his ordered mind fought for a snappy response which would make her laugh but let her know he was not at this precise moment interested.

He opened his mouth but no words at all came out.

Torrance laughed anyway, which had been half his intent. "You know what they say about soldiers," Torrance said, rising from her seat and perching herself on the desk before him. She rested one foot upon his chair and took his tie in strong, delicate fingers, sliding them all the way down before replacing them at the top and repeating the process. "About how we could die any day so make the most of what time we have?"

Again Valentine tried to speak, although his voice came out strangled. He cleared his throat and tried again. "You haven't been in the army long enough to be thinking that, surely?"

She pouted in contemplation. "First assignment they send me to the dinosaur world, Dex. That's what they call this place back home. The forbidden dinosaur world. Like the Garden of Eden, some folks say. Just with more snakes." She smiled, her eyes shining. "The most exciting place in the solar system. And everyone needs a little excitement in their life, right, Dex?"

Torrance had worked slowly, leaning closer to him while at the same time pulling him gently from his chair towards her. Her full, moist lips formed an almost perfect O of contemplation, her cute, rounded face mere inches from his own. He could smell her now, the sweet aroma of honey glaze, and found her presence intoxicating.

But this would not solve anything. These people could very well have been sent here to investigate what had become of the prison guards, and this could have simply been an attempt at interrogation. The most bizarre interrogation he had ever known from the army, he reflected as he stared into Torrance's penetrating blue eyes.

She was playing with his mind, whether she realised it or was doing so only as a by-product of her genuine lust. Valentine needed to be in control of every situation, needed to know everything about everyone before he committed to anything; and he would never let down his guard. Aura Torrance may have been the most beautiful woman he had ever seen, but she was too much of an unknown for him to risk lowering his defences.

"I think a tour of the prison would be best after all," he said, trying not to gaze directly into her eyes but failing miserably.

Her eyes twinkled brighter at this. "It's interesting you still think of this place as a prison, Dex, considering you have no idea what happened to the prisoners."

Valentine was up in an instant, rising with such force that Torrance actually fell backwards, her elbows slamming audibly into the table beneath her. She raised her eyebrows as she looked up at him, and Valentine, flustering over everything he was doing wrong in this scenario, straightened his tie and fumbled over his words. "A tour of our operation, yes," he said. "Then you'll see how serious we are about our dinosaur research."

Torrance's shock and indecision had vaporised by this point, and she walked back to where she had left her armour resting on the floor. She purposefully made a show of bending slowly to retrieve it, and Valentine averted his eyes from the view she was presenting him. She took her time in replacing the armour, as though giving him as much time as he needed in order to change his mind, but Valentine was resolute. Each second ticking by was agony for him, for by this point he wanted nothing more than to throw the young woman back upon the desk and relieve both their frustrations. But Valentine was nothing if not organised, and his brain screamed to him this would have been a very bad idea indeed.

Finally Torrance was ready. She even looked a little annoyed as she faced him once more. He felt he had wronged her in his refusal and hoped he had not just made an enemy. But she smiled regardless, refusing to let him see her true feelings. "Lead on, Mr Valentine."

Valentine winced as he opened the door for her to precede him. Which she did, with head held high.

This, he feared, was going to prove a most uncomfortable tour.

He decided to begin with the actual research area. His people were of course not in the swamp because they wanted to be, but since they were still living in the prison they had through necessity had to make some investigations into the native wildlife. Aubrey Whitsmith was of course the main authority on such things, but even without her there were people who had taken up the task of researching the animals. Criminals, after all, were as much a snapshot of society as any other group. Valentine did find they had more than their average of senseless brutes, but if they did not have people with the skills to survive they never would have lasted as long as they had. While Valentine had access to the records detailing the crimes of each prisoner, all the former inmates knew of one another was that they were all criminals. No one really asked why anyone had been put away, and tended to treat one another as they would were they all free people.

Valentine therefore decided to take the young woman to the man who knew more about the dinosaurs than anyone other than Whitsmith.

"Zebadiah," Valentine informed her while they walked, "can answer all your questions. He's quite a character, our Zebadiah. I think you'll get along well with him."

Torrance did not seem to be paying that much attention, however. Valentine had attempted to take her along the route where they would happen upon as few people as possible. Unfortunately there was no corridor in the prison which was entirely empty at any given time, and they had already passed several people. One of the men they were currently passing was clearly leering at Torrance, and since Valentine knew just why that particular fellow had been incarcerated he should hardly have been surprised.

Once they had passed him, Valentine noticed Torrance was looking over her shoulder while they walked.

"He's a character, that one," Valentine laughed.

"He looked a bit menacing to me," she said, facing front once more.

"Nah, he wouldn't hurt a fly."

"Where's he from?"

"Earth. We're all from Earth."

"Like the prison?"

Valentine forced a smile but could not bring himself to look directly at her. Once again he had panicked and shown a card he had never meant her to see hiding up his sleeve. Valentine was far from an architect, but it seemed there was some artistic flourish which Torrance had recognised. Or perhaps she had just known the prison was not Jovian, even though it was in the Jovian system.

"All right," Valentine said, "I have something to admit to you."

"Oh?" she asked, raising an almost disappointed eyebrow.

"We knew the prison was here when we set off. We'd been instructed there was an abandoned building here we could use for shelter against the dinosaurs. I don't know the prison's history, just that it was already here. I can only assume the prisoners, and guards, were shipped back home and the place abandoned for some reason. Maybe it was decided a world full of dinosaurs was a bad place for a penal colony."

"So why not tell me that at the beginning?"

"And admit that Earth has made at least two expeditions into Jovian space, to land on forbidden ground no less? You finding us here was bad enough, but finding out Earth had dumped a prison here as well would not have gone well for the guys back home."

"So why are you telling me now?"

"Because when I'm around you, things keep slipping out."

She considered this, did not even make fun of his clearly ridiculous sentence, and the playful respect returned to her eyes. "Well, I won't tell if you don't."

Valentine wished he could figure this woman out. In the one sense she seemed to want nothing less than to make him so distracted he could not think straight, yet with every little slip-up she seemed less and less impressed with him. It was as though she had been ordered to press for information but was disappointed whenever he gave any of it up. Valentine had never really understood women and had always tried to steer clear of them. They upset his natural order of things. The sooner Torrance's unit arrived and they did whatever it was they wanted to do and got out of there, the happier Valentine would be.

"Zebadiah?" Torrance asked while they walked, and Valentine realised he had been staring.

"Zebadiah," he said, setting his jaw firm in determination to get this over and done with. Soon, he decided, would not be soon enough.

CHAPTER FIVE

"So," Hudson asked while the two women had stopped for a rest, "what's between you and Valentine anyway?"

Whitsmith glanced sharply at her. Hudson was sitting casually upon a log, munching on a chocolate bar as though the swamp would sit back and wait for her to finish before it became dangerous again. Whitsmith had once asked her why she did that, and Hudson had merely replied that since their chocolate supply was almost gone she didn't want to waste the experience by being afraid of the local wildlife. If something was going to get her it would get her, but at least she would die with chocolate in her mouth. It was an odd philosophy, and Whitsmith had never asked again.

Hudson also seemed to think that just because she was taking the time for a break, it meant she could pry into Whitsmith's affairs.

"There's nothing between us," Whitsmith snapped, perhaps a little too late. "Dex is my boss, that's all."

"Well technically he's my boss too, only I don't call him Dex."

Whitsmith decided she would do the adult thing and simply ignore her.

Hudson crunched loudly on her chocolate, which Whitsmith fancied contained some form of biscuit or honeycomb. She did not have any herself and tried not to think about where Hudson may have got hers. Another crunch and Whitsmith felt her own stomach growling since the only thing Whitsmith had brought with her were some bad-tasting energy bars someone back at the prison made out of swamp reeds or something.

"I'm willing to share," Hudson said, and Whitsmith looked to her then to see the heavy-set woman holding out a finger of chocolate. Whitsmith glanced from the hand to Hudson's face, knowing there would have to be a catch. "No catch," Hudson said, knowing precisely what she was thinking. "Just trying to bond."

Whitsmith did not want to bond with this woman, but another crunch made her mind up for her and she reached for it.

"It's just," Hudson said, pulling back to wave the chocolate finger in a measured pace that showed she was only pretending not to have realised she had retracted it at that precise moment, "if we're bonding like this, we should really open up to each other. You know, about our feelings for certain people. People like ... I don't know. Dex maybe?"

Whitsmith straightened her back and looked into the swamp once more, biting down harshly on her energy bar. Hudson chuckled and leaned back against her tree rest while she ate.

It was only a couple of minutes later that the two women returned to their work. For Whitsmith, however, the break had been far from relaxing. She was angry and did not even know why. Her personal life was none of Hudson's business, and even if she was involved with Valentine it certainly would not be something she would be ashamed of. Dexter Valentine was many things, a lot of them bad, but he was also the man who had kept their little community alive for all this time. If someone else had taken charge, Whitsmith was willing to bet the dinosaurs would have moved in by now.

She caught Hudson smirking her way and raised her chin slightly, wishing Hudson would just mind her own business. Besides, it wasn't as though there was a lot of choice in the prison.

No more was said about it as they resumed their search. Hudson would have been happy if they just returned home with the news that the crocodile had been identified and turned away, if not actually dealt with, but she was willing to allow Whitsmith to play out her hunch. Whitsmith had to admit even to herself, however, that this was all it was. She had nothing concrete to go on, yet her gut instinct about this sort of thing was always right. She knew there was something out here other than a crocodile and she intended to prove it.

A call came in across her radio which told her one of the perimeter guards had found something. The swamp cut out most of the man's speech, but she had a location and that was all that mattered to her. Whitsmith wished they could send up a satellite so they could bounce signals around a little more easily, but if they had the means to launch anything into space she reckoned they would all have left long ago.

Hudson did not complain at all as they trudged their way back to the guard, did not even snidely mention the fact they had been moving around in circles this whole time. Whitsmith did not like to think they had been wasting time, especially because it would give Hudson even greater ammunition to consider her useless, but the truth was it was very difficult to track anything through the swamp.

Whitsmith spoke briefly with the guard once they found him, and she was informed that he had spotted something lurking within the rushes and that when he had taken a step towards it the thing had scarpered. That made Whitsmith consider she wasn't tracking a dromaeosaurid at all, and that it was some small herbivore instead. Certainly if there were any raptors in the area they would not be running away from a border patrol.

"Go take a look," Hudson said tiredly, "since we're here anyway."

Whitsmith did not like taking orders from Hudson, especially since she was intending to take a look regardless. Without even acknowledging her, Whitsmith moved into the rushes the patrol guard had indicated. They rose to her knees and could easily have hidden a crocodile, but Whitsmith was determined not to show her fear. She had her pistol in her hand once more, although hoped Hudson had her rocket launcher primed just in case it turned out to be another deionosuchus.

Swiftly Whitsmith located an area of the reeds which had been pressed flat, indicating something heavy had been lying there. Crouching, affording her a view of what the creature would have seen, Whitsmith looked back to where Hudson waited. Whitsmith could see her very clearly and suddenly realised just how good a point of concealment this was. Whatever had been hiding here, she did not think it would have been a herbivore, yet if it was indeed a predator why would a man taking a step towards it frighten it away? It might retreat to a safer distance, but surely it would not simply flee entirely? And if it had not fled, where was it?

Rising, Whitsmith glanced about her, trying to fathom where the thing might have got to. The swamp was still, the winds providing a gentle sway to the reeds and leaves, but otherwise drawing out nothing amiss. The soft sounds of chirruping insects drifted through the air. Nothing seemed amiss at all.

And then her eyes caught something and she frowned. Ahead of her, almost hidden by the rushes and a nearby tree, she could just make out what appeared to be a dark green head, and an eye staring out at her. Whitsmith could not from this distance identify the species, but the eye seemed large and rounded, which would indicate some form of troodont. There had been a byronosaurus supposedly spotted in the swamp a couple of years back, and, while it had never been confirmed, it was the only form of troodont Whitsmith had ever known to even be suggested living here. Troodonts supposedly did not live in swampland, their long legs far more suited to open lands where they could run like the emus and ostriches they resembled. This world was nothing if not odd, however, and some days Whitsmith even expected the trees to get up and walk away.

The great eye blinked once and Whitsmith felt a shiver run down her spine. She knew she was being watched, but more than that it was as though she was being observed. It was as though the creature was assessing her, and she shivered with the thought that she was naked before its gaze. Troodonts were hunters which reached to an average of around two metres. They were dangerous, certainly, although their prey would not have been large animals the size of humans. Besides which, with Hudson and her guns handy Whitsmith did not really fear attack too badly. If the creature, whatever it was, had fled when the guard had taken a single step towards it, she could not see it would be prepared to launch an attack upon her with Hudson so close by.

Whitsmith continued to stare at what she could see of the head, wishing so much was not obscured by the foliage. The more she stared, the more she frowned. And the more she frowned, the more she began to determine that the thing she was watching was no troodont. Certainly the eye and the texture of the skin were indicative of such a creature, but there was something strange about the cranial structure. It was almost too rounded, and she could see very little indication that the creature even had a beak.

Suddenly the thing was moving. Whitsmith did not know whether she had spooked it or whether it had finished its viewing of her, but for whatever reason the rushes rustled as the creature tore off through the swamp. Whitsmith shouted to Hudson and gave pursuit, determined not to lose the creature. It was keeping low and moving very quickly, suggesting it was running upon four legs. If the thing was indeed a species of troodont she could not see how it was keeping itself so well concealed from her with the rushes being so low.

Charging through the strange grass, Whitsmith kept track of her prey only by the movement of the rushes ahead of her. At one point the movement stopped, presumably as the creature got its bearings, and then it was off once more. Whitsmith plunged ahead at this point, hoping to catch up to the thing, but it was ahead of her too quickly.

"Come on," she urged Hudson, and then stopped, aghast. Hudson was no longer behind her. Whitsmith had charged ahead so quickly that she had lost her protection.

Her eyes turning back to the rushes, which she noticed had become much thicker and taller now, Whitsmith suddenly realised how clever this animal had been. Like the stories of the ancient Will-o'-the-wisps, the creature had drawn her deeper into the swamp with the intention of pulling her away from any help she might have received. And now it had her just where it wanted her.

Whitsmith froze, realising she was in trouble but refusing to lie down to die. She listened for any sound which might help; the insects were still buzzing and the wind was still rustling the rushes, but if it was creature movement and not wind she could not say. Nor could she see anything, could catch no further glimpses of dark green scales or large staring eyes. As her heart thumped soundly within her she half-hoped the thing had taken the opportunity to flee.

But she knew a strategic genius did not draw out the enemy without moving in to finish it off.

A shrieking hiss emanated from the brush to her right and Whitsmith snapped her pistol around in trembling fingers. The wind continued soughing through the long rushes; taunting her, trying to angle the blades for a better view of her upcoming demise. Whitsmith could hear her heart hammering through her eardrums, the incessant pounding of a primitive rhythm foretelling her death.

And suddenly something was leaping at her. Whitsmith raised her pistol and cracked off a shot, the report sounding loudly through the swamp and sending up a shower of birds from somewhere nearby. Whitsmith stood staring at the rushes once more, for whatever had come for her was no longer in her sight. She could not for one moment believe that she had managed to shoot the thing; all she could think was that it had dropped back into cover. And why would it not? It had drawn her so meticulously into this trap and had no need to show its hand until it was ready.

Whitsmith knew she had to get away. She had lost all sense of direction by this point, but even stumbling about in fear would be better than just standing there waiting for the creature to make its move. Selecting the direction she felt most likely to be her point of entry, Whitsmith broke into a run. All she could see were the parting rushes before her; all she could hear was the hammering of her own terrified heart; all she could think of was how easily a drowning woman fighting for the surface would push herself even deeper into the black ocean.

She went tumbling, her leg having snagged on something, and cursed her clumsiness. Ending on her backside, she struggled back to a sitting position. It was then she saw the wound to her leg. There were two deep slashes in her shin, as though a massive claw had torn at her leg even while she ran. Whitsmith had no idea why she could not feel the pain and put it down to the adrenalin pumping furiously around her body. But the pain was irrelevant. If the creature had been able to predict her path with such accuracy it meant it would be watching her even now, waiting for her next move.

Raising her pistol with shaking hands, Whitsmith knew she had no chance of making any shot connect; but she would not die without a fight. Her mind struggled to put a name to the creature stalking her. It was no crocodile, of that much she was certain. But nor could she think of any dinosaur with intelligence enough to be doing what it was doing. That left only one possibility that she could think of. Whatever was stalking her was human.

A low growl rumbled through the rushes then and Whitsmith saw a form stepping through. It kept itself hunched so the rushes would conceal it more fully, but Whitsmith could see it clearly enough.

The thing was thin and tall; with its back straightened it would have stood at around seven feet. It was a pale green in colour, its skin the rough, coarse texture of leather. Its arms were long, gangly almost, while its legs were thick and strong. The creature had a short, almost useless tail protruding from its back, but this was not used for counterbalance as with most carnivorous dinosaurs. For this creature walked upon two legs, with a straight back as though it thought it was some kind of human. The naked creature stared down at Whitsmith with large, bright eyes almost filling its green, rounded face. It bore a large gash of a mouth within which Whitsmith could see the promise of mutilating teeth.

The impossible creature stared at her in something which seemed amazingly like curiosity. It made no hostile moves, yet Whitsmith was not fooled for a moment. She could see the claws of its hands were as sharp as razors, while its clawed feet bore the lethal, slashing scimitar of a dromaeosaurid. Just what the thing was, Whitsmith could not say. It was not natural to this world, for nothing like this had ever existed in Earth's entire prehistory. But then nothing on this world was natural, not even the world itself. No one had ever been able to provide a satisfactory explanation as to how the dinosaurs and other prehistoric life had come to this world, so Whitsmith knew she should not have been so surprised to learn of some kind of dinosaur-man here as well. Perhaps even the origins of this world could be found through this being, whatever it was.

"Whitsmith!"

Whitsmith watched as the thing crouched lower at the shout, cautiousness taking hold once more. Whatever the thing was, it certainly knew that to survive it had to remain hidden. Whitsmith could hear Hudson shouting her name once more as she blundered through the rushes. The creature began to back away, its large eyes focusing on the exact area of Hudson's approach. Whitsmith could only imagine what senses the creature must have possessed in order to be able to detect Hudson's precise location.

Slowly the creature began to back off into the rushes and Whitsmith knew she was losing her only opportunity to study the thing. "Wait," she said anxiously, holding out her hand. "Please, don't run."

The creature looked to her momentarily and Whitsmith detected something almost like regret. But then the beast was gone, swallowed once more by the rushes.

"Whitsmith."

Whitsmith felt the large form of Katie Hudson drop beside her. Hudson held a rifle in one hand, while trying to help Whitsmith with the other. She was kneeling on only one leg, ready to run at a moment's notice.

"Good idea shooting your pistol," Hudson said. "Gave me a bearing."

Whitsmith could not help but laugh. If she hadn't been so afraid she would not have scared away the creature. But the thing had torn at her leg, there was no denying that. Perhaps it had not meant her harm, perhaps it had. There was simply no way of knowing. Not now anyway.

"Did you get a look at what you were chasing?" Hudson asked, keeping a careful eye on the rushes. "Was it a raptor?"

"I don't know what it was." Tentatively Whitsmith tried to stand and found the wound was not nearly as bad as it could have been. If the creature had wanted her dead she would not now be alive to wonder. As she put her weight upon it she felt the pain at last, but only grunted in Hudson's presence. "I need to talk to Dex," she determined. "I think after all these years it's time to explore this swamp properly."

CHAPTER SIX

Once, long ago, there had been a simple man leading a simple life. And that simple man had one day discovered how to transfer a little money here, a little money there, in order to maximise his potential for profit and interest. Sometimes that money had not belonged to him, and sometimes it did belong to him but some of it belonged to the government in taxes. The simple man had over several years acquired a somewhat large sum of money. Then the police had arrested him and he had ended up in a penal colony far from where his money could have done him any good.

Zebadiah grinned to himself as he held a branch through the stout vertical iron bars of the cell. The creature within, a recent acquisition called an erythrosuchus, snapped at the raw meat he had skewered to the end of the stick. The erythrosuchus was a five metre brute with a bulky body and long, snapping tail. Its head was huge compared with the rest of its body and resembled the classic long-snouted, razor-toothed picture always painted of the tyrannosaurus rex and its kin. It was not, however, a dinosaur, for it walked upon four legs as though it was a jungle cat or a crocodile. Indeed, its name meant 'red crocodile', which Zebadiah found amusing since its legs, though thick and powerful, were far longer than any crocodile's he had ever known. The beast always looked to him like it was a dinosaur; just one that walked on four legs.

If he had not been caught stealing so much money, Zebadiah would never have been afforded the opportunity to study such an animal, and every day he woke to thank Jupiter that he had made such a bad criminal.

The erythrosuchus roared at him, its meal finished since the meat was swallowed whole. Whether the animal was still hungry, whether it was angry at Zebadiah for something, or whether it was just laying down its territory hardly mattered. Zebadiah was the one standing free in the corridor and the creature which predated the dinosaurs was behind bars.

It was a wonderful use for the former cells. While most of the cells had been retained as sleeping chambers, those located in the lower levels were larger and designed to contain numerous prisoners at once. They proved to be the perfect areas in which to hold the various animals Valentine intended for pit fights, and it was Zebadiah's job to make sure the animals were kept in a fit and healthy condition so they would be ready to fight should Valentine call upon a specific one.

It was a job Zebadiah took extremely seriously. He did not believe Valentine was an especially cruel man, but he knew some of the inmates here would gladly feed him to the animals if they did not get their promised dose of blood sports.

Besides which, Zebadiah did not see this as a task, but a reward for something he had clearly done right in a former life.

Zebadiah moved between the various cells, feeding the animals and checking their health. He was an old man now, he supposed: somewhere in his seventies probably but he had never really kept count. He walked slowly, with the aid of a gnarled cane whenever he remembered to use it. His wrinkled skin was patchy with brown and white splotches which he didn't think were likely very healthy but had never bothered to get checked out. There were doctors in the prison, but very little in the way of medicines. If someone was dying all the doctors could really do was tell them they were dying, and that was something Zebadiah could have done without. He sported a short, wispy white beard and very little hair; what he did have he had not bothered to run a comb through since the break-out five years earlier. He had most of his teeth left, but an adult human did not need all their teeth in order to eat so he wasn't bothered about those either. In fact, very little bothered Zebadiah. He lived by the philosophy that there was precious little in this world a person could change, so there was no sense in worrying about any of it.

He heard voices then and scowled to himself. Usually he was left to his own devices, but occasionally people would come and bother him. Usually it was a pit fighter trying to bribe him into cutting the legs of the animal they were about to fight, as though he was breeding racehorses or something. Zebadiah had no interests in the fights himself, had never seen a single one of them, but he knew he was kept in work only by their continuing success. That meant sometimes he would have to speak with the various people who came down to visit him.

The voice he recognised belonged to Dexter Valentine and Zebadiah sighed. Of all the people to visit him, Valentine was the worst because he was in charge. Zebadiah found he had to be reasonably polite to the man, always had to answer whatever questions he proposed, and was sometimes told to change the way he did things. Why Valentine was bothering him today Zebadiah could not say, but he hoped to be able to get rid of the man as quickly as possible.

Then he heard a woman's voice and decided Valentine had brought a girl down here in order to impress her. Men had done similar things before, and while it did not seem like Valentine's style he could think of no other reason for Valentine bringing someone with him. Unless of course it was his secretary Aubrey Whitsmith and they had come to do an audit or something.

Zebadiah cringed at the very thought of ever having to do an audit or file reports of any nature.

When the two appeared before him, stepping slowly down the stairs into the dimly-lit underground passages surrounding the cells, Zebadiah immediately noted the woman's armour. It probably meant someone upstairs had developed some new metal and wanted to test it out in the arena.

"Mr Valentine," Zebadiah said with a wide grin. "What a wonderful surprise. You bring me a live meal for the erythrosuchus?"

Valentine looked horrified, while the woman just gazed into the cells curiously.

"You've managed to catch quite a few of these things," she said. "Be careful, Dexter, you may start impressing me soon."

Zebadiah wondered whether she believed Valentine had gone out to capture any of them himself. Or whether he even left the prison at all.

The woman wandered over to one of the cages, taking hold of the bars to peer through at a thick, bulbous creature Whitsmith had brought in only recently. "What's this one?"

"A moschops," Zebadiah explained. "Bite ya fingers off, that one."

The woman's hands immediately released the bars and Zebadiah grinned at how easy it was to control people.

Valentine only looked annoyed, which meant he really was trying to impress this woman. All the more reason, Zebadiah thought, to wind her up as much as he possibly could.

"Private Torrance here," Valentine told him, "is part of an expedition into the swamp."

Which meant she wasn't even from the prison, which was odd. "Oh," Zebadiah said. "If her expedition's in the swamp, what's she doing here? The swamp's out there."

"That's a good question."

Torrance seemed to realise the two men were looking at her, waiting for an answer. She did not take her eyes off the moschops while she answered, as though she fully expected the thing to be able to slink its way through the bars. "That's for the sergeant to tell you, I'm afraid. Like I said, I don't have the authority to ... Is that a T. rex?"

Zebadiah watched her move across to the cell holding the erythrosuchus. The animal had calmed somewhat and was presently dozing in the corner. "No," he said, wondering how anyone could be so dense. "Does it look like a T. rex? It's not even a dinosaur, you stupid girl."

Valentine shot him a glower which told him to shut the hell up, but Zebadiah could not maintain his good nature indefinitely.

Torrance, however, was more concerned with the animal than the gaoler's attitude. "What if it got out?" she asked.

"Well I'd be sacked for one thing," Zebadiah laughed. "Kidding. I'd be eaten."

"The animals can't get out," Valentine put in quickly. "They're only ever removed from their cages when they're taken to the pits."

"Pits?" She looked directly at Valentine now and Zebadiah found a great deal of pleasure in the other man's sudden anxiety.

"Where they fight," Zebadiah said before Valentine could spin her some lie or other. "The prisoners fight 'em for fun. Sometimes they lose and another prisoner gets a new pair a boots."

"What prisoners?" Torrance asked.

Valentine laughed hollowly, glowering at Zebadiah once more to be silent. "Zeb likes the irony of our being trapped here in this prison while we do our research. He calls us prisoners."

"Oh."

Zebadiah considered telling her the truth, but figured that if she was too stupid to see through the obvious lie she deserved everything that was coming to her. Up to and including Valentine getting his leg over, if that was what he intended. Strangely, the man seemed more afraid of her than anything, and Zebadiah wondered whether he should have found out all the facts before plunging ahead into his warped sense of humour over the whole thing.

"When's the next fight?" Torrance asked.

"There's one scheduled for tomorrow night," Zebadiah said. "Some idiot's chosen to fight the erythrosuchus."

"Do you mind if I watch, Dex?" Torrance asked, her entire face lighting up at the prospect. She clutched her hands before her in supplication and Valentine did not know how to react. He clearly wanted to refuse, for he did not want this soldier to see the rowdy, boisterous, bloodthirsty truth of life in the prison. But Zebadiah could also see he was still trying to get into her pants so was more than liable to accept.

"Sure," Valentine therefore said. "If your sergeant lets you stay that long."

Torrance squealed with joy and hugged him before moving back towards the stairs. Valentine pointedly ignored any reaction Zebadiah may have made as he followed her. But Zebadiah, for once, was not thinking about how to make fun of or inconvenience someone. He had seen things in the young woman that perhaps Valentine had not. She was a clever one, throwing off Valentine's senses with all her girly act. As she had departed, however, Zebadiah had caught her steal one final glance at the caged erythrosuchus. It was not a look of fear, of keeping the animal in her sight. Zebadiah could be certain of nothing, but there was something going on in her mind; something he knew he wasn't going to like. Something Valentine would ordinarily have been able to see.

Perhaps when Whitsmith returned, he reflected, they would have someone with sense enough to look into this properly. Whatever the young soldier was up to, Zebadiah knew it would be bad for them all.

CHAPTER SEVEN

Sergeant Zara Cartello cast her eyes about the hall derisively, wrinkling her nose and clearly wishing she was somewhere a little more upmarket. She was a short woman in her mid-to-late thirties, filled out by the bulk of her armour but somehow oddly at ease within it. Across her shoulder, the word *ZARA* was prominently displayed. Her face was rounded, her short dark hair could have done with a wash several months back, but she did not appear to be someone who cared for such things. Her eyes were too small, too thin and too close together, lending her a perpetually suspicious air. She was also far from smiling and as Valentine came down the main staircase to greet her he wondered whether she was even capable of such an expression.

"Welcome, Sergeant Cartello," he said, beaming as brightly as he possibly could. He held his arms wide as though he intended to hug her, but as he reached the bottom of the stairs and caught her dark expression he decided he would prefer to have embraced that red crocodile downstairs. Clapping his hands for want of something to do with his outstretched arms, Valentine noted the dark-haired woman from the roof earlier had accompanied the sergeant back here. Torrance had told him the woman's name was Tana Hunter, which was apt considering only the hunters ever seemed to survive around here.

"Welcome to what?" Cartello asked flatly. "I've camped in homelier tents than this."

"Ah yes," Valentine enthused, "but here you have a roof over your head, and guards at the doors."

"I'll give you that. So," she said, looking at him properly at last, "you must be Valentine."

"Dexter Valentine," he said with a flourish. "At your service."

"And what kind of a name is Dexter Valentine? You sound like something out of a god-awful rom-com."

Valentine forced a laugh, but suddenly wanted to kick the woman back into the swamp and see how she fared the night. That she was carrying an array of weapons and had an unknown amount of reinforcements out there stayed his hand.

"Private Torrance," Valentine said, "is an asset to your unit, Sergeant. You should feel proud to have her."

"Private Torrance," Cartello snorted, "is a young fool who talks too much. She's tried to bed you already hasn't she? Tries to do that with every man she meets. Has self-esteem issues that one. No idea why, useless waste of space."

Valentine bit back the obvious retort about just why Torrance might have self-esteem issues. He also did not know how he felt about the sergeant's assessment of her. He did not know whether to be elated or annoyed that Torrance handed herself out like a booby prize; then suddenly stopped and asked himself why he was behaving like a schoolboy. While it was true that Aura Torrance was without doubt a stunningly attractive girl, the very presence of these soldiers could spell the end to his entire society. At the very least the soldiers would make it common knowledge around the prison that there were parts of this world that were not swamp, and then the prisoners would demand why Valentine had been lying to them all this time. At worst of course they could be here because they wanted to get the prisoners back in their cells.

In short, it was not a time to be thinking with anything other than his brain.

"Sergeant," Torrance said, falling into step behind Valentine. He had half hoped she had wandered off somewhere and not heard Cartello's description of her, but the tension in her body attested otherwise. It was not simply a straightening of the back in order to stand at attention: Torrance was part embarrassed, part angry, and Valentine felt a rush of chivalry in his sudden desire to stand up for her. But antagonising an armed woman with troops at her back was never a good idea and he hoped Torrance would understand she was not worth it.

"You have a report to make," Cartello barked, "or have you found a mirror to do your hair in front of?"

"Mr Valentine runs a dinosaur research centre," Torrance said without any indication that the sergeant's words had bothered her.

"They have some creatures locked away downstairs and other equipment set up to study them. I have no doubt Mr Valentine has been nothing but genuine with me."

Valentine winced, but it was too late to come clean now.

"Fine, fine, whatever," Cartello mumbled. "Valentine. We'll need a place to hole up for a couple of days while we run some routine scans of the area. I'll take your room: it's going to be the most decent one here. Don't get in our way."

Valentine bit his lower lip. "Certainly, Sergeant. Please treat this facility as you would your own home."

"My home's a whole lot nicer than this. Hunter, take a proper look around since Torrance is a damn screw-up. I'm getting some shut-eye."

Valentine got someone to show her the way since he wanted to be out of her presence as soon as possible. Hunter also looked him up and down derisively before moving off to her own errands. Valentine could not understand how he had assessed the situation so badly. Back on the roof it had been Torrance asking all the questions, and now neither of her colleagues seemed to care much for her at all. He supposed since she had been the one with the gun she had simply taken out her frustrations upon Valentine when she had the opportunity.

"How do you put up with that woman?" he asked.

Torrance seemed tense, and he could tell she was embarrassed at his having witnessed the scene. "Sergeant Cartello is just thorough. There are a lot of dangers on this world and it's always best to get a second opinion."

It would have only made her more uncomfortable for him to push further so he said instead, "Well, if your sergeant's resting her weary old bones and Hunter's skulking around to dig up the dirty on me, what do you intend doing to make my life miserable?"

"They're not bad people, Dex. We've just been through a lot lately. We've come a long way and you're the first people we've met in ages. Cartello's probably just forgotten how to talk to people, that's all."

"So once she's had her rest she might be offering to lay the breakfast table?"

Torrance smiled wryly. "No, she'll still be pig-headed and arrogant, but I didn't tell you that."

"Dex!"

Valentine felt an immense wave of relief wash over him as he heard the familiar voice of Aubrey Whitsmith. Suddenly he knew all his problems would be solved.

Whitsmith slowed her approach when she realised he had company, her eyes narrowing in a curious frown. She had come to him with a large, violent woman named Katie Hudson, which was unusual since the two women were far from friends. Hudson was a notable pit fighter with only a minimal amount of defeats and was the perfect choice for a bodyguard out in the swamps; but once they returned to the prison he had expected the two women to part company as soon as humanly possible. He also noticed Whitsmith's leg was bandaged, but, since she was still walking, the injury could not have been that bad so he didn't bother asking about it.

He realised then he should probably make some introductions. "Private Aura Torrance, I'd like you to meet my lifeline. Aubrey Whitsmith: my secretary and foremost knowledge on everything."

"That's quite a claim," Torrance said, extending her hand. Whitsmith seemed to regard the hand as though it was laced with poison, and barely brushed her fingers across it in greeting.

"Who is she?" Whitsmith all but demanded. "Where'd she come from?"

"Private Torrance and her unit are staying with us for a while, so please don't upset them. They have big guns, unknown numbers and a commanding officer with a not-too-sunny disposition."

He knew from experience that Whitsmith could assess a situation in moments, and that was more than enough information to bring her up to speed. She seemed incredibly wary, however, and Valentine knew there was something she needed to say.

Torrance wrinkled her nose. "You stink really bad."

"Eau de moschops," Whitsmith said tartly. "Do you have anything to do with that thing out there?"

"What thing would that be?"

"The theropod that stood upright."

"Theropods couldn't stand upright," Torrance said.

"No one told this one."

"What did you do with it?"

Whitsmith hesitated. "It's dead."

"And it was alone?"

"Yes."

"You're sure?"

"Hudson and I checked the area carefully. There were only tracks from one creature, and we shot that one. Threw its body in the swamp."

"An odd move," Torrance said, "for people studying the wildlife."

"That thing wasn't natural. What was it?"

"I have no idea. Now it looks as though no one will. Excuse me, Dex, I'm going to go give Hunter a hand."

Valentine noticed Whitsmith staring darkly after her as she left and neither of them spoke until Torrance was out of the hall entirely. Whitsmith grabbed his arm and dragged him away from earshot of everyone else, although he noted Hudson had sauntered over to join them. "What?" he asked, shaking his arm free.

"What do you mean what? Who is she? What's she doing here? Why's she calling you Dex?"

"Aura Torrance, staying the night, and because I asked her to. Now what's all this nonsense about an upright dinosaur?"

"I don't know what it was, but it slashed my leg and might have killed me if Hudson hadn't turned up."

"You really should have brought it back, you know."

"It got away."

Valentine blinked. "But you told Aura it was dead."

"So it's Aura is it?"

"Why do you hate someone you've only just met, Aubrey?"

"I don't hate her. I ..." She seemed angry about something, and Valentine sometimes wished he knew how her mind worked. She was a good woman and a loyal friend, but sometimes she did his head in. "Do they have a shuttle?" Whitsmith asked.

"I don't know. Probably, somewhere."

"So we could take it and get away from here."

"Depends how many soldiers they have waiting there. I'm more concerned with this creature you saw. What was it?"

Whitsmith's shoulders sagged and he could see her adrenalin rush fading. What with her confrontation, her almost being killed and now finding out the military were swarming all over the place, she had had a busy day. "It looked like a troodon," she said.

"But what was it?"

"I don't know. A swamp god for all I know." She ran a hand through her grimy hair and looked more anxious than Valentine had ever seen her. "I need a shower and a long sleep. I don't know, maybe I'll think of something in the morning. I take it you haven't given away my bed as well?"

Valentine shrugged. "So far these soldiers don't know what happened here. We need to find out what they want, whether it has anything to do with us."

"What if it does?"

"Then," Hudson said simply, "we kill them."

Valentine had forgotten Hudson was even there, and while he felt revulsion at what she was suggesting, it was the only way to keep themselves alive. Valentine did not like the thought of having to murder an unknown number of people, especially since it would mean a great number of deaths on his own side, but there was likely no other option. Unless of course the soldiers were not here for the prisoners at all. In that case they might finish their work and just leave.

"Let me work on Aura," Valentine said. "I might be able to get something out of her."

Whitsmith looked at him sourly. "Don't let me twist your arm or anything."

Hudson gave a slight cough and they both looked to her to see Private Torrance returning to the hall. Valentine put Whitsmith and her attitude problem behind him and greeted Torrance with a warm smile.

"Hunter's fine as she is," Torrance reported. "I'm going out to check the area. If there's something weird out there it might pose a threat."

"It's dead," Whitsmith said acidly. "I told you."

"And I believe you. But I can't think of any species that ever had just the one member. Do you have motion sensors set up in the swamp?"

"Are you a complete idiot?" Whitsmith retorted. "It's a swamp. There are thousands of creatures out there."

Torrance's smile was tight. "If you could just show me where the tracks were, I can make my checks and get back here before nightfall."

"Actually," Valentine cut in, "Aubrey's tired and a little smelly. How about going out in the morning?"

"How about you show me instead, Dex? You must know your way around out there."

"I'm fine, actually," Whitsmith said, glowering at Valentine and Torrance alike. "I was going back out there anyway, just to make some checks of my own. You can tag along if you like, Torrance. Just don't slow me down."

"Wouldn't dream of interfering."

Whatever Valentine could have said to any of this, he knew it would be wrong. Wisely he chose to remain silent.

As Torrance and Whitsmith headed back out, Hudson checked her guns and looked upon Valentine with a mixture of amusement and pity. "What?" Valentine asked.

"Nothing," Hudson said. "You really are a simpleton Valentine. Don't worry, I'll bring her back safely."

He watched them all go and shook his head. Whitsmith had the finest mind in this place, but sometimes he just wished he understood what went on inside it.

CHAPTER EIGHT

He had been unable to locate Private Hunter, and eventually Valentine surrendered to the fact that he had lost her. He had several people keeping a lookout for her, but he was not confident anyone would find her. He had a feeling that whatever Private Hunter had been told to do, it was not something Valentine was meant to know about. Instead he had gone to spy on his own chambers to see whether the sergeant really was asleep. He was not fool enough to listen in at the door, but nor was he fool enough to have no means of escape from his room. Long ago had he built what amounted to a back door, and presently was he within the connecting passage. The secret door held a two-way peephole, in case he needed to use it either way, and he was using it now. From the peephole he could not get the best of views of the bed, but the curtains were open so there was a lot of light in the room. It was not concrete evidence that the sergeant was awake, but as he listened harder he could detect no sounds of snoring or even the subtle breathing a sleeper makes.

Deciding he had nothing to lose but his life, Valentine unset the lock and gently slid the door open a crack. Peering in, he realised he should not have put his wardrobe in such a position so as to block his view of the bed, but in truth he had never really expected a grumpy soldier to be napping between his sheets.

Sliding the door open a little further, Valentine craned his neck until at last he could see the bed. Which was, oddly enough, empty.

Stepping sheepishly into his own room, he stood at the foot of his bed and scratched his head. He did not like where this was going. First he had Private Hunter vanishing on him, and now Sergeant Cartello was following suit. That they had met up somewhere was obvious, but what were they trying to do? That all depended on why they had been sent to the prison, and the only way of finding out that was getting the information from the soldiers themselves. He just doubted any of them would be willing to give him anything he could use.

Then he noticed a heap of armour dumped in the corner of the room. Wherever Cartello had gone, it seemed she had gone in just her ordinary clothes. Then he saw a pile of ordinary clothes dumped beside the bed and he decided he really didn't have a clue what was going on.

"What the hell?"

Valentine spun about and shrieked, leaping back a pace. Sergeant Cartello had emerged from his en suite bathroom, his toothbrush sticking out of her mouth, her face wearing an expression heated enough to fry an egg. That was almost all she was wearing, actually, for she was standing before him in only her underwear. Her body was as thick and bulky as he had expected, her muscles those of a human tank. Valentine immediately shut his eyes and averted his face, as though by doing both these things he would somehow wipe the image from his memory.

He heard the distinctive sound of a gun being loaded and bolted for the door.

"Just checking everything was all right. Good night, Sergeant." He collided with a wall and decided to open his eyes, struggling with the door handle he had turned a thousand times before. He heard Cartello's cursing all the way down the corridor, although she did not pursue. At last he decided he had run far enough and collapsed against a wall, his breathing haggard, his mind reeling, his every iota of reason telling him he was an idiot.

He stayed there for some minutes, trying to catch his breath. With any luck the sergeant would be too embarrassed to mention the incident when she got up in the morning, or whenever it was she intended getting up. Valentine estimated there were still a few hours of light remaining, so there was every chance the sergeant would wake up sometime in the early hours and come looking for him.

"Have to respect you for that."

Valentine started, his eyes snapping open. Private Hunter stood before him, amusement playing upon her face.

"You already know?" he asked.

"Sergeant called me, told me to find you and skin you alive. If you're going to spy on someone you might not want to do it by standing in the middle of their bedroom."

"My bedroom," Valentine snapped. If he was going to be shot she might at least get the facts straight.

"Well, technically it's the bedroom of whoever ran the prison before you guys got here."

"He's not using it any more," Valentine grumped.

"Evidently. Do you have a bar in this place?"

The question threw him. In the past five years they had attempted to build a small community for themselves, which involved various forms of entertainment. "Yes, of course we have a bar."

"Where'd you get your alcohol?"

"We make it."

She raised her eyebrows.

"Well, we brew the beer and ... crush the grapes? I have no idea actually. I just know we have people who can make alcohol from whatever can be found in the swamp. I tend not to ask too many questions about things like that. Same with the food. Sometimes it's best not to know."

Hunter laughed, and he could see he had indeed made an impression on her. "Then you can buy me a drink."

"We don't have any money here."

"Even better," she said, slipping her arm into his. "Let's go get sloshed."

There were two bars in the prison and Valentine decided to take her to the least rowdy. It had been adapted from a bar area the former guards had used, although a few walls had been knocked down in order to accommodate a greater number of patrons. The actual bar was no larger than it had been, and those in charge of fermenting the alcohol had set bottles to the wall as though they were working in a proper pub. They had beer and water on tap and everything else came from bottles. The bar was one of the most efficiently-run places of the entire prison, which was hardly surprising since it would be the one place everyone would want to get absolutely right.

Valentine found them a table and went to the bar for their drinks. He came back with two pints of what passed for the local beer. It was a little thicker than he had been used to and the colour was a little darker, but it tended to go down all right so he did not question. Hunter regarded the drink curiously, sniffing the thick liquid.

"It's not dangerous," Valentine said. "But that's about all I know of it."

"What fun's a beer that's not dangerous?" Hunter asked, taking a sip. Immediately she scowled, although at her second sip she seemed to be contemplating it more deeply. Valentine found himself watching her in fascination. Aura Torrance had been a strange girl to him – one moment authoritative, the next incredibly flirtatious – but Hunter never seemed to let down her guard. Even while she was tasting her beer he could see her eyes were alert, taking in every aspect of the bar about her as though preparing for an attack from any angle. Valentine had yet to see anything of her he could term even remotely accommodating and wondered why she had asked him here to begin with.

"Well," she said, "it's certainly not watered down."

"If it is, they do it with swamp water."

She smiled at this, although Valentine could tell it was merely to humour him.

"If you don't have money here," she asked, "why do the people behind the bar stand there serving drinks?"

"We have a ... rota."

"Uh huh. This has something to do with those pit fights doesn't it?"

"How do you know about the pit fights?"

"Torrance mentioned them. And no, I didn't tell the sergeant. Truth be told, I don't think Cartello would care, but it's best not to take chances."

Their willingness to hide information from their direct superior told Valentine some important things: for one, that neither of them was blindly obedient to their sergeant. That was useful and Valentine filed it away. "Tell me about yourself," Valentine pressed. "I take it you were conscripted like Torrance?"

"Hmm? Oh. Yes, something like that."

That was not the reply he had been expecting, for he could see Hunter was several years older than Torrance. He placed Hunter somewhere in her early twenties, and if everyone in their region of

Io was conscripted at eighteen that was some length they forced their citizens to take in the army.

"You haven't answered my question about the staff though," Hunter said.

It was a reasonable request, even if was an obvious evasion of the issue. "The staff here," Valentine said, "as with the people performing all the other duties, change regularly. We have no physical monetary system, but we do have a replacement."

"The pit fights? I don't see how."

"People bet on the fights. Those who lose have to work, like behind the bar for instance. Those who win gain privileges, such as extra alcohol rations or food or whatever."

"So I'm drinking your rations?"

"I don't mind. I rarely get such pleasant company."

"Don't think I've ever been called pleasant company before. What do the people doing the fighting get?"

"Notoriety. The best fighters never have to do a day's work in their lives. Unless they want to. Hudson for instance is one of our best, but she likes to get out and about. She doesn't ask to go, she just tells me she's going, which is a courtesy for her."

"How many people do you lose in the pits?"

"Not many. A defeat doesn't necessarily mean death. It's a shame when someone dies, but the system works so we have to keep it running."

"Well it's a good system." Hunter drank more of her beer. "This is actually beginning to grow on me."

"Can I ask you something?"

"You just did."

"Can I ask you something else?"

"This could go on all night."

Valentine decided to just ask. "Why do you conscript? What happened to your country that's made you so afraid?"

Hunter stared into her drink and Valentine could see old hurt in her averted eyes. It was a look he had seen within Torrance, although while the younger woman had concealed her pain with joyful abandon, Hunter was more withdrawn. "Our country was bombed during the Solar War. Bombed heavily. We lost a lot of people. We weren't even involved in the fighting: it was nothing to do with us.

But we were targeted, I'm told, because we were suspected of harbouring enemy soldiers who were using our country as a staging ground."

Valentine had heard similar stories before. The war had been terrible and while it had ended a decade earlier its effects still had not dissipated. Each planet held its own system of worlds and thus far no system had ever gone to war with another. The people who had attacked Earth, however, were not from any such planetary system but had been wanderers looking for a home, or so Valentine had heard. There was always a lot of rumour floating around following wars: rumours and conspiracy theories. Valentine had little time for either. He had no idea what had become of the wanderers, people who called themselves the Lustrum, but he did know they were defeated. In fact, he didn't know that much about the Lustrum at all: only the things every schoolchild of Earth knew. They were piratical villains with silly call-signs of always four letters.

The war had been between the Earth system and these wanderers, but politically there were so many other planetary systems involved it had seemed several times as though the entire solar system would erupt into chaos. Thankfully it had been brought to an end before that could come to pass.

"I'm sorry," he said. "At least Earth won the war."

She snapped her eyes to him then and Valentine felt his breath catch in his throat. Her eyes narrowed. "It was Earth that bombed us, Valentine."

She had no proof of that. Otherwise there would have been massive repercussions: perhaps even a Jovian/Earthen war. No human throughout their species' entire history, however, had ever needed proof to wholeheartedly believe in something. That Hunter was from the Jupiter system and Valentine from Earth hardly made it a very comfortable conversation for him.

"So," he said to change the subject, "what do you think of this world then?"

"It's unstable. It was put together wrong."

"Happens when mankind tries to build a world. Have you been here long enough to experience the really bad quakes?"

Hunter's eyes flashed with recognition of his digging techniques and said, "I've been here as long as my mission's lasted. You didn't get permission to come here, did you?"

"An Earth expedition to a Jovian world? No."

"You do realise once we leave we could tell our government about you and you'd be finished. Arrested as spies perhaps."

"There aren't any artificial satellites around this world, Private. It's a self-contained environment. We couldn't spy on Jupiter from here even if we wanted to. Except, you know, by looking up at it whenever we're outside."

"You say that as though it's a bad thing."

Valentine had to remind himself that Jupiter was so large anyone living on almost any of Jupiter's moons would have a decent view of the planet whenever they looked to the sky. For people like Tana Hunter it was the norm to see half the sky filled with the thing.

"You know," Hunter said, shifting her weight while she thought, "it's quite comforting to have Jupiter in the sky. Reminds me that we have almost seventy natural moons and that most of them have been colonised. Even the very, very small ones. I can't imagine what it would be like on Earth, looking up and seeing only one moon. One moon to offer you protection. When I'm sitting at home, Valentine, I can't just see Jupiter; I can see Ganymede, Europa, Callisto: sometimes even some of the smaller moons. They're my brothers and sisters, Valentine. And, having survived the war, we're all well aware that we have to be there for each other."

Valentine understood the threat without the need for Hunter to elaborate. Everyone knew the power of the Jovian system, simply because it had so many moons. If the Jovians ever decided to invade another system, they would very likely succeed. Valentine liked to think there was too much history on Earth for anyone to risk destroying it, but people didn't care enough for history any more for it to much matter. Nor did they feel much affinity for the world they had all left so many generations ago to colonise their own worlds; no more than Americans or Australians much thought about their origins in England; no more than anyone considered their species' origins in Africa.

In war, people tended to forget quite easily.

He understood entirely now why Hunter had asked him for this drink. She wanted to threaten him in a neutral area which encouraged freedom of speech and thought. She wanted him to know she could kill him any time she wanted to, but that for the moment she was restraining herself. She was, it turned out, very different to Aura Torrance indeed. It was good to know, yet he wanted more than ever now to be rid of these people as soon as humanly possible.

At his belt his radio crackled and Valentine was thankful for the distraction. "Valentine."

"Boss," his bodyguard, Stone, said from the other end. "We need you down here."

He felt relief wash over him and was almost out of his seat before he realised he should ask what the problem was first, just so he wasn't painting a bad picture of himself for Private Hunter. "Anything serious?"

"And then some," Stone grunted. "There's some creature running around down here. Torn two people apart already."

"Creature?" Suddenly Valentine did not care at all for Hunter's company or finding an excuse to leave her. "What creature? Are the doors secure?"

"Didn't come from the outside, boss. It's that red crocodile thing from downstairs. Looks like it's broken out of its cell."

"All right, I'm on my way."

It had never happened before. Zebadiah was such a good custodian of the animals that the very notion he would leave a door unlocked was ludicrous. On a plus note, Valentine's sociopathic mind interjected, it would make the betting on its fight all the stronger, assuming they could recapture it alive. But the creature was messing with Valentine's natural order of things, and there were far too many security procedures to ever allow this sort of thing to happen.

"I'd love to help," Hunter said dryly, taking another sip of her beer, "but Jupiter has to remain neutral in Earthen affairs. You know, I'm getting used to this beer of yours."

Halfway to his feet, Valentine froze. She was too calm, too silently pleased, for her not to have had something to do with this. He could not accuse her of course, for even if he was right there would have to be an investigation and that would mean her people staying even longer, and bringing more soldiers in. But he did not need proof to wholeheartedly believe she had let the beast free. In that way he knew was their entire species linked.

He gripped the table fiercely to fight his rising anger. "Perhaps you should return to your chambers until this matter is settled."

She shrugged. "Kind of like it here. Don't worry, I won't exhaust your entire ration."

"Private, I must insist."

"Sure. Don't you have ... I don't know ... a creature to stop?" She raised her eyebrows and Valentine turned his back on her and marched out of the bar before he could respond with something less verbal and more physical. He had known from the beginning these people would be bad for his routines, but now he just wanted them gone. Any way possible.

CHAPTER NINE

Private Aura Torrance was young and beautiful. Beneath her armour she no doubt had maintained a slim, toned body in line with her military training. She had a smile which lit up her entire face, while her bright, blue eyes were ever inquisitive and curious. She had exchanged almost furtive glances with Valentine; probably would have even laughed at the man's jokes if he ever made any.

Aubrey Whitsmith hated everything about her.

Bringing up their rear, the one-woman powerhouse that was Katie Hudson kept one eye upon them, the other upon the swamp. Whitsmith had no fear of being attacked from any direction, for nothing would get past Hudson. That left Whitsmith and Torrance in the lead, which made for some silent conversation. Torrance had said she had wanted to see where the creature had been spotted, but Whitsmith did not fancy going all the way there. She was tired, footsore and famished: a second long trek into the swamp was simply out of the question. Torrance had no idea where Whitsmith had tangled with the creature, which meant Whitsmith could show her just about anywhere. She even felt Hudson would back her up, or at least remain silent on the matter. Had this been Valentine or anyone else back at the institution, Whitsmith would of course have taken them the full way, but she owed these soldiers nothing and knew they only meant everyone ill. Valentine was playing nice with them up to a point, but underneath he was scared of them upsetting his little world.

If he paid less attention to the young blonde and more to his own work, perhaps he might even make it through unscathed.

"We're here," Whitsmith said, stopping and casting a glance to their rear. Hudson raised an eyebrow, but not so Torrance could see it.

"That wasn't far," Torrance said.

"I never said it was."

Torrance did not question further and removed some equipment from her belt. Whitsmith assumed it was some form of handheld scanner, but nothing like that lived very long in the swamp so she doubted it would work. Nor did she much care either way.

Whitsmith looked about her. The ground was still pretty level and hard, the nearest marshy ground about fifty metres in any direction. There were clumps of bushes about them, within which any number of crocodiles could have been lurking, and there were trees towering above them. The trees in the swamp were all sickly, so far as Whitsmith was concerned: as though even they disliked the foulness of the mire.

"You don't much like this place do you?" Torrance asked from where she was crouched, taking readings from the ground.

"The swamp? Who would?"

"You could always leave."

"We have a job to do," Whitsmith lied.

"I meant leave the swamp. If you're studying the wildlife you can do it just as easily from the mountains or the plains or something."

Whitsmith did not mind the conversation, for Hudson already knew of the existence of the outside world. "How much of this rock have you seen?" Whitsmith asked.

"Aside from the swamp? A fair bit. We've been on the move for a while now."

"Why?"

Torrance glanced at her. "A direct question deserves a blunt answer, Whitsmith."

"You're a funny kid."

"I'm nineteen, grandma."

Whitsmith narrowed her eyes. She was only six years older than Torrance but the gap was wide enough for the comment to annoy her.

"So what's out there?" Whitsmith asked, determined not to let that annoyance show. "Past the mountains I mean."

"Forest mainly," Torrance said without looking up. Her scanner had lights flashing across it and she gave it a bash on the side. That would be the swamp water, Whitsmith thought with satisfaction. "Lots and lots of trees."

"What kind of animals are out there?"

"Pack animals. Coelophysis and utahraptors. A few daspeltosauri and a lot of herbivores." She looked at Whitsmith now. "So tell me, dinosaur expert, a fact about each of those."

Whitsmith narrowed her eyes. She knew Valentine had laid down a cover as their being a research expedition, but the truth was Whitsmith did know a lot about dinosaurs; and Torrance's attitude was only grating further on her nerves. "The daspletosaurus was smaller than the T. rex," Whitsmith said snidely, "but its teeth were larger and its skull probably thicker. The utahraptor was a raptor found in Utah, obviously. The coelophysis was the first dinosaur in space."

"Say what?"

Whitsmith folded her arms and raised one side of her mouth in snide victory. "You forget you're talking to an expert."

Torrance went back to her scans, but Whitsmith could tell she had annoyed her in return. It felt incredibly good.

"Is there anyone else out there?" Hudson asked. Whitsmith had almost forgotten she was even with them.

"No," Torrance said without looking up.

"Not even your unit?"

Torrance stopped fiddling with her scanner and looked back up at both women. She knew she was being interrogated and didn't like it one bit. "Well of course my unit's out there. But aside from that, no." She went back to her work.

Whitsmith stepped away from her, indicating with a jerk of her head that she wanted to talk to Hudson alone. The two women moved a short distance away and Whitsmith whispered, "I think this is a good opportunity to find out what these people are doing here."

"Was hoping you'd ask that. But it would have been better if we'd moved farther away. They can probably still hear her screams from here."

"I didn't mean torture her."

"How else do you want to find out anything? Promise her a daisy chain? Wise up, Whitsmith. We're escaped convicts who've murdered our guards. These soldiers are either aware of that or they're not. If they are, they're here to arrest us; if they're not, they're going to mention us in their report. We can't let any of them leave this place, so at the very least we need to know their numbers.

Personally I think it's just the three of them, which is fine. Torrance dies out here, which leaves only two back at the prison. Communications are bad around here, so even if they have one or two others back at their shuttle they won't get a message through. Then we take the shuttle and get the hell off this rock for good."

Hudson had spoken slowly and each word punched through Whitsmith's brain. They made sense, every single one of them, but Whitsmith did not like the idea of murdering three people, no matter the reason. But nor could they allow them to leave the prison. She looked back over to where Torrance was still having problems with her scanner. She did not like the young woman, did not like her at all; yet to kill her and leave her body to sink into the swamp was not an idea which made Whitsmith feel especially good about herself.

"I was just beginning to respect you, Aubrey," Hudson said. "Don't wimp out on me now."

But wimping out would mean tossing away her morality simply because she was afraid, and that was not something Whitsmith was prepared to do. "We'll interrogate her," she said, "and we'll take it from there. But," she added when Hudson grunted, "we do it without beating her up."

Hudson shook her head, but it was not her call to make. Hudson survived in the prison by recognising the hierarchy. It had been good to her and she had prospered because of it, perhaps more than anyone. She would not risk all of that now just so she could drown someone in the swamp.

"This stupid thing's conked out," Torrance said, shaking the scanner now even as she rose back to her feet.

"This isn't the forest," Whitsmith told her. "Most of your equipment will be dead by now."

"How do you live in this place? Better yet, why?"

"Because it's home."

"Well it's a stupid home."

"No argument there. Where's your shuttle parked?"

"What shuttle?" Torrance asked absently.

"The one you came down in."

"Oh. North somewhere I think. I don't see any tracks of the creature."

"Maybe it cleared them away."

"Normally, yeah, but you killed it and threw it in the swamp."

"Hmm," Whitsmith mused. "Sort of lied about that."

Torrance rounded on her. "You what?"

"So what precisely do you mean by 'normally, yeah'?"

"It's still alive?"

"You're evading my question," Whitsmith said. "You know what these things are, you've fought them before. Hell, you've likely brought them here with you since we've never seen sight of them before. You're chasing them aren't you? Hunting them?"

"We have to get back to the prison, we have to get back right now."

"No so fast," Whitsmith said, grabbing the soldier's arm as she made to rush past her. "First you're giving us some answers."

"You stupid cow," Torrance spat. "If that thing's still out there, we're in dan ..."

Whitsmith's fist slammed into the soldier's stomach, doubling her over despite the armour she was wearing. Pain shot through Whitsmith's knuckles, but she ignored it and cracked her left fist across the younger woman's face. Blood spattered from a split lip, spraying against her perfect blonde hair even as Torrance's face hit the mud. Whitsmith stamped her foot down upon her cheek, grinding her face into the dirt.

And then Whitsmith was falling, landing heavily on her backside as Torrance cut her legs away from her. The young soldier stared dripping hatred at her, her bloody teeth bared, her blue eyes afire. Her face was streaked with blood and mud, a nasty graze and the impression of a boot-print across her face.

Whitsmith suddenly remembered that she may have been young and obnoxious, but Torrance was also a trained killer.

Torrance leaped at her, her hands grasping for the other woman's throat, and Whitsmith met the woman's rage with her own. The two punched out at each other, and Whitsmith felt a metal elbow slam into her nose. She grit her teeth, punching Torrance in the face since this was her only unprotected area. Torrance roared like an animal gone mad and Whitsmith raised her arm to block whatever attack she was about to make, so Torrance bit into her arm. Hard.

Whitsmith screamed, surprised at the nature of the assault and in terrible pain. Her free hand flailed, caught a handful of the perfect blonde hair and yanked hard. She had messed up the girl's face and if she could mess up her hair the fight would have been well worth it.

Torrance released a stream of curses only a teenager in the army would know as she struggled to clasp her hands about Whitsmith's throat. Whitsmith tugged harder at the other woman's hair even as she felt hot, dirty fingers clutching at her windpipe. She heard something tear and hoped it was hair, then kicked out with her knee, catching Torrance in the stomach and sending her off-balance. The two women rolled in the muddy ground, hands tightening about one another's throats. Whitsmith found herself on top and yanked her hand up and down to repeatedly slam Torrance's head into the ground, but with a roar of rage Torrance spun them again to reverse their positions.

Suddenly an explosion rocked the swamp, loud enough to scatter a flock of birds into flight and send several creatures slipping into the brackish waters in fear. The two women froze where they lay, their bodies covered with the filth of mud, sweat and blood in equal parts from both of them. They looked over to where Katie Hudson sat upon a rock, calmly reloading her rifle. There was a look of disdain upon her face and she did not meet either of their gazes.

"You do realise," Hudson said slowly, "how pathetic it is to catfight over a man?"

Her adrenalin rush had been intense, although as the words filtered through Whitsmith's brain she realised Hudson was right. She pushed herself away from Torrance, stumbling to her feet and slipping in the mud to fall upon her backside once more. Torrance rose also, more slowly, her eyes narrowed in hatred, her face a mess of blood and rage.

"You're welcome to him," Torrance said snottily. "He's not worth the trouble." She reached for the gun she had dropped in the fight when they both heard the click of a rifle being cocked. Torrance raised her eyes, her hand halfway to her gun, to find Hudson aiming the weapon at her.

"We still need some answers," Hudson said flatly. "So you're going to tell us what we want to know or I'm going to shoot you."

Whitsmith took the opportunity to assess her own wounds. She was covered in various levels of filth, although sometime during her struggle a light rain had set in. It would make the ground muddier, but if the rain came down strong enough she might be able to use it to wash the dirt from her skin. She knew full well how quickly the rains could come on this world and did not fancy being out during a downpour.

"You're not going to shoot me," Torrance told Hudson calmly.

"Yep," Whitsmith said, tentatively touching her arm where Torrance had bitten her, "she is."

Torrance looked uncertain now, and for the first time since they had met did Whitsmith at last feel in control over her. It felt good, even if it was mainly due to Hudson and her rifle.

"The armour," Hudson said. "Take it off."

"Take off my armour?" Torrance asked, horrified. "You don't understand. That creature is still out here. If you didn't kill it, it's watching us right this minute and we have to ..."

"Armour," Hudson said. "I'm going to count to five. If you haven't made a nice pile of metal on the ground I'm going to shoot you in the head." She raised her eyebrows as if to dare the soldier to think she was joking.

Whitsmith felt an unreasonable sense of elation as Torrance grit her teeth and unfastened the straps holding her gauntlets to her arms.

"Slowly," Hudson warned her.

Torrance spent the next two minutes shrugging out of her armour. Whitsmith noted with no small amount of pride that the breastplate was actually slightly dented, which probably accounted for the tremendous aching sensation coursing through Whitsmith's knuckles. Finally Torrance tossed the last of her armour to the side and stood before them, exposed to the elements. Whitsmith had not known what she had expected Torrance to have been wearing under the armour, but it was not her underwear, nor was it standard army-issue garb. Torrance was dressed in some form of pale blue flight suit, by the looks of it. It was tight, hugging her curves as though it was a lecher's hands, and lacked any footwear at all, forcing Torrance to go barefoot. There were tears in the attire which could well have been caused through their brawl, and already the rain was splashing dirt up her legs even while it plastered her now scraggly blonde hair to her face.

Annoyingly enough, Whitsmith reasoned Torrance actually looked more attractive outside of the suit and was tempted to make her put it back on.

"We need to get out of here," Torrance said dryly, her narrow eyes staring pure hatred at Hudson, all but refusing to even acknowledge Whitsmith was even there any longer. "That thing's coming for us and if it finds us it will kill us."

"It didn't kill me before," Whitsmith said.

Torrance looked to her now. "What?"

"It seemed more curious than anything," Whitsmith continued. "In fact, it even seemed human. After a fashion. What is it?"

"I don't know."

"Where did it come from?"

"I don't know that either."

"You're lying."

Hudson waved her rifle slightly to remind Torrance she was still holding it.

Whitsmith could see the soldier wasn't going to give them anything and said, "It came from the north. Didn't it?"

It was such an obvious thing that Torrance did not even bother denying it.

"What happened up there?" Whitsmith asked. "You said there were forests to the north. Are there more of these things?"

"I don't know," Torrance said through gritted teeth. "Maybe. We ... We found something. An outpost maybe, I don't know. People had been living there anyway. Looks like there may have been some kind of large craft settled for a while. There was a camp with high fences, for all the good they did. We found electrical generators for the fences, but nothing was working. The barriers hadn't kept the creatures out."

"Go on," Hudson urged when she stopped.

"There weren't any bodies," Torrance said, "so whatever happened there, there may have been survivors. Maybe they took their dead, maybe they buried them. Maybe the animals got them. We didn't find much of use there, but we did find that thing. It stalked us, tore two of our people apart before we even realised it was there. It's the most proficient killing machine I've ever seen."

"So you ran," Whitsmith determined. "And it chased you."

"What?" Hudson asked. "You mean you led that thing here?"

"Why didn't it kill me?" Whitsmith asked.

"I don't know anything about it," Torrance snapped, and Whitsmith reasoned she could believe that. "I've never stopped it for a chat, we just ran."

"Perhaps it doesn't like soldiers," Whitsmith surmised. "Maybe it fought soldiers in that camp and it's developed a hatred for them."

"I hope so," Torrance said, "because that would be the only good thing to come from me dropping all my armour."

Thunder rumbled overhead and Whitsmith glanced to the sky. The rains were strengthening. "Come on," she said. "We should head back."

"What about her?" Hudson asked. "We take her back like this, there'll be questions."

"We're not shooting her."

"Just in the legs?"

Whitsmith glowered at her colleague. "It's not at the us or them stage yet, Katie. You," she spat at Torrance. "If we take you back, you don't go telling tales to your boss."

"She's going to wonder where my armour's gone."

"She's right," Hudson said. "Shooting her's the best option for all of us." She smiled. "Oh, Aubrey? It's nice to see we didn't beat her up or anything."

But Whitsmith had no time for such levity. Her mind was racing. The rain was freezing and her teeth were beginning to chatter. She could see Torrance was shivering, her naked feet likely frozen. "We'll head for a marker," Whitsmith decided. There were several outposts surrounding the prison, usually referred to as markers. They were little more than sheds, but they were handy places to stop for a while if necessary. "We'll tie her up while we think of what to do about her."

"Tie me up?" Torrance almost shrieked. "That thing is after me and you want to truss me up like a present?"

Lightning flashed, the rain suddenly pounding them, and Whitsmith knew the time for arguing was long past. Whatever they were going to do, they needed to do it now; and Whitsmith was in charge. "We're heading for a marker," she determined. "Katie. If she resists, shoot her."

Again lightning cracked through the swamp and Whitsmith snapped her head up to the sky. Her eyes widened. Along with the darkness of the storm, night was also rapidly falling so she could not be certain as to what she had seen, but as the swamp was illuminated she could have sworn there was something lurking in the trees, looking down upon them.

"All right, move," Whitsmith said.

Hudson led Torrance away at a brisk trot. Whitsmith remained behind for several moments, staring up into the trees. It was still light enough to make out the trees themselves, although the various shadows cast by their high branches and all-encompassing leaves were mystified by the coming night. Nothing leaped out to cut her down and Whitsmith realised it did not much matter what was out there. If that creature wanted to kill them, it would do so. Torrance had said it had killed two of her people in seconds. Whitsmith believed her.

Tearing her eyes from the darkness, Whitsmith hurried after her companions. The marker would shelter them from the storm, but if electrified fences could not keep this beast at bay, she very much doubted wood and nails would be anything more than kindling for its fury.

CHAPTER TEN

There had been over one hundred species of animals catalogued upon their world in the five years since they had taken over the prison, and the only ones Valentine had ever been interested in were those which were served up to him in gravy. The more dangerous creatures were useful only in that they could be fought in the pits, but that was Zebadiah's territory and Valentine wanted nothing to do with it. If it was up to Valentine they would only ever capture and fight herbivores, but the bouts which attracted the most attention were always the ones where a human being was pitted against a carnivore. As such Valentine understood the necessity for having carnivores locked up in cages downstairs, even if he did not agree with it. He had always been assured, however, that there was no chance of any of them ever breaking out.

He had not counted on someone being stupid enough to just open the door and let the things walk free.

So far as he could determine, there was only the one creature loose in the prison, but that one had been without doubt the most violent and dangerous they had stored away. On his way down to the main hall Valentine grabbed a handheld access port linked into the prison's library and scanned through all the information he could find about the creature on the loose. The erythrosuchus, the red crocodile, was an odd name considering no one knew what colour these animals were. Fossils could tell scientists many wonderful things, but even Valentine knew they did not preserve skin pigmentation. That the red crocodile from the cells was actually red may have been coincidence, genetic manipulation or proof it had an apt name. Valentine did not much care why it was red and was of half a mind to just shoot the thing dead and be done with it. If he did that, however, he would be faced with a lot of angry people, and it could bring his entire system down about his head.

He continued to scroll through the animal's file, but there was precious little of interest. That the creature was a precursor to the dinosaurs and that it was a cross between a theropod and a crocodile was something he didn't care about. That it was considered an ambush predator was indeed useful information, since it would mean it would be good at hiding. There was nothing in the library about how to kill one, but then he doubted many people had ever done such a thing.

There was more information which had been added by his people over the past few years, probably by Whitsmith mainly, but most of that only dealt with its lifestyle and habits. Unless it intended to nest or rear young any time soon, Valentine did not believe any of Whitsmith's research would do him any good. He promised himself he would have a talk with her about priorities once this was over, assuming any of them made it out alive.

As he entered the main hall he could see a scene of carnage. Blood soaked the stairs and Valentine could see an arm hanging loosely over the railing. There were four bodies on the ground floor, all torn apart by savage jaws, with several people dealing with the bodies while others stood about with guns. When they had initially seized the prison Valentine had been thankful to have found such a supply of weapons, and since many of the prisoners had been incarcerated for gun-related crimes they had no shortage of people able to train everyone in how to shoot. Valentine was still not sure it was such a good idea to teach convicted murderers how to shoot someone, but on this world there was very little choice in their survival.

He approached his bodyguard, Anthony Stone, who was directing operations.

"Where did it go?" Valentine asked, trying not to look directly upon the shredded people, nor hear the wailing of any still alive. The smell was something he could not block, however, and wrinkling his nose only struck him as a tad insensitive.

"We're not sure," Stone told him. "I have patrols moving through the corridors. That thing was big, it can't have got too far."

"It could be anywhere," Valentine chastised him. "It's an ambush predator, which means it's good at hiding. Don't you know anything about these creatures?" It was a low blow, but Valentine always had to maintain an air of knowing what he was talking about. It all helped with his control, especially should anyone be considering wresting the institution from him.

Institution, he reminded himself. Since the arrival of the soldiers he had reverted to thinking of this place as a prison all over again. Prison was not a name these people favoured, although it was just a name to Valentine.

"If it's hiding," Stone said, "it might go for dark places. Perhaps we should shut off the lights in some areas to goad it into a direction we want."

"I think it might be a tad cleverer than that, Stone."

"So we lower the temperature. It's a reptile, right? So it's coldblooded. We lower the temperature and it'll become sluggish."

Valentine tried not to scowl. The truth was not all dinosaurs were coldblooded, but he had no idea which were and which weren't. To top it all off the red crocodile wasn't even a dinosaur, and he had no idea how such things stood with creatures like that. What he needed was someone who knew what they were talking about.

"Is there any word on Aubrey yet?" he asked.

"No, boss. You want me to call her?"

"That would help, yes."

Stone pulled his radio and tried her frequency, but there was no response. He tried again, to no avail. "Probably the storm, boss," he said.

"So there's a storm as well is there? Oh joy, this really is my lucky day. Just do a level by level search and bring that thing back down to its cage. Tranquilise it if possible. I'd rather lose a few murderers and bank robbers than a crowd-pleaser like that." He of course spoke this part more softly so no one would be able to overhear.

Stone took some people and headed out after the patrols he had already established. Valentine was left not knowing what he might himself be able to do about this situation. Whitsmith would have known the best course of action, but Whitsmith was unreachable. He briefly considered leading an expedition to find her, but with a storm raging outside it was never a good idea to wander the swamp. He hoped Whitsmith and Torrance were taking care of each other, although he had detected no small amount of antagonism between the two women. Whatever their problem with each other, so long as it didn't break into a shooting match he knew Whitsmith would handle it fine.

Knowing he would be useless on the search for the red crocodile, Valentine decided it was time he did what he was best at. He was in charge here and it was about time he started acting like it.

Grabbing a pistol from one of the women standing guard, Valentine headed back to his bedroom. It was not a long walk, yet when there was an angry monster potentially lurking within every shadow it was like running a marathon. He had received training in the use of a firearm but had never been especially good at it and suddenly wished he had not sent his bodyguard off to organise the search. If there was one thing which was not favoured within the institution, however, it was weakness, and Valentine could not be seen cowering in the corner while everyone else ran around dealing with the threat.

Sucking up his gut, Valentine ran all the way back to his chambers. His reasoning was that if the creature was going to get him it was going to get him. Being an ambush predator there was a chance he might speed past it and be gone before it had decided whether he was worth attacking.

Whether through skill or blind luck, Valentine made it to his room and pounded upon the door. He could have unlocked it of course, for he carried a spare key upon his person, although did not want to antagonise the sergeant any more than he had to. There was a chance after all she did not know what Hunter had done, and he wanted to keep the cranky woman on his side if at all possible.

After a few moments the door flew open. Cartello stood there wearing a shirt and a scowl, and before she could say anything Valentine had pushed his way into the room.

"There's a creature on the loose," he told her.

She was too taken aback to even say anything; not because of what he had told her, but by his sheer brazenness.

Valentine, safe in his room at last, spun to face her, watching for a reaction. "Private Hunter thought it would be worth a laugh letting go one of our research subjects."

The sergeant's scowl diminished slightly, and Valentine was not certain whether this was a good thing. He had been hoping to transfer the woman's aggression onto Hunter, but the sergeant seemed more amused now than anything.

"This isn't funny," Valentine said. "My people are dying out there."

"What creature are we talking about?"

"An erythrosuchus."

"No idea what that is."

"A red crocodile."

"And what do you want me to do about it?"

"Well you're a soldier aren't you? Go shoot it. It's Hunter's fault I'm having to deal with this."

"So go bother Hunter."

"You really don't care do you?"

Cartello rubbed at her tired eyes. "Has there been any word from Torrance?"

"What? No."

"Stupid girl, probably got herself killed already."

"You really have no respect for anyone, do you?"

"You noticed that."

Valentine folded his arms and simply stared at her.

"All right," she finally said with an exaggerated sigh. "I'm not getting any peace until I've taken down your lizard am I?" She moved across to her armour and began to fix it to her body. She struggled into the breastplate, for she was a heavy-set woman and the armour was a tight fit. Not wanting to watch her dress, Valentine gazed about his own chambers, trying to see whether she had broken anything, and his eyes fell upon his computer terminal. He could see it had been accessed and he idly called up the history. It made for interesting reading.

"You've been looking up troodons," he noted.

"Your Whitsmith woman seemed to think the creature in the swamp was connected."

"I'm reasonably sure you were out of earshot when she said that."

"I have good hearing."

Valentine paused. She clearly knew more than what she was telling, but asking her about it would not gain him anything so he did not see the point. Antagonising her would not get the red crocodile hunted down.

"Oh," she said as she finished with her armour and began checking her guns, "I also looked up the history of this place. The prison records have all been wiped, but I managed to find some old data relating to outstanding warrants. I cross-referenced the names with some of the rotas you keep on your computer. Strange so many people who would have been arrested a few years ago would have ended up working in a prison. Ironic, you might say."

Valentine felt a sudden chill wash through him. "It was a government scheme," he said quickly. "Using former inmates to help charter the various animals on this world."

"Well since the entire expedition's illegal, it makes sense." She glanced over at him. "Don't treat me like an idiot, Valentine. Especially when I'm loading my gun. I don't care about you people, and I don't care about the paperwork involved in reporting you. Knowing my luck I'd be sent straight back here to arrest you, so you can stay here and rot for all I care. Once my mission here is finished I'm leaving this world and I tell you now I'm never looking back."

She was being upfront and a part of Valentine even believed her. It would be taking an incredible risk to trust her implicitly, but she was right about one thing: she was the one holding the weapons. Valentine may have had a pistol in his hand, but she was trained to kill with her eyes closed.

"I appreciate your honesty," he said, trying to build a bridge. "If you told me your mission I might be able to help speed things along."

She regarded him with an expression which told him she was seriously considering telling him the truth, but then she finished her weapons check and said instead, "Lead the way, Valentine. Let's see about this red crocodile of yours."

Gripping his pistol, yet knowing it was by far a flimsier lifeline than was Cartello herself, Valentine led the way from his chambers and activated his radio. "Stone, talk to me."

"We've lost three more people on the east side, boss. We think it's headed for the cafeteria. Maybe it can smell the bacon cooking."

"Keep it pinned if you can. Block all its exits. I'm on my way with the sergeant. She'll sort this out for us."

"Stroking my ego," Cartello said once he had put his radio back at his belt, "isn't going to make me like you, Valentine."

"Maybe it makes me feel less nervous. I've never known an animal eat so much."

"It's not eating anything. It's trapped in unfamiliar corridors when it's used to being able to hide in trees or slip into foliage or the marsh itself. It doesn't understand all these walls and especially the ceiling. And people running towards it with guns isn't going to do any good."

It was something Valentine had not considered, yet something he knew he probably should have. Something Whitsmith would have seen in an instant. The creature was killing when attacked, killing because it was scared. He had never before considered that something so monstrous could be afraid. Truth be told, Valentine had never really got that close to the creatures here, but he had always thought of them as everyone did: creatures kids had watercolour pictures of in their fact books. That they were animals was not something he liked to think about; that each could have a separate personality was almost beyond his understanding. He had never been a five metre long reptile trapped inside a building, but he supposed if ever he was in that situation he might have been a little scared as well.

Soon enough they came upon one of the patrols Stone had stationed at the perimeter he had formed. Valentine exchanged brief words with them but there was little they could tell him. He and Cartello continued, entering the final corridor before they would reach the cafeteria. Cartello held her rifle before her as she walked, and Valentine knew if the red crocodile leapt out at them suddenly there was a good chance she could take it down.

Reaching the door, Valentine could hear an incredible commotion coming from within the room. There were no screams, so he had to assume that whatever was happening in there, it did not involve any of his people. That was something, at least. There were after all only a finite amount of people in this institution and the more they lost the more the work would have to be shared out. Truth be told, Valentine would have liked to have lost a few of their number, for there were simply too many people to deal with. Had he been able to compile a list for the monster to devour he would happily have shown it fifty victims or more. After all, the prisoners had mutinied once: there was little stopping them from doing so a second time.

He realised then Cartello was staring at him.

"You want to shut up?" she asked.

"I didn't say anything."

"You were mumbling."

"Was I?"

"You do that a lot?"

Whitsmith had mentioned such to him once or twice and he had always told her she was imagining things. Valentine liked to plan his schemes, but that did not mean he talked them over when he was with company. Just when he was alone.

"Can we concentrate on the problem?" he asked.

Cartello smiled grimly at his discomfort and shouldered the door gently. She entered the room in a crouch, keeping her rifle aimed before her, and Valentine followed, crawling upon his hands and knees. The cafeteria was a large room, the old mess hall from the days of the prison guards. It was not where the prisoners had been brought to eat, for no one would have wanted to continue using that place, but it was still large enough to hide a few monsters. He could see several tables overturned and chairs splintered. A pot of stew was strewn across the floor, seeping through the cracks in the floor. There was no blood that Valentine could determine, so whatever staff had been working here may well have escaped.

Cartello moved slowly across to the service counter, peering behind with her weapon and apparently not discovering anything. She moved about the room more quickly now and returned to Valentine, lowering her gun. "You can get up off your knees now."

Valentine did so, brushing down his trousers and wondering what a sight he must be presenting. He knew he was afraid and didn't like it one bit. Fear was the worst thing a human being could feel because it robbed him of his sense of mental balance and made him look a fool.

"It's not here," the sergeant said.

"Kitchen?"

She followed his eyes to the door behind the counter. It was barely over a metre in width but could easily allow a creature to squeeze through. Cartello briefly reflected on the possibility, then raised her rifle once more and moved across to check. Steeling his nerve, Valentine followed.

The sergeant was just reaching out for the door when they heard a snuffling from the other side. Cartello dived backwards just as the door exploded towards them, the massive form of the red crocodile bounding into the room. Cartello fell behind the counter, her armour dragging her to the ground, and Valentine was left standing in the centre of the room, backing slowly away as the terrible creature regained its bearings.

He had never before been so close to such a beast. Reading that something was five metres long did not prepare him for such a confrontation; for no watercolour could ever do justice to a monster like the erythrosuchus. It stood as tall as Valentine himself, its tail swishing behind, stroking the counter as though it was being used as some form of sensory organ. The skin of the bulbous body was coarse and scaled, and looked as tough as leather but supple as water. Its legs were thick, powerful stumps ending in vicious claws. Its head was almost too large for it to seem real, and turned from side to side by the aid of a thick, flexible neck. That its name meant red crocodile seemed ludicrous, for it did not resemble a crocodile in any form, other than that it walked upon four legs. Its head looked so much like the venerated tyrannosaurus rex, its body so similar in shape, that to Valentine's eyes it seemed simply to be a dinosaur with long enough arms to reach the ground.

The erythrosuchus – it seemed disrespectful not to call it by its true name – shook its head in much the same manner as a dog Valentine had owned many years previously. Then it opened its maw in a wide yawn which revealed a set of sharp tearing teeth stained with the blood of those it had already killed. It was an image Valentine could have done without.

Fixing its eyes upon him at last, the erythrosuchus snorted as though determining its current plight was entirely down to this man, and Valentine felt himself raise his pistol feebly to focus upon the creature. His hands shook, even with both clutching the gun, and he knew whatever shots he fired would only anger the beast, even if he did somehow manage to land one on target.

He wondered just what he thought he was doing there facing the thing in the first place.

The creature lowered its head, the tail rising even as it continued to gently swish from side to side. Valentine could see its eyes carefully watching him, searching for signs of threat. All that kept flashing through Valentine's mind was what he had read in the creature's file: that this was an ambush predator. It was used to pouncing upon prey far larger than a human, which meant its muscles would have to be extremely powerful indeed. That it was crouching before him now meant there was nothing Valentine and his peashooter would be able to do to stop it.

With a roar, the animal leaped and something inside Valentine kicked him into motion. He was upon the floor, scrabbling away, before he had even registered the attack. He felt the huge bulk of the monster pass him by, felt even more acutely the claws which raked his side as the creature's attack grazed him. Valentine tumbled, thrown off-balance, and went crashing into a group of chairs. He lay there, his back propped against an overturned table, staring at the creature as it began to pace to his right, its head turned to face him at all times while it reassessed the situation.

Valentine's resolve screamed at him that shooting the thing might well anger it, that his shot would not even likely connect, but it certainly couldn't put him in any worse a position than he was already in.

Raising his pistol, he squeezed the trigger repeatedly.

The pistol cracked loudly through the contained area, but he had pulled on the trigger too hard, in his fear forgetting not to yank at the thing, and since no wounds appeared upon the beast he could only assume all his shots had missed. A five metre monstrosity stood directly before him and he could not even strike it a glancing blow. He squeezed the trigger again and it clicked on empty, not even a tremendous sound aiding him to give the animal pause.

Valentine was suddenly weaponless against the behemoth.

The report of a gun cracked the air once more and the erythrosuchus staggered, roaring in anger. A second shot sent a spray of blood pluming from its snout, and the creature shook its head as though it thought it was being plagued by a swarm of particularly nasty mosquitoes. Valentine turned wide, anxious eyes to the bar, where Sergeant Cartello had returned to her feet. She was leaning her rifle upon the bar to steady her aim, and he could see blood seeping down the side of her face from a nasty head wound. She looked angrier than he had ever seen her and suddenly Valentine even pitied the poor red crocodile.

The beast at last seemed to associate the attacks with Cartello and charged her, its four feet loping like those of a dog. Reaching the bar, it reared upon its hind legs, clawing at her with its forelegs even as it snapped its massive maw. Cartello dropped, retreating to what cover she could find, and Valentine heard another shot and saw the beast fall backwards as the bullet tore through its jaw.

By this point Valentine had all but surrendered the idea of recapturing the animal. A wounded animal would be a foolish thing to throw into the pits, and he did not much care how much trouble Whitsmith had gone to in order to capture the thing: placing it in the pits was not worth his own life.

He could hear Cartello shouting now, screaming at the animal even as she re-emerged from behind the bar, switching her rifle to an automatic setting before spewing rapid bullets into the thick hide of the beast. Blood spattered the walls and floor as the animal wailed, thrashing about madly. Valentine crawled backwards, aware that even in its death throes the thing was dangerous: if nothing else it would crush him to death should it fall upon him. He watched as the creature attempted to make it to the door, and he felt a small pang of pity for the brute. Having been taken from its home and thrown into a cage, it had escaped only to find itself in alien surroundings. It had fled, retaliated when it had been attacked, and could not find the exit. And now it was being blown apart by some angry woman with a weapon it did not even understand.

Valentine had never before felt any pity for these animals, even those which died in the pits. It was a new experience for him and he did not like it at all.

With a final, sickening wail of anguish the creature collapsed and Cartello ceased firing. She walked slowly from behind the bar, her rifle still trained upon the animal. Its body was now a mess of blood and sinew, and certainly the beast now lived entirely up to its name. Valentine got back to his feet, unable to tear his eyes from the dead creature staring sightlessly up at him. So often on this world it was a case of survival: theirs or the creatures'. But he was beginning to wonder whether they had any right to assume they had priority here.

Cartello fired again, her shot drilling into the beast's brain, and Valentine jumped at the sound, having believed the shooting to be over. She looked over her shoulder at him with a half amused expression at his reaction and he realised he must have yelped or something.

"Job done," she said. "Can I go back to bed now?"

Valentine continued to stare at the proud corpse. "No." He took a deep breath, deciding he would have to man up at last. He was in command here and it was time he began acting like it. Straightening his back and meeting Cartello's eyes he said, "I need to check the cells first. See whether your Private Hunter's let anything else wander loose."

Cartello seemed as though she was going to argue, but conceded the point. They headed from the cafeteria, Valentine giving orders for the mess to be cleaned up. Reaching the staircase which would lead into the large underground cells, Cartello motioned for her to precede him, which was something with which Valentine was in total agreement. They headed down carefully, slowly, but even at first glance Valentine could see nothing else was missing. He checked the cells regardless and found all the locks secure.

"You're sure there's nothing missing?" Cartello asked when he told her everything seemed fine.

Valentine looked about them slowly. "Everything seems in place, yes. I ... Hold on. Something's missing all right."

"Another carnivore?"

"More like a bibliovore."

Cartello stared at him blankly.

"Someone who collects information? Like a ... Forget it: bad word I just made up."

"Just tell me what's missing," Cartello said tiredly.

"Zebadiah. That erythrosuchus was just a distraction. Your Private Hunter's kidnapped Zebadiah."

CHAPTER ELEVEN

The marker was much as they had expected: little more than a shed in which they could shelter from the rain. It was as large as a spacious caravan and contained only one room, which was cluttered with old tools, rusty containers and spare tyres. While Whitsmith set about binding Torrance to a wooden beam attached to one wall, Hudson had taken the time to sift through the various items the marker stored. The swamp had destroyed most of it, the humidity rusting all the metal and weakening pretty much everything else. She struggled to tear the lids off several boxes but found only nails and sowing equipment within. The storm had not abated and the rain battered the roof of the shed, but Hudson was not worried. She could see evidence of several leaks, but in the main the roof was doing its job. She was more concerned with the creature outside which might have tracked them to the shed.

Checking her rifle, Hudson wandered over to where Whitsmith was attempting to tear the wrapper off one of her tasteless ration bars. Her clothes were soaked through and her fingers were shivering in the cold, and that was without taking into consideration the woman must have been terrified. Now they had the opportunity to stop for a moment their adrenalin could level off and they would at last come to realise what trouble they were really in. Hudson was herself wet, they all were, but she had trained herself long ago not to be affected by such things. Whitsmith had not suffered the hardships Hudson had known, but all things considered she had held up well out there. Hudson would never have admitted to Whitsmith that she was impressed, but certainly Whitsmith was not the total waste of space she had sometimes felt.

Reaching into a pouch on her belt, Hudson withdrew what was left of her chocolate bar and tossed it in Whitsmith's lap. Whitsmith stared with wide eyes.

"You've earned it," Hudson grunted. "Just don't go thinking we're friends now or anything."

As Whitsmith tore into the chocolate bar, Hudson turned her attention to Torrance. It was the first time Hudson could see she was actually a teenager. For all her bravado, for all her anger, when her armour was stripped from her she was just a frightened eighteen-year-old girl trembling in the corner. Hudson smiled at the thought that they had taken down one of the soldiers at least, but Torrance only tensed at the silent jibe.

"Who are you people anyway?" Hudson asked. "Why would Io send soldiers here to this rock?"

"I don't know our orders."

"The hell you don't."

Torrance said nothing.

"Whoever they are," Whitsmith said, her eyes watching Torrance carefully, "they're connected to that thing out there."

"Our only connection," Torrance said heatedly, "is that we were attacked by it when we found that basecamp."

"Io wouldn't break the law for no reason," Whitsmith continued. "The penalty for being here is pretty stiff, I hear. The Jovian governments don't take kindly to trespass."

"So what are you doing here?" Torrance snapped. "I know you killed the guards and took over the prison. Doesn't take a genius to see that. Why has no one come looking for you?"

Hudson and Whitsmith exchanged glances. It was a question everyone at the prison had asked many times over the last few years. No one had an answer and no one could stop anyone coming, so there was no sense in worrying about it. "We're not talking about us," Hudson said. "You have a craft somewhere. You have a way for us to get out of here. You're going to tell us where it is."

"Or what?"

Hudson considered that and set aside her rifle to draw a six-inch hunting knife from her boot. She saw Torrance's eyes widen at the sight and kept her movements slow and graceful, allowing the soldier's imagination do her work for her. Hudson crouched beside her, toying with her knife, placing it upon Torrance's bruised and bloodied cheek before drawing the blade slowly across what had been such a pretty face not so long ago.

"We're too far from the prison," Hudson said equally as slowly, "for anyone to hear you scream. Then there's my friend the storm. So why don't you start telling us what we want to know? It'll go far easier on you in the end, girl."

"We don't have a craft," Torrance said, her eyes fixed upon Hudson so she would not have to look at the knife playing across her flesh.

"Of course you have a craft. How did you get here otherwise?"

"We crashed. Our pilot ... wasn't exactly a pilot, but he had more experience than the rest of us."

"They sent you here without a proper pilot?" Hudson tried to work some sense from what the girl was saying, and there was only one thing that seemed like even a slightly realistic scenario. "You weren't sent here, were you?"

Torrance's lip trembled, but she said nothing.

"But why come here if you weren't sent? Why would soldiers come to this world and crash because they weren't given a proper pilot?" When Torrance did not reply she pressed the knife against the girl's throat and said, "That was a question by the way."

"We were running," Torrance said, her eyes forming terrified tears by this point. "We didn't have much choice. We needed somewhere to hide."

"Running? Running from whom?"

"This base you say you found," Whitsmith said, her voice dry. "This military base. You say you looked through it for anything you could use. You didn't happen to find, say, three suits of armour did you?"

Suddenly it all made sense to Hudson and she retracted the knife, falling upon her backside to rest her arms across her knees. She laughed heartily, and Torrance jumped at the sound. "You're criminals," Hudson said. "You crashed here, raided whatever you could, and when you stumbled upon us you just lied. There aren't any more of your unit out there, are there? It's just you three."

"When we found you," Torrance said, "we thought we could use you to help against that creature. We thought with so many people we might at last be able to overpower it."

"You might have mentioned it then," Hudson said.

"We were going to. Cartello wanted to get a good night's rest in first. Hunter ... Hunter's a psychopath. I've no idea why she was being transferred but I can bet it was because she was too dangerous to stay where she was."

"So you were being transferred," Hudson said, "and you took control of your shuttle. Killed the crew?"

Torrance looked away. "That was Hunter. It's why we can't afford to get recaptured. I don't know what Cartello was in for, but I was put away for theft. My boyfriend had me cover for him when the cops got him. Stashed a load of stuff with me and made me say it was mine. I didn't know it was stolen or anything. Anyway, my point is I'm not a murderer or anything, but the instant Hunter killed the crew she made me an accomplice."

"Well we're all in the same boat, it seems," Hudson said, still finding intense amusement in the situation. "Just how many prisoners can this world take?"

"We weren't being transferred here," Torrance said. "We were being moved to one of the outer moons. When we took control of the shuttle, this was the closest place we could reach."

"Which means," Hudson said, "anyone who comes looking for you will come straight to us."

"The world's quarantined," Torrance reminded her. "No one's coming looking for us."

Hudson looked to Whitsmith then. It was all good information, but it did them no good if they couldn't get back to the prison. "Once the storm lets up a bit we'll head out. See if you can find Torrance here a pair of shoes in one of these crates."

The smile vanished from Hudson's face as something struck the roof. The noise reverberated through the entire shack: it sounded as though a branch had broken loose in the storm.

"It's found us," Torrance whispered in terror.

"The shed's coated with a scent to repel animals," Whitsmith whispered. "It can't possibly have found us."

"I get the impression," Hudson said, retrieving her rifle, "we're not dealing with an ordinary animal. Stay with her."

"Where are you going?"

"I'm taking a look outside."

"If you go out there it'll kill you."

Hudson frowned at the genuine terror in Whitsmith's eyes. Showing fear was a weakness, everyone knew that, but she could see Whitsmith was not afraid for herself. Yes, she was being left without a protector, but that was not why her eyes were pleading with Hudson to stay. Whitsmith was afraid for Hudson's life, and Hudson could not fault that kind of fear. Another word for it would have been loyalty.

"I've fought more creatures in the pits than anyone," Hudson said, surprised to find her voice full of compassion. "I'll be fine."

"Then I'll go with you."

"Doesn't take two of us. We have what we need from Torrance and we know no one would miss her. It's your call whether to shoot her or leave her tied up here or whatever."

"We'll decide that together. When you come back."

Hudson said nothing more and headed outside. She had never allowed herself to grow close enough to anyone in the prison to actually call them her friend, but it was nice to think that someone cared for her. Hudson was too happy when she was beating people up to ever make any real friends, and it felt strange to think Whitsmith cared about her at all.

The storm was raging fiercely and as Hudson stepped out in it she threw aside any of the foolish inhibitions of character she may have been growing in the shed. The rain was cold, but the swamp air was warm, and the resulting effect cast a cleansing shower upon her. Hudson closed her eyes, raising her face to the dark heavens, the orange/red glow of Jupiter ever present through the trees. Water cascaded down her face, plastered her clothes to her skin, ran off her weapons harmlessly. The rain was where Katie Hudson felt most at home, and she knew whatever this creature was chasing them it could not survive when facing her in her element.

Bringing the rifle to her eyes, Hudson investigated the roof, but there was no sign that the creature was still up there, even if it had ever been there at all. She wandered about the exterior of the shack, keeping her rifle trained upwards, searching for any signs that the creature had ever been here. She saw something then, brushing against the roof in the wind. The thick leaves of a tree, still attached to the branch, were scraping the roof fiercely. Hudson smiled. Their monster had been nothing more than a few leaves.

She lowered her rifle, deciding she would take a look around the area while she was out here. She knew she would not be able to find any tracks through the storm, but perhaps she could find something of importance regardless.

A sound came from the trees and she dropped into a crouch, her rifle coming to her shoulder. The howling wind was throwing off her hearing, and as rain dripped into her eyes and flashed across her face she could not even see clearly. If there was something in the trees, it was not moving, however, and she debated whether it would be best for her to return to the shed. It would offer her no protection, but at least in there her senses would not be blasted to oblivion by the raging storm.

Backing away slowly, she judged the distance to the door as being around ten further paces. If there was something out there watching her she only needed for it to remain where it was for another few moments and she would be back with the others. Whitsmith could not be relied on to shoot straight, but Torrance was an extra body. Hudson knew trusting Torrance might prove a very bad idea, but if that lizard was still tracking them it was also something Hudson was willing to risk.

A series of sounds snapped her attention around: a swift slap of feet in mud. Hudson swung her gun about but a powerful arm slammed into it before she could pull the trigger. The rifle flew away from her and disappeared in the night, and Hudson felt something slam into her throat. She gasped as she was lifted from the ground, barely making out the form before her. The creature was tall, with dark mottled scales for skin. She could see precious little of its body, for the darkness was stealing everything from her, but its grip was powerful and as Hudson struggled, clawing at the hand with both her own, she realised the creature was also far more powerful than she.

The beast hissed, a waft of misty breath washing over her. She could see twin slits in the creature's head, staring out at her, threatening. A flash of teeth appeared in the pale light and Hudson knew if she allowed her imagination to run away with her she would die.

Keeping her left hand upon the claw attempting to throttle her, Hudson flailed with her right, dropping down the side of her body, grasping for her hunting knife. The creature squeezed more tightly and Hudson tasted blood in her mouth even as her brain began to haze. Then her fingers clasped about the hilt of her weapon and she stabbed horizontally with the blade, sliding the knife easily through the creature's ribs.

And suddenly Hudson was in the mud, hacking and wheezing and at last breathing. Her fingers went to her throat and came away bloodied where the claws of the monster had torn into her flesh, and she sat upon the wet ground staring in all directions, her heart racing, her breathing haggard, as she tried in vain to find her enemy.

Slowly she rose, drawing a pistol from her belt and wishing she had not lost her rifle. She could see nothing of the creature. While it was possible she had killed the thing, she could not expect it and desperately she now wanted to return to the others at the marker. She had no doubt that Torrance had been telling the truth when she said the creature had killed some of her colleagues, and Hudson tried to fathom just what this creature could be. On an unnatural world it seemed there were far more unnatural horrors than any of them understood.

Hudson took a single step back towards the shed before something howled to her side. She trained the gun in its rough direction and fired, the explosion swallowed by the strength of the storm. The creature collided with her, her shot apparently having gone wide, and Hudson felt pain shoot through her chest and underarm as the beast clamped its teeth through her flesh. For the first time in her entire life, Hudson screamed, but the sound was muted by the winds laughing at her predicament.

She angled her gun at the creature's head, but its hand shot out and encompassed the firearm, crushing both weapon and hand. Hudson screamed again as she felt her bones break, and fell once more into the mud as the creature released her, bounding back into the darkness.

Hudson half lay in the mud, her life fluids pouring from her side, her right hand a crushed pulp. Her heart was on the verge of exploding while she panicked, trying to think of something she might do, anything which might save her. She had been outfought and she had no doubt the creature would not let her return to the shed. It was playing with her, goading her to try, and she knew whatever she did she would be playing into its claws.

Taking a firm hold of her knife, Hudson forced herself to her feet. Her body was screaming in pain, she could feel blood bubbling within her throat and suspected the teeth may have punctured her lung. Scanning the area, still could she see no sign of the creature. In all the pit fights she had ever won, Hudson had always been able to see her prey, hear its approach. But this creature was canny and had awaited the coming storm before striking. It had stalked them and bided its time. The pit fights had all been forced and fought on terms Hudson had favoured. Now she was in the territory of this animal and she was being taught the meaning of not fighting fair.

Suddenly she could see it, standing before her and making no pretence of hiding. It stood taller than Hudson: at the moment it even stood straighter. She could make out the knife wound she had inflicted upon its side, but the animal ignored the pain, focusing its attention upon her. The thing walked upon two legs, just as Whitsmith had claimed. It walked with a straight back upon two legs as though it thought it was a human being.

Just what the hell it was Hudson could not say, and she knew she would never find out.

Summoning all her courage and strength, Hudson roared in bestial fury and charged with her knife. The creature simply stood there waiting for her, and as she reached it she stabbed down with the knife, attempting to strike the animal in the chest. But it dropped in that split second, spinning on its heels to slam an elbow into Hudson, allowing her own momentum to carry her through. It was an all-too-human reaction, one which had been trained into it. Hudson spun, slashing horizontally with her knife, but the creature caught her hand, twisting and almost snapping her arm. Hudson fell to one knee, gritting her teeth as she stared up into the coldly curious face of the monster.

Its teeth flashed once more as it grinned, before snapping its maw about her head.

CHAPTER TWELVE

There were people who called Zebadiah strange, sometimes even to his face. He did not care what people thought of him, especially since everyone in his life now was a convicted criminal. It was why he preferred the company of his caged creatures to real people. People could think what they liked about him: it did not bother him in the slightest. Conversely, he did not think much of anyone else, did not form opinions of anyone else. He had some dealings with Valentine and found him concise and utilitarian, which was good considering it meant he left Zebadiah alone more often than not; and Whitsmith was the only other person with whom he had any prolonged contact. Whitsmith was a nice woman who was vastly underrated by her employer. There had been a time when Zebadiah had thought he was actually starting to like Whitsmith, but had then reminded himself that there was a reason she had been in the prison as well. For all he knew she had committed multiple counts of homicide. He did not know and did not want to know.

However, Zebadiah was beginning to form an opinion of someone, and that opinion was not very good.

Private Tana Hunter had taken him to the roof. Zebadiah did not believe he had ever been to the roof, and what with the storm he wished he was not there presently. Thankfully the roof was not a single flat level but formed of many sloping surfaces and hidden alcoves. Whoever had designed the prison had known about the storms, clearly, and had created an intricate system of runoffs for the water, and shelter for anyone who was posted as sentry up there.

He was frozen to his bones and his clothes were damp with a fine spray, but at least he was sheltered from the worst of the foul weather. It was a stone hut-like structure he presently sat within, although was not much larger in volume than a phone booth and only had three walls. He did not like it on the roof, although in truth he would not have been all that bothered were it not for the company.

Hunter sat on her haunches, watching him. She was an extraordinary young woman, for she had such old eyes. That she was a psychopath was becoming more and more evident, and Zebadiah was under no illusion that she would not put a bullet in his head if he refused to cooperate. Her armour was tough, her weapons numerous, and her body close to the peak of human perfection. There was no way Zebadiah was going to chance attacking her directly.

They had remained there together for the better part of fifteen minutes now: one sitting, the other crouching. Hunter stared at him blankly, as though a zombie awaiting orders from her master. It was an incredibly unnerving experience for Zebadiah, but everything he thought to say somehow seemed foolish once it almost made it to his lips and he discarded such thoughts.

Finally he said something anyway.

"Your names are made up aren't they?"

There was a flicker of curiosity in Hunter's face, but perhaps even that was wishful thinking on his part.

Zebadiah cleared his throat and continued. "Tana, Aura and Zara. They're a little ... similar?"

The silence lasted another ten seconds or so, his question lingering in the storm-tossed air. And then Hunter's face broke into a smile which sent chills down her captive's spine. "You know," she said slowly, "that never even occurred to me."

That confirmed something he had long suspected. "You're not soldiers."

Her smile vanished and she stared into him with piercing eyes. "How do you come by that?"

"Because you're wearing stolen armour."

Her stare deepened, became almost lethal.

"Tana, Aura and Zara," he explained, "are Lustrum call-signs. You Jovians didn't fight a war with the Lustrum so you wouldn't have learned things like that. Anyone from Earth with even a passing interest in such things should have picked up on it. Valentine probably would have if he wasn't so interested in that blonde girl."

"Maybe we're just using call-signs and not our real names."

"Maybe you are. But if you were, you'd know what they were. Your armour's labelled Tana, I can see that much from here. You adopted the names thinking they were people names. Which means you stole the armour. That abandoned facility up north must have been Lustrum."

Hunter glanced away and Zebadiah reasoned she had not even known. They had found the armour and stolen it, fabricating their entire life story. Who they really were he neither knew nor cared: he was just making conversation because the silence was killing him. He hoped the truth wouldn't now kill him just as easily.

"So you know more about me than I do," Hunter said, her voice and expression tight. "Torrance or Cartello might have been impressed by that, but unfortunately for you you're talking to the wrong woman."

"Why make Cartello your sergeant?" Zebadiah asked, trying to keep her talking while at the same time mildly curious.

"Cartello's built like an oak. The only armour we could even vaguely get to fit her had sergeant stripes on it. When we found you people we figured we'd play on that."

"Clever."

"Any more questions before I get to mine?"

Zebadiah had been hoping Hunter would have talked long enough for someone to find him. He had watched Hunter release the erythrosuchus and knew it would keep Valentine and his people busy for a while, but had been rather hoping they would have been used to bringing down such creatures by now. If they were competent they would have dropped the beast immediately and returned it to its cell, where they would have discovered Zebadiah was missing. The more time passed the more Zebadiah was coming to realise how incompetent the people in this place truly were.

Hunter took his silence for permission to continue. "What do you know about the creature stalking us?"

Zebadiah blinked. "Nothing. Why would I?"

"Come on, you know about all the creatures here. It's your job to look after them, feed them, keep them clean and happy. You know more about their behaviour than anyone in this whole prison."

"True, but from what I heard about what Whitsmith faced out there, it was a troodont that walked holding its spine vertically."

"And?"

"And? And they don't exist."

"So you're saying we're all seeing things?"

Zebadiah knew he would have to be careful how he answered that. "I'm saying nature could not have created this creature."

"Nature didn't create any of the creatures on this world. Nature didn't even create the world."

"Have you ever wondered why there are dinosaurs here?"

The question threw Hunter, for she genuinely seemed taken aback in thought. No one knew who put the dinosaurs there, or how, or even why. It was assumed they were cooked up in a laboratory and let loose into the forests and swamps. It had all happened generations before anyone now living had been born, so if there was an answer out there it was long buried. Several theories had been put forward over the years, none of them proven. Many things had simply become accepted over time, as with all legends, from Robin Hood to King Arthur. So many factoids were now ingrained into everyone's brains that no one sought to question the very fundamentals of those legends.

With regards to this world, the fundamental question was why?

"I don't know," Hunter admitted at last. "Why would someone put dinosaurs here?"

"Because they could. And maybe they also put something else here, something which had never existed anywhere else. Again, because they could." He paused, but could see she still did not understand what he was saying. "There are no fossil records of this creature. There are no similar animals back on Earth to which we can compare it. When lions were introduced to Io they panicked, went mad. They attacked handlers, their own pride, anything that came to their jaws. That was unexpected, but explainable by the fact that lions had never before existed in such an atmosphere, or with Jupiter hanging over their heads. With dinosaurs we don't have the actual animals to look at and compare, but we can make reasonable guesses as to whether their behaviour here is natural. With this new creature though?" He shook his head. "We haven't a clue."

"And you've never seen it before in your time here?"

"If anyone in the prison had seen it, word would have got to me. The only person here who's seen it is Whitsmith. It didn't kill her. I wonder why."

"Why?" Hunter snapped.

"I ... said I wondered why?" He could see Hunter was wound so tight she was on the verge of snapping, and by doing so would likely ping off a few shots into him without even considering it. "She wasn't attacking it, she wasn't armoured. Maybe it was curious."

"Curious?"

Zebadiah wished she would stop repeating him. "Perhaps it had never seen a human civilian before. Or," he had a sudden thought, "maybe it's the armour it doesn't like. Maybe whoever wore that armour before you did some terrible things to its species."

It was all conjecture, but it was also based on common sense. He could see Hunter was beginning to understand him, beginning to fear he was right. He was all but convinced now these three women had themselves done nothing towards these creatures and that it was after them because of their armour. It was strangely amusing to think it wasn't their fault, although he was not fool enough to laugh in her face over it.

Hunter moved more quickly than he had ever seen her. Still keeping her gun trained upon him, she tore her armour from her body piece by piece, discarding everything as though it was on fire. She shifted the gun to her other hand whenever she needed to, but struggled with the breastplate since she only had the one hand to use. Zebadiah wondered what she thought an old man would have been able to do to her. Eventually she succeeded in stripping the armour entirely and kicked it into the storm in disgust. Beneath the armour she wore dark tight-fitting clothes which may have been some form of uniform, may have been picked up from the same place as the armour. Either way, Zebadiah doubted it was going to do her much good. The animal had her scent, it knew her face, and it wasn't going to be confused just because she had removed her only real defence against its claws.

Again, this was something he decided not to point out.

"Anything else you might know before I put a bullet in you?" she asked, even sounding serious.

"Only that I may not have met those things, but I'm the best thing to a dinosaur profiler you're going to get around here."

"What about Whitsmith?"

"Well, she has the field experience, yes, but I ..."

"She knows everything you do and has field experience?"

Zebadiah paused. "Well, I wouldn't put it quite like ..."

"She's with Torrance," Hunter said, gazing through the storm in thought, as though she would be able to see the other woman through the rain and black night. "Stupid girl, she's probably botched this up as well."

"You two don't like Torrance much do you?"

"Girl's an idiot."

Zebadiah stared past Hunter, out into the night. He tried not to give any reaction, but was certain he could see something out there. A form in the dark night. He concentrated upon the sloped side of the roof, where the rain sloshed into the gutter. There was something perched at the end, like a prone grotesque. The harder he stared the more he was certain he could see the form begin to move, shuffling ever towards the small concealment in which the two of them were contained. Zebadiah could think of no natural creature in this area which could have made it to the roof, since none ever had before. That meant it had to be either this mysterious beast or else someone trying to get the drop on Hunter. Perhaps Valentine had found them and had sent someone to ambush her.

Whichever it was, Zebadiah knew his chances with it would be better than his chances with Hunter. As such he tore his eyes from the form and tried to engage the psychopath in conversation once more. He fought for something to say, tried to keep it normal and free-flowing.

"Nice weather we're having."

Hunter stared at him blankly.

Zebadiah shrugged. "If you like storms, of course."

He risked a glance back into the storm and could see the figure had paused in its crouch. Unfortunately Hunter saw Zebadiah's eyes flicker in that direction and she half-turned to see what he was looking at, her gun still kept trained upon him. She gasped the instant she saw it, swinging her gun about to crack off three shots. The sound thundered within the enclosed shelter, but by the light of the explosions Zebadiah could see the thing was indeed the upright troodont. He watched it leap, evading the shots, even as Hunter took off across the sloping roof, stumbling but not caring as she fled.

Zebadiah was left in silence, wondering why she had removed the armour. If she wanted it not to recognise her as an enemy, shooting at it wasn't such a hot idea.

He listened for any sign of the creature, for he could see very little in the darkness and had only assumed it had chased the psychopathic non-soldier. He knew he should have been panicking, should have been on the verge of a heart attack, but he was not. So far as he saw things, he was in no greater danger now than he had been a moment earlier. If the creature wanted to kill him it would do so: there was nothing he could do about it.

A hiss echoed through the shelter then, the sound of water spattering hot metal. So the creature was still out there, he reasoned, and it was trying to scare him or something. Possibly it wanted him to run out into the rain in a panic, but instead Zebadiah sat patiently waiting to see what it would do. After but a few moments it landed at the entrance as silent as a falling leaf. The creature was indeed magnificent, beautiful even; its muscular almost human form standing imperiously, with back straightened in pride of its achievements. Zebadiah noted it was wounded, for blood poured from its side in what appeared to be a knife-wound. The creature was not infallible then, but nor would it allow an injury to slow it down. Oddly enough, while animals were always at their most dangerous when injured, they tended to find safe ground and stay there. This one seemed to have done entirely the opposite and attacked the enemy in its home ground. Perhaps the wound was fatal and it wanted to take its foes down with it. If so, the creature was far more human than beast, and that, Zebadiah reasoned, was the most frightening thought of all.

"If we had you in the pits," he told the creature without a single tremor to his voice, "we wouldn't have nearly so many heroes among us any more."

The creature continued to stare at him for several more moments, and then lunged for the kill.

CHAPTER THIRTEEN

Valentine had asked the sergeant what Hunter's strategy would be now that she had Zebadiah, but Cartello could not tell him. It was an odd admission for a military leader, and Valentine could not understand how Cartello did not seem to know that much about the soldiers under her command. Locating Hunter was the priority, however, for should he lose Zebadiah he could not think of anyone qualified to look after the animals.

He had dispatched several units to find Hunter, giving them orders to take her alive if possible but that they should preserve Zebadiah's life over hers. Cartello had strangely not countermanded that order, which gave Valentine even more concern over the situation. He could see the annoyance in her eyes, but it was more than that. He realised she was afraid of Hunter, afraid she would do something stupid, and Valentine no longer knew what to think of any of these people.

"Dex!"

Valentine pulled his radio from his belt. The sound was faint, the signal scratchy, but the voice was unmistakable. "Aubrey?"

"Storm's lessening out here," Whitsmith said. "We're almost back to the prison. Listen. Hudson's dead and that thing's probably on its way to you right now."

Valentine felt his blood chill. "How do you figure that?"

"Because it didn't kill me or Torrance so it had to have gone somewhere more important."

Valentine heard Cartello grunt, and she rechecked her weapons nervously.

"Thanks," Valentine said through the radio. "You and Torrance lie low until we take care of this thing."

"Hold on, Dex. You have to watch out for Hunter. Blondie says she's a psychopathic killer. They're not soldiers. They're prisoners being transferred between moons. They stole the armour and got that thing mad. Hunter's not going to like being stalked so who knows what she'll do."

"I have a pretty fair idea on what she might do, Aubrey. Kidnapping for one thing."

"What?"

"Just lie low. I'll let you know if any of us survive." He returned the radio to his belt and arched an eyebrow at Cartello. She was not pointing her guns at him, which he could only take to be a good sign.

"All right," she shrugged. "So we're criminals."

"All in the same boat then."

She frowned and Valentine realised she really was that dense.

"Right," Valentine said, "so we have a crazy woman running around the prison, a hostage and a monster. Zebadiah will have to take care of himself because I think we're going to have to concentrate on the creature."

"Hunter will do whatever she needs to," Cartello said. "She doesn't care about any of us. All she wants is her own survival. She'll use us as far as she can, but will kill us if she has to."

"You're saying she's more dangerous than the monster?"

"No. I'm saying once we kill the monster I'm going to shoot her down as well."

"Oh. And I thought the people here were harsh."

Valentine informed his teams to be on the lookout for the monster as well as Hunter and decided he would be a lot safer sticking with Cartello. He was immensely intrigued with what Whitsmith had said, for if these people had stolen their armour he wanted to know from where. Their guards presumably, in which case those guards would now be dead, but Valentine was beginning to think that there was more going on here than he understood. If there was a chance there were other people on this world, he needed to know.

That could, of course, wait until their problems had been dealt with.

Gunfire sounded in the distance and Valentine tried to work out where it was coming from. Cartello was running by then so he gave pursuit, hoping they would not run into a hail of bullets. The gunfire intensified the more ground they covered, and became intermingled with screams. Wishing he carried a weapon, Valentine knew it was still safer with Cartello, and decided he would re-evaluate once he started to see the bodies.

They broke out into a large open area with cells lining the hall all the way down. The walkways were about two metres wide, moving ahead as a corridor and splitting off every fifteen metres or so in order to connect the two lines of cells. Each walkway was enclosed by metal railing on either side. This left a lot of space in between, which was filled with open air, allowing any patrolmen to use these walkways and peer down the cells on the next level. There were three levels of such cells, and Cartello and Valentine were presently on the uppermost one.

Ahead, Valentine could see two bodies strewn across the floor, their throats torn out with medical precision, their bloody handprints all over the floor where the dying men had attempted in vain to crawl to safety before bleeding out or dying of shock. There were several more former inmates taking minimal cover behind the railing, shooting at the thing which had torn their fellows apart.

It was the first time Valentine had seen the beast, and he stopped short to stare in wonderment at the thing. It crouched upon the railing, its human-like legs coiled and ready to spring. The creature looked upon the gathered troops and hissed, blood and spittle spraying through the air.

Immediately Cartello set herself up in position to lend her own fire to the fray, resting her rifle upon a railing and taking aim. Valentine backed away, not wanting to present himself as a target.

The creature leapt, flying through the air, entirely heedless of the great drop with which it was flirting. Even through the air it moved with far greater speed than Valentine had ever seen an animal achieve and he could imagine it leaping from tree to tree in its native element. It landed amidst its attackers dispassionately, and they panicked, blasting and running and screaming. Valentine watched one man go down, a shot tearing through his leg, another woman clutching her face as blood exploded from her cheek. The creature dropped low, making no overtly hostile moves, and within the span of two seconds three of its attackers were down and the rest fled. The third person to fall was a man who had simply stumbled in his panic. He looked at the creature fearfully, and as it rose, calmly, it tore out his throat. Standing erect, the creature looked about for a fresh target, a swell of pride expanding its chest.

Valentine had never before seen a creature use its prey's fear to such an extent and suddenly knew whatever this thing was it was capable of slaughtering them all.

A gunshot cracked in the spacious hall, the echo resounding from all sides. Cartello's shot took the creature through the shoulder, sending it spinning, crimson ichor spraying up the bars of the closest cell. The creature did not fall into shock, however, and bounded upon the nearest rail, launching itself through the air to catch hold of a second rail, placing it beyond the range of Cartello's rifle.

Cartello lowered her gun without even a hint of emotion.

Valentine felt it would be far easier for all concerned if they just trained their own weapons upon themselves.

"That thing reasons like a human being," Valentine said. "Maybe we could try talking to it."

Cartello arched an eyebrow, the glint of humour to her face.

Realising there were some things he should not say aloud, Valentine kept quiet from that moment and let Cartello work. By this point the creature had vanished entirely and he rather hoped someone had managed to get in a lucky shot. There were so many people running around the prison, shooting anything that moved, that Valentine figured the thing would have to get hit eventually. Its skill was still something which astounded him, for it had displayed not simple animal ingenuity but human-trained strategy. If it was clever, perhaps indeed it had taken instruction from someone; but if so who? And why?

He realised Cartello had moved off by this point, and he watched her. She moved slowly across the walkways, her gun held to her eyes, ready to shoot the thing the instant it reared its head. Valentine leaned on the rail before him, glancing down to the two levels below. He could see people moving around down there as well, hunting for this creature. It was wounded now, so it might well be heading somewhere it could hide and tend to its wounds. Until it got there it would be extremely dangerous, but at least Cartello had shown the creature could be wounded; and anything that could be wounded could be killed.

He watched as Cartello glanced into one of the cells, which was a sound strategy since they were dark, utilitarian places. Just the location the creature might have chosen to rest. Apparently she found nothing, for she kept moving.

A strange scratching came to his ears and Valentine looked about, trying to pinpoint the source. Finally he looked down, and started as he saw the creature, scampering along the underside of one of the walkways, using all four of its limbs, and heading straight for him.

"It's here!" he shouted frantically and several people on the level below began firing. Valentine dropped as the bullets whizzed about him, throwing his arms across his head. He tried to scuttle back, away from the danger zone, but he had only moved a metre or so when a dark form exploded before him. The creature landed upon the walkway ahead, dropping into a crouch and hissing at him. Its shoulders were hunched, its long arms held to the side, vicious claws poised, and Valentine could see the terrible injury to its shoulder which marked its otherwise unblemished body. He also noticed something else.

The creature possessed opposable thumbs. Even Valentine knew what an evolutionary leap that was.

"What are you?" he asked, terrified but weaponless. His only recourse was to reason with the creature, even though he knew it would do no good. The creature gave no indication that it could understand his language, that it had even heard him in fact. It shuffled towards him, eyes alive and alert. He could see the thing was enjoying the attack, that it revelled in this sort of encounter, and Valentine knew there was nothing he could say which would make any impression upon the creature at all.

Frantically he tried to think of anything he held which might help, but all he had of any use was his radio. The creature regarded him with a curious, lopsided stare. It knew he was unarmed, knew he posed no threat, and had elected to examine him, much as it had Whitsmith. It had not attacked Whitsmith, but then it had been frightened off by Hudson's arrival: Valentine was no longer under any illusion that it would not have torn Whitsmith apart had not her companion arrived at the best of moments.

"I can offer you a deal," Valentine said. "You let me live and I'll get someone to teach you a few more moves. I know someone must have taught them you, I know you must have had human contact sometime in the past." He was sweating now, for the creature was so close its curious claws brushed against his leg. It leaned its face towards him, sniffing, as though searching for a specific scent. Valentine sucked in his breath, his heart on the verge of exploding. He valiantly tried to think, tried to work out how he could survive this. But he could not. This creature was strategically the greatest warrior ever known, the perfect soldier trained by master sergeants.

But if that was true, if it had indeed been trained, it must have had discipline instilled into it, and harshly.

Valentine shouted as loud as he could, "Attention!"

The creature's reaction was instantaneous. Its grin faded and it snapped bolt upright for a single instant before Valentine could see anger flash across its face. The reaction had been instinctive, but now it was furious and stared at him as though it had at last found that which it had sought all this time.

The air erupted and the creature pitched forward. Valentine screamed as the thing came for him, crushing him with its full weight. Valentine struggled against it, feeling its claws tear into him, and he continued to scream and scream even as he flailed uselessly in his death throes.

And then the creature was torn from him and Cartello threw the body aside. "Clever that," she grunted. "Getting it to stand up so I could get a clear shot."

Valentine was alive. His brain fought for clarification, for a reason behind why he was alive, but it did not matter. He was alive, and that was all he cared about. As Cartello helped him to his feet he looked down at his shredded suit, the material torn by his own struggles with the dead claws, and then focused his eyes upon the gaping wound in the side of the creature's head. Its huge eyes stared out emptily now, and Valentine shuddered at the very thought of what the thing might have been.

"I almost wish it didn't work," Valentine said in a small voice.

"Why's that?"

"Because it means someone trained this thing, Cartello. And if someone trained it, they may well be training an entire army."

CHAPTER FOURTEEN

Her boss had told her to stay away, but Whitsmith had never much liked taking orders. Dexter Valentine may not have been what she would have considered a good man, but he was a halfway decent one, and that had to count for something when every second person was a murderer. That Valentine wanted to protect her only pushed Whitsmith on even harder to help him. As she approached the main entrance to the prison, however, Whitsmith glanced to her companion and could not help but feel it wasn't Whitsmith Valentine wanted to protect so badly.

"It would help if you gave me a gun," Torrance complained for the dozenth time.

The storm had passed and the rain had reduced to a trickle, but the two women were still soaked through and cranky. Finding what was left of Katie Hudson had made Whitsmith violently sick, and having to deal with Torrance whining all the way back was not helping her mood. She knew it was only common sense to give Torrance a firearm, and in truth she did not expect the girl to shoot her in the back or anything. It was the very fact that Torrance kept asking for one, however, that made Whitsmith not hand one over. Whitsmith had never been a particularly spiteful woman, but Torrance was bringing out all the worst qualities in her. It was just another reason to despise her.

Whitsmith unbolted the main gate to the prison and pushed it open. There was no point in having a lock on the gate since there were officially no other people on this world: the only things they were keeping out were the dinosaurs and their prehistoric friends.

"I'm going inside," Whitsmith told her. "You can come if you like, but that creature's going to be in there. Your best bet for survival would be to take off through the swamp. Head west. The swamp ends soonest that way."

"Without a weapon?"

"If I give you a weapon do you promise to get out of my life?"

Torrance set her shoulders firm and scrunched her face in a very juvenile, petty manner. "I wouldn't last five minutes on my own. At the very least I need to collect Cartello, but I can't see Dexter throwing us both out when all this is done."

"Oh, because you know *Dexter* so well." She put such sweet emphasis on the name she felt ashamed of herself even as she did it.

Torrance blinked. "Please don't tell me you're still jealous. I was only all over him because I was distracting him. I couldn't have him thinking too much about who we were and where we came from."

"Dex wouldn't be interested in you anyway, blondie."

"Why? Because I'm younger and hotter than you?"

"You're a fad, that's all."

"Which is more than you've ever been with him."

Whitsmith forced herself not to rise to the bait. She knew what Torrance was doing. She wanted another roll around in the mud so she could get her hands on a weapon. If Whitsmith was smart she would just put a bullet through the girl's knee and leave her out here for the wildlife. But Whitsmith wasn't that far gone yet. She had spent five years trying not to lose her morality and she wasn't about to let some teenage hussy destroy her resolve.

"In or out?" Whitsmith asked, holding the gate.

Torrance stepped in without a word and Whitsmith slammed the gate, shooting the bolt. She motioned with her gun for Torrance to precede her.

Whitsmith's radio chose that moment to crackle and she brought it up to her ear. "Dex?"

"Good news," he said. "Or at least some good news anyway. The creature's dead."

"You sure about that?"

"Unless it can gather up its brains where they're spattered all over the floor. Now all we have to worry about is Hunter and you can come back."

"Already back, Dex. Never was good at doing what I was told."

"Aubrey," he said, sounding truly worried, "it's not safe here. Hunter kidnapped Zebadiah. She let a reptile loose and doesn't seem to care who gets hurt."

"Why'd she kidnap Zebadiah?"

"No idea. Because she's a nut-job?"

"Zebadiah?" Torrance asked, concerned. "He knows about the dinosaurs. She probably thought he could tell her about this creature."

"He didn't even know it existed," Whitsmith snapped at her. "Now shut up."

"Wait, wait, wait," Valentine said. "She may have something there."

Torrance folded her arms and huffed. "Got more than your girlfriend anyway."

"My girlfriend?" Valentine asked. "I don't have a ... Never mind. We have two dinosaur experts here, Aubrey."

Whitsmith barely heard him. Between the two of them, Torrance and Valentine were flaring her cheeks with fury. "I don't know why I bothered coming back to help you, Dex. Of all the ... You know what? You're welcome to this blonde little tramp. I hope you have ugly babies together."

"Babies? Aubrey, just listen to me. We have two dinosaur experts and ..."

"Yeah, so? Zebadiah and me, I know that already. What do you want? A medal for the bleedin' obvious?"

"And you've also met this creature," Valentine continued. "Twice now. And survived both times."

He sounded frantic but Whitsmith wasn't about to let him change the subject that easily. "I'll scout out a nice place for you to have your honeymoon. Somewhere you can relax on a nice beach: I'm sure it'll be perfectly safe for you to just lie out in the open."

"Aubrey, what are you going on about? You've survived the creature and ..."

"And I'm beginning to wonder why I bothered with that either."

"Whitsmith," Torrance said, her eyes wide.

Whitsmith stared daggers at her. "One more word from you, missy, and I'm shooting you where you ..."

A gunshot tore through the air, making Whitsmith physically jump. Torrance flew backwards, blood spraying in the air. She landed heavily, rolling on the ground, screaming. Whitsmith felt fear wash through her entire body like a shivering wave. She looked down at her gun, shaking in her hand. She had not even realised she had pulled the trigger: she had become so callous she had shot the woman without even knowing it.

"Drop the gun."

Whitsmith glanced to the side, where Tana Hunter stood, levelling her own pistol upon her. Hunter's eyes were intense, focused, and entirely without mercy.

"Drop the gun," she repeated. "Now."

The gun fell from Whitsmith's trembling fingers. Perhaps relief should have washed through her in the realisation she had not been the one to have pulled the trigger, but all she could hear was the soft weeping of Torrance lying in a pool of her own fluids.

"And the radio," Hunter said.

Whitsmith unhitched the radio and let that fall also.

"You're the dinosaur expert," Hunter told her straight. "And, as your boss just said, you've survived the creature. Twice. You're going to show me how to track it and how to kill it."

Whitsmith opened her mouth to tell her the creature was dead, but realised that would negate the psychopath's reason for keeping her alive. Similarly she would be instantly killed were she to convince Hunter she would be of no use against the thing.

"All right," Whitsmith told her. "I don't know what it is precisely, but I can tell you how I survived it. Twice."

"You only need to tell me once."

Whitsmith fought for something with which to reply to that.

"That was a joke," Hunter said flatly. "You were supposed to laugh."

Whitsmith laughed. Sort of.

Hunter shook her head. "No, you don't laugh after I tell you it was a joke. That just makes me look stupid."

Whitsmith stopped laughing. "Uh, can we just get on with tracking this creature of yours?"

"Sure. But first, that whimpering's getting on my nerves."

Whitsmith watched as Hunter turned her gun upon Torrance. She did not like Torrance – in fact, it seemed no one much liked her – but Whitsmith could not watch as someone shot her to death while she lay wounded on the floor. "No!" Whitsmith shouted, and Hunter raised a questioning eyebrow. Whitsmith thought quickly. "We might need her. This creature's tracking the three of you, right? Well, we'll need her as bait. Unless you want to volunteer yourself?"

Hunter considered that for all of two seconds before training the gun upon Whitsmith once more. "All right. Pick her up. She's your responsibility. If she annoys me too much, I'll shoot you instead."

Whitsmith swallowed back a retort, again wondering why she bothered with helping people. Moving across to the downed young woman, Whitsmith quickly assessed the damage. The bullet had struck Torrance in the arm and passed straight through. The wound was bleeding and didn't seem to want to stop. Whitsmith swiftly formed a tourniquet by tearing off Torrance's sleeve. It was soaked and caked with dirt, but it was all she had to work with. Torrance was crying, wincing and what very much sounded like howling. Whitsmith would have liked to have considered her a weak woman for behaving in such a way, but Whitsmith herself had never been shot so would not condemn someone who had been.

"Listen to me," she said, talking quietly so Hunter would not overhear. Torrance did not seem to be listening at all, so Whitsmith grabbed her face with both hands and forced her eyes to focus. "Listen to me, Aura. Hunter's going to kill us both, do you understand me? She's going to kill us both. I can't get us out of this, but I can buy us some time. Dex will save us. Do you understand? Dex will save us."

Torrance seemed to comprehend at least some of what she was saying, because she nodded, although her eyes were not focused at all and Whitsmith suspected she was in shock or something. She was hardly a doctor but it seemed the most logical answer.

"Now, you have to stand," Whitsmith told her. "I'll help you, but you have to stand."

Placing her arm about the young woman's back and hooking her hand under her arm, Whitsmith was able to lift her from the ground. Torrance's feet gave out beneath her, her legs not seeming to want to work, although as Whitsmith steadied her she was able to put some weight on them. Whitsmith threw Torrance's arm over her shoulder, realising she was going to have to help her a lot more if she wanted her to walk anywhere.

Then she realised Hunter was staring at the two of them with something like wonderment in her eyes. "Gosh," she said, "it's like watching sisters kiss and make up. Start moving."

Whitsmith bit back her retort. Torrance was heavier than she looked and Whitsmith struggled to move with her at all, although after but a few steps did Torrance seem to understand their lives were on the line and she was able to literally pull her own weight. They moved ahead of Hunter, who trailed them with her gun in hand.

Whitsmith could faintly hear the scratchy voice of Dexter Valentine calling to her through her radio. Calling to her, not Torrance. Perhaps she should have taken that as a victory. Instead she just wished this had been a segregated female prison in the first place.

CHAPTER FIFTEEN

"You must have some idea what she might be trying." Valentine was becoming frantic now. The remains of the creature were being removed but the prison could not return to normal until Hunter was taken care of. Stone had regrouped with Valentine and Cartello, and Valentine could not think of a worse bodyguard who only appeared once the threat was dead. Following the death of the creature, Cartello seemed in two minds of whether to stay. Valentine had pleaded with her, saying Hunter was deranged and might well come after Cartello later. He had argued they should take her down while there were so many numbered against her. Cartello had seemed to accept the argument and had stuck around, at least for the moment. Unfortunately she was not proving much in the way of help.

"Don't really know her," Cartello admitted. "Kept to herself mostly."

Valentine had tried to raise Whitsmith on the radio several times since the transmission had been cut off, and the continued silence was only making him certain his secretary was in terrible danger. Hunter needed her knowledge of dinosaurs, but as soon as she realised Whitsmith knew nothing about this strange reptile she would put a bullet in her and be done with it. Torrance would have been of no use to her at all, and Valentine was all but resolved to her having been killed already. Even this possibility did not seem to stir Cartello to action.

"You don't care about much, do you?" Valentine asked. Over his years at the prison Valentine had only been able to hold things together because of his own sociopathic tendencies, but with Whitsmith's life at stake even he was willing to throw them aside and focus on saving lives. Cartello did not even seem to have that little compassion in her soul. He briefly wondered why she had been incarcerated, but had been playing that game for five years now and had long since ceased caring for the answers.

A crackle sounded at his belt and Valentine answered the radio. It was a report from one of the search teams. It seemed they had located Zebadiah and were bringing him down. Valentine said he would meet them and the three of them headed to the hospital room. It was a large area containing several beds, only one of which was currently in use as they arrived. Medical equipment was stored and used in this room, and sometimes surgery was even performed. Creature attacks seldom left survivors, which was almost fortunate for the poor souls who were wheeled in here. They only had one surgeon in the prison, and that was a former inmate who had delighted in making unnecessary incisions in her patients because she liked to see people suffer. Valentine did not know her back story and honestly did not want to. She was the only person in the entire building with the necessary skill to put people back together. She was also a very good reason for never wanting to get hurt in the first place.

Thankfully the good doctor was nowhere in sight as Valentine approached the team leaving Zebadiah lying on the bed. The old man's clothes were soaked through with rainwater, his body having stiffened in death. Valentine could not even see any marks upon him, so whatever had happened he had not been savaged by the beast. A proper assessment was probably out of the question, but he suspected Zebadiah had died of a heart attack. Kneeling beside the prone form, he leant his elbows upon the bed and wondered whether a prayer would do the man any good. He did not know any of Zebadiah's religious beliefs, had never really spoken to the man outside of his professional capacity. There were so many people in this prison Valentine did not know simply because he had not wanted to know them. But whatever their crimes, some of them were decent people, and he asked himself how many more would have to die before he accepted that the pasts of everyone on this world needed to be buried forever.

"I wonder whether it was the creature that got to him," Valentine said in a small voice, "or Hunter."

"Why don't we ask him?" Cartello said.

"What do you mean?"

Cartello prodded the old man in the side with her gun. "Wake up, you old coot."

Zebadiah stirred, his brow furrowing. His eyes opened tentatively and at first Valentine thought he was witnessing a miracle. Then the truth dawned on him and he got back to his feet.

"Zebadiah, wake up," Valentine demanded, shaking him.

Zebadiah mumbled something and rose to a sitting position. He blinked several times, looked about him and seemed genuinely even more surprised than Valentine that he was still alive.

"What happened?" Valentine asked.

"That woman of yours," the old man told Cartello, "is insane."

"Quite possibly," Valentine said. "What happened?"

"That creature attacked me. Or sort of did anyway." He frowned. "It lunged for me, but then pitched forward. Its side was giving it jip. Anyway, after it pitched over it seemed to decide I wasn't worth killing and it took off. No idea where it went."

"Because you fainted," Valentine supplied.

"Like to see you do any better."

"What's jip?" Cartello asked.

"Pain."

"Why was its side in pain?"

"I don't know," Zebadiah said. "Maybe the big honking knife wound?"

"Knife wound?" Valentine asked, confused. "But there wasn't any knife wound. The only injury it sustained before it died was the shot Cartello fired through its shoulder."

Zebadiah shrugged, not much caring.

Valentine's eyes widened. "It's a different creature. There are two of them. And we ... we just killed its friend. Maybe even its mate."

Cartello did not seem at all bothered by the possibility and just rechecked her rifle.

"Would you stop doing that every two seconds!" Valentine snapped. "The damn thing's loaded fine."

"Just get itchy fingers when I'm not doing anything," she said. "So we still have a creature to hunt as well as Hunter."

"If anyone," Valentine warned, "says anything about Hunter becoming the prey I swear I'll scream."

He noted Stone closed his mouth very quickly indeed.

"Where are you going?" Valentine asked, for Cartello was already halfway out the door.

"Seems to me," she said, "we have two things left to hunt. Might as well go looking for one."

"But which one are you going after?"

"Whichever I manage to track first. You keep trying your girlfriend. Maybe she'll answer."

"Aubrey's not my girlfriend."

"No business of mine."

And she was gone. Valentine stared after her in abject horror. She had simply walked out on him when two young women were facing imminent death. But there was nothing he could do about it. He couldn't fight, he didn't have the first idea on how to even properly throw a punch. But Whitsmith was out there, and he would not allow her to die while he sat around doing nothing.

He held out his hand to Stone. "Give me your gun."

"Which one?"

"A ... small one."

Stone drew a pistol, turned it and handed it over. He looked confused, even partly amused. Valentine ignored him as he tried to work out how to properly hold the thing. Eventually he gave up and shoved it inside his belt.

"Uh, sir?" Stone asked. "It's going to take a lot more than that to bring down either Hunter or that creature. I think you should lock yourself in your room while I lead a team out after them."

"I'm not hiding while my secretary's out there, Stone."

"I'll find her. And if she's alive I'll bring her back."

Valentine tried not to wince at that statement. Whitsmith was alive, she had to be. Hunter still thought she needed her, and that would keep her alive. If only he had some clue as to where Hunter might have taken her.

His eyes widened as a thought struck him. He didn't need to know where Hunter was, he didn't need to know at all.

"Come on," he told Stone. "I have an idea."

His plan should work, in theory. It all hinged on just how bad that storm outside had been.

CHAPTER SIXTEEN

The ground was strewn with soil and straw, but beneath there was a layer of rock. The chamber was around fifty by fifty metres and entirely vacant of any furniture, obstacles or anything else. There were two doors: one of ordinary size, the other somewhat larger. The walls of the chamber were tall and sturdy, ending at around ten metres in a railing which travelled the entire length of those walls. Whitsmith had no idea what the original use for this chamber might have been, but Dexter Valentine had seen its potential as soon as he had laid eyes upon it. He had termed the area the pit and it was here that former prisoners set their strengths against the various horrors Whitsmith captured from the outside world. The pit would not be used until the current crisis was over, which meant they should remain undisturbed. It was a sound, strategic plan for Hunter to have brought them to the pit, Whitsmith had to admit. It was also ironic, she felt, that she had been brought here to die, just as Whitsmith had brought so many animals before her.

Torrance was not doing so well. She had not spoken much since Whitsmith had laid her against the wall. The single gunshot had sapped the girl of her strength and colour, and no matter what Whitsmith did she could not stop the bleeding. She had seen enough animal wounds in her time to know there was a good chance Torrance would die without immediate medical attention, but sorely doubted Hunter much cared. As for Hunter herself, she had taken a quick look around the pit, to determine its strengths and weaknesses, before returning to Whitsmith with her gun levelled.

"All right," Hunter said. "You need to start talking."

Whitsmith ignored her. She was knelt beside Torrance, putting pressure on her wound, blood seeping through her fingers. Torrance's breathing was haggard, her body was exuding sweat which would have given the storm fair competition. For some reason Whitsmith could not stop the blood flowing and she feared Torrance had some form of condition. Her eyes were unfocused and afraid, and Whitsmith felt a pang of pity for the girl she had never liked.

"I said you need to start talking."

"I heard you the first time," Whitsmith snapped. She was going to die, they both were, so she could not see any reason to be nice to her captor. "You haven't asked any questions yet." Whitsmith continued to put pressure upon the wound and held the girl's hand if only for comfort. There was still warmth flowing through that hand, although the strength of her grip was waning fast. "Get me a doctor," Whitsmith said, "and I'll tell you everything."

"You'll tell me everything or I'll shoot you."

"And what will that get you?"

"Fine. I'll shoot her."

Whitsmith looked at Hunter then. She stood angrily, her gun covering them both. She was a woman not used to being spoken back to, a woman who felt secure behind the barrel of a firearm. She was everything which Whitsmith had always found despicable about her company in this prison, and could only laugh at the sense of humour Jupiter had to send only more prisoners to this world.

"What are they?" Hunter demanded.

"The creatures?" Whitsmith realised she was going to have to start lying, so said, "They don't have a name. Not an official one anyway."

"They're Lustrum aren't they?"

"Lustrum?"

"We took this armour from a Lustrum camp to the north. Either the Lustrum ran away from these things, or they created them."

Whitsmith could not think of any reason why the Lustrum would be involved with these creatures at all. The Lustrum had gone to war with the Earth years ago and had fled at the closing of that conflict. Where they had gone no one could say, but certainly if they had taken root on this world she felt she would have known about it. There would have been some clue over the past five years. Unless this was just such a clue.

"All right, yes," Whitsmith said. "The Lustrum created them."

"And they turned on their creators."

"That's about it. Frankensteinosaurus."

Hunter's eyes narrowed and Whitsmith decided she probably should not bait the woman so much.

"I need to contact the Lustrum," Hunter continued. "They have a space-worthy craft and I mean to take it."

"I thought you said the camp was deserted?"

"It was. But they have to have left a token unit behind."

It was wishful thinking, but Whitsmith did not dare tell her that. She was herself insanely curious as to what this abandoned basecamp might have been, but if Hunter and the others had found it deserted it was a good bet there was still no one there. But that was not exactly what Hunter would want to hear.

A sudden thought struck Whitsmith.

"Have you noticed I don't much like Torrance here?"

"What does that have to do with anything?"

"Humour me."

Hunter did not seem in a humouring vein, but she replied through clenched teeth regardless. "I did notice. Probably because she's younger and more attractive, no?"

Whitsmith was almost impressed that Hunter could be such a cow even under these conditions. "She's also named Torrance," Whitsmith said, purposefully vague.

Silence consumed the arena for several moments.

"So?" Hunter finally asked, taking the dangling bait.

Whitsmith smiled inwardly. "I have a file in my chambers. I have a lot of files in my chambers, but I have a file about the Lustrum. We found it when we got here, but it never occurred to us they had a base out here somewhere. That file mentions the name Torrance."

Hunter stared at her and Whitsmith silently willed her to put two and two together. "So you're trying to tell me Torrance is a Lustrum?"

Whitsmith wondered why the woman felt the need to say it aloud when Whitsmith could not have been more blindingly obvious. "If you want real answers about these creatures, Hunter, Torrance is the one who can give them to you."

"Wake her up."

"Wake her up?"

"Shake her or something."

"Shake ... Hunter, the girl's lost a lot of blood. She needs a transfusion, she needs surgery, she needs a ... I don't know what she needs, but whatever it is I don't exactly have the equipment in my pocket."

"So this is a ploy for me to get her to a doctor?"

And an obvious ploy at that, Whitsmith felt. But it was also the only chance Hunter had of even possibly finding out the truth, and she knew Hunter would not be able to take the risk that Whitsmith was telling the truth.

"Stand away," Hunter said. Whitsmith reluctantly obeyed and Hunter approached the dying girl. With her gun still trained upon Whitsmith, Hunter withdrew something from her belt. It was a syringe, so far as Whitsmith could tell, yet injecting Torrance with anything would not do her much good. But there was something it could be which might do Hunter some good.

"That's a stimulant isn't it?" Whitsmith asked worriedly. Some strange form of drug had started appearing with field medics about ten years earlier. It was some form of adrenalin boost mixed with a truth serum, although Whitsmith did not know the specifics. It provided a sudden rush of life to a dying patient, long enough for that patient to report urgent information. It had been developed to be used on dying soldiers, so their allies could find out enemy strengths. It did not save the lives of the soldiers being injected, but could save the lives of any following. Once the rush wore off the cells died more rapidly, killing the soldier. For this reason it had become a banned substance in almost every civilised culture.

Hunter clearly did not care.

"You can't give her that," Whitsmith said urgently, realising her lies had just caused the death of the girl she was trying to save. "I made it up. Torrance doesn't know anything."

"We're about to find out."

"No, seriously. I lied."

Hunter sighed. "Whitsmith, I'm going to kill her anyway once this is done with. It doesn't matter all that much how she goes, OK?"

Hunter had spoken so callously that Whitsmith felt sick to her stomach. She watched as Hunter drew the liquid from a small plastic bottle, watched as Hunter tore the sleeve off Torrance's good arm. Whitsmith stared in horror of what she had done and decided in that moment that she didn't care what happened now. She may not have liked Torrance, but Hunter's killing ended here.

With a primal roar she had learned from a gorgosaurus she had captured last year, Whitsmith launched herself at her foe. Hunter palmed the syringe, swinging her rifle around to slam the butt into Whitsmith's stomach. Whitsmith doubled over, her brain screaming at her, her mouth filling with a bitter, coppery taste. Her face exploded in pain as Hunter kicked her in the head, sending her reeling to land in a painful heap amidst the gravel. Whitsmith strained to stare down at where Torrance was stirring. Hunter snorted disdainfully, crouching once more and preparing the injection.

Whitsmith fought to rise, fought her own pain, but she knew even if she got to her feet there was nothing she could do. Hunter was a killer who had survived all this time in the swamps and forests of this world. There was nothing someone like Aubrey Whitsmith could do against her.

An explosion of wood erupted from behind Whitsmith at that moment and she turned her head to see the massive doors yawning wide. A five metre bulbous form lumbered into the arena, charging with the speed of a freight train, its fat body heaving as it ran in great leaps in order to drag its body along.

Hunter dropped the syringe and brought her rifle to bear, but even despite its bulk the creature was swifter. It swung its flappy, thick neck – the victor of so many mating rituals – and slammed the hard flesh into Hunter. She was blown from her feet, her body slamming into the wall of the arena, her rifle clattering away. The creature reared and roared, thudding its forefeet down and almost crushing its enemy. Hunter barely managed to evade the attack, although once more it struck with its neck, battering her a second time against the wall. Whitsmith could see her face streaked with blood, her eyes filled with anger, and she punched out at the creature's flat snout. Her blow only seemed to anger the creature, however, for it slammed her a third time with its neck, rearing once more and this time bringing its heavy feet down upon one of her legs. Hunter's scream tore through the entire arena and Whitsmith heard the sickening sound of crunching bones.

She was also very much aware that Torrance was lying dangerously close to the odd combat.

"Aubrey!"

Whitsmith felt hands grabbing her, steadying her. She looked up, startled, into the eyes of Dexter Valentine. He grinned broadly, his relief pouring from him in waves.

"Dex?"

"Dexter and his moschops to the rescue."

He said nothing more, for Whitsmith threw her arms about him, pressing her lips to his in an embrace she knew Katie Hudson had predicted long ago. Valentine stiffened in shock, but in moments she felt him relax under her embrace. Then he stiffened again and pulled away.

"What?" she asked, confused.

"Uh ... Just, that I think I might be making someone jealous?"

"Jealous?" Whitsmith asked, entirely lost now. She followed his gaze to the raging moschops, which had left Hunter where she had fallen and was now focusing its attention upon her and Valentine.

"I remembered the accident you had with the moschops hormones," Valentine said nervously. "When we collided in the corridor and they spilled all over you?"

"I remember you pawing at my chest, Dex."

"Yeah, kind of hoped you'd forgotten that."

Whitsmith realised what he meant though. He had released the moschops so it would follow her scent, and when it had arrived it had found Hunter being aggressive so had dealt with her. And now that was done with it could see Whitsmith in the arms of another man.

"Surely," Whitsmith whispered, her eyes never leaving the creature she did not want to antagonise, "it can't think I'm a moschops. I mean, do I look like a moschops to you? And think very carefully before you answer that."

"I think it's confused. It can smell a mate, but can't see a thing."

Valentine was right. Now things had calmed somewhat, the moschops was looking around in all directions, trying to figure out why this strange bipedal creature smelled so good. Whitsmith heard Torrance groan and knew they had to end this quickly or she would die.

"I'm going to draw it away," she told Valentine, releasing him entirely. "Get Torrance to a doctor."

"You're going to what?"

"It's all right, I deal with these animals all the time, right?"

Valentine looked about as convinced as she felt.

"Aubrey, there's something I need to tell you."

Whitsmith shook her head. She was not at all certain what she was herself feeling at that moment, but adrenalin and near-death were playing huge parts in her emotions and she could have done without Valentine suddenly deciding he was in love with her.

"Just get Torrance to the doctor," Whitsmith said.

"Aubrey, this is important. There's another ..."

Whitsmith ran before Valentine could say another word, although even as she took her first step she began to wonder how that sentence would have ended. Another woman? Was that it? Was he trying to tell her he still fancied his chances with Torrance? She had no idea how she felt about that and just thought it was a good job she was already running.

She could hear the bellow of the moschops behind her, followed by the thunderous padding of its heavy feet. Whitsmith bolted through the huge doors and did not stop running. She had no idea what the moschops intended to do when it caught her, but a thousand horrific images flashed through her panicked mind, and the kindest of them would have been her being pounded to pulp like Hunter before her.

The doors led to a short tunnel which broke out into a larger chamber, also kept empty. The animal pens were not too far away, but Zebadiah had not wanted them kept too close to where they would be fighting in case they were spooked by the noise of dying creatures. There was a door in the wall through which it was far too small for the moschops to squeeze, and Whitsmith flung it open, barrelling through and striking her elbow against it in her haste to be away.

Whitsmith drew to a halt with a gasp. Before her, crouching in the shadows and tending to its wounded side, there was a bipedal reptile she had been promised was dead. The creature raised its head in her direction and hissed savagely, its eyes taking on a flicker of recognition and hatred.

Without a second thought, Whitsmith spun and bounded back into the other room, ducking the thick throat of the surprised moschops to stumble over her own feet in her haste to get away. Running as fast as she could, Whitsmith fled back towards the arena, having a fairly good idea now of what Valentine was trying to tell her there was another of. She wished she could feel relieved he had not been talking of another woman after all.

CHAPTER SEVENTEEN

Aura Torrance was dying. Valentine had seen enough death in his time to know when it lay before him. Her skin was almost white, her breathing shallow and weak, and blood continued to pour from her wound. He could see where Whitsmith had made a good enough effort to bind the injury and create a tourniquet, but she clearly knew nothing of doctoring. Unfortunately Valentine knew even less. He had radioed for assistance, demanded their doctor be sent to the arena at once, but knew help would come too late. Torrance was losing body heat, and it did not matter how much Valentine rubbed her hands or wrapped her in his own suit jacket, he knew he would never be able to restore warmth to her. He looked upon her face, so young and full of promise. Her cheeks were grimy and soiled, there was a graze down the side of her face which appeared to have been caused by a boot. Her lips, so full and cherry red before, were now thin and turning blue as they dried out. Her entire body was shivering and Valentine held her tightly, fighting back tears. Over the years of his confinement he had seen many people die, but none of it had ever bothered him before. He had never cared for anyone, not until Torrance had walked into his life. Aubrey of course, he had always cared for Aubrey, but she was just Aubrey.

Torrance's face twitched and her eyes flickered open. Valentine smiled at her, forcing his sadness away. "Hey," he said, his voice cracking. "Couldn't keep away from me, eh?"

She attempted a smile, but her face lacked the passion to be able to make it pleasant. "Hunter?" she asked.

Valentine glanced over to where Hunter's body lay crumpled and unmoving.

"Kind of like kneaded dough."

Torrance did not find joy at his words, but then Torrance was not someone who would ever find death amusing. He could see forming words was a strain for her and fought for something to say for the both of them.

"Everything you told me," he asked. "Was any of it true? All that stuff about Io and conscription?"

Her eyes closed, and her voice was fading. "Does it matter?"

"I just want to know who you are, Aura. I want to know the real Aura Torrance."

"Aura's a name that came with the armour, Dex. My name's Becky."

Valentine smiled a genuine smile. "Becky."

"Becky Torrance," she said, her voice almost too small to hear now, "was a messed-up kid who made mistakes."

"Kids make mistakes, Becky. It's what helps them grow into adults."

"Cute, Dex." She even managed another smile. "Whitsmith."

"She's not here."

"Good. Look after her, Dex. She's sweet on you."

"Aubrey? I ... I'm getting that impression."

Torrance convulsed and Valentine panicked, but the spasm passed and he could feel her slipping away even more quickly. "Cartello was right about me, Dex. I never contributed anything, I was always just in the way. I was never any good for anything."

"You contributed to me, Becky," he said, his voice cracking. He could feel his face was wet with tears. "All my life I've worked with numbers and profiles. I never got to know people, real people. They were just statistics to me. You helped me see what people are really like, Becky. You helped make me realise I'm human. Can you see that?"

But Torrance did not reply. Her face was set in a peaceful calmness, her hand was limp in his grip. He had no doubt she had not heard a word he had said. And she had died in the firm belief that she was a nobody.

"You know you're better off without her, stupid girl."

Valentine looked across to see Hunter's broken body attempting to right itself. One of her legs was entirely crushed, and blood soaked her torso and face, but she had managed to get to her good foot by using the wall as a backrest. She had brought a pistol to bear. All her previous show of egotism had been beaten out of her, but as she levelled the weapon shakily upon Valentine he realised she still thought she was walking out of this.

"When that doctor gets here," she told him, "the three of us are leaving. Any funny business and I shoot you. Do you under ... What are you doing?"

Valentine had collected Torrance's body in his arms. He looked at Hunter for several moments, shaking his head. "Becky wasn't the pathetic one, Hunter. Because even dead she has someone who cares enough to get her out of here."

Hunter's face took on a look of terror and Valentine knew she was finally accepting the reality that she was going to die in this pit.

"Goodbye, Hunter," he said. "Pretty soon no one will even remember you existed."

He turned his back upon her and moved towards the single-door exit. He had seen Hunter's shaking hands and knew with the realisation of her death they would only tremble further. Hunter shouted obscenities at his back, promising to wreak all kinds of vengeance upon him. Then she pleaded, promising him in her desperation so much reward. But she could not shoot him, even if she could hold her aim. She needed him to survive, and to shoot him was to shoot herself. And the only thing Hunter loved in life was herself.

With a sudden yell, Whitsmith appeared from the massive doors and Valentine watched as she tore across the arena, waving her arms at him, shouting for him to keep moving. Then Valentine saw what was giving chase and he needed no other urging. Carrying Torrance as he was, Valentine could not properly run, but he would not relinquish her body. Whitsmith reached him moments later, surprising him by taking some of the weight, and together they made it to the door. Valentine turned back to see the bipedal reptile bounding across the arena. Hunter fired at it, her shot pinging into the ground, and the monster recognised the threat and turned its full attention upon her. Valentine did not tear his eyes away as the creature ripped out her throat in one savage horizontal slash. Hunter's cry was brief, and as she fell, blood gurgling in her throat, she looked up at Valentine pleadingly, so far across the arena.

Valentine turned away. Whitsmith had the door open by this point and he handed Torrance to her. "Go," he said.

Whitsmith stared at him in horror. "What?"

"It's going to follow," he said calmly. "I need to slow it down."

"Dex, you can't stay here and ..."

"Aubrey, I've never done anything selfless in my entire life and I just watched a good woman die in my arms. I have the opportunity to save the life of the only other woman I care about on this whole world and I'm going to take it. Go. Please."

Whitsmith looked over his shoulder, and he knew she could see the creature beginning to stalk him. Her eyes found Valentine's once more and she kissed him again. He allowed himself to savour the moment, knowing it would be the last time he ever saw her, and as she pulled away he could see the tears welling in her eyes.

Without another word, Valentine closed the door upon her and turned to face the monster.

It was still around ten metres away, sitting in a crouch and observing him. Perhaps it was searching for weakness, perhaps it was trying to work out whether he was holding a weapon. He suddenly remembered he had taken one from Stone and drew his pistol. He had to assume it was loaded because he had no idea how to check. Holding the weapon at arm's length he steadied his hand as much as he could and pulled the trigger.

Then he yelped as the gun all but exploded in his hand, the bullet flying into the air. It was the first time Dexter Valentine had ever fired a gun, and the ricochet tore up his arm and left his hand stinging. The gun itself lay on the floor where he had dropped it.

The creature seemed to raise its eyebrows as though asking whether that was his big attempt at survival.

"Attention!" he shouted, but this creature either did not have the same conditioning as the other or else did not care at all for his commands. Placing his back to the door, Valentine tried to calm his own raging heart and said, "Well, it was worth a try."

The creature rose to its full height, moving towards him in the same way a human being would walk. What it was he could not say: nor did he even care any more. He had already slowed it enough for Whitsmith to get away, for her to find the protection of some people with some really big guns and the knowledge of how to use them. He had played his role and was now prepared for the curtain to fall.

The reptile reached to within a metre of him, snarling and sniffing him, always searching for something. Always trying to learn. Valentine felt his body shivering and somehow he still had control of his bowels. It would be something of which he was certain Whitsmith would be proud when she buried what was left of him.

Apparently having finished its assessment, the creature bared its razor fangs and stared at him directly in the eyes.

That was when its head exploded.

Valentine cried aloud as blood spattered his face, his tongue. The creature hesitated upon its feet before it toppled, slamming into the ground and spilling its brains clear across the floor. Valentine stood staring, his mind fighting to make sense of what he had seen twice now in one day.

"Got him," Cartello said, and he looked up to see her crouched by the railing behind which people would gather to watch the pit fights. "Worked so well last time, thought I'd give it another shot. Literally."

"How ... How long have you been there?"

Cartello shrugged, checking her weapon.

"There's no one left to shoot!" Valentine shouted. "You don't need to check your guns!"

She paused, considering his words, then checked the rifle anyway. "Always more enemies out there, Valentine. Welcome, by the way."

Valentine collapsed against the door, sinking to the ground and spitting dino-man blood. He sunk his head into his hands, his entire body collapsing as he began to weep. It was over, and he at last knew what it was like to be a man.

EPILOGUE

"So Cartello just left?"

Whitsmith stood before Valentine's desk, a report in her hand. Valentine himself sat behind the desk, of course, filling in reports. A day had passed since Death had stalked the former prison and things were getting back to normal. The moschops was back in its pen, the reptile-men's bodies were cleared away and burned, along with what was left of Hunter. They had never even discovered her real first name, although Whitsmith knew none of them cared. Rebecca Torrance had been buried in the prison cemetery along with the victims of the two creatures. Only Hudson's body was missing, for that had been left outside and would have long been picked clean by animals.

Cartello was the only loose end, so far as Whitsmith could see, and Valentine had just very calmly informed her the faux-sergeant had gone.

"Yep," Valentine said without looking up from his writing. "Said she wanted to see the world. Wasn't about to stop her."

"Did you at least give her a radio?"

"She didn't want one. I'm sure she'll be fine, Aubrey."

"Oh."

She had never known Valentine to be this distant from her and knew it had to do with Torrance. She had spent so long being jealous of the girl that she felt bad about the entire affair. Especially the rolling around in the mud, pulling her hair and stamping on her face thing.

"You don't have any work to do?" Valentine asked, still scribbling away.

"I wanted to talk to you about something."

"Moved on. You know me, Aubrey, nothing gets to me."

She did not know whether she wished that was true. "We need to make a decision about this abandoned base to the north."

"If it's abandoned, it's no problem."

"Hunter said it was Lustrum."

"I heard that too. Doesn't make it true; and it doesn't make it any less abandoned."

"Shouldn't we check it out or something?"

Valentine sighed, his pen even stopping long enough for Whitsmith to realise he wasn't actually writing any proper words. "It's been five years, Aubrey. If anyone was going to come here they would have done so by now."

"Yeah, but we have no idea why no one's ever come to check on the prison. I mean, we killed the guards five years ago and no one's even turned up to ask why."

"Leave it, Aubrey."

"But don't you want to know why? Even just for peace of mind?"

"It's sometimes best we don't know."

He still had not looked up, and now resumed his writing. Whitsmith narrowed her eyes. There was something about his tone, about his demeanour, which did not sit well with her at all. She knew Valentine better than anyone, better perhaps than he knew himself, and she could sense there was something big he was holding from her.

"You know, don't you?" she asked. "You know why no one's come sniffing around?"

Valentine said nothing.

"I don't believe this," Whitsmith whispered, astounded by the possibilities this opened up. "How could you just sit on information like this? Don't you think the rest of us have a right to know?"

He looked up now, and Whitsmith felt suddenly ashamed. His eyes were red, his lips were dry and he looked far more scared than she had ever seen him before. "It won't change anything," he told her. "Nothing ever does."

"I'm sorry," she said, feeling bad for questioning his motives when he was so obviously grieving. "Torrance was ... well, she didn't deserve what happened to her."

"She was a good woman. Can't you even bring yourself to say that little?"

Whitsmith wished she could, but to do so would be to lie, and she knew Valentine was very good at knowing when people were lying.

"She was wrong about you," Valentine said, his voice stern only because it saved it from choking. "She told me to look after you, Aubrey. She told me you were worth it."

Whitsmith blinked. "She said that?"

"Yes. She's not quite the monster you thought is she?" He looked back down to his papers. "Now get out and do some work, Miss Whitsmith. I'm too busy right now to chat to my staff."

Whitsmith hung her head and left his office. She had fought Torrance so much, she was wishing now she had instead got to know the young woman. Perhaps they could have been friends, or even the sisters Hunter said they were like. But that was gone now, in the past, extinct. And nothing extinct ever returned.

Carefully and gently, Aubrey Whitsmith closed Valentine's door behind her.

Printed in Great Britain
by Amazon

55892679R00298